PRAISE FOR THE AUTHOR

THE THIEF TAKER

'Captivating, vivid writing. Descriptions come straight off the pages and permeate deep into your senses, and a truly electrifying pace. Quinn is a brilliant new talent!'
— Peter James, international bestselling author

'A fast and dangerous ride through Restoration London where plague stalks every street and death is hidden behind the iron-beaked mask of a plague doctor. Sharp, atmospheric and sumptuous.'
— Simon Toyne, author of *Sanctus*

FIRE
CATCHER

ALSO BY C.S. QUINN

The Thief Taker series

The Thief Taker

C.S. QUINN

FIRE CATCHER

THOMAS & MERCER

Published by Thomas & Mercer, Seattle

www.apub.com

Amazon, the Amazon logo, and Thomas & Mercer are trademarks of Amazon.com, Inc., or its affiliates.

ISBN-13: 9781503947887
ISBN-10: 1503947882

Cover design by bürosüd° München, www.buerosued.de

Printed in the United States of America

To Simon and Natalie.

London, 1666

London is a city of half-timbered houses and wooden shacks. In the narrow backstreets, astrologists predict the future and alchemists conjure wonders. Traitors' heads line London Bridge, where witches sell potions and gamesters turn cards. The river flowing beneath lands a daily cargo of smuggler gangs and pirates.

England has traded her Republic for a monarch of the blood. But London's wealth lies in the guilds, which regulate trade and set prices. And already, there is talk among Londoners that blood is a dangerous currency.

Prologue

London 1649. Seventeen years before the Great Fire.

Sally's heart was pounding as she opened the chest. She heaved the papers into its dark belly and her candle flame hovered over them. These documents held secrets worth killing for.

She knew the risk she took in stealing them. The disused sea chest was the safest place to hide the papers until she could call on the protection of the magistrate. Its ocean duties were long relinquished and it was too heavy to be moved or sold. As far as Sally knew, no one in the household ever looked inside the great trunk.

She pulled back her candle and the papers fell into darkness. Sally shut the lid and turned the key with shaking fingers. Hewn of a dense teak, the chest was impenetrable. Only fire could breach the interior, and even that by slow degrees. All of London would have to burn before the contents were at risk.

Pocketing the key, Sally felt for the heavy shape through the fabric of her apron.

Its head bore a symbol of a crown and three knots. The sign of the Sealed Knot – the Brotherhood whom she had served until she discovered their dreadful secret.

A sound from the doorway made her start. Sally turned to see her two boys were eyeing her from the threshold. She hadn't dared leave them in their slum home whilst she took the papers. But she'd taken pains to ensure they were ignorant of her purpose.

'I told you to stay downstairs,' she hissed. 'What did you see?'

The eldest eyed the chest. 'Why did you hide Master Blackstone's marriage certificate?' he asked.

Sally cycled through the safest next step.

She knelt by the older boy.

'Rowan,' she said carefully. 'Tell me exactly what you saw.'

His eyes flicked to the chest, then to his younger brother Charlie, trying to establish how much trouble he was in.

'A marriage paper,' said Rowan. 'For Master and Mistress Blackstone.'

Sally hesitated, trying to decide how best to protect her children.

'Stay here,' she said, trying to keep her voice from shaking. 'I'll only be a moment.'

Sally stepped out on to the landing, pulse racing, to the locked door of her mistress's dressing room.

The household was sleeping. She could grab her little bundle of possessions and with the money she would get for them, secure sanctuary for long enough to tell her story. Master Blackstone was an important man. She would need all the resources at her disposal to persuade the authorities to search his house.

She crept to the door with the heavy bunch of housekeeper's keys in her hand. The warm circle of candlelight fell on the lock. Behind the door were the belongings that had been held in trust since Sally had entered the household. No light shone through the keyhole, but she still paused to reassure herself all was silent inside before unlocking the door and stepping into the room.

Sally washed and dressed the lady of the house daily, combing her hair and warming her pearls on her own throat. She knew every hiding place of the chamber, and moved easily to the jewellery box, picking out a gold chain from which a small key dangled.

Turning it in the dresser she opened the drawer and retrieved a bulky roll from the back. When she'd started her service she'd been made to give over a scant parcel of possessions as security that she wouldn't turn thief. She breathed out in memory of her little clutch of embroidery, coins and the pewter mug which she had not seen since she'd entered service for the Blackstones. Snatching them up, she turned to see a long shadow had fallen across the doorway.

Sally felt the breath constrict in her chest. The pewter mug dropped from her grip, ringing like a death knell on the wooden floor.

Blackstone's dark figure loomed in the half-light. He wielded an eight-armed candelabra and amber flames danced over his heavy features.

'Sally,' he said with chilling calm. 'I never thought to catch you stealing.'

Blackstone had returned from civil war starved to a yellow skeleton by siege. He had regained his muscular frame and more during peacetime, lending his face a swollen quality. War had punched a ruthless savagery into his eyes.

'I . . . ' Sally hardened her voice. 'It is my bundle I take,' she returned. 'Belongings that are due to me is all.' She tried to summon bravery. 'I no longer serve this house,' she added. 'I know what you did.'

From her vantage point by the bed she could see he swung his own bunch of keys, slowly, dangerously. 'That will be for the hangman to decide,' he answered.

Sally blanched. 'It is my own possessions I take,' she repeated.

'I don't speak of your trinkets.' Blackstone's voice had dropped to a furious hiss. 'I am missing some papers.'

The accusation sat thickly in the air. Sally swallowed. She hadn't thought he would notice them missing until morning. But of course he would check obsessively. Whoever held the papers had England's darkest secret in his power.

Blackstone took a step forward and as he did, Sally saw the candlelight catch his eyes. In that moment she knew he meant to kill her. He would easily find her sons hiding in the adjacent room. The realisation stripped away a life of learned servitude.

'Your wife, Teresa,' cried Sally. 'Your unholy marriage has driven her to dark magic.'

Blackstone hesitated.

'Blood-ash,' continued Sally. 'Ground into your family tree, over your sister's face. It's death magic, old and powerful.'

'You lie.' Blackstone's heavy features were tight with pain. The flames in his candelabra trembled.

Sally lunged with a ferocity she didn't know she had. For a split second Blackstone was caught off guard. He sidestepped clumsily and the candelabra twisted from his hand. It fell heavily to the wooden floor, its clutch of candles breaking away.

Fire rolled in eight different directions. The richly decorated interior flared in circles of low illumination. One candle came to rest against thick drapes and the flame ebbed briefly before advancing upwards.

In the next moment Sally hardly knew what happened. Only that there was fear in Blackstone's face and flames at his feet.

Letting her scant possessions fall, Sally raced past him. Flinging open the door where Rowan and Charlie were hiding, she grabbed both her sons by the hands. They all three ran down the back stair and out into the starry night.

Breathlessly, Sally and the two boys hastened along the honeycomb of dark and winding track which led from the house down to the riverbank. The way was strewn with washed-up debris and Sally's foot landed awkwardly. A shard of broken cartwheel lodged in the mud pierced her calf. She choked back a cry of pain and staggered on. Blackstone hadn't seen her boys. She could put them safe.

Her calf ran with blood and the biting pain had risen quickly to excruciating. Sally took a ragged breath. They were on the riverbank, where heavy industries dumped their refuse into the Thames. Her eyes landed on the brewery. She'd visited it a few times to collect beer for the house. Brewers were burly men built to shovel hops. They worked through the night. Maybe the men there could protect her. Sally headed for the dark building.

Her leg sparked agony with each step. She gritted her teeth as she limped the final distance. The thick brick walls and square windows seemed to promise sanctuary. It was only as she neared the large door she realised her mistake. It was Sunday night. Cromwell's Puritan Republic had banned brewing on the Sabbath. The heavy door was locked. Wild panic rose in her chest. Blackstone would kill her children. Sally closed her eyes tight, trying to pull an idea from the raging thoughts.

There was a small grating in the door. She tried to push her hand through, to raise the catch from the inside. But it was no good. The metal bars were too narrow.

She let out a bitter sob of defeat, slamming a fist against the heavy door.

A warm hand tugged at hers.

'Mama,' said Charlie. 'I can fit my hand through.'

She turned to him, hope blooming.

'Do you want me to?' he asked.

Sally nodded. She lifted him and Charlie's tiny hand slid easily through. He pressed the catch up and the door fell ajar.

Sally let out a sob of relief. She pulled open the large door just as Blackstone emerged from the house. Two candles had been wedged back into his candelabra at hasty angles, shadowing his enormous frame.

Offering up a prayer she pushed her children into the brewery and slipped in behind them.

A close beery smell hit her and Sally made out the domed copper pot-stills, ranged like giant beehives across the packed-earth floor. Desperately she circled one, but there was no way to climb inside. Then as her eyes adjusted to the dark she noticed a stack of empty barrels at the far back of the brewery.

Sally raced for them, pulling her children. They were easily large enough for her small boys, and she thought her slim frame might fit in one too.

Lifting Charlie she placed him carefully inside. Then she did the same with the elder, Rowan.

'We play a game,' she said brightly. 'We shall hide in here. Whosoever is quiet longest will get an orange.'

Sally began climbing inside the third barrel.

'A whole one?' asked Rowan.

'Yes, but you must not say a peep,' Sally cautioned, finger to her lips. They could hide until morning, she thought, pulling in her skirts.

Outside the brewery footsteps approached. Sally froze. Then she saw the blood trail, glistening. Despair washed through her. It would lead Blackstone straight to them.

Dread blooming, Sally climbed silently from the barrel. She knew what she must do.

Sally turned to her youngest.

'Charlie, I have something for you to keep,' she said, struggling for composure. The little boy looked steadily back at her, uncomprehending.

She reached into her apron pocket and withdrew the large key. Taking a ribbon from her hair she fashioned a necklace and looped it over his head.

His gaze dropped instantly to the shiny object, and he gripped it wonderingly. The key was double sided, foreign looking, with blades fanning out like wings. The top was wrought in a strange symbol pattern, like a crown, looped over with knots.

The sound of a shoulder slamming into wood resounded through the brewery. Then a loud splintering as the door began to give way.

The boys glanced uncertainly towards the noise. Sally wrestled to appear calm.

'Keep it well, Charlie,' she whispered, trying to hold back the grief that squeezed at her throat. 'This key guards the sacred secret of the Sealed Knot. If the wrong man discovers it, England will fall.'

Charlie's small face was stern with responsibility.

'I'll guard it with my life,' he promised. Sally's eyes filled with tears.

'Not a peep,' she reminded them. 'Hide here. I'll come get you, when the game is over.'

The brewery door creaked open. A yellow orb of light flared out, multiplied in the copper pot-stills.

'I will return,' whispered Sally, and with a final choking sob kissed them both on the head. Gently she replaced the lids.

Sally closed her eyes, took a breath and stepped away from the barrels. At the sound of her movement Blackstone's light held steady, listening. She took a breath and walked towards the nearest still, drawing Blackstone away from her boys. In moments he was on her.

Sally stifled a shriek as his strong arms pinned her, wheeling her back against a pot-still with a clang.

'The papers.' His voice resounded with tight fury around the empty brewery. Blackstone's candles had fallen to the floor in the struggle, and the light cast upwards, giving him a demonic cast.

With effort Sally kept her eyes on Blackstone, and away from the barrels where her boys hid. His hands tightened painfully on her trembling shoulders. 'Tell me where the papers are!' He shook her so that her cap tumbled from her head. Without waiting for an answer he plunged his hand into her stays in search of the concealed documents.

Sally struggled vainly against the attack, and after contenting himself she wasn't carrying anything on her person Blackstone wrenched his fingers free, tightening his grip on her arms. 'You have cost the lives of your children,' he hissed. 'I know you have nowhere else to hide those papers. Believe me, I will find them in your Blackfriars slum home.'

Something else seemed to occur to him and his eyes ranged the brewery. Panic surged in Sally.

'You are a coward and a thief,' she shouted. 'You shall go to hell.'

Blackstone's gaze rested back on Sally.

'Your witch will burn with you,' she continued. 'I know what you have done and what you are. The Sealed Knot will find you out.'

Uncontrolled rage was animating Blackstone's features.

'Their revenge will be brutal,' Sally said. 'The marriage will be found out.'

She gasped as he fastened his hands around her slim throat.

'Your wife . . . wears the dark crown . . .' she managed as her vision began to swim. She felt his hands tighten further, as though he meant to wring the curse out of her.

'It is too great a risk to me to let the hangman carry out this duty,' said Blackstone, as he watched her lips purple and her eyes bulge. 'People may talk, though the words are of a thieving servant. And as you know, I can well conceal one extra body.'

As the world darkened Sally thought she could see a shape, reflected in the shining copper, picked out in the widening gloom. A crown and a loop of knots. And then the world closed around her.

It took Blackstone a moment to assure himself of her death and as the anger passed he realised his mistake. He should have kept her alive. Now he would have to find out her children in the slums. Cursing in frustration Blackstone shouldered Sally Oakley's limp body and headed for the door. He could dispose of her and find out her sons before dawn. Then his papers would be back under lock and key.

Inside their barrels the two boys sat quietly. The older was already whimpering but Charlie gripped his key tightly. It was only hours later that he too began to cry in a steady hopeless rhythm.

Chapter 1

London 1666

The bitter smell of coffee hit Charlie like a slap. He waited for his eyes to adjust to the gloom. The leaded windows were tarnished by oily fumes. A cosy cauldron fire lit the thronging table of coffee drinkers.

Charlie grasped the makeshift rope bannister and made the last few steps up the rickety wooden staircase into the coffee house. The babble of animated voices poured forth as he stooped through the narrow doorway.

Reflexively Charlie drew in his bare feet and straightened his brown-leather coat. Close fitting with a flare to mid-thigh it hid patched breeches, an oft-mended shirt and all his worldly goods besides.

'Coffee?' A burly man at the cauldron was waving a ladle menacingly. He wore an inexpertly wrapped turban in an attempt to appear Turkish.

Charlie peered at him through the array of curios which hung from the ceiling. There was an unidentified scaly creature, horns and tusks of varying lengths and a number of odd-shaped rocks. All were tinted brown and caked in dust.

'Alchemy ingredients of the purest sort,' grunted the cauldron ladler, following the direction of Charlie's gaze. 'We have your unicorn horn. Your salamander.' He waved his hand at the chattering coffee drinkers. 'And all the mysteries of the universe to discover.'

Charlie eyed the tar liquid in the cauldron. It belched with ominous oily bubbles.

'I'm here for the card maker,' he said.

The cauldron ladler's eyes dropped to the key at Charlie's neck. He eyed the shape at the head, a crown looped with knots.

The cauldron ladler wiped sweat from his forehead. 'You're the thief taker?'

Charlie hesitated. As a thief taker he caught criminals and stolen property for a fee. Not everyone in London welcomed his profession.

'I thought you'd be taller,' continued the coffee man. He frowned at Charlie's brown eyes and dusty-blond hair through the fug. 'I suppose I can see it. You have a certain poetry to your face. Despite the scar.'

Charlie smiled in reply. In his youth a bucking horse had left him with a scarred lip, bent nose and permanent unease around riders. He turned away from the cauldron man and surveyed the coffee drinkers.

Charlie spotted the card maker, a tidily bearded man with modest lace at his well-laundered cuffs. He was listening politely to a loud noble. Charlie began to make his way down the crowded table when another familiar face leapt out at him.

Charlie squinted in disbelief. 'Bitey?'

The old man was a friend from the Bucket of Blood bare-knuckle tavern. Charlie couldn't imagine what he was doing in a coffee house.

Bitey grinned back a greeting, revealing the hand-carved wooden teeth which had earned him his nickname. His squat frame was armoured with its usual grime-toughened layers. Charlie's gaze dropped, looking for Bitey's pet pig, which had a tendency to ram the unwary at knee height.

'Where's Juniper?' asked Charlie, failing to spot the animal among the legs of the seated drinkers.

Bitey scratched the narrow portion of face between beard and eyebrow.

'She swam away, Charlie,' he said. 'Up river. I took her for a dip in the Thames and she scented something on the wind. Lifted her head and took off west.'

Charlie raised an eyebrow. 'I didn't know pigs could swim.'

'They are not good swimmers, Charlie,' agreed Bitey sagely. 'But they can make a distance if they set their mind to it. And Juniper was always determined.'

'What brings you to the coffee house?' asked Charlie.

'I hoped the alchemists could return my piggy,' said Bitey. 'The best minds gather here to talk. That which is lost shall be found. That's their creed is it not? Besides,' he added with another wood-filled grin, 'coffee houses are a secret thing. They make a man feel dangerous.' Bitey pulled his battered tricorn hat lower, making his fury of eyebrows and beard more pronounced.

'They're hard to find,' conceded Charlie, remembering the grace and favour he'd deployed to track this one. 'Upstairs rooms. Narrow staircases.'

'Our Merry Monarch would shut them all down if he could,' agreed Bitey. 'He fears plots.' The old man scratched his beard. 'Civil War was years back,' he said, 'but there's plenty men who'd have kept Cromwell's Republic. 'Stead of bringing back a King with his jewels and whores.'

Bitey adjusted his hat.

'I heard about Maria,' he said.

3

'That was a long time ago now,' said Charlie. 'She left back in spring.'

'You don't think there's a chance you'll mend things?' said Bitey.

Charlie shook his head. 'She wanted something I couldn't give her.'

'What was that?'

'Peace of mind,' said Charlie distractedly. He was looking towards the card maker.

'Shame,' said Bitey. 'I liked her best of any of 'em.'

Charlie's gaze flicked again to the card maker, whose companion was now jabbing an enthusiastic finger at the heavens. The card maker looked up and noticed Charlie. His eyes went to the sack on Charlie's shoulder and lit with hope.

'Charlie Tuesday!' he replied, raising his reedy voice with difficulty above the throng. 'I expected to see you in my premises. How did you find me here?'

'It wasn't easy,' admitted Charlie, moving closer. 'Even for a thief taker.'

The card maker was looking eagerly at the sack. With a heave, Charlie laid it on the floor.

'Your missing print plates,' he said, as the contents hit the wooden boards with a clang. The bag fell open, revealing an array of playing-card faces etched into brass.

The card maker's face split into a huge smile.

'I can hardly believe it!' His hands fell on the contents. He eased out a Jack of Spades and Ace of Clubs, turning them this way and that. 'I thought they were lost forever. However did you find them?'

Charlie shrugged. 'Mud from St Giles. A few questions.'

'I can begin work again,' said the card maker happily. 'I'll finish two packs today. Who was the thief?' he asked, still smiling down at his returned print plates.

'Two young girls from the St Giles slums,' said Charlie. 'Desperate types. Not yet twenty and barely a tooth left between them. Skin and bone.'

'What explanation did they make when you caught them?'

'The usual,' said Charlie. 'They'd been gifted the plates. Couldn't remember who by.'

'Gifted playing-card plates?' snorted the card maker in disbelief.

'Any lie is worth trying when the noose hangs near,' said Charlie.

'They're on their way to Tyburn then,' said the card maker with satisfaction. 'I will go watch them swing.'

'They went yesterday,' lied Charlie. 'Hanged with the religious sect who plotted to assassinate the King.'

'A shame,' said the card maker. 'But I am glad enough to have my plates back. You are a man of your word.' He reached for his hanging pocket and then paused.

'But I'm forgetting,' said the card maker. 'What would you say to a trade? Information for pay.'

'I'm a thief taker,' said Charlie, holding out his hand for payment. 'If it's a rigged dog fight or a boxer with the pox, trust me, I know it.'

'No,' the card maker licked his lips. 'It is something else.' He pointed. 'About your key.'

Charlie hesitated. The secret of the key still haunted him. He'd tracked his mother's killer last year. But Blackstone had died of plague before answers were found. The locked chest had vanished with him.

Charlie was London's best thief taker, but this was the one mystery he hadn't yet solved.

'What kind of information?' he asked.

'Somebody was in here,' replied the card maker, 'asking about the symbol on your key.'

Charlie considered. You didn't say 'somebody' if a man had come looking. And no respectable woman came to a coffee house. Which meant she was a whore. Or a spy.

The card maker waited hopefully, fingering his hanging pocket.

'I'm listening,' Charlie decided, withdrawing his outstretched hand.

'There was a girl here,' said the card maker. 'Dressed fine, but whorish. Like those who hope to be the King's mistress. She was asking about the symbol on your key. Drew it with chalk,' he added.

Charlie cocked his head thoughtfully.

'Why was she looking for the symbol?'

'I only overheard part,' admitted the card maker. 'She was asking about the Magnus Opus. Then she drew your key. Said she was looking for information.'

'The Magnus Opus?'

'It's an alchemist's idea,' said the card maker. 'Latin. They argue over what it means. An elixir of life, gold from lead.' He shrugged. 'Many men are obsessed with its discovery. But she was the first woman I'd heard asking.'

'Pay me half,' Charlie decided, 'and tell me where she went.'

The card maker hesitated. 'I lost some business with my missing plates. I was hoping . . .'

'Half,' said Charlie, flexing his fingers meaningfully. He watched as the card maker counted out coins into his hand. Then he looked up expectantly.

'She left with a man,' said the card maker, as Charlie dropped the coins into his coat.

'She found a man who knew about the symbol?'

The card maker shook his head.

'He was just some drunk lord. He offered to pay for her . . . her company,' continued the card maker, making an obscene gesture with his hands.

6

'And?'

'She accepted. Bartered for a sum that made us whistle. The man suggested they go to Fetter Lane. He said there were rooms there. Rooms where men can . . .'

'I know them,' interrupted Charlie.

'They might be there still,' said the card maker. 'If the man wants his money's worth.'

Charlie nodded his thanks and made to leave.

'He paid enough,' the card maker called after him, 'to keep her all week.'

But Charlie didn't hear. He was already heading back down the stairs.

Chapter 2

Fetter Lane was an oppressive jumble of chaotic wooden buildings. Charlie knew it well. There were three possible buildings where the girl might be. His attention fastened on a flame deep behind a dirty window. The steady amber of a fine wax candle. The kind a wealthy man might buy.

The window was too grimed to see through. Charlie moved to the badly built wood wall and fixed his eye to a gap between the boards. His heart missed a beat. There she was. Red silk. The girl was undressing. Charlie watched transfixed as the red silk moved lower and lower, revealing two buds of white breast against the sun-browned collarbones.

A stray calf barged Charlie, knocking his eye from the crack in the wooden wall. For a moment he was back in the oppressive filth of Fetter Lane. The calf stumbled away, re-joining its herd on their switch-driven journey to Smithfield Market. He refastened his eye to the crack in the wall.

The girl had paused to take a deep drink from a cup of wine, making a smiling toast to someone out of Charlie's eye line. Then she resumed her sashaying undress.

Suddenly her gaze locked with his. Charlie stared back, unable to break the contact. Then she stepped across the room suddenly and out of sight. Charlie tried to swallow but his mouth was dry. He strained to see further into the darkness. She was sitting astride something. A chair or a lap. On her naked back was a crescent scar. It dipped in and out of view like a livid crimson moon rising and falling.

An unusual movement drew Charlie's attention to the girl's hand. It was dancing over the man's fingers in a familiar technique. So she was a jewellery thief. A good one. Charlie watched as she extricated a ruby ring from the unwitting wearer. Then the girl's hand came out with a deliberate carelessness, knocking over one candlestick and then another. Charlie shook himself back to reality as the flames danced against the dry wood of the house. He looked right and left along the tiny street, and then back in at the little scene, where the candles smouldered threateningly and then leapt into life.

'Fire!' A shout came hoarsely from inside the house. There was a hammering on the inside wall. 'Fire!'

In the alleyway the people froze in their morning business. Laundry women, hod carriers and pie men stood wide-eyed in panic. Charlie looked back to the crack in the wall. The girl had seized her opportunity to pickpocket a weighty purse and in a little jump she ran from the room, grabbing a silver candlestick as she fled.

A man stumbled into view, his fashionable breeches and shirt undone, face slack with confusion as the flames crackled around him. An expensive wig was perched atop his greying hair.

Beside Charlie a door banged and the girl tripped past light as a bird, with one hand holding her shift over her breasts. The other clutched her dress, and the stolen goods, to her body.

The girl turned a quick glance behind her and then halted suddenly. She was staring at him open-mouthed. For a brief moment Charlie was taken aback. His soulful brown eyes and fair hair appealed to certain women. Particularly in the context of candle-light and strong drink. But the kinked nose and scarred upper lip lent a bandit quality. And Charlie's frame, whilst passably tall and muscular, was of a wiry configuration best suited to running and street-fighting. He was nowhere near handsome enough to stop a woman in her tracks.

Then he realised. The girl wasn't staring at his face. Her attention was fixed on the key he wore around his neck.

Her expression was of pure terror. Slowly her lips mouthed two words.

'*The Brotherhood.*'

Chapter 3

The boy stumbled in the dark cellar. Fasting had left him weakened. Starved.

Rough hands pushed him onwards.

A red shape grew out from the dark. A demon. Then the boy's eyes made it out.

A hooded figure. Master Blackstone was wearing the red cloak of the Brotherhood. His bulky form made him monstrous. Candlelight winked behind Blackstone, casting his face in shadow.

Fear pulsed through the boy. He'd drunk nothing but the bitter initiation wine and his stomach boiled. Shadows in the dark seemed to shift and bloom. There was a smell too. Like a butcher's alley.

Blackstone's icy blue eyes seared out. There was a deadness to them. The boy had heard whispers from higher initiates. It was said Blackstone had made a secret marriage. That his wife wore black on their wedding day. They'd heard Blackstone scream in his sleep of a sister killed by death magic.

The boy clutched an offering in white knuckles. His feet butted against a soft mound on the packed-earth floor. Dread flooded through him. A body beneath his feet. But when he looked there was nothing there and confusion tore at him. Then Blackstone's eyes were on his. A chill ran through his soul.

'Kneel,' said Blackstone. 'And tell us why you come.'

The boy hesitated. He couldn't trust his legs to kneel. Then hands were at his shoulders, forcing him down. His knees hit the cold earth and he trembled.

'Parliament sent men,' began the boy. Words felt thick and unfamiliar in his mouth. 'They tried to make us attend the Protestant church,' he continued. 'We could not pay the fine. They took my brother to the Clink prison.'

Quite unexpectedly, hot tears rushed forth. He was a long way from his warm, safe home now.

Blackstone nodded at the familiar tale. Everyone knew what happened to Catholics in the Clink. Parliament's heavy-handedness was pushing young Catholic men into rebel factions across the city.

Blackstone threw back his hood. The boy flinched. It was true then. Blackstone was a living ghost. A man who couldn't be killed. Plague had left him a fearsome sight. Bubo scars ate their way across half his scalp, leaving a mess of shiny bald wheals in their wake. His remaining clumps of thick black hair were a livid contrast to the purple and red contours.

'Make your offering,' said Blackstone. He held out a jewelled chalice in which a dark liquid swirled.

The boy uncurled his fingers and dropped his offering into the chalice. A chunk of lead. There was a hissing noise. A funnel of steam poured upwards from the chalice. Blackstone raised it, touched it to a candle and a font of blue fire roared forth.

Instinctively the boy moved back. It was true then. Blackstone had powers. He knew dark alchemy.

'The offering is true,' said Blackstone. Blue light swirled over his face.

Then the flame died out and Blackstone's features fell to darkness again.

'Now,' said Blackstone, 'you face the Bringer of Death.' He was moving towards a curtain the boy hadn't noticed before. An unmistakable shape loomed behind it. The boy's stomach twisted.

With deliberate ceremony Blackstone drew back the curtain. Hot bile rose in the boy's throat.

'Look on one who had failed this rite,' said Blackstone.

Chapter 4

Nailing Charlie with a stare as if to etch him in her memory, the girl spun on her heel and sprinted off down Fetter Lane.

Charlie was about to give chase when the sound of crackling flames stalled him. The city was a warren of wood buildings built virtually on top of each other, and Londoners lived in constant fear of fire. People on the street were already panicking.

Charlie's conscience pricked at him. The locals would be unlikely to muster the rationality needed to tackle the blaze. With a frustrated glance at the escaping girl, he span in the opposite direction. There was a laundry stall on the street, and in a few quick strides Charlie was by the water butts.

'Which is wool?' he demanded of the laundress, who was standing open-mouthed in terror at the rising smoke. She turned to him like a sleepwalker. Charlie seized her roughly by the shoulder.

'Wool,' he repeated. 'Which holds the woollen clothes?'

She pointed and without waiting for permission Charlie plunged an arm into the tub and seized forth a load of sopping clothing.

'Bring the butt,' he commanded. The laundress hesitated and then moved to obey. Charlie sprinted off with his armful of wet wool without waiting to see if she followed.

There was a roar from the house as Charlie blazed through the doorway. The man inside was swinging one way and then another. He held an upended bottle of wine. Around him the flames burned blue on the sugary residues.

Charlie made a rapid assessment. Working quickly with the wet wool garments, he doused one fire and then another. Steam rose as fire spluttered resentfully beneath the sopping clothes.

As Charlie suffocated the last flames, the washerwoman sidled clumsily into the house with her water butt.

'Throw it there,' directed Charlie, pointing to a charred wooden wall. She looked at him in confusion.

'There's no fire there,' she said.

Charlie seized the water butt just as the flame flared. He threw it at the wall and the fire retreated, hissing discontentedly.

Behind them a younger woman in a mob cap arrived carrying her own pail of water. The fire was smoking in submission now but she threw her water anyway.

The three of them stood silent for a moment, bonded by mutual heroism as the final splash of water fell on charred wood.

'How did you do that?' the washerwoman asked Charlie. 'You knew where the flame would come.'

'Lucky guess,' said Charlie.

'It was no such thing,' announced the younger woman. 'I know you, Charlie Tuesday. You were a cinder thief.'

'That was as a boy,' said Charlie, giving her the uncertain smile he reserved for women-he-might-have-slept-with. 'I value my neck more greatly nowadays.'

He was eyeing the younger woman, mentally debating.

Did we? Didn't we?

The washerwoman was looking at him with disapproval. Looting burning buildings was frowned upon, even by commoners.

'I grew up in the Foundling Orphan Home,' explained Charlie. 'Hanging is better than starving.'

Understanding dawned on the washerwoman's face. Everyone knew about Foundling Home soup.

The younger woman gave Charlie a hopeful smile.

We did, he decided.

'All of London dry as a bone and candles lit when there is sunlight,' announced the washerwoman, eyeing the aristocrat slumped dejectedly in a chair.

'And my babes asleep only a few houses away,' added the younger woman, her voice quailing as the chance for drama occurred to her.

'The fire is out now,' said Charlie firmly. He could see the women were sizing the aristocrat up for compensation, and judged the man had suffered enough for his stupidity. Charlie turned to the aristocrat.

'The purse was of value to you?' Charlie asked. It was an odd thought. The man's clothes suggested a few lost coins would be nothing more than an inconvenience.

'It was a ring,' said the man. 'She took a ruby ring of great importance.'

Charlie thought of his key. The crown looped with knots. His whole life he'd searched for the mystery of what the symbol meant. The girl. She *knew* something. Something that frightened her deeply.

'If you'll allow me to help you, sir,' said Charlie slowly. 'I may be able to return this property to you.'

'What are you?' asked the man. 'Part of the Watch?'

The two women exchanged glances. Since Cromwell's army had been deposed and King Charles reinstated, the Watch were a figure of fun among Londoners. They had not successfully tracked a criminal in over three years.

'God forbid,' said Charlie, with a wide grin. 'I am a thief taker.'

16

Chapter 5

'The girls are all asleep,' explained Mother Mitchell, leading Charlie inside a richly furnished salon with a distinctive tang of male sweat. 'So we may talk in here.'

Two women were slumbering on the floor, arms slung over one another, faces flushed. The fire grate hadn't been swept and wine cups lay all around.

'They won't wake,' said Mother Mitchell. 'What is it you need?'

'I'm looking for a girl,' said Charlie, following her ample frame through a doorway carved with cherubs and wreaths. Beside the silken skirts, Charlie's seamed breeches and muddy feet looked conspicuously out of place.

'But of course it is always a girl,' she said, seating herself on a gold-legged chair and drawing the enormous folds of her silken gown around thick legs. Mother Mitchell had once been a famous courtesan, and the striking cast of her younger features could still be traced in the older face. But she had embraced the authority of her ageing body, expanding outwards until she echoed the proportions of the wide court dresses favoured in her youth. Heavily constructed ringlets of greying dark hair framed her face like a military helmet, whilst her unchecked moustache and eyebrows served as a whiskery warning that she was no longer for sale.

'Here, boy. Pass me my tobacco.' Mother Mitchell was gesturing to a marble mantelpiece littered with spent candle stubs. She coughed from the depths of her lungs and waited as Charlie passed her the silver box.

There was a girlish shriek from upstairs. Mother Mitchell raised her eyes to the ceiling then back to Charlie. She extracted a slim white pipe from the folds of her gown.

'Have you tried to find Maria?' Mother Mitchell asked, after a moment's pause.

'No,' said Charlie.

'She'd have you back,' said Mother Mitchell, 'if you'd only offer the poor girl a little stability. It's not much to ask.'

'I'm a thief taker,' said Charlie.

'That isn't the reason,' said Mother Mitchell. She nodded to the key around his neck. 'It's because of that. You won't let it go. You're obsessed by a mystery you can't solve.' She rearranged her skirts. 'No sensible woman can plan a future with that looming large.'

When he didn't answer she laughed her creaking phlegmic laugh.

'I have known you since a boy,' she said. 'Who else will tell you if not me?'

Mother Mitchell tugged out a pinch of tobacco and pressed it into the silver-edged bowl of her pipe. 'I thought it would last,' she continued, without waiting for an answer. 'I truly did.'

Charlie said nothing. There was something wrong in him, he knew. Maria was beautiful, clever and much too good for him. For a short time they'd been truly happy.

But the more Maria pressed for an ordered life, the more Charlie yearned for his thief taker's hand-to-mouth transience. And much as it burned him, he knew Mother Mitchell was right. At the heart of every argument with Maria was a truth Charlie couldn't admit.

How can I settle down, when I don't know who I am?

'Maria was good for you,' added Mother Mitchell. 'I remember the actress. How many fights started over that one?'

'None that I did not finish,' said Charlie evenly.

She shook her head. 'If you could only think with your head, Charlie Tuesday, you could rule the world.'

Charlie didn't disagree. Women always seemed to be his undoing. Women and the extra-strength ale sold after Lent.

He unravelled a small purse from inside his shirt and removed several coins. Her eyes glittered as she took them.

'Who do you seek?'

'I saw her this morning on Fetter Lane,' he began. 'She was with a man in one of the rental rooms. A better type of building.'

Mother Mitchell grunted. 'A kept woman?'

'More in thieving,' answered Charlie after a moment's thought.

'Pretty, was she?'

The answer came to Charlie in a rush. 'Beautiful.' A memory of the girl's mesmerising eyes and long dark hair flashed in his memory.

'A street prostitute?' asked Mother Mitchell.

Charlie shook his head. 'Her dress was silk. Well made. And the wine they were drinking. It was too good. Much better than a man would buy for a common prostitute.'

Mother Mitchell nodded at this.

'Any marks? Smallpox scars?' she asked.

Charlie ran the image of the girl in his mind.

'No smallpox,' he said finally. 'But she had a scar on her back. Red raised. Shaped like a scythe.' He motioned the shape.

Mother Mitchell rocked back and forth as if trying to urge a memory forward. Then her face broke with sudden enlightenment. 'Lily Boswell!' she announced. 'Aye, that is your girl.' Her face darkened. 'You must stay away from Lily Boswell. She is deadly.'

Chapter 6

The stink of the cellar washed over the boy. Blackstone's red-clad figure loomed over him like a demon. Hanging behind the curtain was someone the boy recognised.

'He failed the rite,' said Blackstone. 'You share his fate if you show his weakness.'

The boy's heart was racing. He'd tried to look away and found he couldn't. A young carpenter's apprentice from St Giles hung in bloody tatters. A rictus of pain was frozen on his dead lips. Fear rose hot and thick. The boy had not realised, until now, what it truly meant to fail the initiation.

'He dropped his arm,' said Blackstone, taking in the mangled remains with pleasure. 'When the Bringer of Death was upon him.'

The boy saw Blackstone was holding a wooden block. A hard ball of terror tightened in the boy's stomach. He knew part of what must come. He'd seen the scars on the other recruits.

The boy felt his forearm seized. Blackstone pressed the block on to his arm and raised the chalice again. The boy looked down. The wood bore a shape, cut out like a stencil. A crown looped over with three knots.

'When I was a boy,' Blackstone said, 'my father made tests of my faith. He burned my fingernails to yellow stumps. But I never renounced my Catholicism.'

Blackstone paused, letting the image sink in. The boy swallowed, and his eyes flicked to the dead recruit hanging.

'Are you a worthy son of the Brotherhood?' asked Blackstone. In a smooth movement, he poured liquid from the glass goblet over the exposed skin on the boy's outstretched arm. The boy drove down a shriek of agony. It burned worse than any fire he'd ever known. Every instinct screamed to run from the cellar, to plunge his arm into cool water. But the hanging recruit grimaced a warning.

Blackstone left a long pause. 'During the Civil War,' he continued, 'Catholics fought for the King. England's true father. When we lost, Cromwell's Republic hunted and killed us.'

There was a deadly hush in the cellar. All the boy could hear was his own laboured breathing. He tried to form silent words between the breaths.

Hold firm. Hold firm.

'Now King Charles is reinstated,' Blackstone continued. 'The escaped heir we risked our *lives* to secretly toast, in cellars and outhouses. He cavorts with whores and unclean women. Dishonouring his good Catholic Queen.'

Blackstone's dead eyes suddenly flashed. 'This false King is no father to us,' he spat.

The boy's forearm was shaking uncontrollably. His teeth were gritted hard. He squeezed his eyes tight shut, trying to drive back the pain. But it came on and on in relentless waves. A boiling heat that knew no mercy.

He couldn't stand it any longer. He must drop his arm. Rub at the boiling agony.

'Do you swear to keep our secrets?' demanded Blackstone.

The boy couldn't speak. He managed to nod. His arm was shaking uncontrollably.

I can't do this.

The boy knew he was about to fail the rite. He would join the terrible remains.

Whatever Blackstone does to failures, it couldn't be worse than this.

But as the corpse's gluey eyes stared back at the boy, he knew it wasn't true.

Blackstone was staring at him hungrily. Then his pale eyes widened suddenly, as though he saw something unexpected in the candle flame.

Blackstone whispered something barely audible. A woman's name. The boy thought he said: *Teresa spills blessed blood.*

Then something else.

She wears the dark crown.

Through his agony the boy felt something shift in the atmosphere behind him. It was well known that Blackstone had a wife who'd died at her own hand. No church would bury her and other recruits whispered Blackstone was maddened by thoughts of her in hell.

An unmistakable odour of burning flesh was wafting through the cellar. The boy could feel his arm bubbling. He couldn't do it. He couldn't bear any more pain. Swaying on his feet he knew he was close to a faint. The boy made to move his arm.

Blackstone was holding something now. A leather pouch decorated with strange letters.

Blackstone was saying words. 'The Elixir.'

Unstopping the pouch Blackstone poured a stream of liquid on to the boy's arm. He let out a whimper. The Bringer of Death had burned deep into the muscle. And the Elixir brought heat before relief. There was a wet hiss and a vinegary smell rose up.

Slowly the boy stopped trembling. He let out a breath and stared at his arm. Blackstone stepped forward and embraced him.

And in that moment with the blood pounding in his ears, the boy felt a surge of emotion that took him by surprise. He was filled with love for the Grand Master.

Blackstone straightened, giving his newest recruit a paternal pat on the shoulder.

'You have passed the first test,' said Blackstone proudly. 'Your new name is Jacob, ward of the Sealed Knot.'

Jacob. The boy rolled the title around his mind. He'd been Peter Carpenter before. A simple furniture-maker's son.

'Jacob was one of the first biblical sons,' said Blackstone. 'You must be obedient, always, to your Grand Master. Never question, always obey and your rewards will be great.'

Jacob nodded.

'More tests will come,' said Blackstone. 'The more you pass the more truth you will learn. Fail and you have seen your fate.'

The pain in Jacob's arm was already fading. He was hungry now for the secrets he'd been promised.

'Our faith has finally been rewarded,' said Blackstone. 'Last night a fire started on Pudding Lane. An accidental blaze, but we may use it for our purposes.' He waited for this to sink in. As the lowliest recruit, Jacob had been building fireballs for weeks. He'd not been told when the plans would begin. Jacob was now of a select few who knew the truth. He swelled with pride.

'I have claimed the fire in the name of the Sealed Knot,' continued Blackstone. 'Today the King will receive news that we will burn London to the ground, unless our demands are met.

'The true faith shall rise again,' said Blackstone. 'And what shall we do, with those who defy us?'

'They will burn in holy fire,' Jacob replied, automatically delivering the familiar words.

'Yes,' agreed Blackstone. 'We will burn them.'

Chapter 7

'I once tried to tempt Lily to work for me,' Mother Mitchell was saying. 'Before I discovered her true nature.' She sucked hard on her pipe and looked as if she might say more. Then she shook her head and blew out smoke.

'Do not chase that girl,' warned Mother Mitchell. 'She is a bad business, and a gypsy besides.'

Charlie considered this. Gypsies were godless people. They were lynched in the countryside. Londoners crossed themselves if they saw one.

'Lily Boswell might even be a match for you, Charlie Tuesday,' added Mother Mitchell with a small smile. 'She can pick a pocket fast as lightning, and is as good a card sharp as I've ever seen.'

'Better than me?'

Mother Mitchell smiled. 'Even so, she is dangerous.'

'Where is this Lily now?' asked Charlie.

Mother Mitchell rearranged her bulk on the gold-legged chair. 'You should not wish to find her, Charlie,' she repeated. 'Not where she goes. Even a thief taker would likely be in danger.'

'I have friends everywhere,' said Charlie, extracting another few coins.

'London Bridge,' said Mother Mitchell, taking the money and closing her lips back around her pipe. 'On the west side is a clutch of tailor's shops. Take the third. It has a blue door. In the back are gaming tables. Ill-hidden, but safe enough as they are managed by murderers and cut-throats. The last I knew, Lily was employed there. They are always in need of a handsome girl who is quick with cards to cheat the men from their money.'

Charlie nodded thoughtfully. London Bridge was a treacherous place even for a thief taker. Hardened criminals routinely escaped into the milieu of ancient wooden buildings. Murdered corpses were thrown nightly from the stone arches into the dark waters of the Thames.

Mother Mitchell seemed amused at his discomfort. 'Why is it you must find her?' she asked, puffing steadily.

Charlie hesitated. 'She knows the symbol on my key.'

Mother Mitchell's eyebrows raised then lowered again. 'Still seeking your mysterious lost papers?'

Charlie was turning his key in a tightly balled fist.

'My mother died for those papers.'

'A marriage certificate for Blackstone and his wife. Seems a strange thing to die for.' Mother Mitchell met his eyes, and something maternal passed over her face.

'Do you remember when you came to me as a young boy escaping the Foundling Orphan Home?' she asked. 'When you worked a few errands for this house?'

Charlie nodded.

'You told me you were homeless,' said Mother Mitchell. 'Do you remember what I said?'

'You said, home is where the heart is.'

Mother Mitchell nodded. 'Home is where the heart is,' she repeated. 'Whatever those papers hold, they will not tell you who you are. Let it be.'

'I did not realise you'd become philosophical in your old age,' said Charlie.

Mother Mitchell shrugged good-naturedly. She caught his expression and sighed.

'I've told you all I know of the Sealed Knot,' she said. 'They were a group of nobles formed during the Civil War. That was seventeen years ago. Whatever purpose they had is likely long won or lost.'

'Then why would Lily recognise their symbol?' pressed Charlie. 'She said something of a brotherhood,' he added, remembering the fear in her face.

Mother Mitchell huffed a little.

'You cannot move for secret fraternities in London,' she pointed out. 'The guilds all have some foolish initiation or other. Men love to dress in cloaks and pretend they know secrets.'

Charlie smiled, acknowledging the truth of this. 'She was asking about a Magnus Opus,' he said. 'In the coffee house.'

'Alchemy?' said Mother Mitchell disapprovingly.

'You tell me,' said Charlie. 'It's something to do with making gold.'

'Magnus Opus means "Great Work",' said Mother Mitchell. 'Some of my nobles prattle about it. They squander fortunes in search of some alchemy secret.'

'Do you believe in it?' asked Charlie.

'I believe in gold I can see.' She thought for a moment. 'It doesn't surprise me,' she said, 'that Lily Boswell makes business in that silly myth. Ample opportunity to fool men from coins.'

'But how might she know of the Sealed Knot?'

Mother Mitchell looked thoughtful. 'If Lily Boswell knows something of the Sealed Knot, then you truly should forget your past,' she said finally. 'Dark and dangerous things surround that girl like spectres.'

They were interrupted suddenly by the rustle of skirts. Charlie looked up to see a round-faced young girl, decked in the most incredible finery for the time of day and thickly painted with make-up.

Mother Mitchell looked up sharply. 'Why do you come unannounced, child?' she asked. The girl yawned in an unconcerned kind of way.

'I need the carriage,' she said. 'Mr Gowrie will be at Bishops Gate today.'

Charlie was watching the girl in fascination. He had never got over the strangeness of hearing the thick accent of the slums in the finery of high society.

'Mr Gowrie was last night at Crutched Friars Mansion,' said Mother Mitchell. 'Do you know what they do there, girl? They fume mercury. For syphilis. Your Mr Gowrie will have lost his nose and lips to the pox before the year is out.'

The girl put her hands on her hips.

'A woman cannot catch the pox from a man, you told me yourself,' she retorted.

'In any case, there was news of a fire last night,' added Mother Mitchell. 'On Pudding Lane. The smoke may cause the Smithfield Market animals to bolt. I shall not risk my carriage.'

'The Mayor himself attended that fire,' protested the girl. 'He said a woman could piss on it. Pudding Lane is close by the river. They'll have easily doused the flames by now.'

'We'll see,' said Mother Mitchell with a wave of her hand. 'Without the King's authority, people won't pull down houses for firebreaks. Pudding Lane is dry wood all the way to Cheapside.'

Charlie rose to his feet as their voices pitched to a full-scale argument. Neither woman noticed. As he slipped back into the hallway he could hear the heated exchange raging.

He should make for London Bridge quickly, he decided. Pudding Lane was nearby. Charlie headed back down the gilded hallway mentally mapping his route. Fire could spread fast in the city. And paper burned.

Chapter 8

The smoke from Pudding Lane was sticking in Charlie's throat. Cinders whirled in the air. He eyed the direction of the blaze. Pudding Lane had once been a grisly backstreet of cheap butcheries, but recent years had seen fragrant bake-houses replace stinking meat shops. The whole street would be ashes by the time the fire was extinguished.

From his bankside vantage point, Charlie redirected his attention to London Bridge. Even with his connections to the criminal underclass, he avoided the crossing. The farthing for a boat to cross was one of the few financial outlays he paid willingly.

The bridge had become an outlaw village, its twin banks of high buildings sheltering criminals in their dark embrace. The towering wooden edifices of shops and lodgings were daily threatened with fire, collapse or wholesale consumption by rats. There was hardly a visitor to the city who had not had his pockets picked on the crossing.

Scattered at the entrance were stalls selling cheap ribbon and lace. They crawled with Catholic beggars, evident by their long hair, rosaries and colourful clothing. Civil War veterans hobbled on wooden limbs or sat with stumps splayed accusatorially outwards.

Charlie stopped to buy a pipe of gin from an elderly woman with ulcerated legs. Then, taking a few short gulps of the fiery liquid, he stepped out of the light and into the dark of London Bridge.

A dank smell closed around him. Drivers armed with heavy pistols drove their horses on into the murky depths, whilst a ragged and wild-eyed populace now outnumbered the bargain-ribbon shoppers on the outskirts. Roadside sellers here sold sheaves of tobacco leaf and bales of coarse wool. A pitiful little meat stand had a blood-spattered board of roughly butchered chicken and a thick stench of guts piled beneath.

Charlie noticed several pairs of eyes had begun regarding him with interest. It was time to get off the thoroughfare.

He spied a yellow-faced girl, barely more than a toddler, and beckoned her over. As she approached he saw that in her free arm she clutched a baby, its head lolling large from a tiny rag-swaddled body. Charlie crouched down and extracted a farthing from the carefully concealed purse in his shirt.

'Do you know the tailor's with the blue door?' he asked.

She nodded mutely.

'Can you take me there, off the main street?' He pressed a coin into the filthy hand. Her face broke into a wide smile and she made an odd delighted little curtsey.

'Yes, sir,' she said attaching her hand to his with surprising strength.

She dragged him bodily along, the baby's head swaying as they weaved through the thickly lodged stalls and into a narrow alleyway.

They followed a darker and smaller lane which ran parallel to the main street, exposing the backs of buildings which were almost entirely rotted away.

As they emerged back on to the bustling bridge the girl pointed proudly to a swinging sign showing a needle and thread over a blue door.

'There,' she said, grinning as Charlie handed over another coin. He looked at the parchment-skinned baby whose features were making expressions in slow motion.

'Wait,' he said as the girl turned to go. He handed over the piece of cheese he'd been saving for his midday meal and she beamed before vanishing back into the alley.

Charlie took in the shop warily. It looked to be a serious gambling den. Two mangy dogs were tied by the door, growling over a muddy bone. The windows were open holes with wooden bars and a high blood splatter decorated the frontage.

Charlie paused to check no one was looking before dousing himself in the dregs of his gin pipe. Then he pushed open the door and stepped inside.

A tailor sat cross-legged on the dirty floor. He looked up as Charlie entered.

'I take no new business,' said the tailor.

Charlie dropped into a practised hustle, playing the shifty-eyed gambler and scratching behind his ear as though his lice were bothering him.

'I come for the gaming tables,' he said in a low voice. His host's expression drew even less welcoming.

'There is no gaming here,' he said. 'Best you try your luck further along.'

'I have coin enough to play any man,' said Charlie, thickening his tone to a drunken lilt, and making a lurch forward. The tailor recoiled slightly at the smell of gin, then, without taking his eyes off Charlie, rang a small bell at his side. Almost immediately a burly man cut deep with scars appeared.

Charlie quelled the urge to run. The large man sidled close to the tailor, and to his relief, Charlie heard snatches of 'new' and 'addled'.

There was a long pause as the guard assessed Charlie.

'What do you play?' he asked finally.

'Anything I may place a coin on,' said Charlie loudly.

The guard gave an amused grunt.

'We play at Hazard,' he said. 'The price is ten shillings a throw.'

Charlie nodded, but his stomach twisted. Only a handful of villains could afford those stakes. Worse still, they played at dice, so his card sharping would not help him.

'Something amiss?' challenged the guard.

Charlie shook his head, making to step past him. 'Ten a throw,' he replied. 'I have enough.'

The guard held out a rough hand. 'And a shilling to see inside,' he added.

Charlie kept his face impassive as he handed over the money. He had barely enough left for a single throw.

'That way,' said the guard, dropping his hand.

Charlie headed through a doorway closed by sacking, and found himself not in a room, but a half-finished shack tacked on to the back of the tailor's shop. The three-sided shelter of rotting wood opened out on to the Thames, and a stiff autumn breeze rolled in off the boat-laden river.

Under this drafty refuge the gamesters huddled on their haunches, flinging grubby dice and coins into the centre. Charlie noticed with a sinking feeling that Lily was not among them. He had until his money or luck ran out to discover her whereabouts.

Charlie squatted among the men, noticing inch-thick slices of whirling river between the ill-fitted floorboards. Engrossed in their game, they barely looked up.

There were five gamblers in total, and all bore the signs of being staunch villains. Magpie-markers of ill-gotten wealth glinted on them. A tricorn hat here, silver shoe-buckles there. Two looked barely old enough to be considered men at all. They must be pickpockets, trained from when they were old enough to walk. The others looked older and tougher. One wore a worn leather eye-patch. Another's bald head was patched with silver from a skull fracture.

The round of dice came to an end. Slowly they scrutinised him, one by one.

Recognition sparked in the single eye of a man with an eye-patch. 'I know you,' he said. 'You are the thief taker.'

Chapter 9

King Charles lay sprawled in bed. It was already mid-morning but the wine seemed to still be swirling in his head. Louise Keroulle was beside him, her naked plump limbs sprawled out from the sheets. His eyes rested on her sleeping face. Louise's childlike features looked so innocent in repose. He never would have guessed the demanding rages of the woken woman.

In the middle distance a door slammed. And before Charles could register what it might mean, two large hands grabbed Louise's soft curling hair.

He sat up in alarm as his mistress's head was wrenched back and she was pulled bodily from the bed. For a fractional moment Charles thought the dreams had returned and he was in the middle of a waking nightmare. Cromwell's armed men. His father's head rolling on the scaffold.

Then, as Louise crashed loudly to the rug, he saw a familiar face. Barbara Castlemaine was wrestling a now wide-awake Louise from the sheet in which she was still partially wrapped.

Charles watched in dull amazement as Louise shrieked in outrage, her little fingers digging into the other woman's auburn hair.

Barbara batted her away with a blow that made Charles wince, and followed up with a succession of ringing slaps.

Charles had not seen Barbara for many months, not since their argument over the dukedom he'd given their third child. He should have foreseen she would burst back into his life in a storm of violence and retribution.

'Barbara . . .' began Charles. But his attempt to placate seemed to make her angrier.

'Get out!' Barbara raged at Louise. 'You dirty French whore.'

Barbara was tall and well built to Louise's short chubbiness, with an angry streak which cast the other woman's rages as dull petulance. She had seized the skin on Louise's rounded upper arm, and in her fury seemed not to realise this prevented her opponent acceding her wishes.

'You call me whore?' blustered Louise, 'Where is your husband? How many bastard children have you had by the King?'

In answer Barbara delivered a blow to the side of Louise's head.

Louise's face cycled through fear, outrage and affront. She looked at Barbara, then to Charles.

'I cannot deal with Barbara when she is like this,' admitted Charles with less regret than he might have. 'Better to do what she says.'

Louise was breathing heavily, her small breasts rising and falling. Barbara released the unthinking hold on her arm, causing Louise to fall again.

'What is she doing here?' Barbara raged.

Charles sat up a little in bed. At the height of her famous temper, his longest-serving mistress was a gorgeous spectacle. The sultry violet eyes smouldered in fierce fury, and her copper hair blazed. She put Charles in mind of an avenging goddess.

'She was keeping me company,' he said mildly, 'whilst you were bedding the rest of the court.'

Louise had risen to her feet and snatched up a corner of sheet to cover herself. Her eyes flicked between the King and Barbara.

The movement drew Barbara's attention and she made another enraged grab towards Louise's curling hair.

'You fat French bitch!' shouted Barbara, missing by an inch as Louise darted out of reach with surprising speed for her size. Louise burst into tears and a torrent of French expletives poured forth. Charles raised a calming hand, but she rushed from the chamber, pulling the sheet tighter around her body as she ran.

With her opponent vanquished, Barbara had calmed. She seated herself on the King's large bed, arranging her skirts carefully.

Charles was still mentally calculating how much it would cost to buy back Louise's good humour. The people had started to openly protest about his spending on women. As a Catholic, Louise's expenditure was particularly resented.

'She ran fast for a chubby girl,' Barbara observed, her shapely eyebrows furrowed.

Charles gave a sigh which was mixed with a laugh.

'What do you want, Barbara?'

She tossed her head coquettishly.

'Why do you imagine I want something?'

'You always want something,' said Charles evenly. 'All women do. Money. Jewels. Titles for your children.'

'*Our* children,' said Barbara, anger rising in her voice. She seemed to check herself and her voice softened.

'Perhaps I wanted to see you,' she suggested. 'Perhaps I missed you.'

She put a hand up to his shaved head.

'You cut your hair,' she said sadly.

'Six years on the throne is all it has taken to turn my hair white.'

Encouraged, Barbara leaned over and took his long white fingers in hers.

'Do you remember,' she began, 'the night we met, where you put these fingers?'

Charles swallowed. He had forgotten how quickly Barbara's conversation could turn to seduction. It was one of her most alluring qualities, and had kept her in his bed for so many years, despite a succession of beautiful young women.

Barbara leaned forward so her face was level with his. Even at twenty-seven, having birthed four of his children, she was so very, very beautiful.

'I was barely sixteen,' she whispered, moving his hand down. 'When I met the exiled King. Roaming in Holland with not a penny to his name. I was the only one,' she breathed, stroking his cheek. 'The only girl who truly loved you before you were King. You need never doubt me.'

Her hand had moved to her skirts, and Charles noticed the ring he had bought her was missing. The jewel had been bought at great cost from the Spanish Ambassador. He had heard rumours she'd sold it, but had not believed it until now.

'Tell me why you came back,' replied Charles, stopping her hand. In addition to seducing half his court, Barbara often hawked his most expensive gifts as revenge for his philandering.

'Why should Lucy Walter's son have a dukedom?' Barbara demanded.

Charles shook his head slowly and sighed. Always it came back to this.

'We have talked of this,' he said. 'Monmouth is my eldest son and I have great love for him.'

Barbara's wide mouth set hard like stone.

'You don't help his character,' she said, 'with your indulgences.'

Charles waved a hand. 'I was a young man once,' he said. 'He'll grow out of the giddiness.'

'You swore you loved me best,' spat Barbara. 'You swore it. Is this what the word of a King is worth?'

Charles spread out his hands. 'Lucy and I were barely eighteen. She was nothing to me. You can't be jealous of a fifteen-year-old boy. Our sons have dukedoms too.

Is this why you came back?' he asked, his voice softening. 'To start the old wars again?'

Barbara tilted her head and smiled a little. It was his favourite expression of hers. The one that reminded him, despite everything she'd done, Barbara loved him in her way.

'I fear for you, Charles,' she said after a moment. 'What happened to the young man I met in Holland? Who swore that when he was King, he would right his country's wrongs?'

'He encountered politics,' said Charles sadly. 'What happened to the young girl who waited for me naked, in the upstairs of a Dutch tavern?'

'She had four of your children,' returned Barbara with a smile. Then she frowned.

'You have heard of the fire?'

Charles nodded. 'A bakery by the river. The Mayor says a woman could piss on it.'

'There is a gale blown in to fan the flames,' said Barbara. 'It's still burning on Pudding Lane. And there is a Catholic faction who claim the blaze as their vengeance.'

Charles shrugged.

'Every day there is a new rebel faction,' he said. 'The Protestants hate me for protecting the Catholics. The Catholics hate me for not doing enough. You can't move in London for men calling for my head.'

'This faction is different,' said Barbara, her violet eyes serious. 'They call themselves the Sealed Knot.'

Charles stiffened. 'How do you know this?' he asked.

'I hear all the whispers,' said Barbara. 'There's nothing talked of in court that passes me by.'

There was a long pause.

'You never told me,' said Barbara finally, 'why the Sealed Knot followed you to Holland.'

Charles was silent and thoughtful.

'I felt so sure they were all dead,' he murmured finally. 'All but Amesbury.' His mouth had set in a hard, grim line.

Barbara chewed a finger. 'I will send for Amesbury,' she said. 'Perhaps he can intercede. They were all dangerous men,' she added. 'You must be careful.' Her eyes were softer now, full of fear.

Charles felt a spreading sense of fear. Barbara had no idea how dangerous. Or how deeply he was in their debt.

Sensing his unease, Barbara's soft fingers closed on his. Charles kissed them gratefully. She always could read him better than anyone else.

'I'm glad you're back,' he murmured.

Barbara smiled and folded him in her arms. Charles breathed a little easier, letting her comfort him.

'Do we know anything more?' he asked. 'About the Sealed Knot faction?'

Barbara shook her head.

'Only that they issue demands like all the others.'

'What demands do they make?'

'Give back what is ours,' said Barbara. 'Or we'll burn London to the ground.'

Chapter 10

'You're a thief taker?' The gambler with the skull-plate was glaring.

Charlie swallowed. He could already sense the outsized guard bristling.

'You had John Noilly hanged for murder,' said the man with the eye-patch, waving a knowing finger. 'Little Kitty from hereparts was the girl killed.'

Charlie let his eyes slide to the open water of the Thames. Two swift movements would be all that was needed to dive into the safety of the river.

Unexpectedly the man leaned over and gave Charlie a well-meant thump on the back. 'God bless you,' he said. 'Kitty was one of ours, and our sort never sees justice left to the likes of the Watch.'

Charlie felt a rush of relief.

The eye-patch leaned over and scooped up the dice, all business now that he had decided to accept the newcomer. 'We start a new round. Main number is six,' he said, hurling the dice down with a clatter.

Charlie instantly discerned the fall of loaded dice. His eyes followed the sleight of hand. The eye-patch and the skull-fracture were fleecing the younger men. Charlie breathed a little easier. If the men were cheating, then he could follow the course of their feints to stay in the game.

———

They played for an hour, during which time Charlie was careful to win and lose evenly, following the loaded dice as it feinted between the players.

'The Catholics are the cause of it,' the eye-patch was saying. 'They touch their rosaries and are forgiven murders. Now they throw fireballs.'

'They spread lice with their long hair and fancy clothes,' agreed skull-plate, spitting. 'This city is a stinking hole. The King should do something. Pull down the old wood buildings. Stop the smithies and their sparks. But he is cock-deep in whores whilst Londoners are up to their ears in shit.'

'The King *thinks* to rule,' said eye-patch, 'but it is the guilds who run this city.' He rubbed his thumb and finger together. 'Money,' he clarified, 'is London's King.'

He licked his finger and raised the eye-patch to reveal a scarred pink socket.

'Tried my hand at carpentry,' he said, 'without thinking to join the city guild. The Carpenters' Hall sent men. Said I must apprentice with them or trade outside the city.' He tapped his missing eye. 'Words were exchanged,' he concluded.

'I always thought to join a guild,' agreed skull-plate wistfully. 'The barber-surgeons maybe. Learn the secrets of a craft.'

'I should like to see you in a honest trade,' laughed the eye-patch. 'With all the ragged apprentices.'

'I would buy guild membership,' retorted skull-plate. 'I almost had the fee once.'

'Stick at stealing and gaming, my friend,' said eye-patch with a wink of his good eye. 'It suits you better.'

Charlie was steeling his nerve to ask about Lily when one of the players called for drink.

A female voice sounded behind the gamers and Charlie froze. But when he risked a glance upwards, he was disappointed to see an ordinary-looking girl lugging a small barrel of sherry on her hip. She made a little shriek as one of the gamers ventured a hand up her calf and stepped hastily away from the group.

Charlie watched her go. 'What is become of the other girl?' he asked conversationally. 'The one who played her hand here? By the name of Lily.'

The temperature of the gaming den seemed to drop by several degrees.

Charlie pretended to scrutinise the dice whilst studying their reactions. The older men wore practised poker faces but their affected nonchalance didn't seem to be hiding a great deal. One of the younger pickpockets knew something though. He had visibly twitched at the mention of Lily.

After a long pause the eye-patch spoke up.

'That was when old Mooney ran the place,' he said, his eyes fixed on the falling dice. 'Lily brought 'em in off the streets. Drunk ones. Rich ones. She was a demon player and robbed 'em blind. Things is different here now. We play a straight game for our kind alone.'

'Where is Lily now?' asked Charlie.

The eye-patch sucked at his teeth. 'Last I heard 'a Lily Boswell, she was on the hunt for some treasure,' he said slowly. 'That's how I heard it.'

'That's not right,' corrected the skull-plate. 'It's a ghost she chases. A man who can't be killed.'

Charlie logged this. 'Do you know where she is now?'

The eye-patch shook his head. 'You are best leaving well enough alone, lad.' He gestured to the skull-plate. 'See Lister? He got a knife in his belly courtesy of that one.'

The skull-plate nodded aggrievedly and they both returned to play without elaborating.

Charlie's attention settled back on the young pickpocket. He was a shambling sort of youth, gangly and awkward, with long limbs splayed at odd angles. The boy had been worrying a coin in his hand and now he stood.

'I have business to attend,' he muttered, in a tone casual enough for Charlie's practised ear to sound an alarm. The boy knew something.

Possibilities raced through Charlie's head. He'd have to bide out his time and follow the gambler. Perhaps he could question him in some safer part of London.

But he needn't have dwelt on any of these options because the young gambler, for all his gracelessness, was more astute than Charlie had given him credit for.

The boy lurched with sudden speed through the sacking doorway. The other gamblers looked up only briefly, as if this turn of events were an hourly occurrence. Neither did they seem particularly shocked when Charlie abandoned his winnings and raced out after him.

Chapter 11

The boy was already far ahead into the thick of the crowd as Charlie burst from the tailor's shop. Cursing, he forged forward in pursuit. They dodged past tattered stalls and heaps of wares. People were packing up, leaving the Bridge, Charlie noticed. The fire must be serious then, if stall holders and shopkeepers were deserting.

The boy pushed through a group of courtesans bartering with a ribbon seller and made it off the Bridge. Charlie followed.

The wind had picked up. And as Charlie broke into the loud daylight of King William Street, he froze in horror.

The Pudding Lane fire, which had been dying back, was a sky-high sheet of flame. Fire had engulfed Fish Street. The Fishmongers' Hall blazed high, dropping hot cinders on to the dry roofs of Swan Lane. Two young cinder thieves were dancing through the flames, pillaging ceremonial fish carvings and candlesticks.

A ragged line of firefighters were assembled, ferrying slops of Thames water into the angry maw of the fire from a few small buckets. Elsewhere more innovative locals were tossing milk and beer towards the burning bakeries.

Ahead of Charlie was a blazing curtain of flame. The escaping boy cast a brief, terrified glance back, and then ran for a narrow gap in the fire. He made it through with Charlie hot on his heels. But as the boy's skinny frame vanished into smoke, the flame billowed wider in a sudden gust of wind.

Charlie hesitated. The battered leather of his close-fitting coat was thick enough to deflect flame. Fastening the row of tiny buttons, Charlie steeled himself and plunged towards the flames. A rush of hot air enveloped him and he emerged, dark-blond hair singed and scalp sweating, the fire behind him.

He was just in time to see the boy turn right, towards Leadenhall Street. Despite Charlie's rapid pace the boy, animated by fear, was proving a fast competitor.

Charlie slipped into the more considered pace of the long distance runner. The boy seemed to be slowing now, ducking through the maze of smaller alleys rather than maintaining a straight sprint. But as he turned back out through Bishops Gate and fled north, Charlie realised he was heading towards Leadenhall Butchers' Market.

Ordinarily this would have been an expert move. The boy could slip into the sea of animals and traders. But with the fire so close it marked desperation. The market would be chaos.

A wall of noise hit Charlie as they spun through Bull's Head Passage. Spurred by the fire, traders were deserting with their stock. A mayhem of sheep and cattle coupled with the men shouting, cursing and hitting at the herd with sticks poured forth in a torrent. Smoke and ash whirled in the air, whipping the animals into a terrified frenzy.

During the pursuit the boy's shirt had ridden up and was flapping loose in the breeze, and Charlie was within a few yards of grabbing hold of it. But his target swerved suddenly, heading towards the cattle herd. The boy hesitated, judging his point of entry. Then he plunged into a maelstrom of hide and hooves.

The boy vanished for a moment, before reappearing bloodied and filthy on the market side. He paused, locking eyes with Charlie, and then raced into the market building.

Charlie watched for a moment. In his panic the boy had flung himself through where the herd was thinnest. A better place to cross was the most crowded, where animals moved slowest.

Charlie scanned where the cows were bottle-necked, pitching against one another in their haste to move forward. There was a windowsill at waist height.

In two moves Charlie had one foot on the sill and another on the flat back of a jostling cow. The animal bellowed in outrage, twisting so Charlie had to fight to keep his balance. He stepped both feet on to the terrified cow, and in an ungainly four-limbed manoeuvre, he began stumbling over the backs of the cattle, in the direction of the market entrance.

A cry of fury went up from one of the drovers, and Charlie ducked a flying stick. As he reached the edge of the tussling herd, all the cattle-herders were roaring obscenities. Charlie dodged a calloused fist, slid down the final cow and sprinted into the market building.

Chapter 12

Charlie scanned the wide expanse of Leadenhall. Under the market's majestic medieval beams, the boy was nowhere to be seen.

The high wind whipped through the market corridors, channelling vast plumes of smoke through the walkways. Charlie coughed, squinting to see through it.

At the periphery were a few remaining animal pens, their livestock crammed in so tightly that hooves lifted from the ground. Deeper in, a handful of traders were hastily concluding their business. They made a tableau of stench-laden scenes, scraping guts, boiling bones, or cutting the throats of animals into tin buckets. Gore-splattered boys, ferrying buckets of blood to be boiled into black puddings, made rapidly back and forth.

With no sign of the escapee, Charlie's gaze dropped to the ground. The market floor was littered in muck and straw and dappled with the endless footprints of the traders and customers. A mix of prints from both bare and shod feet had been pressed into the slurry.

Forcing himself to slow, Charlie took in the array. Making a mental grid system of the market floor his eyes tracked systematically along the sludge-covered pathway. And then he saw it. The far-apart tracks of feet which had sprinted.

Quickly, he homed in on the prints, picking up the trail. At one point the boy seemed to be heading out towards the city. But a smeared imprint showed him veer back towards the bone boilers and pudding makers.

Now the trail ran out, dropping to a walking pace and muddied among the feet of the hard-working pudding boys.

Turning into the reeking smoke of the trade Charlie made his way thoughtfully along the stalls, as if making a selection of the best producer. A man carrying a pail of intestines looked across at him in annoyance.

'You'll not get a pudding here now,' he said. 'All will likely be burned to the ground by tomorrow.'

Charlie ignored him, cruising slowly along the row. He was greeted by a variety of confused or annoyed glances – each vendor clearly thinking along the same lines as the first. But as he suspected there was a pudding-maker who did not look up. A man who seemed all too well engaged in his business of adding the oats and bran to the blackening pails of liquid.

Charlie eyed him for a moment before stepping forward and sliding his last half crown carefully on to the well-worn wooden counter. 'I'll not hurt the boy,' he said, dropping his voice to an almost indiscernible whisper. 'I mean only to return some property.'

The vendor's head remained carefully down, and Charlie kept an anxious eye on the gleaming array of cleavers arranged around the stall. Then the man looked up, passing his hand unconsciously over his forehead to leave a bloody smear. Something in Charlie's expression must have convinced him, because he slowly slid the coin into his fist. Then with a tiny motion the man nodded to the back of his shop. Silently, Charlie moved past him.

A small fire filled the back room with the stench of boiling bones, and a stack of carcasses in various states of being skinned were heaped towards the back corner. Charlie surveyed the scene. One of the glassy-eyed cows seemed to be breathing of its own accord.

In a lightning movement, Charlie pounced, throwing his arms around the twitching carcass. Inside the animal something struggled violently, and the boy's face emerged from beneath the head of the cow, where the flesh had been slit stomach to sternum.

'You know something of Lily Boswell,' said Charlie as he wrestled to contain his hostage. 'She has information for me.'

The boy's tussling lessened slightly. 'I don't know her,' he said, eyeing the fleshy prison. 'God's truth.'

'You don't have to lead me to her,' Charlie said. 'Only tell me where she is.'

'She will kill me.' The boy was struggling again. 'Those gypsy girls grow up hunting with bows and knives.'

'And I will kill you if you do not tell,' said Charlie gruffly. 'So you may die now for certain, or later for maybe.'

The boy hesitated and Charlie shook the carcass, causing the cow's head to nod in violent agreement.

'Tell me where she is.'

'I don't know, I swear it,' said the boy.

Charlie lowered his voice.

'Do you know who I am?'

His captive shook his head.

'I am Charlie Tuesday, the thief taker. You have heard what people say? That I have a sense for when people are lying.'

The boy swallowed.

'Lie to me again,' said Charlie evenly, 'and you will join this pile of carcasses.'

Chapter 13

Blackstone fingered the torture tools.

'I've been here before,' he said, eyeing the thick, heavy walls of the Clink prison.

'In what capacity?' asked the gaoler nervously. He'd forgotten how large Blackstone was. He seemed to take up the entire cell. The muscular bulk had been heaved into plain black breeches, thick leather boots and gauntlets. A black woollen tabard skirted his protruding belly, banded by a broad silk sash. His cavalier hat stayed firmly on his head, despite the close confines of the Clink.

He wore the clothes of an old Royalist general. But the pale eyes, sunk deep into his fleshy face, were those of a killer.

Blackstone gave a grim smile.

'Both capacities,' he said. 'I was here for a long, long time.' He inhaled deeply and pointed to a brazier of burning tar. 'The smell of pitch,' he said, eyeing the dirty smoke, 'still sickens my stomach.'

The gaoler scratched nervously at a flea bite. He often brokered black-market goods, but was regretting agreeing to this transaction. Something was very wrong with this dead-eyed man.

'It's hard to think of you . . . that way.' He managed.

'Cromwell took revenge on the King's generals,' said Blackstone. 'We were crammed in here. Starved, tortured.'

His eyes clouded slightly. They rested on a sharp-looking iron implement.

'Then,' he continued, 'I was employed to extract secrets from Royalists. My . . . experiences you see.' He smiled sadly at the pincers in his hand. 'They made me better qualified.'

'Do you have the cauldrons ready?' he asked.

'We have two,' said the gaoler carefully. 'We had a problem finding lead.'

Blackstone picked up a wickedly toothed wooden vice.

'You've made some improvements,' he noted. His eyes were cold.

The gaoler nodded. Sweat had broken out on his forehead, though the cell was cool.

'Torture is a wicked business,' said Blackstone.

The gaoler nodded uncertainly.

Blackstone lifted the vice and eyed it against the candle flame.

'New?' he suggested. 'There's no blood.'

The gaoler nodded. 'We've better tools than any other gaol,' he said. 'There's no man in twenty years the Clink hasn't broken under torture.'

'No man?'

'There was one,' the gaoler corrected himself. 'A nobleman.' The gaoler sniffed. ''S one of those legends,' he says. 'I don't believe it. The story is they used every tool on him for two years. He never gave any names.' The gaoler gave a scoff of derision. 'I've never met a man lasted more than two weeks.'

Blackstone replaced the vice. 'He was real,' he said. 'They called him The Unbreakable. Torturers tried each device in the Clink and even fashioned some new ones. The man never uttered a word.'

'You were one of the torturers?' asked the gaoler, sounding interested.

'I am the man they couldn't break,' replied Blackstone.

The gaoler's eyes widened.

'I'm a different man now,' added Blackstone. 'I'm a father. Of a kind.'

'Children are a blessing,' offered the gaoler uncertainly.

Blackstone nodded. 'And we must protect them.' In a sudden movement he grabbed the gaoler's throat. The gaoler twisted helplessly under Blackstone's grip. But his skinny frame was no match for the enormous man.

Deliberately, Blackstone forced him back into a leather chair. The gaoler struggled in horror as leather straps were fastened over his wrists. Blackstone scooped up the iron pincer.

'You hurt one of my boys,' said Blackstone, wielding the pincers. He raised a hand as the gaoler made to protest. 'You came to his house and took his brother. For being Catholic.'

'Many boys,' said the gaoler, his voice quavering. 'Parliament makes us . . . Catholics must be kept in line.'

Blackstone gave him a cold smile. His eyes were burning. 'Catholic women and children too? I hear all.' He tapped his head.

The gaoler shrank back. 'I can give you . . . information,' he gibbered. 'Of interest.'

'I know everything in the prisons,' said Blackstone carelessly, his eyes ranging the array of tools. He selected a sharp-edged hammer.

'Amesbury is looking for you,' blurted the gaoler. 'He suspects you build an army against His Majesty.'

Blackstone's face darkened. Amesbury was one of the turncoats. He hadn't thought about that in a long time. They'd fought together for the King. Blackstone, Amesbury and Torr had been Brothers of the Sealed Knot. Sworn to return the King to the throne. Before Blackstone made the unholy marriage and all the darkness descended.

'Why does Amesbury suspect I plot against the King?' he demanded.

The gaoler was shaking his head. 'I ask no questions,' he said, looking helplessly at the cuffs. 'I just supply lead. Tell me nothing, I beg you. I will never hurt another Catholic.'

'After the war I had just enough money to buy a guild place,' continued Blackstone, ignoring him. 'They taught me a craft. Gave me permission to trade. I worked my way up to the Mayor's office.' His eyes dulled. 'But that is not where true power lay. Not for a Catholic.'

Blackstone pulled off his hat. The gaoler recoiled. Shiny wheals and scars had eaten away half the skin on his scalp.

'I burned with plague,' he said. 'I cannot be killed. Now I build my army of fallen angels. We will drag the King down to hell.'

'I will not tell . . .' began the gaoler.

'You?' laughed Blackstone. 'A Protestant gaoler, who'll help a Catholic plotter for the right price? You'll keep my secret?'

The gaoler's face said it all. He knew too much.

'We have a kinship, you and I,' said Blackstone, gesturing to the prison cell. 'We understand things other men cannot. Or should not,' he corrected himself. 'We know great secrets.'

Blackstone moved back.

'I find the most terrible thing is the shame,' he said. 'Not yours. You become the monster all too easily.'

His blue eyes looked thoughtful.

'But their shame,' he said. 'The men you hurt. That's what chills the soul. Pissing themselves and crying for their mothers. You carry it always. Do you find that?'

The gaoler nodded but Blackstone could see in his eyes it was a lie.

'Then after a time,' said Blackstone. 'You come to need it.'

Thoughtfully he picked up the wooden vice.

Blackstone attached the vice to the gaoler's knuckle.

'Broken bones are painful,' he said. 'But it's the joints. The tendons. That's where agony really lies.'

The man began shaking his head, sweating.

'Knuckles make a noise,' continued Blackstone. 'You never forget it.'

The gaoler's gaze dropped to Blackstone's hands. Two of his large knuckles were a flattened mess of scars. He looked back up at Blackstone's face.

'Please . . .' he said, 'I've been nothing but loyal.'

'Tell me what you know of Amesbury,' said Blackstone.

'We imprisoned a young boy for thieving,' said the gaoler, the words coming out in a rush. 'This afternoon. We only showed him the tools and he told us everything.'

'Everything?'

'He worked for the Earl of Amesbury. As an informant. He was trying to find Torr. To get to you.'

Blackstone's mind ticked over this, turning it this way and that. If Torr were found, could it be a problem? He pictured his old ally, marked with mystic tattoos, alchemy tools in his strong hands.

'If you should need someone to kill Torr . . .' began the gaoler.

Blackstone laughed.

'You are not the man,' he said.

He moved back and the gaoler's body relaxed slightly. He tugged hopefully at the leather cuffs. Blackstone looked at them and then raised a hand for the gaoler to be patient.

Blackstone nodded. 'Do you tell yourself stories?' he said, 'of the men you torture?'

'I don't know . . .'

'We all have ways of squaring it with ourselves,' continued Blackstone. 'Let me tell you my way.'

Chapter 14

There was a pause as the boy visibly assessed his options. He looked at Charlie then to the wider meat market.

'I deliver things to her,' he said finally. 'She pays me.'

'What kind of things?' Charlie demanded.

'Information.'

'About?' Charlie tightened his hold on the boy.

'A brotherhood!' yelped the boy. 'She's looking for a brotherhood.'

'What kind of brotherhood?' prompted Charlie.

'Alchemists,' said the boy. 'She says they're powerful.' The boy swallowed. 'They have a secret which could change the world.'

'And how are you helping Lily to discover this brotherhood?'

The boy hesitated, and his eyes shifted almost imperceptibly to his chest. Thief taking had honed Charlie's attention to small gestures. In an instant his hand was at the boy's shirt, pulling free a paper hidden there.

'What is this?' he demanded.

'I don't know,' said the boy, 'I can't read.'

Charlie eyed the paper, careful not to loosen his grip on the boy. He didn't want to admit he couldn't read well himself.

At first glance he saw words arranged in a circle. Names, perhaps.

'This is for Lily Boswell?' asked Charlie. 'This is the information she wanted?'

The boy nodded mutely.

'Where did you get it?' asked Charlie.

'One of the rebel factions. They meet by the Thames.'

'A rebel faction?'

'Catholics,' clarified the boy. 'They are mostly poor boys. From Whitechapel, near the tanneries. But they have a leader who is a noble. They say he is a ghost. A ghost who can't be killed.'

Charlie was piecing things together.

'Does the group use this symbol?' He held up his key, tightening his other arm on the boy.

The boy's eyes widened and he nodded.

'They have it burned on to them. Here.' The boy gestured with his forearm.

Charlie's face darkened.

'When were you to give this to Lily?' He waved the paper.

'Today at noon. She'll take a carriage to the Palace, I'm to meet her there,' he admitted.

'The Palace?' In his surprise Charlie released his grip slightly. Lily must be joining the parade of women hoping to catch King Charles's eye. It made sense that a girl as attractive as Lily would try her luck. But it seemed beneath her.

Sensing his distraction, the boy made a sudden twist, slipping free of the carcass. Charlie made a grab, but the boy, slick with entrails, slipped from his grip. He skidded across the bloody floor and fled into the market. Charlie watched him go, deciding he had extracted all he needed. He moved his attention to the paper.

His eyes travelled over the ring of words. It was a round robin. Of the kind sailors write so as no one man is held culprit for challenging the captain. A round of names circled a short paragraph of script and a number four.

But the number was different to how it was usually written. The four had a kind of curly tail. Like a symbol.

Charlie sucked at his scarred upper lip and began slowly making out the names. These were surnames he was familiar with – Smith, Cutler, Skinner. Commoner's names. Men who worked for a living. This fitted with what the boy had told him. Poor Catholics. But the paper did not. What impoverished Catholic boy could write?

Charlie's gaze fell to the longer script, which was written in the shaky hand of a semi-literate. He read it carefully, trying not to move his lips as he read. Charlie froze.

'The Sealed Knot ask their Grand Master Blackstone,' said the writing, 'not to use alchymy to fire the city.'

Blackstone.

His gaze went back to the document. He licked his finger, dabbed at the ink and tasted it. A cheap kind made from burned tar and honey, which flaked within weeks of drying. This writing was not old.

He turned it back and re-read carefully. *Alchymy.*

Charlie assessed what he knew.

Blackstone had contracted plague and vanished last summer. Charlie had assumed him dead and buried, his possessions burned.

He'd made an uneasy promise to Maria that he wouldn't pursue the mystery. But his thief-taker instincts had always gnawed away at him. Eventually they'd driven a split between them.

What if Blackstone lived?

The paper seemed to suggest he'd not only survived the plague, but had built a following of Catholic boys.

Fire swirled in Charlie's mind. If Blackstone lived, then the chest his key opened could still be somewhere in London. Charlie thought of the growing fire, and his stomach turned.

Flames were sweeping through the city. He needed to get to the Palace.

Chapter 15

The moment Charlie arrived at Whitehall he knew he'd been misinformed. The flag at Barbara Castlemaine's grand apartments was raised. The King's most famous mistress allowed no parades of women. There was no other way a commoner like Lily could get inside the Palace.

Charlie eyed the hotch-potch of Palace buildings, thinking. His eye idly rested on some anti-Royalist graffiti. A naked image of the Queen, graphically suggesting she was barren because of the Pope's illicit attentions.

Something had always seemed amiss about Lily going to the Palace. Charlie replayed his conversation with the boy. The informant told the truth. Charlie was sure of it. He took out the round robin and studied it. It wasn't yet noon. Charlie decided he had time to pursue another line of enquiry.

Expensive shops with colourful carved-wood frontages were ranged opposite Whitehall. An apothecary sign swung outside one. It was the only shop whose diamond-pane windows were black with soot. As he neared, thick yellow-green smoke curled from the doorjamb.

Charlie knocked, and when no answer came, opened the door to a fug of choking fumes. He squinted through the eye-watering haze. After a moment his eyes adjusted to the gloom, and he made out the tall shape of Sebastian Longbody.

'Charlie Tuesday!' A twitching mouth was the closest thing Sebastian did to smiling. Facial expressions were bothersome with so many ideas raging. 'Only this week I used those herbs you returned to me.'

'It was one of my most interesting cases,' said Charlie.

Sebastian tilted his head and squinted through the smoke. His huge eyes were yellowed and staring. A tall black hat and white collar marked him of the Quaker religion and his jet cloak was pocked with round burn holes. A shock of wild brown hair gave his skeletal frame a scarecrow air. He stood in front of a large table scarred with the burns and stains. Behind him were ranged flasks of every size and colour.

'A moment.' Sebastian held up his hand. Then he tipped a flask, dissipating the curling yellow smoke.

Charlie approached the table. A crucible burned with embers. Smoke seized at his chest and his head swam.

'Opium,' explained Sebastian. 'Smugglers are bringing huge bales from India. It is a good painkiller mixed with wine. Burning makes it better still. Don't stand too close,' he added, waving Charlie away. 'It addles the mind if you aren't used to it.'

Charlie took a judicious step backwards.

'Your potions are still keeping you in favour with the King?' he asked, eyeing the colourful flasks.

'How else does a Quaker keep a shop?' said Sebastian. 'London is not known for religious tolerance. People say Catholics are throwing fireballs.'

'Catholics are blamed for the fire?' asked Charlie.

Sebastian twitched his strange smile. 'If not the Catholics then us Quakers,' he said, 'and if not Quakers then the foreigners. Is that not how it is with Londoners? We must all be Protestant or burn.'

He shook his head.

'Things are changing in England,' he said, tapping his black hat. 'Cromwell split religion apart.'

Charlie took the round robin out of his pocket. 'How much do you know of alchemists?' he asked. 'Might their arts be used to fire the city?'

Sebastian tilted his head at the paper.

'You wish me to discern something from this?'

Charlie nodded and Sebastian peered.

'Why are the names arranged in a circle?'

'It's a round robin,' said Charlie. 'A sailor's tool. They write their names in a circle so none can be held ringleader.'

Sebastian blinked his yellowed eyes slowly at the paper.

'Common names all,' he said. 'No nobles. Men who work a trade.' He frowned at the writing. 'The Sealed Knot ask their Grand Master Blackstone,' he read, 'not to use alchymy to fire the city.'

He looked up at Charlie.

'Treason?' he asked.

'I don't know,' admitted Charlie. 'But I think they may use some alchemic means. There's a number four. Here. Could it mean something?' He pointed.

Sebastian raised the page and mouthed silently.

'That's no number,' he said eventually. 'It's a symbol. For lye.'

'An alchemist symbol?' asked Charlie.

Sebastian's brow furrowed. 'Yes. But lye is no alchemist thing. Every laundress in the city has a barrel for whitening linen.'

'Could it be used to cause a fire?'

Sebastian considered this.

'Not to my knowledge,' he said. 'Lye is made from soot. But you can't set it alight. In chymic law lye is named as a common substance. Along with wood and potash. And I don't believe an alchemist would use it.'

'Why not?'

'I'm an apothecary, not an alchemist,' said Sebastian. 'We are sciences which collide. I supply them. They supply me. But from my dealings with them, they are haughty in using higher metals. The only low thing an alchemist mixes is sulphur.'

Charlie considered this, trying to make sense of it.

'An alchemist would never use lye?'

'You'd have to ask an alchemist,' said Sebastian. 'It is possible some rogue chymist would attempt his own creations. But those I have encountered are a close-knit community. True alchemists are obsessed with rare ingredients. They believe only the purest will reveal the universal marriage.'

'Marriage?' repeated Charlie.

'Some alchemist belief,' said Sebastian with a shrug. 'I am not certain what it means. Only that alchemists talk of the universal marriage a great deal.'

'Could they mean an actual marriage?' asked Charlie, thinking of Blackstone's papers.

'I have no idea,' said Sebastian.

'What of the Magnus Opus?' asked Charlie. 'That's an alchemist pursuit isn't it?'

Sebastian looked confused. 'I assumed you know all about it.'

'Why would you assume that?' asked Charlie, thinking he may have misheard.

'Magnus Opus is the great work,' said Sebastian slowly. 'It's otherwise known as the search for the Philosopher's Stone. And you carry the symbol for it. On the key around your neck.'

Chapter 16

The gaoler struggled in his restraints. The walls of the Clink prison seemed to be closing in on him.

Blackstone moved to the brazier of pitch and lifted a smoking ladle.

'My wife, Teresa,' he said, 'should have liked it down here.'

The gaoler's eyes widened slightly.

'She was very beautiful. Long blonde hair,' Blackstone gestured a sweep along his back. 'White as she aged, but still lovely in its way. She died. Last year.'

'I'm sorry for it,' stammered the gaoler.

Blackstone waved away the condolences. A sudden memory of his dead wife lurched out from the shadowy corners of the cell.

'Your sister is dead.' Teresa's eyes were open wide. 'I killed her.'

Her mouth made a bizarre smile. She held a bloodied corn dolly in her hands. 'You mustn't say such things,' said Blackstone carefully. 'My sister's death was a tragedy. It had nothing to do with you.'

'You thought your sister an angel,' replied Teresa. 'But she speaks to me from the grave. She wears a dark crown now.'

Teresa smiled up at him evilly. She shifted her candle and Blackstone saw something ranged around her. Thirteen wedding blessings. The wooden statues were burned to charred nubs. She'd arranged them in a kind of circle and symbols had been drawn in the ash.

'Your sister told me everything,' Teresa said, staring down at the corn dolly. 'When I took her blood. She told me what your father did to her. How he defiled her.'

Blackstone's stomach turned icy. He tried to ease the corn dolly from her hands but Teresa pulled it away protectively. 'Powerful blood,' she was saying, 'powerful blood. I took your sister's blood. Now her dark crown is mine.'

'Teresa . . .' Blackstone tried to reach for her, but she drew back, hugging the corn dolly to her.

Blackstone shook the images away. He needed to gather his thoughts. 'She was a good wife and loyal,' he continued. 'Noble blood. Raised properly in a Catholic family.' Blackstone's eyes flickered slightly. 'Women must have such strictures,' he said, 'or they fall to their baser natures.' Revulsion was twisting his bloated features.

'No church will bury her body,' Blackstone continued. 'They say she made a suicide.' Thoughts seemed to crowd into his head suddenly, hot and heavy. He'd survived plague. But recovery toyed with his memories, rending and spitting back fragments.

Blackstone remembered nothing of the months before the illness. He'd come to consciousness in a churchyard. Then returned home to find Teresa's body. Her hands on a knife struck deep in her belly.

Had she driven the blade herself?

Blackstone couldn't remember.

'A great sin against God,' offered the gaoler.

Blackstone's eyes flashed.

'Things happened to my wife during the war,' he said. 'Protestant men got to her. I never found them,' he continued, eyeing the ladle of pitch thoughtfully. 'After the horrors that befell my family, I thought I could protect Teresa. I couldn't.' He shook his head. 'Dark cellars. They were her favourites. She didn't like to go outside.'

He moved back to where the gaoler sat and brought his face closer.

'So when I see a Protestant like yourself,' he said, holding the ladle high, 'good short hair, plain clothes, I think you could have been one of those men. You fought for Cromwell, didn't you?'

The gaoler opened his mouth to reply just as Blackstone ladled the hot liquid into his lap. He screamed. A high squealing sound.

'That's how I used to make it right with myself,' said Blackstone. 'I thought to myself that you could have been one of those men.'

The pitch was cooling and the gaoler breathed hard. His eyes rose to Blackstone, pleading.

'Now,' said Blackstone. 'I think of the boy you hurt. Jacob. I see his face when I explain to him how revenge was taken. That he needn't be afraid and helpless any longer.'

Blackstone ladled more pitch on to the arms of the chair. Then he puddled it around the legs.

'You could have been,' he said. 'You might not even know it. How many Catholic women did you have? As a soldier during the war?'

Blackstone shook his head at the sweating gaoler. 'After all the men you've broken. You'd be one of the easy ones.'

He sat back looking hungrily at the gaoler's face.

'Two years I sat where you sat,' continued Blackstone. 'I knew each tool and implement like the old enemies they were. And I never breathed a word of my brothers. You've given everything away already.'

'Pitch cools quickly,' said Blackstone as the gaoler breathed hard in fear. 'But it will catch alight with the smallest flame.'

'No!' the gaoler shouted in terror and began to buck in his seat.

Blackstone brought out a small sack of coins and rested them on the table. 'From the time of the old King,' he explained, bringing out a handful and letting them trickle back into the sack. 'Lead tokens.' He removed a battered coin and examined the stamp. 'No longer legal tender.'

He looked at them thoughtfully. The gaoler sat motionless now, uncertain as how to reply.

Blackstone removed a glass bottle from his cloak. It was filled with a dark liquid.

The gaoler began to twist in the chair.

'Bringer of Death,' said Blackstone, holding it up to the light. Sweat broke out on the gaoler's lip.

'This is a prison,' said the gaoler, 'you must do no dark magic or devilment here. It's the law.'

Blackstone moved to stand behind the gaoler and moved his chair slightly.

'I told you I was here a long time,' he murmured. 'I sat here. Where you sit.' He adjusted the chair again. 'Exactly here.' Blackstone's eyes panned for something on the far wall. Then he pointed.

'See that mark?' Blackstone moved to a spot on the stone wall which bore a splatter of aged blood.

'I remember looking at it, when I sat where you do now.' He touched the blood. 'I remember looking at it so long it seemed to shift and move. I fancied it was the shape of an angel. And I thought . . . I thought if there was a merciful God, he would give the angel a sword, so he might take off my head.'

Blackstone tilted his gaze.

'But the mark is still here, as you see.' He paused. 'It doesn't look like an angel to me any longer.' Blackstone gave the blood-stain a last curious tap. 'Just a mark on a wall.'

He moved back to the bag of coins and the dark bottle.

'So,' said Blackstone. 'I learned to make my own holy angels. And devils.'

He raised the bottle and swirled it. 'The most common of substances,' he said, 'can have surprising uses. I call this liquid Bringer of Death.'

Blackstone moved nearer the gaoler. 'The slightest drop will burn the skin,' he said. The gaoler shrank back. 'Add metal,' said Blackstone, 'and it will make a demon – a devil's breath which glows blue when you light it.'

Blackstone regarded the Bringer of Death. 'And if you capture the demon inside a bottle,' he continued, 'you don't even need a flame. It grows so hot, the Bringer of Death fires on its own.'

The gaoler's eyes were tracking from Blackstone to the bottle, trying to understand what was happening.

Blackstone unstoppered the bottle and dropped a handful of coins inside. The liquid began hissing furiously. A jet of steam issued forth.

'The devil's breath,' smiled Blackstone, re-stoppering the bottle. He gave it a shake as the liquid continued to boil furiously inside.

Blackstone placed the bottle in the gaoler's lap.

'I've timed it,' he said. 'You can never be exact, of course. But my estimate is you have twenty breaths left in your body. Then the bottle will explode in flame and blue fire will pour forth.'

He smiled at the gaoler.

'Tell me,' he said, 'after I leave this room. Do you think that angel will come for you?'

The guard was tugging furiously at the leather straps.

'No,' said Blackstone turning to leave. 'I don't think so either.'

Chapter 17

'Your key,' said Sebastian, eyeing Charlie. 'The crown and knots. They make a circle within a circle. The crown is the square. And this is a triangle. See?'

Sebastian dipped his finger in the crucible and drew a rough shape in soot.

'The Philosopher's Stone,' he said, pointing. 'The shape of your key is the same. It's hidden in the crown and knots. But it's there.'

Charlie looked at his key. Sebastian was right. The shape matched. 'What does it mean?' he asked.

'The story of the Philosopher's Stone is clouded in myth,' said Sebastian. 'Some say deliberately so. It's said to be the apple from the Garden of Eden. Or the cornerstone to Solomon's Temple. Myself I think these fairy tales to hide its true meaning.'

'Which is?'

'The stone has mystical powers, but men disagree on which,' said Sebastian. 'Some say it can grant eternal life. Others claim it can turn lead into gold or dissolve gold. In any case, it's an exceptionally powerful substance and alchemists are obsessed with discovering it.'

'Alchemists seek a holy stone which makes magic?' Charlie couldn't believe it. The alchemists he knew were eccentric but highly intelligent.

Sebastian shrugged. 'Alchemists love to speak in riddles,' he said. 'Likely they've deliberately mixed truth with fact to disguise their true goals. Allegory, especially, they are fond of.'

'Allegory?'

'Where a story symbolises a real thing,' said Sebastian. 'The green lion who ate the sun is popular currently.'

At Charlie's blank expression he quantified.

'I forget you're not a coffee-house man,' he said. 'The green lion is a substance which can dissolve gold,' he explained. 'A green liquid. You see? The green lion eats the gold sun?'

'I didn't think anything could dissolve gold,' said Charlie.

'They haven't discovered it yet,' said Sebastian. 'When alchemists dissolve gold into matter, they can then discover how to make it from base materials.'

Charlie was thinking. Marriage. Gold. He was sure there was something there.

'Why not ask your brother Rowan?' suggested Sebastian. 'I should have thought he'd have a great interest in alchemy. Discovering riches from worthless things,' he waved his hand airily.

'Rowan disappeared last summer,' said Charlie. 'When plague was high.'

Charlie tried not to think about Rowan too deeply. He'd last seen his brother selling quack plague cures in Moor Fields. Then Rowan had mysteriously vanished.

In his more honest moments, Charlie conceded the likelihood that his brother lay in an unmarked plague grave.

'I see.' Sebastian paused. 'I am sorry for it. My own two brothers vanished during the Civil War. It is a strange thing to grieve and hope at once.' He lifted his eyes to Charlie's. 'Even a familiar place can feel strange when people you love are gone from it.'

Charlie looked away. Sebastian rubbed at his thatch of hair and changed the subject.

'I can't think of any other alchemists whom you might ask,' he admitted. 'Isaac Newton dabbles. King Charles is a believer. He funds a secret alchemy chamber beneath the palace. I supply it occasionally. Through the tunnels underneath the Palace. Along with treatments for the pox.'

Charlie looked thoughtful. Something had just occurred to him.

'Crutchfriar's Mansion,' he said, 'that's where they treat the pox with mercury?'

'Quicksilver for the pox,' said Sebastian with a sniff of distaste. 'A bad business. And expensive.'

'But people don't say Crutchfriar's do they?' said Charlie, thinking aloud.

Sebastian looked at him strangely. 'The smoke is bothering you,' he suggested, fanning the air with his skinny fingers. 'It can muddle the thoughts.'

'What would you call Crutchfriar's Mansion?' asked Charlie.

'They call it the Palace,' said Sebastian. 'A Londoner's bad joke. Commoners can't afford mercury treatments. But many courtly men visit the fuming tubs.'

'The Palace,' said Charlie. The boy didn't say the Royal Palace, he remembered. Perhaps he meant the Pox Palace. Where men have their syphilis fumed away.

Charlie nodded to himself. He was suddenly certain this was where Lily planned to go. It made much more sense than a royal appointment. Crutchfriar's only treated men. But the warren of discreet rooms afforded a number of illicit possibilities.

The only problem was it was now nearly noon and Crutchfriar's was the other side of London. Quickly Charlie cycled through his mental map of the city. If the fire was now at Gracechurch Street, there was only one route Lily could realistically take to Crutchfriar's by carriage. With luck he could still catch her. Nodding his thanks to a baffled Sebastian, Charlie set off at a run.

Chapter 18

No one could remember a time before the London Stone. But everyone knew, if the stone split, the city would fall.

Charlie stared at the tall Roman column. The usual milieu of ballad singers, beggars and merchants swearing oaths had deserted. But the wide street of Poultry was chaos.

He'd been expecting to see two carriages at most making their ponderous journey through the London traffic of riders, carts and pedestrians. But Charlie had not accounted for the fire. Every citizen within a half-mile radius of Cheapside was deserting with their worldly goods. People had goods piled on their backs, their heads, or in handkerchiefs suspended from sticks. Donkeys, cattle and sheep pulled makeshift sleds laden with goods. Families had loaded clothes, furniture and bric-a-brac on to sheets, bearing them like rafts through the tide of people. And among it all were countless carts, buggies and carriages of various shapes and sizes.

The tips of the flames at Cheapside could be seen colouring in the sky in the middle distance, like some ominous portent of hell. And the ash had been carried on the breeze, thickening the air and whipping further panic into the deserting citizens. It was complete madness.

Charlie assessed the traffic. Eight coaches. He let his eyes scan the jostling, terrified crowd. A fist-fight was taking place in the thick of it, over a bundle of possessions which had split and scattered. Horses snorted, their eyes bulging. Charlie eyed them warily. By the time he fought his way to the first coach, he would lose another. And that was if he managed to avoid flying hooves and riled-up escapees.

Charlie assessed the coaches carefully. There was nothing to give away Lily's whereabouts. One in eight. Charlie was a gambling man. He didn't like those odds. If Lily got inside the fumigation house she could vanish into the warren of treatment rooms. And slip out of one of the many exits without a chance of being followed.

Charlie's attention shifted to the wider scene. A fat ballad singer was sitting by the London Stone, on the side where oaths and announcements were made.

Usually ballad singers howled favourite songs on request for a penny. But today there was no one paying for music. The singer was sat on her haunches, surveying the crowd morosely. Seeing her gave Charlie an idea, but he had no penny to enact it. He would have to improvise.

The singer had stood and was shuffling from foot to foot as Charlie approached, easing the pressure on her knees. She wore a tatty apron over a grubby wool dress which her bulk had shortened to knee-length. Her greying hair was pushed haphazardly inside a round frilled cap.

The singer eyed Charlie hopefully as he approached. She had a hare-lip which grossly plumped half of her mouth, revealing a large portion of surprisingly white upper teeth.

'You charge a penny a song?' asked Charlie.

The woman nodded and began straightening her cap ready to begin.

'How should you like to earn fivepence?' he asked.

Instantly her expression shifted to suspicion.

'You know of the Bucket of Blood?' said Charlie.

'Aye.' The woman's voice was husky from over-use. 'The bare-knuckle fighting place.'

Charlie nodded.

'There will be a fight tonight,' he said. 'One man has been paid to go down. I could tell you his name in exchange for a song to the crowd.'

The singer considered this. Her calloused finger ran along the top of her apron where he suspected she kept her coins.

'The fire will not stop the fight,' said Charlie, pressing the advantage. 'If the devil himself fanned the flames, it would not reach Covent Garden so soon. Besides,' he added. 'You'll sing no songs today. This information is the best money you can hope to make.'

The woman's lip bobbed in a strange expression.

'You'll swear it on the Stone?' she suggested.

Charlie nodded and placed his hand on the Roman column. The Latin markings were worn smooth where other Londoners had done the same.

'I swear I tell you true,' he said.

She nodded.

'Very well,' she said. 'What would you have sung?'

'No song,' said Charlie. 'You must call to the crowd that the King comes.'

The ballad singer twisted her head to look.

'He is never seen in the city,' she said excitedly. 'Which direction does he come from?'

She caught the expression on Charlie's face and her twisted mouth made a little perturbed dance.

'I shall be lynched,' she protested, 'for telling a mistruth.'

'You can be long gone before they realise,' assured Charlie. 'On your way to Covent Garden to place a bet,' he added enticingly.

The singer gazed out on to the crowd for a long moment before making her decision.

'The King is coming?' she confirmed. 'How many times?'

'Wait until I'm at the head of the crowd,' said Charlie. 'Then call it three times. Loud.'

The singer patted the London Stone. 'It will be done,' she said.

'John Gracey,' said Charlie. 'This evening. The Bucket of Blood. The second round. I swear it.'

The singer nodded her thanks and Charlie slipped away towards the crowd. Behind him he heard the singer bellow the words with more force than he could have thought possible. Almost immediately excited shouts of the King's approach were taken up through the crowd.

'The King is coming!' seemed to echo all around, and immediately heads snapped in the direction of the singer.

Charlie waited patiently as the rumour surged and just as he had hoped, heads began to pop out of the carriages. He counted them off carefully. A young couple. An old lord. Two ladies… And there she was. At the window of a finely decorated carriage, peeking through the curtain. Lily Boswell.

Chapter 19

Charlie had forgotten how beautiful Lily was. She looked out of the carriage for only for an instant, and then the curtain was back. Charlie had to force himself not to stare at the blank window. Instead he pitched into the swelling crowd, and began beating his way towards the carriage. Even the blinkered horses were twitching with nerves. Charlie plotted a course wide of their back legs.

He reached the large wheels of Lily's coach after a sustained effort. Taking advantage of the thick crowd, he slid underneath the carriage. Charlie had learned in his boyhood to stow under carriages for sport. The trick was to fix your feet into the front planks and hold on to the axle. It was harder now he was nearly six foot and scared of horses, but he managed it.

The carriage gave a sudden spurt and he found himself looking up between the gaps in the planks, directly at Lily. Her dress was the kind worn by courtesans. Red silk stretched low and tight around the body. It was low cut, displaying a mass of necklaces. And from his angle he could see indecent flashes of white underclothes. The wide skirt was embroidered with large gold flowers.

Up close he could see Lily's skin was toffee-coloured, plump against sultry dark eyes with a rosy pout which was exotic rather than beautiful. The kind of face that would do for a mistress but not a wife.

Charlie manoeuvred for a firmer position. A button from his long leather coat ricocheted against the carriage. Lily looked down. Charlie ducked back, but when he glanced through again he saw she held something. A handkerchief.

The way she was holding it caught his attention. Lily's knuckles were white and her hands were trembling. Something about this handkerchief frightened or angered her.

From the underside Charlie could only see the back of the stitches – clusters of faded thread. They made a fish tail shape. A mermaid, he thought.

He was struck with a sudden certain knowledge that he'd seen the mermaid before.

There was something so . . . *familiar* about her. Charlie stared, wondering where he might have seen the handkerchief. Nothing came to mind, which was unusual. Usually his memory was perfect.

The mystery of it taunted him. How came Lily to be holding a handkerchief he'd seen before?

Her brown hands turned the cloth. Charlie spotted a ruby among the cheap rings which adorned her fingers.

She chewed her lip, toyed with a mass of charms and pearls at her throat, then stuffed the handkerchief in her dress, wiping at her eyes angrily. She'd been crying, Charlie realised.

The carriage began to turn a corner, and Charlie felt his feet begin to ease out of the creaking planks. He looked back to see there was now a knife in Lily's hand. She seemed to wield it as naturally as fingers, tapping her chin with the blade, and using the tip to absent-mindedly scratch her arm.

The carriage swayed to a halt before turning towards Crutchfriar's and Charlie took a chance. He dropped from the underside of the carriage and glanced up to assure himself the driver was preoccupied with nudging the horses forward into the thick traffic. Then Charlie straightened, opened the door of Lily's carriage and stepped inside.

———

Lily looked up in alarm. In an instant her knife was at his throat.

'I'm no robber,' said Charlie, impressed at her speed.

Lily's eyes flicked to the front of the coach and her knife held firm.

'I have something of interest to you,' he said.

She hesitated, looking him over. The knife pressed a little firmer.

'I remember you from Fetter Lane,' she said, her eyes resting on his key. 'You're not wealthy enough to buy my time,' she added, glancing at his bare feet. 'So what could you have of interest?'

'Information,' said Charlie, 'from your boy on London Bridge.'

The pressure of the knife eased and she sank back a little into her seat.

'So tell me quickly. Before I change my mind. The driver is employed by the Earl of Amesbury and fought at the Siege of Colchester,' she added, nodding to the front of the carriage. 'So don't think to cross me.'

Charlie drew out the round robin he had intercepted. Lily's eyes widened and she went to snatch at it, but Charlie was too fast for her. He tucked it back inside his coat.

'I took it from your messenger,' he said.

Lily sucked her teeth in annoyance. 'That is mine,' she said.

'Yours by right of having stolen it?' retorted Charlie. 'Then it is just as much mine.'

She moved to open the carriage door and Charlie raised his hands.

'Hold. I will give you the paper.'

He held it out and she snatched it up triumphantly under Charlie's glaring gaze.

'A few minutes of your time,' said Charlie, 'is all I need.'

Lily smiled, relaxing back slightly. The knife rested in her palm like a snake ready to strike.

'The paper bought you entry to the carriage,' she said, tucking it into her dress. 'My time costs money.'

Charlie paused, and her eyebrows raised.

'I've no money,' he admitted. The knife twitched and her expression darkened.

'But perhaps we could come to an arrangement,' he added quickly, as her eyes glanced back towards the driver. 'You play at cards?'

The smile twisted sideways and Charlie knew he had struck the mark. It was often a weakness of card sharps that they could not resist a gamble.

'What do you propose?' she asked, failing to keep the glow of interest from her eyes.

'Three tricks,' said Charlie. 'Whatever game you choose. If I win best of three, then you tell me what you know.'

'And if I win?'

'If you win, I tell you what I know about this key.' He lifted it, watching her expression carefully.

She hesitated. Her eyes followed the shape of it.

'Double sided,' she said, watching his expression. 'A foreign key?' She was staring at the shape at the head now. The crown looped with knots.

Charlie was silent. Lily watched his face and he knew she hadn't discerned what she'd hoped from his expression. She turned the cheap rings on her fingers, considering his face.

'That's not enough,' she decided. There was a pause as she considered. 'If I win, you give me that key.'

Chapter 20

The Earl of Clarence blinked against the rising steam. Floral fragrances wafted gently from inside the bathhouse. Rose and saffron, he thought. He eyed the King's fashionable silk clothing which hung jauntily outside. His Majesty's wig was new. Jet-black, elaborately curled and the size of a small sheep. Barbara Castlemaine's influence.

Next to it was Amesbury's military cloak, sturdy and worn from the years.

Slowly Clarence shrugged off his elaborately jewelled coat. He hesitated then pulled down his silk breeches, revealing aged legs mottled red with veins.

Clarence's portly belly swelled out beneath his shirt. His hand rose to his snowy wig. A servant waited patiently to take it, but Clarence baulked at the last moment. Without expensive clothes his wig was the last sign of his authority. He batted away the servant rudely and stepped into the bathhouse.

'Clarence!' The King's disembodied voice hailed him from the steam. 'Come tell us of the fire,' he called.

Clarence shuffled forward. The bathhouse had been styled like a Roman marquee. An old stable interior had been tented with white linen and decked with fragrant flowers. A glass pitcher of white wine sat on a bed of ice. Clarence bristled. He'd spoken against the expensive ice house in Parliament.

For a moment Clarence could only see the Earl of Amesbury. The old general was seated with scarred elbows rested on muscular thighs. Shirtless, his chest was bull-like, latticed with war wounds. Amesbury had retained his heavy breeches, thick boots and sword.

There was a quick movement and Clarence saw Amesbury's pet monkey flit from view. The old general had acquired it in the colonies and claimed not to notice when it bit people.

A cloud of steam cleared and the naked royal body came into view. King Charles was sat on a bench with his legs splayed forward. Without his wig the monarch's strong features were even more prominent. Heavy black brows arched over dark eyes and a well-groomed little moustache framed his wide lips. It was a striking, well-made face. Though his large rounded nose dwarfed all.

'As you can see,' observed Amesbury, nodding to Clarence. 'His Majesty is every inch a King.'

Clarence realised he had been staring and blushed furiously.

'What news of the fire, Clarence?' asked Amesbury. 'We hear Catholics throw fireballs.'

'Your Majesty,' began Clarence, trying to look anywhere but the impressive royal groin, 'I represent Parliament. The fire is under control. Your Palace at Whitehall is safe.'

Amesbury sat up. Sweat had plastered his greying hair across his forehead, but he didn't seem to notice the heat of the bathhouse. His scarred torso rolled with perspiration.

'Are you mad, Clarence?' said Amesbury. 'The wind whips it to a frenzy. You must pull down buildings and quickly.'

'A man's property is his own,' said Clarence. 'Londoners won't give permission for their homes to be levelled.'

'So I hear,' said Amesbury testily. 'But the King can overrule them.'

Clarence raised a hand. 'Asserting your rule wouldn't be wise, Your Majesty. The political situation in the city . . .'

'London burns,' stormed Amesbury. 'We must act and quickly.'

Clarence eyed Amesbury and then the King. 'Amesbury is bred in a time of war,' he said. 'No one doubts his military brilliance. But this is not a military matter. A little fire is all.'

'And the fireballs?' asked Charles.

'A rumour,' said Clarence firmly.

'Be careful, Clarence,' said Amesbury easily, 'that your quest for parliamentary advancement doesn't endanger the city.'

'A warning from a military turncoat?' spat Clarence waspishly. 'The man who seeks only the winning side.'

'A wise man sides with me then,' said Amesbury, rubbing a line of sweat from his forearm. 'How many marriages did it take for you to avoid battle?'

Clarence's face turned, outraged.

'I suppose it takes courage of a kind,' added Amesbury. 'Having seen your wife.'

'My services to the Crown were noted,' spluttered Clarence. 'How dare you imply I shirked war duties!'

The King held up a tired hand. He considered for a long moment.

'Amesbury,' he said, 'use what people you have in the city. Discover if fireballs are being thrown. But I fear Clarence may be right about troops,' he added, signalling a servant to refill his wine goblet. The King plucked a grape from a platter, crunched it noisily, then spat pips.

'What, then, do you propose, Clarence?'

'Do nothing,' said Clarence. 'Any action will incite the people to riot.'

'Better they riot than London burns to the ground,' said Amesbury.

There was a rustle of fabric and a breath of cool air wafted through the humid bathhouse.

'Clarence,' said a low female voice. 'How nice to see you in my bathhouse.'

Clarence twisted in horror to see Barbara Castlemaine.

His eyes widened in alarm. What was she doing here?

The King's longest serving mistress was in a state of utter undress, her thin white shift plastered to her curving body by sweat. Patches at her breasts and groin were completely transparent but a huge swathe of jewelled necklaces afforded rudimentary modesty. Behind her came two maids dressed in flimsy open-shouldered shifts.

With effort Clarence drove down his fury. Things were slotting into place. Meeting in the bathhouse. It was her doing. She wanted to impact on policy. The damnable woman had engineered this scenario to wrong-foot him.

'A bathhouse is one way to spend His Majesty's allowance,' said Clarence, trying not to stare at Barbara's shapely form.

Amesbury roared with laughter.

'You see, Barbara,' he said, 'Clarence is always the politician.'

Barbara strode over to the King and planted a lingering kiss on his mouth. The necklaces dangled forward tantalisingly and he reached for her. But she retreated and reclined on the cushion-strewn floor of the bathhouse. Her maids knelt and began massaging perfumed oils into her bare legs. Charles leaned forward for a better look. His previous pensive expression had melted away.

'Lady Castlemaine is here, but not your wife?' said Clarence to Charles with a brittle laugh.

'The Queen was much sheltered before her marriage,' said Barbara. 'Portuguese Catholics are *very* proper and won't set foot in the bathhouse.' She gave the King a disarming smile. 'But they understand their husbands must have some pleasure.'

'Lady Castlemaine designed this bathhouse as a present for me,' said Charles, watching the women caress Barbara's naked thighs. 'The flowers and jewels,' he gestured vaguely to the elaborate swags of pearls and fresh flowers which ornamented the tented ceiling, 'were her idea.'

Sweat broke out on Clarence's upper lip. His eyes switched to Amesbury. How was the heat not bothering him? He wished desperately he had dispensed with his wig.

'Lady Castlemaine is very generous,' said Clarence archly, 'to share herself with your two advisors.'

Charles tipped back his head and laughed.

'That's exactly what I like about her,' he said. 'Why should I care who sees, Clarence? She's my mistress, not my wife.' He peered forward for a better look. 'A man should always have a pretty view,' he concluded.

'Your Majesty,' Clarence said, wrestling for control of the situation. 'I will convey it to Parliament then, that you will leave the firefighting to us.'

'Are you sure that's wise?' asked Barbara lazily, lifting her head slightly. 'There is talk the fire may ford the Fleet river and head for Whitehall.'

Clarence held up his hand.

'The soft hearts of women,' he said, treating Barbara to a patronising smile, 'would see us endanger His Majesty's throne. Fire cannot cross water. Whitehall is safe.'

Barbara lifted her pretty eyebrows and flipped on to her belly. The maids began working her lower back. She gave a cat-like smile of pleasure.

'Since the Civil War,' she said, 'many old soldiers keep gunpowder in their cellars. My understanding is only a woman's kind. But I hear black powder can send flaming materials some distance.'

There was a pause as this sunk in.

'The Royal Barge hasn't had an airing in a few weeks,' Barbara observed casually. 'Perhaps a trip along the river, Charles. Just to see the blaze for ourselves. Amesbury should come,' she added generously.

'The King has already agreed . . .' began Clarence, his mouth a slim line of rage.

'The river would be a good place to view,' said Charles, lifting a thoughtful hand. 'Perhaps we should at least see the blaze.'

'Lady Castlemaine's fine dresses will be stained with smuts and smoke,' said Clarence desperately.

Barbara gave a musical little laugh.

'Oh you mustn't worry about my fine dresses,' she said. 'You've said it yourself, Clarence. I am so rarely in them.'

Clarence turned to the King.

'Your Majesty, I must advise strongly against Lady Castlemaine's fancy to see the fire. Your barge on the Thames could cause alarm.'

But the King was hardly listening.

Barbara twisted her head over her shoulder to where the nearest maid was massaging across her naked buttocks.

'Be sure to work deep between,' she said, eyeing the King. 'His Majesty is particularly keen I am to be oiled there.'

She moved her eyes to Clarence and winked.

Clarence's hands were balled in fists of rage. He wiped away a fresh crop of sweat from his red face. Barbara Castlemaine may have won this battle. But Charles's bastard son, Monmouth, was responsible for the Royal Barge. Monmouth was spoiled and difficult. And he hated Barbara. Clarence would have some sway yet. He would win the war.

Chapter 21

Lily was assessing his reaction like a practised card sharp. Charlie affected nonchalance but knew in his heart she'd seen through it.

'You don't know what my key opens,' he said. 'How could it be of value to you?'

'The key is my price.'

Charlie assessed his options.

'I'll wager the key,' he agreed after a moment, 'but the winner of each trick gets to ask a question. Three questions in all.'

'You shouldn't test me,' she said, pointing to the front of the carriage, 'I can take the key anytime I choose.'

'Maybe, maybe not,' he said, smiling. 'I'm stronger than you.'

'I'm faster.'

Charlie shrugged. There was no harm in letting her think it.

'So take it,' he said, 'but you wouldn't know how I came to carry it.'

This time he had struck gold. A tiny muscle in her cheek twitched.

'Very well,' she said. 'If you wish to lose at cards then so be it.'

She drew a pack of cards from her skirts. Charlie took a seat opposite hers.

'We play at fours,' she said, handing him the cards.

He smiled. All Fours was a classic choice for a card sharper. It involved a dizzying set of rules and the kind of memory and attention which slipped after a few drinks.

Charlie sorted the pack, and made a show of checking for spots and marks which would allow her to cheat. She watched him, seeming amused.

'I've no need to cheat,' she said easily. 'I'm too good.'

'Even the best players lose sometimes,' said Charlie.

'Not unless they mean to.' She took back the cards and began dealing.

Charlie took up his six cards. She fanned the top cards of the pack, and he realised she was testing him to see if he knew the more complicated rules of play.

He debated pretending not to notice, but decided she was too astute for that. Best let her think him good, but not realise how good.

'Trick rules,' he said. 'If you deal like that one of us could count cards.'

She nodded and swept the cards to the bottom of the pack without a word, though there was a glimmer of admiration in her eye.

They played in silence, both assessing the other. Charlie hadn't reckoned on how good she was. He watched her carefully. It all hinged on whether she was holding a Jack. With so little experience of seeing her play, he could not yet be sure of reading her expression.

'Why did you take the ring?' he asked.

She glanced up at him.

'The purse and candlestick were a feint,' he said. 'You took them to disguise yourself as a thief. It was the ring you really wanted. Why?'

She pursed her lips and he thought he detected annoyance. No Jack in her hand, he decided.

'Tell me what your key guards,' said Lily.

'You haven't won the hand yet.'

Without answering, she laid her cards. There was the Jack. The smile on her face was maddening.

'Papers,' he said, trying not to let his surprise show. 'My key unlocks a chest containing papers.'

'What kind of papers?'

'I . . . My reading is not good,' he said. 'I only saw them for a moment. There was a marriage paper among them. For Thomas Blackstone and Teresa Blackstone.'

He scrutinised her reaction but she was so hard to read. Each time he thought he'd seen a tell, it slid away like a snake in long grass. It was infuriating and fascinating at the same time.

Lily shuffled and re-dealt.

This time Charlie had learned enough of her play and the cards in the deck to better her. Combined with a lucky hand, he took the trick and was gratified to see a wave of frustration pass over her face.

'I win,' he said.

'So you do,' she said, looking as though she could not quite believe it. 'You may ask me your question then and I will answer truthfully.'

'Show me the handkerchief you were looking at,' he said. 'Before I got into the carriage.'

'You were watching me?'

'From beneath the carriage,' he admitted. 'A street rat trick to steal a ride.'

'I shall have to learn that one,' she murmured. 'But you may not see the handkerchief. Your win grants you a question only.'

Charlie paused to be sure of his question.

'What do you know of the symbol on my key?' he asked finally.

Lily pursed her lips.

'It is the sign of the Sealed Knot. They were a group of nobles formed during the war,' she said. 'The cleverest and most deadly men. Their purpose was to protect the King. But they fought, and some of them broke away. Travelled to Holland. They consorted with mystics. When they returned, they were said to have powers.'

'What powers?'

Lily hesitated.

'One question is all you won.' She re-dealt.

The questions were firing through his head at such speed that he hardly noticed when Lily laid her winning hand.

'You have lost,' she said, with a slightly disappointed smile. Then she held out her hand for the key.

Slowly, Charlie unwound it from his neck and handed it over.

Her fingers closed on it victoriously, watching his face.

'This key is very dear to you,' she decided. 'Perhaps you think to find me and take it back.'

Charlie said nothing.

'Have you ever been inside the fumigation house?' continued Lily. 'It is a maze. Once I am inside, you will never see me again.' But she sounded less confident now.

'I will,' said Charlie, and was pleased to see a flicker of disquiet in her face.

Lily slipped in beside him. It was a novel sensation to have the swathes of silk pushed up against his body. He could smell her rose-water scent as she leaned in close.

Then he felt a sharp pain against his ribs.

'Feel that?' said Lily. 'I hold a knife at your chest.' Her voice came low. 'Come looking for me again, Mr Sealed Knot, and I will carve out your heart.'

Charlie smiled.

'That might work on your lordly men,' he said easily. 'I grew up in Cheapside where the women would have your pretty guts for garters. Besides,' he added. 'You told me you will be impossible to find.'

Lily holstered her knife, looking furious.

'So I will be,' she said.

She slipped out of the carriage and vanished into the fumigation house. Charlie watched her go. Then he smiled. It had been easier than he thought to trick a trickster.

During play he had scented the playing cards with lavender oil – a favourite thief-taking subterfuge that had never failed him yet. Whichever door Lily touched in the fumigation house would be marked.

It never did to overplay your hand.

Chapter 22

Blackstone eyed the Wax Chandlers' Guild on Lothbury Street. The heat from the flames could already be felt. But the thick stone walls offered protection.

Candlemakers were running in and out of the Guild Hall, ferrying boxes of half-dipped candles. Two clergymen from the nearby church were staggering past with a six-foot candle elaborately carved with scenes of the crucifixion.

Blackstone smiled and moved towards the entrance. He turned the bottle in his cloak. Bringer of Death.

The candlemakers were only adding fuel to his pyre.

Men were digging a pit to bury goods and Blackstone's stomach lurched. He was remembering a different pit. A different time.

'Your sister?' asked the gravedigger.

Blackstone nodded impassively. He let the body drop by the open grave. The head fell back revealing blackened features.

Blackstone could see the gravedigger thought him heartless. He didn't care.

Too much had happened for him to grieve for this death. Soldiers had come. He'd heard his father's screams. When they started on his mother Blackstone knew. He would become a soldier and take his revenge.

'Burned after death?' suggested the gravedigger slowly. 'She didn't move her arms to keep the flame from her face.' He crossed himself. Witches made spells by burning corpses.

Blackstone's eyes flicked up sharply. He was thinking of his wife. Beautiful Teresa and the thirteen blessings. All burned to ash.

Blackstone forced his thoughts back to the present. The torture of plague had burned through his body, sending thoughts and memories spooling into inaccessible corners. Something about the fire in the city . . . It seemed to be bringing them back. But erratically. In sudden snatches.

'Hold,' said an agitated-looking guard as Blackstone approached. 'Guild members only.'

He was eyeing Blackstone's rosary in obvious dislike.

'I bring a message from the King.' Blackstone showed his seal.

'Even so,' said the guard, 'only guild members are allowed in the building. We have secrets to protect. Our brotherhood has sacred practices.'

Blackstone pressed his index finger to his chest in the secret sign.

'Truth is light,' he said, 'light the way.'

The guard glared suspiciously.

'I don't recognise you from the guild dinners,' he said. 'Where are your wares sold?'

'I supply the King's household,' lied Blackstone. 'I'm often away from the city.'

The guard seemed disappointed by the reasonableness of the explanation.

'I'll need to search your cloak,' he said. 'We can't be too careful. There's rumours of Catholics throwing fireballs.'

He gestured Blackstone should open his cloak, and pulled at his hanging pocket roughly.

'What's this?' asked the guard.

'A little lead is all,' said Blackstone, 'for making pigment.'

The guard rubbed it against his lips, tasted the metal and returned it.

'And this?' He drew free the bottle and peered at the dark liquid inside.

'Wine from Italy. You may try some.'

The guard thrust it back at Blackstone.

'I'm an Englishman. A good Protestant. I don't drink foreign filth,' he said, eyeballing Blackstone aggressively.

'As you wish,' said Blackstone good-naturedly.

The guard looked as though he would have liked to say more. He stepped aside muttering '*papist*' under his breath.

Blackstone took in the high carved-wood ceilings of the hall. Candles winked from every corner. Rolls and slabs of beeswax had been carefully stacked in one corner, etched with their owner's mark. Boxes of fine candles in straw were stacked all over.

It could hardly have been more perfect.

Chapter 23

The fumigation house had once been a medieval manor. But the rickety half-timbered building had since been engulfed into the wider city by a patchwork of buildings and lean-tos. Now it was part of a grimy, meandering alley consisting mostly of brothels.

A tented porch had been erected around the doorway to protect the identity of arrivals. As Charlie watched, a sedan chair sidled to a halt outside it. A guard stepped out and hastily drew the porch curtain around the entire sedan. The chair lurched as it off-loaded its mystery passenger into the mercury-laced corridors beyond. Then the doorman uncovered the vehicle and the carriers ushered it away.

Charlie had already decided there was no point trying for illicit entry. Mercury was expensive. The fumigation house was heavily defended against burglars.

Reaching into his coat, Charlie fashioned himself a makeshift nose-covering from string and a spare piece of hessian and made purposefully for the entrance. The guard stepped forward, noticed the nose covering and fell back a little.

'Mercury starts at a guinea,' said the doorman, casting a suspicious eye over Charlie's bare feet and weathered coat.

'I won at the bear pits,' said Charlie, deducing from the door-man's accent that he lived south of the river. 'Old Samson went down yesterday.'

The doorman's mouth twitched. 'I heard of that,' he said after a moment. 'Wish to God I had bet. My cousin won enough to eat meat for a month.' He opened the curtained porch.

'Shame you're not as lucky with the pox as you are with money.' And he laughed loudly at his own joke as he waved Charlie along.

Charlie stepped through the dark tented porch and into the manor. Inside was a wood-panelled corridor lit by gently fuming braziers. Ahead were three wooden booths, of the kind used in Catholic confession. But instead of decorative panelling, each had an artistic woodcut of a syphilis treatment.

One showed an unnecessarily graphic representation of a lotion being applied. Another depicted four men next to a fuming amphora. The third had a smiling man sat in a tub with flames underneath. Prices were chalked on the wood. He was expected to select a treatment and pay inside the relevant booth.

The middle booth was occupied. As Charlie watched, a nervous-looking young man emerged. He was clutching a wooden token and made his way morosely to a set of stairs at the end of the corridor. Waiting a moment, Charlie followed.

The man vanished up the stairs and Charlie paused again. Above the stairwell hung a tapestry map of the building. Each floor echoed the payment booths with pictures of amphoras and fuming braziers. It seemed the higher you climbed, the more expensive the treatment.

Checking the man ahead was out of sight, Charlie lowered his head to the bannister. There it was. Lavender.

Lily had passed this way.

Ascending the stair Charlie reached the first floor, where a wood door barred the way. He bent and checked the handle, but there was nothing. The bannister upwards bore the oil. So he kept climbing.

At the second floor he was rewarded with a clear scent. The stairwell opened on to a wide landing with a multitude of doors beyond. This seemed to be the mercury bathhouse level. There was a row of large doors leading to a fuming room. Next to each was a small cupboard, in which mercury could be fumed through.

An eerie sound of crackling flames and groaning men echoed along the corridor. There was a distinctive scalding aroma.

After seven doors, Charlie's detective work was rewarded. He sniffed again to be sure. This was it. The room Lily had entered. Charlie made another check along the corridor, and moved to peer through the keyhole.

Shuffling closer he strained to see further into the room. It looked as though someone might be moving around on the other side, but it was difficult to see. He caught a flash of red silk and his heart beat faster. Righting himself, Charlie eyed the adjoining fuming cupboard. It was linked to the larger room by a grill. As silently as possible, he slid the latch and eased himself inside.

Chapter 24

'What was that?'

The snap of Lily's voice assailed Charlie as soon as he closed himself inside the fumigation cupboard. He froze, immobile, hardly daring to breath. The fuming chamber was divided from the room by a metal grill, affording him an excellent view into the adjoining room. And inside the dark cupboard he was invisible.

The walls of the fuming chamber were peeling and stained reddish brown from mercury fumes. A selection of low wooden stools were ranged in a semi-circle to allow several occupants to be treated at once.

Lily was sat on one, her red skirts arranged around her legs. On the next was a bullish man, dressed plainly but well, in a thick leather coat and boots. He wore a swooping cavalier's hat and a moustache in the style of the King. A pet monkey sat on his shoulder.

Charlie linked the facts together. Military clothes, large muscular body. Dressed like a soldier of fortune good enough to forgo political allegiance. Sword worn with the self-possession of experience.

An inconstant general with a pet monkey. The Earl of Amesbury.

So Lily was a spy, Charlie deduced. Working for Amesbury.

'Did you tell them not to fume us in here?' Lily's voice came again.

Amesbury waved a thick hand. 'They have instructions to leave us well alone,' he replied.

Lily was staring in Charlie's direction, but so far as he could tell, she couldn't see into the dark confines of the cupboard. For a moment he thought she meant to investigate, but then she walked to an unlit brazier ready-filled with tinder.

Charlie caught his breath. He had seen a flash of his key, looped around her wrist by the ribbon. Lily had taken out a tinderbox and was lighting the brazier. She turned and began speaking to Amesbury again. Charlie strained forward to hear as the cracking of burning wood rose.

'Find Torr,' Amesbury was saying. 'You'll know him by the mystic tree tattooed on his chest and neck. Discover what he knows of Blackstone.'

'You're sure Torr was a friend of Blackstone's?' asked Lily.

'They were friends,' said Amesbury slowly. 'War can change things. Blackstone gambled everything fighting the cause. His estates, his fine name. His wife's large dowry. All were lost to Cromwell.'

'Where will I find Torr?' asked Lily.

'One of my informants told me a place,' said Amesbury. 'I can't say for sure he'll still be there.'

The wood spat sparks, drowning out the next words.

Charlie watched as Amesbury handed Lily a piece of paper. She studied it carefully. Then she leaned forward and dropped it into the brazier. Charlie watched helplessly as it burned away to ash.

'The faction of the Sealed Knot which travelled to Holland,' said Lily. 'Torr was one of them?'

'Torr was one of the Brotherhood,' agreed Amesbury. 'He was always interested in mysticism, alchemy, things of that nature.'

'Their powers . . .' began Lily.

'It's more legend than fact,' said Amesbury. 'I don't know how much is true. The Sealed Knot Brotherhood consorted with alchemists and mystics in Holland. It's said they learned of the highest alchemy.'

'Lead to gold?' said Lily.

Amesbury nodded.

'The universal marriage. The duality at the heart of matter. Lead into gold.'

Lily looked thoughtful.

'Can such a thing really be?' she asked.

'Stories get twisted,' said Amesbury, 'particularly where alchemists are concerned. But the Brotherhood had secrets which could make them very rich men. Their papers could make vast wealth from nothing. That was how I heard it.'

'But their secret was lost?' said Lily. 'Blackstone hasn't the power to make lead from gold now?'

'Some say the young King Charles grew fearful of the Sealed Knot's powers and destroyed their workings,' said Amesbury. 'Others tell it that Blackstone's own maid hid the papers.'

Lily considered this. She was fingering the key at her wrist, Charlie noticed.

'Is this why Blackstone needs soot?' she asked eventually. 'He tries to recover the secret through experiment?'

Amesbury shrugged his great shoulders.

'I don't know,' he replied. 'My intelligence is that he has stolen fifty barrels. Perhaps he tries to re-create the lost alchemy.'

Lily frowned in thought.

'You were of the Sealed Knot too,' she said. 'Surely if they could make vast riches, you would know of it.'

Amesbury shook his head.

'We fought among ourselves, after the King's death,' he said. 'Fine brave men that we were,' he added. 'Blackstone and his troops were held under siege during the war. There are only whispers of what happened. They ate cats, candles. Some say worse. I didn't recognise Blackstone when he returned. His starved body had grown gross. And his eyes . . . He wasn't the man I knew.'

'Do you think he's dangerous?' asked Lily. 'If his men are making fireballs . . .'

'Every man of the Sealed Knot was dangerous,' said Amesbury. 'We protected the monarchy at all cost. There was nothing we wouldn't do. But Blackstone . . .' Amesbury considered. 'He wasn't the bravest. But he was the most ruthless and fearless. There's a rumour he survived plague and it unhinged him. Confused his thoughts. Robbed his memories.'

'If Blackstone has switched loyalty,' said Lily, 'his skill at warfare could now threaten the King.'

'I don't know if Blackstone is dangerous to the King,' said Amesbury. 'Certainly he is one of those who has reason to be. If Blackstone has those papers, then he could be the destruction or salvation of England. Whichever he wills.'

Amesbury stood.

'The King needs me,' he said. 'The fire spreads. This will be another blow to his authority. Perhaps the last.'

Lily nodded as he moved to the door.

'I will discover what I can,' she promised.

Amesbury nodded and left. Lily sat for a moment, watching him. Then she pulled out the same handkerchief that had been in her lap in the carriage.

This time Charlie had a clearer view. There was a siren, or a mermaid, picked out in simple stitching with long hair flowing down her back. Something about the stitching made him catch his breath. He was suddenly sure he recognised the seamstress. Charlie tucked the revelation away for future use.

Lily stared at the handkerchief.

'I will find you,' she said. And then she folded it up and tucked it back in her dress.

Chapter 25

A commotion sounded from the back of the Candlemakers' Guild. Three guildsmen were wielding an eighteen-foot iron fire-hook with difficulty.

Blackstone moved towards them.

'I come from the King,' he said, showing his royal seal. 'The palace says the fire will be out by morning. There is nothing to fear.'

The nearest chandler eyed Blackstone with suspicion. His hair was cut short in the Puritan style and his plain clothes suggested he would rather Cromwell had stayed in power.

'What would the King know?' he said. 'We hear His Majesty has not even been to see the blaze.'

'The King must call for buildings to be pulled down,' intervened a second chandler. He was a young apprentice of the kind Blackstone was familiar with. A Catholic slaving for the lowest guild privileges. 'The gale has whipped the flames too high to save Cheapside,' said the apprentice. 'If buildings are pulled our hall will be spared.'

Blackstone smiled. 'On the King's instructions every guild is expected to buy a fire engine. Where is yours?'

The Puritan looked uncomfortable.

'It was an expense we meant to meet next year,' he admitted.

Blackstone looked meaningfully at the elaborate ceremonial hall. 'A fire engine you should have,' he said. 'If your guild keeps only an old firehook, then you only have yourselves to blame. Only the King may grant authority to pull buildings and he does not,' he concluded.

The guildsmen watched with dismay as he walked away from them. Blackstone smiled to himself as they began bickering about the best course of action. Moving to the north-western corner of the hall, Blackstone's gaze fell on three barrels.

His guild contact had obeyed all of his instructions. The consignment had been left in the allotted place. The barrels were marked as containing bales of candlewick. But Blackstone knew different. Each held six pounds of gunpowder.

Carefully he took out his bottle and unstoppered it. Then, checking he wasn't being watched, he dropped the chunk of lead into the open mouth. The bottle began to hiss loudly. Blackstone stoppered it quickly and placed it on the ground.

Then he turned and walked out of the guild.

As Blackstone made his exit the guard made a mocking sign of the cross and spat.

Blackstone hesitated. He judged he had a few seconds to spare. In a smooth movement he grasped the guard by the throat and wrenched his head up and back. The guard's neck snapped cleanly. His head lolled, an expression of shock frozen on the dead features.

In an easy movement Blackstone slung the corpse back into the guild. A few chandlers were looking at him open-mouthed. Blackstone moved swiftly down the entry steps and on to the safety of Lothbury. A chandler had just started to shout for his arrest when the explosion hit.

The first blast blew a cloud of splinters and fire from the entrance of the guild. Then a deep rumbling came from the belly of the hall. As the other barrels fired the building twisted, shook and then exploded in flames.

Turning on his heel, Blackstone's vast bulk swung away on to Ironmonger's Lane. He vanished into the shady backstreets as the Chandlers' Guild continued detonating behind him. A cloud of smoke had risen high above the city and was settling fiery dust and ash over the surrounding wooden roofs.

The crackle of flames brought another feeling, a purity. Blackstone felt sure Teresa's sin would be purged. Burned away. He could not quite get his mind around the memory. Blackstone grasped at it and it twisted away, dancing at the edges of his conscious. The nearest he could describe it was a taste or a smell. Something bitter on the back of the tongue. Dry, *papery.*

Chapter 26

Charlie watched Lily tip water on the brazier, sending up a plume of angry smoke. He debated the next best step. Wait until she was in the stairwell, he decided, and catch her there. The enclosed space would muffle any noise and he could take back his key without risk of the house guard.

Lily exited the room and Charlie listened to her footsteps make their way down the corridor. Then he quietly opened the door to the fumigation cupboard and slid out.

A rustle of skirts alerted him just in time to a powerful kick aimed squarely towards his groin. Charlie dodged to the side and the foot connected hard with his thigh, lifting him from his haunches and sending him sprawling to the floor.

He looked up to catch a glimpse of Lily's furious face before she descended on him in a tumult of blows to the side of his head. Charlie raised his arms to protect his head, hoping to wait out the assault, but as the violence rained down, it became clear she had no intention of slowing the attack. Instead she began to layer the volley of kicks with a vocal crescendo built mostly of profanities.

Charlie rolled to one side as her tiny foot cracked repeatedly into his collarbone. He needed her to ease up the attack before he could press his advantage.

'Does Amesbury know,' he gasped, 'you carry Blackstone's handkerchief?'

The onslaught abated slightly. Charlie lunged his legs forward, wrapping them bodily around Lily's skirts and bringing her tumbling to the floor. He caught a flash of pure hatred in her expression as she fell past him. Charlie turned quickly, pinning her down with her arms tightly beneath her and placing a hand over her mouth.

He looked back and forth along the corridor but all was silent. Lily was quiet suddenly, as if the fight had gone out of her, and very slowly he took his hand away from her mouth so she could speak. She looked oddly limp, her dark eyes trained on his. Then he saw the knife.

'Get off me,' she said, 'and I'll consider sparing your life.'

Charlie's hand shot out, pressing at the tendons of her wrist. She gasped and her fingers opened, letting the knife fall. She glared at him furiously.

'I told you before,' said Charlie. 'I'm not one of your perfumed lords.'

'The house is guarded,' she said, glaring. 'I need only scream.'

'So scream,' said Charlie, balancing his weight to pin her down and working off the key at her wrist. 'And,' he continued, waving the freed key and refastening it around his neck, 'you'll never get to keep half of what this key opens.'

She was silent for a moment.

'You're offering to give me half of what your key opens?' she said eventually.

'You have information which could help me,' said Charlie. 'I heard you. You're working with Amesbury to find Blackstone.' He dangled the key. 'I'm looking for Blackstone's chest.'

Lily thought about this. 'So you need my help?'

Charlie smiled. 'I don't need your help. I need your information.'

'How do I know the key opens anything of value?'

'Because you already know what it unlocks,' said Charlie. 'Amesbury told you.'

A cycle of emotions flitted across Lily's face.

'The secret of the Sealed Knot?' she said finally. 'Lead into gold. But you said the chest contained marriage papers.'

Charlie hesitated, wondering whether to admit there was no tangible treasure in the chest.

'Alchemists speak of a universal marriage,' he said. 'They are obsessed by it. Amesbury told you himself. And alchemists use allegory and codes.'

Lily looked unconvinced.

'The chest is a Dutch sea chest,' persisted Charlie. 'It holds papers which Blackstone has killed to discover. Does it not make sense that those documents hold the sacred secrets of the Sealed Knot?'

He waited for this to sink in.

'Let me up,' she said. Carefully he shifted his weight, keeping a close eye on her knife hand.

'Swear it then,' she said, sitting up. 'Swear you will give me half.'

'I swear it.' He extended his hand.

She took it, seeming pleased with the arrangement.

Lily rose to standing, examining her red dress for damage.

'How did you know about my handkerchief?' she asked, adjusting the low front.

'Because I know who stitched it.'

Lily's dark eyebrows furrowed.

'It was embroidered a long time ago,' said Charlie. 'By my mother.'

Lily's eyes snapped to his.

Charlie nodded. 'I'll tell you all I know,' he said. 'Only if you swear there'll be no double-dealing. You'll tell me true in your part.'

Her face darkened in affront.

'Is that what you think of gypsies?' she demanded. 'Perhaps you think we steal babies as well?'

Charlie said nothing. He'd heard they ate them.

Chapter 27

Charlie took the handkerchief and smoothed it out. He tried not to be disconcerted that it was warm from Lily's skin.

'I recognised it the first time I saw it,' said Charlie, turning it in his hands. 'I just wasn't sure why.' His hands ran over the threads. 'I must have seen it as a boy,' he added.

'Who was your mother?' asked Lily sharply. 'Why was she embroidering for Blackstone?'

'She was a maid in his household,' said Charlie. 'I didn't think I remembered anything about her. But I remember seeing this mermaid.'

'Your mother was Blackstone's maid?' Lily's mind was working. 'The maid who hid his secret papers?' she guessed. 'So the stories were true?'

Charlie nodded. 'That part at least.' He turned his key thoughtfully.

'Where did you get the handkerchief?' he asked.

Lily swallowed, then her jaw jutted out defiantly.

'Blackstone used it to blindfold my father,' she said, 'before executing him.'

The handkerchief lay accusingly in Charlie's hand.

'My father spied for the Republic,' explained Lily. 'He got information to win against Blackstone's men. But Blackstone could not bear to be bested by a gypsy. After the war he came back to take his revenge.'

Lily swallowed, picked her knife up off the floor and stowed it in her skirts.

'My brothers got back my father's body. He had been blind-folded. With that.'

She nodded towards Charlie's hand.

'But then my brothers vanished. So it falls to me.'

'It won't bring your father back,' said Charlie. 'Revenging your-self on Blackstone.'

Lily's eyes flashed. 'Gypsies have always been persecuted,' she said. 'My mother died at the hands of a lynch mob. But we always pay our dues in the end.'

'So you hope to find Blackstone and kill him?'

'I don't hope,' corrected Lily. 'I will serve him the same as he did my father. And I keep this handkerchief to close his eyes in the last moment.'

Charlie nodded. 'That's why you spy for Amesbury?' he said. 'To find Blackstone?'

'One of the reasons.'

'Blackstone killed my mother,' said Charlie after a moment. 'For hiding his papers. It's why I can't read so well,' he added. 'She taught my brother letters, but died before it was my turn.'

'A maid who could read?'

Charlie shrugged. 'Some learn.'

'So you seek your own revenge?' asked Lily.

Charlie shook his head.

'I've had done with thoughts of that kind. But I mean to dis-cover the secrets of this key.' He held it up. 'I think it's what my mother would have wanted.'

Lily took back the handkerchief.

'Do you know why your mother sewed it?' she asked.

Charlie shook his head. 'Do you?'

'No. I don't think it matters.'

Charlie looked back at the handkerchief. The mermaid's tail was stitched with seven letters cascading downwards. They were the same style as on the London Stone.

He tilted his head.

'Roman numbers,' he said. 'The mermaid's tail is a date.'

Lily nodded. '1649. The year the old King was beheaded. It commemorates something. Perhaps a battle.'

'1649 and a picture of a mermaid,' said Charlie. 'Does it mean anything to you?'

Lily shook her head. 'I never thought about it. Would it tell us anything about Blackstone?'

'Women stitch handkerchiefs for all kinds of things,' said Charlie, handing it back. 'It could be a battle as you say. Most likely it doesn't mean much. Just a work to employ idle hands. We should go find Torr. Where did Amesbury say he was?'

Lily eyed him warily.

'First tell me what you made of this,' she said, removing the round robin.

Charlie glanced at it.

'Not so much,' he said.

Lily raised her eyebrows.

'Perhaps something about the names,' said Charlie grudgingly. 'Working men all. How came they to write?'

'The handwriting isn't good,' Lily pointed out.

'Even so.'

'What of that?' asked Lily, pointing to the number four. 'Alchemy?'

'I asked an apothecary about the symbol,' said Charlie. 'He says it represents lye. Thinks alchemists wouldn't use such a low substance.'

'You didn't ask an alchemist?'

'Not yet.'

'Do you know any?'

'A few,' said Charlie. 'They cluster on Nile Street. No one wants an alchemist in the city walls,' he added. 'They cause explosions. But they've managed to hold their ground.'

Charlie looked back at the round robin. Nine names.

Something was buzzing at the edge of his brain. There was a pattern. A pattern he could not quite see.

He pushed the round robin back to Lily impatiently.

'I've told you what I know,' he said. 'We lose time. Where is Torr?'

'Fleet Street,' said Lily. 'In a tavern called the Cheshire Cheese.'

'Fleet Street,' said Charlie. He eyed Lily. 'The marriage street,' he added. 'Where a minister will marry you for a few pence.'

'I know what a Fleet Wedding is,' she snapped.

Charlie raised his eyebrows at the uncharacteristic slip. Perhaps Lily had fallen foul of a Fleet Wedding. She didn't look the type. Her composure returned so fast he wondered if he'd imagined it.

'Will the fire reach Fleet Street?' she asked.

'It could,' said Charlie. 'The Fleet River is a good firebreak between east and west. But with the fire so high and the wind so fierce, cinders could drop. Many roofs are wood shingle. And plenty of old soldiers keep gunpowder.'

'Then we should go now,' said Lily.

Chapter 28

Clarence greeted Louise Keroulle with a wide smile. He ushered her in quickly, lest they were seen. The King's French mistress was enchantingly pretty up close. Much younger than Barbara too, Clarence noted with pleasure.

Clarence allowed his eyes to roam the plump rounded breasts and tantalising shape of her body.

'You think the tide may turn against the King?' asked Louise, pouting her little lips. She didn't sound as unhappy as she might have.

The Earl of Clarence flinched.

'I said no such thing,' he said.

Louise pointed. 'Your clothes say it,' she said. 'You wear Royalist pomp. But you keep your collar the old Republic style. In case the political tide turns again.'

Clarence concealed his surprise with a cough.

'But of course you are French,' he murmured. 'You have a talent for fashion.'

Louise smiled. It was the first kind thing which had been said to her since Barbara Castlemaine's return.

'I can help you?' she asked. 'That is why you send for me?'

Clarence's rounded features shifted to a calculating expression.

'You dislike Barbara Castlemaine?' he asked.

Louise's eyes narrowed. 'I hate that woman.'

Clarence nodded. He moved to place a hand on the white skin of Louise's delightfully plump arm. She didn't recoil, but her face suggested it took her some effort.

'She is disgusting,' said Louise. 'Barbara catches Charles with . . . with whore tricks. Offering herself however he wants.' Louise lowered her voice conspiratorially. 'Barbara boasts about the filthy things she does with him. She laughs about it.'

'She has no decency,' agreed Clarence carefully, 'but sadly men are weak. Even Kings.' He moved a little closer to her. 'Perhaps I could discover some of Barbara's tricks. Tell them to you, so you might use them.'

'What would an old man know of such things?' retorted Louise rudely. 'No trick would best Barbara in any case. She is without shame. Last summer,' she added, 'she spread a letter around court. Saying that I made love to my own brother, George. He had to leave England,' she continued furiously. 'I am sure it was her. Barbara. Trying to weaken me. To lessen my friends.'

Louise shook her head so vigorously that her shining brown curls made a flurry around her face. 'She wants to push me out,' she concluded. 'But I'll not go. Not because of her. But people still say,' she concluded in an outraged whisper, 'that George 'ad me from beehind,' her pronunciation grew more French in her fury, 'there,' she pointed to Clarence's desk, 'on that table.'

'It sounds like the kind of lewd falsehood Barbara would say,' agreed Clarence. Although in reality, he had to admit it wasn't. Barbara was ruthless, but she liked people to know who had beaten them. Secret rumours weren't her style.

'Barbara hates me too,' said Clarence. 'Because I see her true motives. She wants to go out on the Royal Barge so people will love her. So her illegitimates might fare a better chance for the Crown.'

'Charles said that would never be,' said Louise. 'England won't crown a bastard.'

'We executed a King,' said Clarence. 'England does as she sees fit.'

Louise's soft forehead rippled.

'You love the King?' Clarence asked soothingly.

Louise nodded, her curls bouncing.

'Yes, I love him.' Tears filled her eyes. 'I have loved him since I arrived in court.'

'Barbara Castlemaine has come between you?' Clarence's expression was sympathetic.

'Yes.' Louise sniffed, and she turned to Clarence with outrage in her face. 'She struck me! Here.' Louise tapped the side of her face.

Clarence nodded.

'She is hated in Parliament,' he soothed. 'It is well known Barbara's only pleasure is spending the King's money and gaining advancement for her children.'

'They are *not* his children,' spat Louise. 'I hear the stories. She opens her legs for all the court.'

'Yes,' agreed Clarence.

'Four children the old sow has birthed,' continued Louise, her voice rising. 'She must hang so low between her legs, a man need not raise her skirts.'

'Quite . . .' began Clarence, his face colouring.

'And she is *old*,' fumed Louise. 'She has a whisker on her chin, like a witch. I have seen it!'

'I'm sure she has many such . . .'

'And she does secret things,' continued Louise, her tone dropping. 'Things she hides from Charles.'

Clarence's jowls wobbled in interest. He'd heard rumours that Barbara plotted against the crown, but had never believed it.

'Secret things?' he inquired, trying to keep his tone neutral.

'Yes,' breathed Louise, excited to have captured her audience. 'Dog's piss, she uses, on her face.' Her eyes were narrowed in spite. 'For wrinkles,' Louise concluded, her expression making clear the scandalous nature of such behaviour. 'Barbara works all kinds of disgusting potions and balms into her old face,' she added. '*Lady* Castlemaine doesn't dare tell Charles the expense.'

Clarence tried not to let his disappointment show. The depths of female vanity never shocked him.

'The question is,' interrupted Clarence, 'how can we help the King to see reason?'

Louise calmed slightly at this. 'Reason?' She pronounced the word in such a way that Clarence wondered if her English was failing her.

'How can we help His Majesty see that Barbara is bad for the country?'

'I don't know.' Louise was crying again. 'I have tried. Charles is kind. But I see in his eyes he thinks only of her. I *hate* her.' Louise's face had turned beet red.

'Do you know the King's eldest son? Monmouth?'

Louise nodded, her face twisting. 'He's horrid,' she said. 'Monmouth lies about everything.'

'He takes after his mother,' said Clarence. 'You've met Lucy Walter? Middle-aged woman. Dresses like a French harlot?'

Louise gave a little laugh. 'No French harlot would clothe herself so vulgarly.'

'Perhaps you could talk with Monmouth,' said Clarence, encouraged. 'He keeps the Royal Barge. Barbara wishes it readied for the King to view the fire.'

'So if the Royal Barge weren't available . . .' suggested Louise, catching on.

'Precisely,' agreed Clarence.

Louise toyed with a bouncy curl. 'Barbara would be humiliated,' she said, taking obvious pleasure from the thought, 'in front of Charles.'

Clarence smiled at her encouragingly.

'Why can't you speak with Monmouth?' she said eventually, frowning at the thought of speaking to him.

Clarence coughed.

'I'm a boring old man,' he said. 'Monmouth is a boy. News from a pretty girl is much more interesting for him.'

'So this is politics,' said Louise. 'Charles said I should learn it. I suppose if I want to stay, I should.'

Clarence said nothing.

'Where would I find Monmouth?' said Louise.

Chapter 29

As Charlie and Lily arrived at the head of Fleet Street their route was blocked. Refugees from Cheapside and Poultry intermingled with crazed Fleet Streeters trying to remove their possessions. The tall black-and-white buildings were crawling with ropes, bundles and intrepid householders. Each diamond-paned window had clusters of desperate Londoners, fighting to lower valuables. The small doorways were crammed with smartly dressed servants hauling out furniture. Shopkeepers were removing stock. Tavern owners were rolling away barrels of ale. Coffee houses threw sacks of beans from upper windows.

'It seems no one told Fleet Street residents,' said Lily, 'that their street won't burn.'

Charlie looked east where the bloody maw of the fire towered. The sound of the distant flames was deafening. He'd never seen flames so tall.

'Perhaps it will burn,' he said, eyeing a man inching along the half-timbered exterior of a five-storey Fleet Street house. 'We should hurry. If we could get to Shoe Lane there are gardens behind. We could get into the Cheshire Cheese that way.'

'How do we get to Shoe Lane?' said Lily. 'The crowds are too thick.'

'Behind the Fleet Prison,' said Charlie, 'the Fleet River narrows to a ditch. Timbers run across to brace the buildings either side. We can cross that way.'

He was eyeing Lily's skirts.

'I can climb as well as you,' she said shortly. 'And I know the way to the Fleet Prison.'

───────

They cut back up into Fleet Lane, behind the sturdy walls of Fleet Prison. From the barred windows came wails of prisoners petitioning to be freed. Gaolers guarding the entrance had already begun releasing a steady stream of debtors. No one expected the fire to stop at Cheapside.

'This way,' said Charlie, beckoning Lily over a stone wall bordering the Fleet River. Though the flames looked half a mile away, he could feel the heat of the fire. The air was warm and still.

Lily was covering her mouth.

'This isn't a river,' she accused, glaring at the stinking slurry. 'A river moves.'

Charlie glanced up river.

'It looks like a cart and horses pitched in upstream,' he said. 'They block the flow. People are too busy getting their goods out to clear it.'

'That doesn't explain the stink.'

'The prisoners make their waste here,' said Charlie, his eyes watering from the smell. 'And the households. The hot summer has dried it out.'

'And the heat of the fire,' said Lily, wiping sweat from her forehead. 'I feel it even here.'

Banked by brick houses and high prison walls the Fleet was barely more than a reeking ditch. Thick timber beams braced the buildings all the way along. Each was slimed over and slippery. Filth streaked downwards from toilet holes on either side.

Charlie judged the best crossing point and dropped down. His toes slid in the ooze and then held firm.

'Be careful here,' said Charlie. 'It's as slick as ice.'

He balanced and then walked quickly along, holding out an arm for ballast. Behind him Lily's face was scrunched up in disgust. She took out her knives, then made across on all fours, using the blades for traction.

'Two knives,' observed Charlie as she righted herself, holstered the knives at her hip and scaled across the adjoining wall.

'Four,' she said. 'You'll never see the other two.'

'Remind me never to cross you.'

'Or put a hand up my skirts. Which way now?'

'This way,' he said, pointing west. 'To Shoe Lane.'

As Charlie suspected, the cobblers had long ago deserted with what meagre possessions they had. The street was almost empty and it was easy to cross the gardens to the alleyway leading to the Cheshire Cheese.

From the back of the tavern they could see the commotion inside. There were four floors, and a jettied fifth which Lily pointed to.

'The top floor,' she said. 'That's what Amesbury's contact said.'

Charlie's gaze ranged the building, searching for a way in. Near where they stood were two small doors leading to a wood store. Opening one door could lend them a little height to climb on to the half timber.

He stared back up at the leaded window of the top storey. A gaggle of women were in a flurry behind it. Charlie recognised their black-and-white clothes. They were Quakers.

Charlie took them in. 'I don't think Torr is here.'

'Why not?'

'Those women are Quakers,' he said.

'And?'

'Quakers are against churches and kings,' said Charlie. 'Can you imagine a Catholic Royalist in their midst?'

Lily took the point.

'So Amesbury's contact was wrong?' she said. 'I don't see it.'

Charlie eyed the top floor which jettied out over the road.

'Amesbury's contact was a Catholic boy,' he said. 'So I assume he didn't write this address?'

'No,' said Lily. 'It was a picture.'

A new possibility dawned on Charlie.

'A picture of the different floors?' he said.

'Yes,' said Lily. 'There was no misunderstanding,' she added, sounding insulted. 'A cross for the floor where Torr was. And a sign for the Cheshire Cheese.'

'But a cross can be any way up,' said Charlie. 'What if you read the plan upside down?'

'Then Torr would be in the main tavern,' said Lily, pointing to the ground level window. 'That couldn't be.'

Charlie shook his head.

'What if, instead of a top floor, Torr had a cellar?'

Lily's gaze dropped down.

'Fleet Street is a merchant and tavern place,' said Charlie. 'Most buildings have big cellars for stock. Which would mean,' he added, pointing to the wood-store doors. 'Those doors could be the way in.'

Lily was there before him easing open the doors. A wooden ladder led downwards. Below was dank, empty and deserted. Charlie hesitated as Lily beckoned him over.

'You're afraid of cellars?' she asked.

'Strange memories of them is all.'

Lily blinked her dark eyes and lowered herself on to the ladder. He saw her vanish into the gloom.

Charlie pushed away an image of Blackstone's wife Teresa, in her cellar of ribbons and poppets. He was never quite sure if it was a memory or a dream. Charlie knew he must have lived in Blackstone's house, whilst his mother worked as his maid. But he had no clear pictures of that time. Only frightening flashes.

He flipped a leg over the edge and climbed down the ladder. The bottom rung was broken and a stale chemical aroma greeted him. By the slim shaft of daylight Charlie made out a large table on its side. Signs of a struggle perhaps.

He could just make out the centre of the cellar. There were a few barrels there. But all beyond was black.

Charlie listened carefully. He could hear Lily's light breath and the faint rustle of her skirts. But every now and then he thought he caught something else. Like the faintest inhale and exhale. As though a monster slept deep beneath them.

'Where are you?' he hissed, moving reluctantly away from the sunlight.

There was only silence in reply. Charlie felt his heartbeat quicken. Then a tinderbox flared.

'There's no one down here,' said Lily, appearing at the other end of the cellar. 'But you'd better come and look.'

Chapter 30

Charlie moved past the barrels in the centre of the cellar. Lily was standing by a wide stone hearth peppered in burn marks. A collection of dusty rings on the floor suggested a number of flasks had been cleared out.

The glow of Lily's tinderbox was in no way reassuring. Dark corners loomed. Weak lines of sunlight shone down from the tavern floorboards above.

Not quite regular, thought Charlie, noticing a broken pattern in the lines of light. There were marks too, on the far wall. Four points where a cross might have hung.

'What do you make of this?' asked Lily, prodding at the stone hearth. 'Alchemy?'

Charlie switched his attention to the hearth. It looked to him like an alchemical set-up. Colourful burns pock-marked the stone. A crucible for heating metal was lain on its side. But there was another smell on the air besides chemicals. Incense.

'Maybe alchemy,' he said. 'But I think this place is a secret church.'

Lily turned to him, raising her tinderbox. Charlie was pointing to a pitted area of ground.

'I can smell incense on the air,' he said. 'And see there.'

She raised the flame.

'Four points where a cross was nailed,' he said. 'And the ground is more worn here as though a body of people shuffled. Less at the back where the priest stood. Incense smoke marks on the ceiling.'

'Then what of that?' asked Lily, waving her tinderbox towards the hearth.

Charlie approached it and saw symbols carved carefully into the stone.

There were circles arranged in a pattern. But they didn't have the look of witchcraft. The arrangement looked older somehow. It was surrounded by crystallised marks.

'Runes?' suggested Charlie, running his hand over them. Each circle had a strange symbol in the centre of it.

Lily shook her head. 'The circles mark the Tree of Life,' she said. 'I recognise it. Gypsies sometimes use it,' she added. 'With tarot cards.'

'You think they were telling fortunes here?' asked Charlie. It seemed unlikely. Fortune-tellers in London clustered by the Sign of the Merlin's Head and conned silly maids out of pennies.

'Tarot is about contemplation.' Her hands plotted the circles. 'This is Kaballah. The soul's path. It's an ancient way of understanding God.'

Charlie studied it.

'A sect then?' he said uncertainly. 'A mystic sect?' Sects were common in London since Cromwell. Mystics believed God could be experienced with no church or priest.

Charlie was looking back at where he imagined the altar to be.

'They experimented with fire,' observed Lily, touching the scorched hearth with her toe.

Charlie's gaze switched to the stout barrels in the centre of the cellar. He moved to investigate.

'Bring the flame over here,' he called.

The barrels flared into soft light. Charlie took out his eating knife and levered off a lid. Inside was a dark black powder with a very familiar smell.

'Gunpowder,' he said, leaning closer to confirm the odour.

He waved Lily back with her flame and resealed the lid.

Charlie shook away the feeling that sorcery was afoot. It was time to view things practically.

'Gunpowder,' he said. 'In a secret church or sect. So perhaps Torr plotted. There was a struggle down here,' he continued, approaching the upended table. 'And the bottom rung of the ladder is broken. Something removed by force. Or someone.'

He dropped to his haunches, considering.

The circles on the hearth. Incense. Alchemy.

Charlie moved back to the alchemy hearth, certain there was more to be gleaned from it. Then he stopped short, listening.

'What is it?' asked Lily.

'Shhh,' he held up a hand. There was that noise again. Like tense breathing. 'You hear that?'

Lily listened. 'I hear the wind,' she said. 'The gale is up.'

'That's not it.' Charlie turned back to Lily. 'Something's not right.'

Charlie scanned the dark cellar. The floor was packed earth. The walls damp-slicked brick. His eyes looked up to the ceiling seeking out the anomaly he'd noticed earlier. The pattern of light was wrong. Straight line, straight line. Then an interruption. As though something were blocking the light.

Charlie walked to the central point of the cellar. His hands began gently probing the beams. Dust and cobwebs dropped free.

Lily moved towards him with the tinderbox but Charlie had stopped. His fingers were working something free.

'You've found something?' Lily's flame lurched in surprise. 'A book?'

'I think it's a register,' said Charlie, pulling it down. 'Not well hidden,' he added with a sense of growing unease. 'Not well hidden enough.'

He opened it and a clutch of papers fluttered free. Lily stooped and picked one up.

'Empty marriage certificates,' she said. 'For Fleet Weddings. This must be how Torr was making his money. A few pence for sailors and silly women to marry.'

Charlie was staring at the certificates.

'I've seen a marriage paper like that before,' he said. 'It's the same as my mother hid.'

Charlie eased open the large book to reveal a list of names in crabbed text.

'So Mr Torr was a minister,' he said slowly. 'The same minister who performed Blackstone's marriage.'

Chapter 31

A bathtub had been placed in the centre of Barbara's sumptuous chambers. The steaming water swirled with rose petals. She lay back, letting her long auburn hair eddy and drift.

There was a knock at the door and Barbara sat up in her bath.

'Come,' she called.

Monmouth strode self-importantly into the room. He was dressed like a gaudy clone of the King, in a slash-sleeved brown-velvet coat, short hose and white stockings. Silver brocade, flouncing ribbons, frothy lace and jewelled buttons decorated every available edge and opening.

He was so preoccupied with making an imposing entrance that he was halfway through a courtly bow when he noticed Barbara was naked. He stopped short, mouth working comically.

Barbara's smile grew wide.

'Monmouth,' she said. 'Don't be bashful. Come closer.'

'You summoned me?' Caught by the arresting sight of Barbara, Monmouth's tone didn't achieve the disdain he was hoping for.

Barbara let out a throaty laugh. 'I should like to get to know you better.'

'I do not recognise your authority,' began Monmouth, his eyes swinging wildly for a suitable resting place, 'to request my presence. I am the first son of a King. You . . .'

In reply Barbara stood. Warm water cascaded down her naked body. Monmouth began blinking rapidly.

'We all know what I am,' smiled Barbara, her eyes alive in their depths. 'And why should you recognise me?' she added, stepping gracefully from the bath and sashaying to where he stood. 'I am nothing to the King's eldest son.'

Monmouth flushed. His eyes lighted briefly on a filigree desk, flicked down to the thick rug and back to the cherub cornicing.

Barbara's smile grew wide.

'Don't be bashful,' she said. 'I do not mind you looking. You are a grown man now. Fifteen and married. I imagine you often look on your wife's naked body.'

She eyed him carefully. 'Perhaps not so often,' she concluded.

Monmouth opened his mouth to reply, but she took his face in her hands.

'Let me look at you,' said Barbara. Monmouth had inherited Lucy Walter's long-lashed dark eyes and pouting mouth, giving his face a girlish quality.

'Such a handsome boy,' decided Barbara, lifting his chin gently. 'You have a lot of your mother in you. Those pretty dark eyes.' Her face flickered.

'They say I have my father's countenance,' said Monmouth, entranced by the touch of her fingers.

Barbara smiled. 'Oh, courtiers will say things to flatter.' She assessed him again. 'Perhaps a little curve on the nose,' she decided. 'And of course you wear your hair like Charles.' Her hand caressed his curling brown locks.

He picked at the pearl detailing of his slashed sleeves, then began toying with his silver buttons.

Barbara smiled. 'The human form is a thing of beauty. You have seen my portrait in the King's rooms?'

Monmouth let out a breath. 'Yes.' He was looking determinedly at her face now. She was gleaming with sweat from the warmth of the bath and her auburn curls were damp.

'Well then,' she leaned in to whisper at his ear. 'You have already seen all of me.'

Monmouth swallowed.

'You must tell me which you like best,' she added, her violet eyes sultry. 'My body in the portrait or that in the flesh.'

Monmouth allowed himself a glance along her body. She was perfect. The little curve of her white belly. The soft pink hue of her nipples.

'The flesh,' he admitted.

'Such a handsome boy you are.' She placed a hand on his shoulder. Then locking her gaze to his, she moved her hand down slowly.

'But you are quite the grown man now,' she observed.

'Yes.' Monmouth attempted to deepen his tone.

Barbara smiled and walked across the room to her couch.

'Come and sit with me,' she invited. 'We'll have some wine.'

Monmouth's legs moved of their own accord to the sofa. He sat beside her rearranging his crotch embarrassedly.

She poured him a glass of red wine and he took it clumsily and gulped.

'Slowly,' she instructed. 'Savour it.'

He slowed his gulps to reflexive sips.

'They say you are trying to have my title taken,' he said, wrestling to take control of the situation.

Barbara laid a warm hand on his thigh. Reason fled.

'Why should I do that?' she asked, circling her fingers. 'Are we not friends, you and I?'

'I . . .' the rush of warmth to his body had hit his brain like a warm fog. 'That is . . . what they say,' he managed.

'I see.' Barbara sat back. 'Do you know what else they say about me?'

'No.' Monmouth gulped more wine.

She leaned in. 'They say that after four children, I am tighter.'

Monmouth froze, the wine goblet halfway to his mouth. His lips were moving slightly, trying to fit what he thought he'd just heard with reality.

'See for yourself,' Barbara suggested. She relaxed back again, letting her legs fall apart.

Monmouth's eyes swam. His lips parted slightly. He was floating in a dreamlike haze of lust. Barbara Castlemaine's naked legs were parted. She smiled seductively.

'Do you think they're right?' she asked, moving a hand to caress her thigh. 'Children haven't changed me?'

Monmouth nodded mutely.

'So tell me,' Barbara continued silkily. 'Who says I try to disinherit you?'

'Clarence,' he mumbled, the wine beginning to work on him now. 'And he says you've turned Catholic.'

Barbara's violet eyes flashed. She sat up a little straighter, letting the gap between her legs close.

'Religion has fallen apart since Cromwell,' she said airily. 'Charles and I were in Holland, we saw it all. Enlightenment. Mysticism.' She gave a little cough of disdain.

'Men in cloaks telling fools they may experience God.'

'I thought mystic sects taught ancient secrets,' said Monmouth, curiosity piquing his young voice.

'They make death rituals,' said Barbara, 'so a man might have holy visions without priest or church. I hope you have no interest in anything of that kind,' she added sharply. 'What would Lucy Walter say? England's prettiest little liar.'

Monmouth flinched at the mention of his mother's nickname, but didn't defend her. Loyalty to his mother had been defeated by his acute embarrassment of her.

'She says I should stay away from heretics.'

Barbara nodded.

'Your mother is right.'

She thought for a moment. Her bare legs drew apart a little again.

'Should you like to play a game?' she said.

'Yes.' Monmouth drank more wine. 'Though I am not so good at cards.'

She laughed. 'It is not cards we play at.'

An uncertain blush rose in his face.

'Take off your clothes,' she said silkily. 'I think we should get better acquainted, you and I.'

'My father . . .' began Monmouth.

'Oh, do not be so silly,' clucked Barbara. 'Your father and I . . . Well you have heard what we do. He takes his lovers where he chooses and so do I.'

'But he . . .'

She raised a finger to his lips.

'Charles will be pleased,' she said. 'His eldest son must be properly educated in such things. Such a noble boy cannot be left to the fumblings of a whore or servant.'

She lowered her eyes at him.

'You haven't yet? With your wife . . .?' She left the question hanging.

'Of course I have!' said Monmouth.

'I don't speak of your enjoyment,' said Barbara. 'I talk of hers.'

'I . . . There have been many times,' blurted Monmouth. 'I can hardly count them.'

'That is an unappealing quality,' said Barbara sharply. 'To lie. Be careful you don't take after your mother. People have already begun to speak of your untruths.'

Monmouth blushed red.

'I council for your own good,' said Barbara. 'Lucy is famed for her tall tales. Courtly people begin to speak of your exaggerations.'

She assessed his face.

'You are an ambitious boy,' she said. 'I imagine you tried with your wife. But you did not win her. I can always tell.' She slid a finger under his chin and raised his gaze to hers.

'I can teach you things you can hardly imagine,' she whispered, her fingers working to loosen his shirt. 'Things your wife will beg for. Tricks which will make you irresistible to women.'

A deep blush was spreading up Monmouth's neck, but he didn't stop her.

'If you think of it,' observed Barbara as Monmouth's youthful chest was revealed by inches, 'I could be like a mother to you.'

Monmouth began to unbutton and Barbara's hands moved to help him.

'You poor boy,' she crooned, stroking the side of his face. 'Your own mother deserted you. I know it all.'

'But my relationship with your father . . .' she said, letting his shirt fall to the floor. 'Means I can be a very loving mother to you.'

She moved his hand to her naked breast and planted a gentle kiss on his lips. 'Should you like that?' she whispered, keeping her face close to his.

Monmouth hesitated.

'Shall we play it, that I am the mother and you the son. And you shall sit in my lap whilst I play with you?' she suggested.

Monmouth said nothing but his body was betraying him.

'Come sit,' she said. 'We'll play. I will teach you to always listen to your mother.'

Chapter 32

'I thought Blackstone was a noble,' said Lily as Charlie looked at the marriage register. 'Why not marry properly in a church?'

'Three kinds of people make a Fleet Wedding,' said Charlie. 'Sailors, paupers, and people with something to hide. We already know Blackstone killed to conceal those papers.'

Lily was staring over Charlie's shoulder at the record-book. His finger hovered over the first marriage in the book. He made out the familiar names.

'There,' he said, mouthing the words with difficulty. 'Torr married Teresa and Thomas Blackstone. In 1649.'

He looked up at Lily. 'That's not right.'

'What do you mean?'

'The marriage certificate my mother hid,' said Charlie, 'showed Blackstone married later.'

'The dates are different?'

Charlie nodded. 'According to this book, Blackstone married in 1647. The papers I saw had him married in 1649.'

'You're sure of that?' asked Lily.

'I've got a good memory,' said Charlie. 'For numbers and things I've seen. Not writing.'

Lily accepted this without question.

'So Blackstone married twice?' she suggested.

'To a woman of the same name,' said Charlie.

'A different wife then? The same name. Teresa is common enough.'

'I don't think so.' Charlie was struggling for memories. 'If Blackstone married legitimately, then why hide the second wedding papers?'

'The book says they married on a ship,' said Lily, showing herself a better reader than Charlie. 'See? "At sea" is the place.'

She looked at Charlie.

'I thought a Fleet Wedding must take place on Fleet Street?'

Charlie shook his head. 'A minister can make a wedding wherever he wishes.'

His eyes scanned down the register.

There was an answer here. He could feel it. A rush of excitement blazed through him. This book would lead them to Blackstone. But the writing was making his head hurt. And some other intuition was shouting at him to pay attention. Cool air was pouring down from the cellar opening, blowing over them in an insistent breeze.

Charlie suddenly realised what the sound of breathing was. The cinder thief in him matched it instinctively to the disturbed air flow. Suddenly everything made sense. The powder barrels. The badly hidden book.

Charlie moved quickly to the cellar wall and pressed his palms against the plaster. The wall was warm. It wasn't breathing he could hear. It was distant fire.

'Torr didn't hide his register,' he said grimly. 'Someone else stuffed it in the rafters. To be sure the book would burn. They've fired the cellar next to this one to cover their tracks.' Charlie surveyed the barrels of gunpowder. 'This cellar has been mined for destruction.'

Chapter 33

Charlie turned to Lily. 'We need to get out,' he said, tucking the marriage papers in his leather coat. 'Now.'

But as they made to leave a leather bottle dropped down from the open cellar door. Lily and Charlie looked at one another. The bottle bounced, rolled and began hissing furiously. Then the cellar entrance slammed shut.

'What is it?' asked Lily, staring at the bottle.

'Some kind of firebomb,' guessed Charlie, shrugging off his leather coat to smother it. 'Designed to light the powder kegs.'

He was halfway to the bottle when it exploded in blue fire. A spray of flame arced towards the gunpowder.

Charlie twisted, throwing his coat towards the barrels. The leather fell heavily across them, shielding the contents. Liquid trails of blue fire danced across the battered coat then died.

Lily cautiously lowered her arms and surveyed the cellar. The spray of fire had pooled and extinguished harmlessly on the earth floor.

'It's not real fire,' she said, eyeing the dark room in puzzlement. 'It didn't last.'

'I think it would have been real enough to light gunpowder,' said Charlie. He brushed down his coat and heaved it back on. The fire in the adjoining cellar had increased to a roaring sound now. It seemed to come from all around.

'We need to get out.'

Lily was already halfway up the ladder.

'We're shut in!' she cried, slamming her fist hopelessly against the door. 'There's something heavy blocking it.'

'Whoever planned this is taking no chances,' said Charlie. He moved to the edge of the cellar and began feeling the walls.

'What are you doing?' asked Lily, watching him.

'These cellars join up,' said Charlie, making an exploratory test with his knuckles. 'There's often not much between them. It's a common robbery,' he added, pressing his cheek to the wall. 'Break into a goodwife's cellar to get to a goldsmith.'

Charlie moved back and tapped. As he'd hoped it was a thin stud wall, with the thinnest smear of horsehair plaster separating the two cellars.

'The cellar on this side is cool,' he said. 'We can break through . . .'

His words were drowned out by the sound of falling rubble. Plaster on the adjoining wall had crumbled away. A red tongue of flame leered from the next cellar.

Charlie knelt, raised his elbow and knocked a small hole clean through the wall at knee height. 'We need to keep the marriage register safe,' he called. 'Whoever burns this place wants to be sure it flames.'

Lily dropped from the ladder, retrieved the register and ran to kneel beside him. Charlie reached a fist through and tugged away at the crumbling plaster. Lily watched for a second, looked back at the powder barrels then removed a knife from her skirts and began plunging it into the plaster.

'Keep it low,' he said. 'Easier to crawl.'

The dull roar was now a menacing crackle, lighting them both in an orange glow.

'You go through first,' said Charlie, pushing Lily towards the gap. 'You're smaller and you can light the way.'

Lily crawled through, shedding plaster as she went.

The fire was growing up the inside cellar wall now. One spitting beam was all that was needed to blow the whole cellar sky-high. Quickly he tunnelled through after Lily.

The tinder-dry air was replaced with a rich salty smell. Someone had used the adjoining cellar to protect their valuable foods from fire. There were shelves and shelves of cheese and cured sausage wrapped in cloths.

Charlie stood to see Lily's waving tinderbox was already halfway up the ladder. She was balancing precariously, holding her flame to see the opening with an outstretched hand. As she shifted to push the cellar door open the marriage register tumbled from underneath her arm.

'Get the book!' she shouted, moving her flame down to illuminate it. Charlie scooped it up as Lily shoved the door with the flat of her hand. A shaft of sunlight blasted through the dark. Charlie reached the bottom of the ladder as Lily's skirts disappeared out of the top. He raced up the first two rungs, his eyes fixed firmly on the welcome daylight. Then the explosion hit.

It blew the bottom of the ladder clean away and jerked free Charlie's grip. He swung wildly, one hand clinging on. The marriage register tumbled headlong into the flames. Kicking his legs back Charlie grabbed hold of the broken ladder with his other hand. Man and ladder hung precariously for a moment. Charlie's knuckles were white. He pulled with all his strength and made it up another rung.

A second blast ricocheted through the cellar and a wave of heat scorched his legs. Charlie knew in that moment he wasn't going to make it. He couldn't get himself out of the cellar. Then Lily's two small hands seized his forearms and wrenched him upwards.

Charlie fell out of the top of the cellar on to welcome cool earth. He rolled, righted himself and looked to where Lily was standing waiting for him.

'I thought you didn't need my help?' she said.

'I didn't,' said Charlie, feeling for his key. 'I was testing your loyalty. Come,' he added, moving them both away from the cellar. 'There are more powder kegs to blow.'

He assessed their new location. Better to go back up Shoe Lane, he decided.

'Where's the marriage register?' asked Lily.

Charlie pointed back to the blazing cellar.

'It might have led us to the chest,' said Lily disappointedly. 'The book had names of a dozen other people who knew Torr. Now we have nothing.'

Charlie studied his leather coat.

'The blue flame wasn't like normal fire,' he said, looking at the row of small buttons along the front. 'No scorch on the leather. No tarnish to the buttons. We should go to Nile Street,' he decided. 'An alchemist might tell us much.'

They turned out on to Shoe Lane to discover a clutch of Londoners had gathered. The flames of the Cheshire Cheese had quickly caught the row of tall houses and now three roared with fire. Charlie realised too late how they must look, emerging from a cellar covered in smoke and cinder smuts.

A brown-toothed merchant was already pointing a finger at Lily.

'Foreigners!' he shouted, eyeing her toffee-coloured skin. 'Here are the villains who fired Fleet Street.'

People began to join the shout and Charlie's stomach rolled icy with dread. Behind them on Fleet Street, heads had turned and people were drifting towards them.

It didn't take much to start a mob attack in London.

'She burned the cellar!' the man continued, turning to the people around him. 'She comes from the Pope to destroy London!'

Lily opened her mouth to protest but Charlie pressed her arm.

'Don't say anything,' he hissed. 'Protest and you'll make it worse faster.'

'Then what should I do?' whispered Lily helplessly, looking at the assembling crowd.

Charlie's face twisted in terror and his finger shot high to the heavens.

'By God!' he shouted. 'A fiery comet! It's God's judgement on us all!'

The crowd's gaze swung upwards as one and Charlie grabbed Lily's arm.

'Run,' he said.

Chapter 34

Jacob was shaking his head in denial. He fingered the crown and knot wound on his forearm. The boys were making fireballs in Master Blackstone's house. And his fellow initiate Enoch, blind in one eye from an accident as apothecaries' apprentice, was telling him tall tales.

'Rats only,' he said. 'There's nothing in Master Blackstone's cellar.'

'I tell you I hear things,' whispered Enoch. 'There is something down there. I hear him talking to it. Late at night when everyone sleeps.'

Enoch swivelled his one good eye to the cellar trapdoor. Since his first visit, he never wanted to go through it ever again. But he knew what he'd heard.

'Fine houses like Master Blackstone's,' suggested Jacob uneasily, gesturing to their comfortable dwelling, 'make noises.'

Enoch didn't answer. He rolled the fireball from the fat and stashed it in a neat pile with its fellows.

'You're imagining things,' said Jacob, sounding firmer than he felt. 'Master Blackstone never goes into the cellar, 'cept for initiations.'

'He does,' insisted Enoch. He looked up at Jacob and his vacant red-white blind eye shifted too. 'I've heard him. He takes food down for it too.'

'There's nothing in the cellar,' muttered Jacob. 'Keep working.'

'You think you'll be initiated to the higher level,' said Enoch, catching on. 'If you work hard and obey. Don't ask no questions.'

'Good sons obey the father,' said Jacob, parroting their brotherhood vows. 'They do not question.'

Enoch had the ghost of a smile on his starved features.

'You really want to take the second initiation?' He was looking at Jacob's still-livid forearm burn. 'Think you'll survive it? Go a level higher? Become a Steward?'

'I want to learn truth,' said Jacob.

'But you don't know what you'll have to endure,' said Enoch, rolling another fireball.

'Do you?' Jacob was curious, despite his vow not to question the rites of passage.

Enoch scanned Jacob's face with his good eye. 'Starvation,' he said darkly. 'Locked in the cellar 'til your belly bloats and you see things.'

Jacob blanched. There was no worse pain than hunger.

'And you're not told nothing good at the end of it,' continued Enoch, knowledgeably. 'I heard one of the higher initiates talking.' He gestured towards the handful of better-dressed recruits known as Stewards. They'd been tasked with arranging lead cauldrons over various points of the city and were examining a rudimentary map.

'Papers,' concluded Enoch. 'That's all they get told. There's papers with legendary powers, lost, somewhere in the city.' He squinted his bad eye. 'Not worth knowing,' he said. 'And,' he waved a finger, 'I don't think Master Blackstone wants any of us low boys as his higher folk. Have you noticed? All the higher initiates are finer than us.' Enoch tapped his head. 'I think,' he concluded, 'all the Steward places are filled.'

'Master Blackstone is an honourable man,' said Jacob uncomfortably. 'He looks after us. Protects us. He found the gaoler who hurt my brother,' he added, loyalty brimming up. 'Paid him vengeance.'

'He's good at that, vengeance,' agreed Enoch. 'But he doesn't like questions.'

'Good sons . . .' began Jacob.

Enoch waved him down. 'Good sons, good sons,' he said. 'But a good father. Does he make his sons traitors, without their say so?'

'He wants to bring down the King who betrayed us.'

'Never asked us though, did he?' said Enoch, drawing a hand over his stomach. 'Your guts ripped out and shown to you,' he added, making a ghoulish mime. 'If they find you.'

Enoch looked at Jacob.

'When he recruited me,' said Enoch, 'from the St Giles slums, Blackstone told me we'd be working to follow our Catholic faith freely. I thought him a dark angel. He never mentioned no firing of the city.'

'It's the bigger plan,' said Jacob uncertainly. Though he had to admit his experience had been the same.

'You're from St Giles too?' added Jacob with interest.

'Most of us are,' said Enoch. 'The Sealed Knot looks right nice to boys like us don't it? Pledges and mottos. Best mottos you make in St Giles is "every man for himself".'

Jacob smiled. 'Or, don't sacrifice yourself for others,' he grinned, thinking of the cut-throat slums. 'Stop talking,' he added, flicking a nervous glance at the Stewards.

But Enoch was insistent. 'Don't you ever question why we're never allowed in the cellar? It'd be a right enough place to store fireballs wouldn't it? In case anyone ever came looking.' He scratched the back of his neck, where lice nested deep in his snarled hair.

''S a cellar, nothing more,' grunted the other boy. But there was something in his voice now which suggested doubt. 'We've all been down there anyways,' he added uncertainly.

'For initiation,' said Enoch, his bad eye twitching. 'In the dark. With barely candle flame to see by. And a lot of screaming.'

They were both silent at this. What Master Blackstone did to boys who failed the initiation was something none forgot.

'He keeps us afraid,' said Enoch. 'That's his thing isn't it? Fear. He thinks it keeps us predictable. But what if there's something truly bad down there. Some demon?' He crossed himself. 'Some sulphur-reeking monster,' he concluded, 'ready to drag us all down to hell?'

'There's nothing down there,' said the other boy. But he didn't meet Enoch's good eye. He was making fireballs at double the speed.

'Have you ever thought about it?' asked Enoch quietly.

'Can't say as I have,' replied Jacob, affecting nonchalance. 'I'm a heavy sleeper.'

'Not the cellar,' said Enoch. 'Leaving. Have you ever thought about leaving?'

Jacob looked automatically to the Stewards.

'Shut *up*, Enoch,' he said, giving him a shove. 'I mean it. I don't want to end up down in that cellar. You neither,' he added.

'You have thought about it,' said Enoch. 'Of course you have.' He turned back to making the fireballs. 'We all have,' he concluded. And his gaze drifted back to the locked cellar door.

Chapter 35

Charlie and Lily raced over Lud Gate Hill in the direction of the Great Fire. Behind them an angry mob surged.

'You've made them angrier by tricking them,' panted Lily as they sprinted towards the burning shell of Cheapside. 'They'll tear us limb from limb when they catch us.'

'They'll have to catch us first,' said Charlie, weaving north on to Fleet Lane. 'This way.'

The crowd was swelling behind them, attracting angry Londoners drawn by their shouts.

'We're heading towards the Fleet Prison,' protested Lily. 'They'll corner me and throw me straight in gaol.'

'Not if we get there first,' said Charlie as the Fleet loomed into view. 'We can hide in the gatehouse. It's the last place they'll look.'

He slowed his pace as they approached the entrance and took her hand. Lily glanced helplessly over her shoulder. The thick of the charging crowd had not yet appeared.

'Walk normally,' Charlie said as they approached the portcullis of the gatehouse. 'We don't want to seem to have arrived in haste.'

They slipped past the open portcullis as the first pitch of the crowd lurched past the Old Bailey. A gaoler stood up, squinting at the shouts of the mob in the distance.

'No visitors,' he said, pointing back towards Cheapside. 'The fire will be here by nightfall. We've already freed fifty people. Be on your way.'

Charlie glanced back down Fleet Lane. He could see the brown-toothed merchant at the head of the charge. Lily didn't stand a chance if they stepped out of the gatehouse now.

'You remember me?' Lily said to the gaoler.

Charlie swung round in shock.

'Lily Boswell,' she added. 'I sat for my portrait with you before I was imprisoned here.'

The gaoler scrutinised her and then sucked his mottled teeth.

'Hundreds of felons I commit to memory,' he said, eyeing her. 'But I remember you right enough. We played at cards.'

'I beat you at cards,' she corrected him.

His eyes narrowed.

'What do you come for?' he said testily. 'You were set free. I owe you nothing.'

'Only news of the fire,' said Lily. 'And I won't tell your wife of the prisoner with the dark hair,' she added meaningfully as the gaoler opened his mouth to suggest payment.

'We had word from the watch that the fire goes north,' said the gaoler. 'No one does a thing about it. Only looks to their own goods and caterwauls. We got a few extra felons I suppose,' he conceded begrudgingly. 'Looks like we may have another,' he added, pointing to the approaching crowd.

A few other gaolers were gathering at the gatehouse now, drawn to the noise. They always enjoyed theatre of this kind. And often they got a prisoner to keep.

The crowd was barrelling towards the prison, attracting angry Londoners as it went.

'Anyone caught?' asked the gaoler, looking at his ragged companions.

A gaoler with a peg leg was peering out into the crowd.

'Hard to see,' he said squinting. 'Certainly they are blood-thirsty enough.'

'To what purpose?' said Lily's gaoler disgustedly. 'When the King orders the release of felons.' He wrinkled his nose without waiting for a reply.

'Ninety felons' faces,' he complained tapping the side of his head. 'Ninety. Then there's visitors besides. It's not easy work making sure the wrong people don't wander out. Them in the Clink have it easy,' he added. 'Closed cells. A bunch of keys.'

'How far north is the fire?' interrupted Charlie, mapping Nile Street where the alchemists practised.

'Right up to the London Wall,' said the gaoler. 'And now they think it might go further west. Talk of it crossing the Fleet. And if the London Stone should burn . . .'

Charlie and Lily exchanged glances.

'Nile Street is gone then?' said Lily. 'The alchemists have fled?'

'Nile Street, Whitehorse Yard,' said the gaoler listing them off. 'Alchemists are long gone and good riddance. God's mysteries are not for men to unravel,' he added.

The mob had arrived outside the prison now and the guards milled hopefully by the door. Charlie saw Lily was holding her breath. Then the people streamed past without stopping.

'Looks like whoever they had in mind has escaped,' said the gaoler disappointedly. 'Already they break away.'

Lily let out a perceptible sigh of relief.

The gaoler spat in the dust.

'I suppose it's for the best,' he decided. 'If we're not allowed to keep men here. Bridewell Prison guards will be making a pretty penny,' he added wistfully. 'The crowd has already turned over three Catholics and a Frenchman who were throwing fireballs,' he explained. 'And we get an extra penny for gaoling a treason.'

'Can we go out through the prison?' asked Charlie. 'The crowd is thick on Lud Gate. It would do us a service to use the Snow Hill entrance.'

The gaoler straightened, scratching his groin.

'I suppose there's no harm in it,' he said. 'This prison will be empty by tomorrow, if the King gets his way.'

He laughed mirthlessly.

'That's what we get for bringing the monarch back,' he said. 'We were better under Cromwell.'

Chapter 36

'Tell me again, James,' said Arabella, closing her brown eyes tight. Her long limbs were ranged languidly across the sheets.

'I love you,' said the Duke of York smiling down at her. He wore a long white shirt, carelessly untied at the neck and nothing else. His rosary half concealed a deep scar from his latest seafaring battle.

James had the same large rounded nose and hooded eyes as his brother the King. His hair was brown and waving, in contrast to Charles's black curling locks. And it never ceased to amaze James how his indifferent looks drew women, now he was royal. But to the surprise of everyone at court, he'd chosen plain Arabella above far more beautiful girls.

Arabella opened her eyes again. 'It's no good,' she said. 'There's no conviction in your voice.' She gave a theatrical sigh. Her smooth features puckered. 'You won't do, James,' she told him. 'You'd best go back to your wife.'

James fell back on the bed laughing. 'What if she won't have me?'

'She will.' Arabella stretched out her legs on the white sheets. 'You're heir to the throne.'

James smiled at his mistress. Arabella's royal connections were low. She had a knightly father and a duke for a brother-in-law. But the moment they'd first met, he knew. She had an angular body and a face that was handsome rather than pretty. But this had never stopped her popularity with men. She was the most entertaining woman he'd ever met.

Arabella thought for a moment, turning a twist of fine brown hair. 'Was your wife with you and Charles in Holland?'

James shook his head. 'She was the only person who wasn't,' he said. 'Shiploads of people arrived to pay their respects. If it hadn't been for father's beheading, it could have been the greatest time of our lives,' he added, looking wistful.

Arabella looked at him with interest. She reached to the side of the bed and poured wine into a goblet.

'Better than being brother to a King?' she asked, passing it to him.

James took a sip, then ran a hand down her long body.

'We had no royal obligations,' he said. 'Plenty of people to buy us drinks and food. And boatloads of pretty women desperate to bed the heir and his brother. We spent four years drunk.' He smiled at the memory. 'Then the Sealed Knot came,' he added, his face falling. 'They were a Royalist faction sworn to return Charles as King.'

'They wanted you to invade England,' suggested Arabella, 'instead of pretty girls? What monsters.'

James laughed a little, but a ghost of unease was in his eyes.

'One was an alchemist,' he said, remembering. 'A good one. Man named Torr. Charles has an interest in such things and visited his experiments. Then something happened. The Sealed Knot unleashed something. Something powerful. Afterwards, no one would speak of it.'

'They conjured a demon?' suggested Arabella.

'Perhaps,' said James. 'Charles only told me of a room with smoking crucibles and liquid metal. But I heard whispers. Lost treasure. Wealth beyond a man's wildest dreams.'

'Then what happened?' asked Arabella, enjoying the story.

'Nothing.' James shrugged. 'It all seemed to be forgotten. Charles was bedding Lucy Walter and that took all his interest. The Sealed Knot grew tired of waiting for their future King to involve himself in plans to reclaim his country.'

James frowned in thought. 'I mentioned it to Charles years later,' he added. 'He said the Sealed Knot secrets had been destroyed.'

'If I'd been Charles,' observed Arabella, 'I should have busied myself with the soldiers, rather than a silly girl.'

'But you're a clever woman,' grinned James. 'Charles was an eighteen-year-old man. And Lucy was very pretty back then. Extraordinary chest.' He mimed two domes. 'Charles thought himself very fortunate. Until he found out about Lucy's other men,' added James, grinning.

'But by then Lucy had birthed him a son,' murmured Arabella, pulling the sheet higher to cover her small breasts. 'It is a clever thing, to win the favour of a future King when he is low,' she concluded, taking back the goblet and drinking wine. 'I would have done the same.'

'You were barely born,' said James, folding her naked body in the crook of his arm, and tugging the sheet down again. 'Does that make me a dirty old man?'

'Yes,' said Arabella unhesitatingly. 'It does.' She touched her stomach and something shifted in her face. 'A dirty *Catholic* old man,' she added pointedly.

'I would never have converted,' said James. 'But I wasn't expected to be King at the time. Charles had just married. We didn't know then that Catherine of Braganza couldn't . . .'

Arabella sat up a little. 'So the problem is with her then?'

James looked shocked. 'Of course. Charles has five children.'

'I don't mean that,' said Arabella. 'I thought . . . Talk at court is that Charles doesn't like his Queen. That he can't bear to bed her. She *is* strange.' Arabella was picturing the pint-sized Queen. 'She looks like she's in mourning. She *stinks* of incense and garlic. You can smell it a mile away. And that *hair*. I can't see how a man would get close.'

'Charles likes her well enough,' said James, settling back. 'Well enough for that anyway,' he said.

Arabella laughed. 'Men amaze me,' she said. 'Could you do it? With the Queen?'

James thought about it. 'If I were King,' he said. 'And it was my duty.'

'You wouldn't struggle to perform? Garlic breath?' prompted Arabella.

'I'd turn her the other way,' said James. 'The Queen is such an innocent she wouldn't know any better. But I'd need a drink inside me.'

Arabella tipped back her head and laughed.

'What of the King's other women?' she asked, her eyes sliding to his. 'Which of those . . .?'

'Barbara,' said James unhesitatingly.

'I heard you had an eye for false hair and cleavage,' suggested Arabella archly.

'Lucy Walter?' said James. 'Everyone has had Lucy. I was lucky to escape with my life.' He shook his head.

'Every dress she wears is a present from the King of Spain,' said Arabella. 'Surely such regal connections must appeal?'

James laughed, then his face turned serious. 'Lucy's lies are a joke,' he said. 'But Monmouth is beginning to take after her. He's spoiled.'

'He's ambitious and arrogant,' said Arabella. 'Protestant too.'

She tapped James's rosary meaningfully.

'English people might prefer a bastard to a Catholic,' Arabella observed.

'Monmouth knows his place,' said James uneasily.

'Is he really Charles's son? There is talk.'

'He might be. Charles thinks he is. But Charles is a romantic. Lucy was open to most comers at that time.'

'You are no gentleman,' smiled Arabella, 'to talk of your lover so.'

James leaned closer, running a hand along her slim body. 'I'm not,' he admitted moving closer. 'And that's the way you like me.'

Chapter 37

'What should we do now?' asked Lily as they made into the wide courtyard of the Fleet Prison. 'Nile Street is all burned. And we don't have the marriage register.'

'You never told me you were in prison,' said Charlie. 'What was your crime?'

'Trusting the wrong person,' said Lily, in a tone which made it clear she'd answer no more questions.

Charlie picked at a patch of his dusty-blond hair which had been scorched in Torr's cellar.

'We know that Blackstone made two weddings,' he said.

'Fleet Weddings,' added Lily. 'Not proper church ones.'

'And perhaps to the same woman,' continued Charlie. 'One during the Civil War and one after. Why?'

'Dowry?' suggested Lily. 'Amesbury said that Blackstone spent his wife's dowry on the royal cause.'

'You can't claim a dowry twice,' said Charlie. 'No matter how many times you marry a woman. Once it's spent it's spent.'

He tapped the scar on his lip. 'You said they married at sea.' Charlie thought for a moment. 'Aboard ship and free of port. No noble marriage is made that way.' Something else occurred to him.

'Blackstone's marriage was the same year as the date on your handkerchief. And Blackstone's chest is a Dutch sea chest.'

Lily shrugged, taking the handkerchief out of her dress. 'So the mermaid signifies his marriage?' Her face suggested the improbability of this.

'Not a marriage,' Charlie said slowly, touching the image. 'I think this mermaid could be a ship's figurehead. Women embroider them for good luck, before a ship sets sail.'

Lily looked again at the handkerchief.

'So she commemorates some ship's voyage?' said Lily, tapping the mermaid.

'Yes,' said Charlie. 'And the bearer sailed on the ship.'

'So Blackstone's ship was called the Mermaid?' Lily sounded intrigued. 'But what can that tell us?'

Charlie shrugged. 'It could tell us nothing. Or it could tell us a great deal. If we can find the ship's captain, or a fellow passenger, perhaps they will remember Blackstone.'

Lily looked disappointed. 'How could we know that? The ship sailed seventeen years ago.'

Charlie rubbed the kink in his nose.

'We can find out about the ship. If we go to the most dangerous man in London.'

Lily smiled at the description. 'What does he sell? Black powder?'

'Information. The Oracle,' said Charlie, 'is a legend in the shadow trade.'

'The shadow trade?' asked Lily.

'Smuggling, piracy,' said Charlie, waving an airy hand. 'High-profit trades and a risk of a painful death. The Oracle keeps information on every ship and cargo to leave and enter London. He is famed for it. It is said his records are better than the papers made by Customs House.'

'Why does he keep records of ships?'

'He sells information,' explained Charlie, 'and makes predictions which he sells for profit.'

'What kind of predictions?'

'Whether the price of lace or brandy will rise or fall,' said Charlie. 'Which goods will be the most profitably smuggled. Smugglers visit The Oracle before planning their time on the tides.'

'Won't he have fled London from the fire?'

Charlie shook his head.

'The Oracle is in the Shadow Market. The entrance is under Pickled Herring steps.'

'The south side of the river?'

Charlie nodded. 'The bad part of town. No fire there. The Shadow Market is in the tunnels beneath. You can only get in by river.'

'Do you know him? This Oracle?'

'I had some dealings with him a few years ago,' said Charlie. 'I think he'll remember me. But he's . . .' Charlie tapped at the side of his head.

'Insane?' suggested Lily.

'Not Bedlam insane. But prone to visions. And bad fits of temper.'

'You say he's dangerous?'

'He's powerful and unpredictable. Which makes him the most dangerous man I know.'

'You're sure he'll remember you?' said Lily uneasily.

'He's still got the scar.'

Lily adjusted the knives under her skirts.

'Wonderful,' she said sourly.

'First we need to get to him,' said Charlie. 'The only way is by river. Every man jack in London will be trying to get a boat.' He thought for a moment.

'We should walk to Charing Cross steps. They're the furthest public wharf up river. More likelihood of a boat.'

Chapter 38

Clarence's fat little legs propelled him down the muddy slope.

'Why is the barge readied?' he said. 'There was no order . . .'

Barbara Castlemaine slid from behind the nearest boatman.

'I gave the order,' she said. 'Monmouth was indisposed.'

Clarence drew himself up to his full height. Though even by that stretch Barbara was a clear head taller.

'You have no authority,' he said smugly. 'The Royal Barge is under Parliament's purse. We must have clear writing from the Keeper of the Barge.' Clarence permitted himself a little chuckle. 'From what I hear,' he added, 'Monmouth has no great love for you, Lady Castlemaine.'

'Young men are changeable in their affections,' said Barbara. She took out a roll of paper and tapped Clarence with it. 'See for yourself.'

Clarence unrolled it to see Monmouth's signature and seal. His lips tightened into a thin angry line.

'I thought you said Monmouth was indisposed,' he managed.

'Oh, he is,' said Barbara. 'Too much strong wine. You know how young boys are. Monmouth and I are better friends nowadays.' She winked at Clarence, put a slim finger in her mouth and sucked it suggestively.

Clarence fought to keep the shock from his features. She couldn't. She wouldn't have.

'I hear you've been meeting with Louise,' said Barbara with an affected yawn. 'But you have a lot to learn about ruthlessness. Ah. Here's Amesbury. He can school you in that art.'

She smiled widely as Amesbury's thick boots tramped through the mud of the Royal Wharf. He wore thick leather boots to mid-thigh, and a heavy military cloak. He looked as out of place as was possible before the decorated barge.

'Lady Castlemaine sent for me,' said Amesbury, at the unasked question on Clarence's face. 'You seem to have forgotten I'm to be present in military matters.'

'This is hardly a military matter,' hissed Clarence, glancing at Barbara and then Amesbury in fury at the ambush. 'A little fire is all.'

'Lady Castlemaine,' Amesbury bowed, ignoring Clarence. 'You've prepared us a feast for the eyes.' He regarded the Royal Barge with its huge swags of red and gold velvet. 'Striped tulips,' he added, looking at the deep floral displays on deck. 'Very rare I'm told.'

'You can't keep the disapproval from your voice,' laughed Barbara. 'But you are cleverer than Clarence for trying to hide it. Yes, the tulips are rare. And very expensive. As was the velvet. I've also ordered the finest French wines, dressed sides of meat, poached fish and hot-house fruits. Oh, and ice to keep us all cool. From the icehouse which Clarence spoke against in Parliament.'

She gave a beatific smile.

'I think it so important that His Majesty is seen to be King,' she said. 'That is what the people want from their monarch. Majesty and fine things.'

Amesbury said nothing.

'Where is the fire now?' asked Barbara. 'Oh, not you,' she added as Clarence opened his mouth to speak. 'I can't trust a word *you* say. What intelligence do you have, Amesbury?'

'The King comes,' said Amesbury. He nodded in the direction of the Palace. 'Better you don't hear it before him.'

Barbara's eyes flickered. She gave a slight smile, adjusting the low-cut shoulders of her dress.

'See how well he looks,' she said approvingly as the King approached.

Charles was attired valiantly with a silver-handled sword attached by a slash of shining leather across his chest. His enormous curling wig was topped with a rakish wide-brimmed hat.

'Like a dashing highwayman and a romantic cavalier all at once,' said Barbara.

'Better you'd dressed His Majesty as an English King,' observed Amesbury. 'Rather than a Frenchie one. If you seek the love of the people.'

'This is fashion,' said Barbara. She eyed Amesbury's boiled-leather coat. 'I could hardly expect you to understand.'

Chapter 39

Charing Cross steps were in chaos when Lily and Charlie arrived. The wide, muddy steps down to the river were thick with frightened people loading goods.

'It looks as though Bedlam has emptied on to the river,' observed Lily, looking at the turgid river. 'There's no boats to be had.' She pointed to a group of desperate people hurling their belongings into the Thames. 'Those folk hope their possessions will float down river and might be fished out later.'

Charlie was looking up to where smoke was blotting out the sun.

'It's midday,' he muttered, 'the sky looks dark as dusk.'

Wind blowing from the water was so strong that the women were fighting to keep their skirts down, and Lily was nearly blown off her feet as a gust swept her petticoats high over her head and then buffeted them back around her legs like a disapproving mother.

'Seven magpies,' said Lily, counting a line which had settled near the riverbank. 'Seven for a secret never to be told.' She added glancing at Charlie. 'A bad omen.'

'Or,' said Charlie, 'it signifies that the Hatton Garden berry bushes are full of refugees fleeing fire. I don't believe in omens,' he added.

At the water steps the burning city smell was intermingled with roasting meat. Butchers from Smithfield were griddling chops which would be spoiled before the markets reopened. Hungry Londoners were queuing to buy them at half price.

'People bury their goods,' Lilt observed as two sweating men worked with shovels to dig a pit.

'Every boat, cart or wagon for twenty miles is used,' explained a woman with a wide basket of fish on her head. 'Only the rich can afford it.'

She tilted her basket hopefully towards them, but Charlie shook his head.

'How far is the fire along the river?' asked Charlie.

'They stopped it at London Bridge,' said the woman. 'Firebreaks. But it raged all along Cheapside. They try and hold it back at the Fleet. But it goes north to Lothbury and the Stock Exchange makes a bonfire tall enough to carry sparks all over the city. Now they fear the London Stone. And everyone knows what happens if the stone cracks.'

Lily looked to Charlie.

'The city will fall,' he said. 'It's an old legend. The Stone was put there by the Romans to protect London.'

Lily raised an eyebrow. 'I thought you didn't believe in omens.'

Charlie looked at the river steps jammed with frantic refugees loading hastily bound goods from boats. 'How many houses do they say?' he asked.

'Three hundred and more besides,' said the fish-wife, resettling her basket and looking past them for possible customers. 'And still it burns bad. All of Fish Street and Cannon Street are burned, and it makes its way along Thames Street like a great rampaging monster with this fierce wind behind it. You'll not get a boat unless you've gold,' she added, glancing to the water. 'This last half hour the people turn frantic.'

'It's hopeless,' said Lily, staring out on to the crowded river. 'Those boatmen are only taking people with huge purses of money.'

They watched as a scuffle broke out between two families surrounded by household goods.

Charlie assessed the steps. Bickering Londoners surged and elbowed. He estimated over a hundred people fought for ten boats.

Charlie looked along the riverfront.

'Ferries are all taken,' he muttered, 'but there's another docking area for commercial boats.'

Lily watched a handful of sweating men heaving wine, animal skins and lengths of timber at speed across the wharf.

'We don't need a row boat,' Charlie decided. 'We can stow on a lighter-craft. The kind shunted by a pole,' he added, pointing to the flat-bottomed boats.

'The wine lighter is too valuable to risk passengers,' he said. 'And the timber is too heavy. But the animal skins . . .' He watched as heavy bales of furs and leathers were tossed on to the deck. 'There would be enough room for a few passengers.'

'The lighters won't take commoners,' said Lily, eyeing the gold crest on each boat. 'Only guild merchants or nobles.'

Charlie was looking thoughtfully at the gold embroidery on Lily's red silk dress.

'You should have learned to wear shoes,' Lily was saying. 'Your coat is fashionable cut. Wide cuffs, flared at the bottom.' She mimed the shape. 'It covers your cheap shirt so we need only borrow a pair of stockings.'

'My legs are too thin,' said Charlie. 'And bare feet are useful.'

'What possible use . . .'

'You don't look noble either,' interrupted Charlie. 'But a mistress of a noble. Perhaps.'

His eyes were roaming the crowd. They settled on a wealthy man in a blue doublet. A lord or a duke, Charlie thought. He was holding up a weighty purse, pushing past a slew of poorer people.

'Something might be done for passage,' Charlie decided, watching two harassed-looking servants follow the lord with a chest and several bundles. 'Could you distract that lord? Work a deceit on him?'

Lily's eyebrows arched.

'I forgot,' said Charlie mockingly. 'You are London's best trickster.'

She nodded, a faint smile on her lips.

'You truly think you could convince that lighterman to take us?' she asked.

Lily looked at the scrum of people waving coins at the boats and again at the lighters.

Charlie was looking at the riverbank, where old barrel hoops and broken cart parts lay caked in dried mud.

Charlie's eyes moved back to Lily.

'That depends,' he said.

'On?'

'How clean are your underclothes?'

Lily's eyes widened.

'Clean,' she managed, 'and too expensive for your concern.'

'Good,' said Charlie. 'You need to take them off.'

Chapter 40

Blackstone eyed the woman.

In the darkness of the street, she had seemed to look very much like Teresa. She had long blonde hair, like his wife on their wedding day. But in his candlelit cellar she looked more like what she was. An ageing whore with a cheap wig and cork cheek-plumpers to pad out her sunken face.

'What is thish?' asked the woman, manoeuvring the cork balls in her mouth with difficulty. 'Witchcraft?'

There was a hint of terror in her laboured consonants.

Blackstone followed the direction of her gaze. He supposed Teresa's cellar did look intimidating to the initiated. The dank room was filled from floor to ceiling with her talismans. Corn dollies. Sheaves of ash and elm steeped in rank water. Bloody ribbons and tattered feathers.

'Put this on,' he said, handing her a crown of leaves in reply.

The woman took it and settled it over her rats-tail wig. She seemed relieved at having a more obvious role.

Her eyes ranged for somewhere to sit. She looked at Blackstone, trying to assess him. His huge body was well dressed in black, with a cavalier's hat and sturdy boots. Something simple, she decided, was what military men usually wanted.

'Should you like me to play a harvest maid?' she suggested. 'Or a fairy queen?'

Blackstone removed his hat. Her eyes widened at the shiny rash of scarred sores between clumps of black hair.

'Speak only when I tell you,' said Blackstone. He began removing his large leather gauntlets. The woman shut her mouth. Fear animated her features.

Blackstone took her in. The dark crown. The green dress. A horrible memory of his first woman tunnelled up. The cloying perfumed flesh. Hot and sickly, like overripe fruit. The rotten-sugar taste of the sin rose up in his throat like bile.

'Women need a stern hand,' said Blackstone, taking her in with distaste. 'Or they fall to sin and drag men with them.'

He was remembering his gentle sister. The measures his father had been forced to take to keep her obedient. His sister was a good, pure Catholic. This Protestant whore symbolised everything that was wrong with England.

'As a boy I was haunted by the idea of sinful women,' Blackstone added. 'The disgusting things they let men do to them. My own strange compulsion to rut with them. I've mastered such thoughts now.'

He approached a shadowed part of the cellar and threw off a cover. A harsh squawking sound echoed forth. The woman started. He had a bird in a cage. A raven, she thought, by the noise it was making.

'Get up,' said Blackstone. The woman rose uncertainly. More and more things were tugging at her instincts now. She desperately wanted to leave.

Blackstone closed his eyes and breathed in the familiar smell of Teresa's room. Something inside of him twitched to life.

'Lie there.' He pointed to the damp ground. The woman moved forward. This was more familiar territory. She arranged herself, prostrate with her skirts over her head.

'Not there,' came his voice. 'There.'

She drew her skirts down in confusion. He was pointing a little to the side of where she lay. And then she saw it. Some sort of . . . circle had been made. Candles and dead things. Her blood turned icy. He was a witch. She sat up.

'I'll not be part of a spell,' she managed. ''Tis a burning crime.'

Blackstone looked down. Then suddenly he was on her.

'You dare?' he whispered. 'Defy me? With your withered body and scabbed soul. Do you think you're worth *anything* compared to her?'

The woman was looking around the cellar in terror. She couldn't understand who he was speaking about. But she knew her mistake now. He was a madman. From experience it was better not to fight. Let him do what he wanted and get out.

She lay back, shaking, and drew up her skirts again.

Blackstone's eyes widened.

'You think I want you for that?' he was laughing. A chill, dead sound.

'What then?' she managed.

'You,' said Blackstone, 'will return my wife to me.'

He was looking around the cellar now.

'Her poppets,' decided Blackstone. 'She cannot return without her poppets.'

He turned away and seemed to vanish in the darkness. There was a scraping sound and then he eased free a large preserving jar. Blackstone placed it gently on the ground and then brought out another.

'There,' he said, after a third was brought. 'Your poppets.'

The woman had backed as far as she could away from the glass jars. One of her cork cheek-plumpers had made it to the front of her mouth and it fell to the ground soundlessly. She didn't attempt to retrieve it.

Floating in the jars . . . Women burned such things.

Chapter 41

Charlie knew Lily could hustle. But he hadn't bet on how good she was. He watched in awe as she laughed and flirted with the man in the blue doublet. Never trust an actress, he reminded himself.

They'd fashioned a bundle of valuables from Lily's underskirt. And she laboured so convincingly under the weight of it, Charlie would have helped her himself.

He watched as the nobleman assisted Lily to set down her possessions, pointing to the ferry he'd just hired.

The first part of the plan in place, Charlie made towards the lighter boats. The next step was to convince the lighterman that Lily was a favourite mistress to a wealthy lord.

By the time Charlie had made the deception and pushed back through the crowd Lily was holding a tankard of ale and a griddled pork chop.

'I found a lighter,' he said. 'So we may go now.'

'Then take my bundle,' Lily shot back haughtily, full into character. She turned and laid a hand on the blue doublet. 'You were so kind,' she whispered seductively. 'Perhaps we may meet up river? Hatton Gardens?'

As the lord's servants watched the exchange, Charlie picked up Lily's bundle. Then he heaved it off towards the lighter-wharf with her following behind.

A burly man was slapping a bouncing barrel across the wharf as Charlie approached. 'Have a care!' he bellowed, heaving the barrel upright and slamming it on to the deck of the lighter.

Charlie moved away and hailed the lighterman on the animal skins boat.

'Quickly then,' barked the lighterman. 'I'm almost loaded.' He dumped down a heavy bale of leather, sending up dust from the furs beneath.

Lily appeared, still clutching the pork chop, and looked from the bundles of furs back to Charlie.

The lighterman eyed the pork chop. Ladies didn't eat in public.

'You're sure she has coin?' asked the lighterman, looking at Charlie uneasily.

In answer Charlie heaved the bundle on to the deck. It clanked expensively.

'She's well favoured,' he replied.

The lighterman sucked his teeth and nodded.

'Four pounds when we reach St Catherine's Dock then?' he said. 'As we agreed.'

Lily glanced at Charlie, but he was nodding.

'And a stop at Bermondsey to gather her sister,' he added. The lighterman picked up his pole. 'All aboard then. I've to get these furs to Medway.'

Chapter 42

'Lucy, you have to stop this.' The Duke of York was trying his best to be kind. But Lucy Walter could test the patience of a saint. The King's first mistress had arrived in her usual eye-wateringly inappropriate dress, demanding transportation for her goods.

'I must have a cart,' she blazed. She was breathing dramatically, a dash of her ageing nipples nudging above deep-pink silk. 'I am mother to the King's firstborn son.'

'The King tries to save the city,' said the Duke of York. He was trying not to stare at Lucy's substantial bosom, hoisted to within an inch of its life by garishly embroidered corsetry.

'Let me past,' demanded Lucy, rearranging a curl of cheap fake hair. 'I know Charles will hear me. I must have a carriage and carts.'

James blocked her way and Lucy blew out her cheeks in frustration. She had been an exceptionally pretty woman, dark-haired and shapely. But almost two decades after her affair with Charles, her famous looks had drooped. Now it was the vulpine cunning in her dark eyes that was most noticeable. James felt sorry for Lucy. She wasn't a clever woman. Her bad dress sense and wild stories made her a joke in court.

'Lucy, if you need a cart I suggest you speak with your husband. Or Lord Buckingham,' James added meaningfully.

'My husband and I haven't spoken for many months,' admitted Lucy. 'Some court gossip told him his heir is Buckingham's.' She looked furious. 'Charles has a duty to protect me. For the love we once bore one another.'

'Charles cannot give you what he doesn't have,' soothed James.

'This necklace!' Lucy's voice rose hysterically, clutching at some bright jewels at her throat. 'Was a gift from the King of France himself! Rubies from his own personal mine in Versailles. If my goods burn, he'll likely declare war.'

James rubbed his forehead.

'Lucy,' he said exasperatedly. 'You've never met Louis XIV. Nor are rubies mined in France. Charles doesn't owe you a debt. He's been very kind to you already.'

James was watching her carefully. He could never tell when Lucy's mercurial temper would erupt. She was full of childish spite when angered.

But instead of storming into a rage, Lucy gave an affected sob.

'To Monmouth,' she protested. 'Charles is kind to our son. Not me. Never me.'

'You weren't kind to him either,' said James. 'If you remember.'

'It was lies,' huffed Lucy. 'I was faithful to Charles.'

'I saw you myself,' said James, exasperated. 'You were hardly discreet.'

'Monmouth is Charles's son,' continued Lucy, her voice rising. 'I swear it on all that is Holy.'

The Duke of York raised his hands. He hadn't meant to get into all of this.

'No one doubts Monmouth's paternity,' he lied. 'Charles himself acknowledges him. I only meant . . .'

But Lucy had sensed the potential for a scene.

'I am the mother of Charles's firstborn,' she continued, her voice raised theatrically. 'I have expectations which must be met. A carriage. Carts.'

Servants were watching openly now. Lucy made to push past the Duke of York again. He barred her way bodily.

'London burns,' he said, 'we have not time for your drama.'

Lucy gasped, her mouth a square of rage.

'*You*,' she shouted, 'you speak to me of theatre?'

James opened his mouth to reply but she spoke over him.

'Everyone knows of your secret marriage. All of England you've jeopardised.'

Lucy narrowed her eyes.

'Does she know how kind you were to me once?' she added in a breathy whisper. 'Your Catholic wife?'

James breathed out hard.

'Charles cannot see you,' he said through gritted teeth. 'Go back to your husband.'

Lucy turned so sharply her enormous skirts propelled her by their own momentum.

'Charles shall hear of this,' she threatened. 'He is not so heartless as his brother.' She raised her voice to include the nearby servants.

'And I didn't tell you true,' added Lucy spitefully, as she stormed away. 'Charles is much bigger.'

Chapter 43

The lighter jolted as the choppy waters nudged it, causing Lily to shriek in alarm. She grappled for Charlie's arm and righted herself.

'Frightened of water?' he said, holding her steady as she positioned herself on a stack of furs. He was surprised.

'You can't trust it,' she said, settling herself more comfortably. 'Same as unmarried men,' she added, looking pointedly at his hand on her arm.

'How do you know I'm not married?' he said, removing the hand.

'You have that dangerous look men get,' said Lily.

Once they were safely loaded, the lighterman raised and plunged his pole in the easy automaton of the well-practised hand, taking them out into the centre of the river.

'Was it recent?' asked Lily as their boat drifted into the thick flow of heavily laden boats. 'The woman,' she quantified, at Charlie's confused expression.

'Spring,' he said, after an uncomfortable pause. 'A long time ago now.'

'Someone was unfaithful?' Lily guessed.

'She was too reliable,' said Charlie moving to survey the river. 'It brought out the worst in me.'

'I can see that in you,' decided Lily. 'You need a woman to solve.'

On the horizon, smoke pumped steadily upwards in black plumes tipped with orange flames.

'It's like the river to the underworld,' said Lily as the lighterman raised and lowered his pole. 'Where the dead are ferried away.'

She was studying the mournful passengers in the surrounding boats. The rolling smoke made them vanish and reappear like pale ghosts.

They rounded the curve in the Thames. The water swirled amber and red now reflecting the towering inferno on the bank.

Even Lily's mouth dropped open in amazement. The entire bank, from Bread Street to the head of London Bridge was on fire, in one seamless ugly arc of flame. It leered forth in a myriad of forked tongues.

'Look at the red way it burns,' said Lily, blinking and spitting against the torrent of air-borne ash and soot which hit their faces as they turned into the straight.

'Aye,' said the lighterman sadly. 'It's not like the fine yellow flame of a fireplace. Here is as bloody and malevolent a fiend as ever breathed in the city.'

He paused to right the little craft and send it straight towards London Bridge. 'They'll scarce be a spare hedge to sleep under tonight,' he predicted.

Charlie stared out at the flames.

'See that?' Lily was suddenly standing, pointing. 'Blue fire.'

The flame flickered, surged up and then died almost as quickly.

'And another,' said Charlie.

As if in answer another blue flame surged up on the riverfront. Then it was gone.

'What does it mean?' asked Lily.

'Blackstone uses some alchemy to further the flame,' guessed Charlie. 'Or perhaps to signal.'

He watched as a blue flare appeared deeper in the city. Then a sudden explosion rumbled in the depths.

'A signal,' said Charlie. 'I'm sure of it.' He was watching a tower of flames tunnel up. 'The signal is made, then one of those exploding bottles dropped. Like in Torr's cellar.'

Lily nodded. 'It's a plot then,' she said. 'Someone has placed gunpowder throughout the city.'

They exchanged glances.

The current dropped off suddenly.

'Why does the river slow?' shouted Lily over the noise of the fire. She was looking anxiously at Pickled Herring steps in the distance. The lighterman was grunting with effort as he wielded his great pole.

'London Bridge waterwheels make a partial dam,' said Charlie, raising his voice in turn. 'The big pillars and the jetties slow the water too,' he added, pointing to the wooden platforms built around the thick stone arches of the bridge.

Breathing heavily with effort, the lighterman punted them south towards Pickled Herring steps and the fire volume decreased to an ugly rumbling.

Charlie looked anxiously at Lily. Her elfin face was contorted in dismay at something in the sky over Thames Street. A flight of pigeons fluttered over the burning church of St Laurence Poultney.

'Why don't they fly away?' she asked, her dark eyes sad.

'The church keeps nest-boxes for them,' said Charlie. 'For pigeon pie.'

'They're frightened,' said Lily, and Charlie was surprised. It was the first time he'd entertained the idea she might have emotions.

'They'll be burned,' said Lily, covering her mouth with her hands.

They watched as the birds fluttered in confusion over the burning roofs. Then one by one their wings singed and they plummeted into the fire below.

'First place of calling,' cried the lighterman. 'Pickled Herring steps.'

Chapter 44

Blackstone knelt by the ageing whore. She'd accepted her fate now, he thought. Women like her always did.

She lay wide-eyed on the cellar floor. Her wrists were bound with blood-splattered white ribbon. The harvest crown was wedged over her rats-tail wig. Blackstone was winding a length of ivy around her legs. The bare skin was creped and veined, but it didn't matter. She was a vessel, nothing more.

He drew out a knife. The woman closed her eyes and began to pray. Her lips tumbled over the Lord's Prayer and then back again.

'White for rebirth,' said Blackstone. 'Is that not how it is?' he patted her wrist. 'And see? I have brought fresh ivy. From the house over the river.'

His grip on her wrist intensified. The cold knife pressed into her arm.

'From air and water, earth and fire,' he incanted. 'I am the magic. I am the power. Do you remember? Your words? As Sally Oakley taught you.'

Blackstone was at her torso now, winding more ribbon.

'Green for fertile hopes,' he said. His hand rested there.

Then the woman felt the knife at her wrists again and tensed. But to her surprise the ribbons fell away. She sat up, rubbing her freed wrists, eyes darting to the cellar exit.

Then she saw the blood. Her wrist was pumping a steady stream. Blackstone loomed close. He laid a white feather in the pool of warm blood. It darkened as it soaked up the crimson liquid.

'Dirty blood,' he said. 'I offer this dirty blood. I ask for your blessed blood to flow through these veins. My one true wife,' said Blackstone. 'Teresa.'

The woman managed a halting smile. His hand moved to stroke her crown. Then he brushed her forehead gently with the bloodied feather. She thought he made a Satan star and shuddered.

'For you I do this,' said Blackstone. 'For you I chance my faith.'

She nodded uncertainly.

'I invoke you,' said Blackstone. 'I command it.'

The woman knew what was happening now. He was a widower. Driven mad with grief, conjuring his dead wife. She steadied her breath. If she could play along, she might survive this yet.

Blackstone was staring at her intently. She tried to adopt a loving expression.

'I have seen your face,' he said. 'In my dreams. You must tell me . . . Tell me you are not in hell.'

The woman blinked back at him in shock. She hesitated and Blackstone nodded she should speak.

'I am not . . . not in hell,' she said slowly, struggling to keep a tremble from her voice.

Blackstone nodded.

'I fear it,' he whispered. 'I have seen you with demons. They do terrible things. After the war . . . What the men did to you . . .'

He looked up at her to reassure himself.

'The devil plays tricks,' he nodded. 'You are with the angels. God is merciful and has forgiven you.'

Blackstone felt the familiar urge sweep through his body. His hands moved down.

'It was no sin what we did,' he whispered, unlacing her dress. 'And I kept our children safe as I promised you.'

At the mention of children, the woman's face flashed. Had he imagined it? No. Blackstone was certain. Teresa was there. Listening.

He took her hands and raised her to standing.

'You must sit,' he said. 'In your favourite place. I will bring your dollies and your magical things.'

He guided her to a corner and pushed her gently to the ground. The woman sat without protest. Her arm was growing cold, she noticed. Soon too much blood would be lost.

Blackstone knelt and gathered an assortment of corn dollies and dead mice.

'Here.' He pushed them towards her. Mutely, the woman took the dolls. She tried not to show the horror she felt. Her eyes flicked to the cellar door.

'I never told you,' said Blackstone, 'why we went to Holland. Why I forced you to make the marriage.'

He swallowed.

'The Sealed Knot swore to protect the King,' he continued. 'But after the war . . . Not everyone stayed loyal. Factions broke away.'

Blackstone sighed.

'I swear to you,' he said, 'when we journeyed to Holland my cause was true. We meant only to reinstate King Charles as the rightful heir.'

He rubbed at his eyes and took a breath.

'What we learned in Holland. It was too much temptation. I stole the Brotherhood's sacred secret for my own.'

Blackstone breathed out.

'I thought . . . The idea of having everything back,' he said. 'Being reinstated to some fine estate. Then Sally Oakley stole away dreams of that kind.'

He patted her hand.

'Please, Teresa.' Blackstone took her hand. 'You must forgive me. I will take revenge on those who harmed you.'

Sensing an opportunity, the woman deepened her voice.

'I do not seek revenge,' she intoned haltingly. 'But you must do no more sin. I command it from my heavenly place,' she improvised. 'Free this poor woman.'

Blackstone closed his eyes tight. 'The marriage we made . . .' His voice was tight.

'A joyful time,' replied the woman.

Blackstone's eyes flicked open. She saw at once the spell was broken.

181

Chapter 45

'Never seen anyone alight here,' said the lighterman thoughtfully, 'in all my years on the river. Heard things though, about Pickled Herring steps.'

'It's a fast way to her sister's house on Bermondsey,' said Charlie, helping Lily to the front of the lighter. The wooden ladder up to the jetty was caked in seaweed and slime. He was looking forward to helping her and gestured Lily should climb up first.

'So you might look up my skirts?' she said. 'You go.'

'I only thought the ladder looked slippery,' said Charlie innocently.

'You'll be back directly?' said the lighterman, as Charlie climbed slick rungs of the ladder. 'If London Bridge burns there'll be riptides. Bad ones. I won't get the lighter through.'

'We leave the bundle of fine plate,' said Charlie, pointing. 'So we must have your word you won't turn thief.'

As he stepped on to the mouldering pier a reek of warm damp rolled out from the space beyond. In the middle distance he could see a pin-prick glow of a lantern. The sign of the Shadow Market beyond.

Charlie turned to help Lily on to the jetty, but she was already behind him. He put out a cautious foot, testing the soft wood beneath. His toes touched the edge of a splintered void.

'There is a safe route over the old planks,' he murmured, reaching for Lily's hand. 'I think I remember it.'

'I don't need leading,' said Lily, pulling away her fingers so his hand settled on her wrist. But she let him guide her nevertheless as Charlie stepped carefully into the muted gloom, feeling out the repaired planks.

'Tread only where I do,' he warned, as the dark swallowed them entirely. 'New wood is laid in a pattern. Two planks and then it shifts one left. One plank and back again.'

'Is this to stop the customs men finding the market?'

Charlie snorted. 'Threats and bribes stop the customs men finding the Shadow Market. The rotted planks are down to lazy carpentry. This whole place will fall into the Thames in a few years.'

They heard a shout of annoyance echo out from behind them.

'The lighterman has checked your bundle,' said Charlie. 'And found flint rocks and broken barrel hoops.'

'Will he come after us?'

'He can't leave his animal skins outside Pickled Herring steps,' said Charlie. 'Besides,' he added, 'his lighter was headed up river in any case. We've barely cost him an inconvenience.'

They had reached the lantern now, and the dripping darkness expanded into the orange glow of an oil lamp. There was packed earth beneath them now.

They turned past the lamp and found a rope ladder with a trap-door at the top.

'This is it,' said Charlie, pointing up. 'The Shadow Market.'

Chapter 46

As Charlie and Lily manoeuvred themselves through the trapdoor, a huge cavern opened up before them.

'Welcome to the Shadow Market,' said Charlie, gesturing to the commotion of goods and sellers. 'If it's shipped to London, you can buy it here.'

The huge market was damp, cave-like and lit by yet more greasy-smoked oil lanterns. Lily's eyes were moving over the chaos of commodities, packed every which way. Alongside each stack of goods was a seller, face shadowed, mouth mechanically shouting their wares.

'I never knew so many fine things came to London,' she said, uncharacteristically cowed by the mayhem before them. She was looking at a woman with a missing eye hawking rum. 'That's fine rum and brandy she sells.'

'She won't pour you a dram for a penny,' said Charlie, looking where port, wine and brandy barrels of varying shape and size were stacked. 'This isn't Cheapside. You buy barrels and bales.'

The cacophony of shouting sellers was made more bewildering by the haze of dark smoke which hung on the air. Black corners seemed to lead on forever, and dimly lighted tunnels spiralled out into hidden places. In one direction were bales of silk, bundles of lace and linens. Another had spices, tobacco and towering white sugar loaves.

Charlie stepped forward, past a sack of spilled peppercorns which a seller was optimistically trying to scoop up from the damp ground.

'Where does that lead?' asked Lily. She was pointing to a rudimentary pulley arrangement operated by a counterweight. The hoist levered a tea chest upwards and out through a gap in the braced-wood ceiling. A scrawny donkey laden with coffee sacks loitered nearby.

'Perhaps some smugglers wait above,' guessed Charlie. 'Waiting for their share to be hoisted to street level. No names no faces.'

They watched as a stocky man loaded three sacks of coffee into the large tea chest. He wiped his brow then slapped the donkey's hind-quarters. The animal brayed loudly, turned and bit him on the hand.

'Do you know where this Oracle resides?' asked Lily. 'It's a labyrinth down here.'

Charlie nodded, surveying the sellers. His eyes lighted on some bales of colourful feathers. 'This way,' he said, leading her towards one of the many tunnels.

They entered a wide earthen corridor filled with dried fish and preserved-fruit sellers. A few slim dug-outs at ground level held slumbering bodies. They passed by barrels of syrup figs and salt cod.

'Here.' Charlie stopped by a hanging line of butterflied herring. He smelled the air. 'This way.' He took Lily's hand and ducked under it, bringing them through a tiny gap between two stalls.

They emerged in a hidden corridor lined with wooden cages. Monkeys and parrots chattered. Mounds of tusks, shells and horns were ranged on all sides.

'Alchemy ingredients and rare animals,' explained Charlie. 'We come to the more expensive part of the market.'

Lily eyed a bale of dried-out poppy heads.

'Opium,' said Charlie, remembering the fumes from Sebastian Longbody's apothecary shop.

'Nobles take it with wine,' said Lily. 'As a tincture.'

'It's stronger to smoke it,' observed Charlie, noting the dried leaves. 'Easier to smuggle too.'

'Why so hidden?' asked Lily, looking back to the bustling fruit sellers. 'Doesn't The Oracle like to be found?'

'Dangerous men must be careful of strangers,' said Charlie. 'It's the price you pay for infamy.' They were passing more menacing-looking traders now. Men with pirate and smuggler injuries, openly armed.

'He lives deeper still,' added Charlie, 'in the part where the gem sellers trade. There's no honour among thieves. They keep a close guard.'

There was a low growling up ahead. Charlie and Lily broke out into a low corridor where a pack of snarling dogs were tethered.

'They're not well kept,' said Lily as they approached where the animals guarded. Deep scars and missing lumps of fur marred the pack. A huddle of vicious-looking men in a patchwork of stolen armour ranged near the dogs. One lurched forward drunkenly.

'Password,' he said, sizing Charlie up.

'No honour but bounty,' replied Charlie, holding up a hand. The man fell back, eyeing them both suspiciously.

They passed by the dogs and men uneasily, into the cavern beyond.

'It's difficult to see,' whispered Lily as the gloom closed around them.

'Your eyes adjust,' said Charlie.

They'd entered a cavern lined with wooden lock-up frontages. Each was lowered to reveal a merchant, fat taper candles and crates of uncut gems.

'This way,' said Charlie, pulling Lily back from the glinting stones. 'The sign of the black cockatoo.'

He pointed to a hanging bundle of red and orange striped feathers.

'It's a little affectation of his,' added Charlie as Lily looked at the sign. 'He was on a ship that voyaged from the New World.'

'A smuggler's ship?'

'It wasn't a voyage of exploration.'

'It's so dark,' said Lily. 'Where are the oil lamps?'

'He doesn't like them,' said Charlie. 'The Oracle's been down here so long, strong light hurts his eyes.'

They both came to a halt. Standing beneath the feathers was a huge man whose face seemed made entirely of scar tissue. He eyed them coldly as they approached. A strong smell of brandy emanated from his thick wool-clad body.

'I have business inside,' said Charlie as the man reached to tighten the strap on his wooden arm. 'He knows me.'

'You've made a meeting with The Oracle?' asked the guard.

'He knows me,' repeated Charlie. 'Tell him the thief taker is here.'

Chapter 47

The Royal Barge floated serenely on the Palace dock. Servants jogged up and down the gangplank. Lush rare flowers and swags of fabric bobbed as they made the final preparations to embark.

'Firebreaks,' said Amesbury. 'We should send troops to make firebreaks.'

Clarence looked horrified. 'The people will fear an invasion. They will arm themselves and attack in the confusion."

The King rubbed his face thoughtfully.

'Let's board the barge then,' he said. 'See the city. Perhaps reports have been exaggerated.'

'Your Majesty,' Clarence made a low bow. 'Lady Castlemaine has arranged the barge very prettily.' He eyed her cunningly. 'But if this is a military matter as Amesbury says, then surely the trip down river is no place for a lady?'

'Perhaps you're right, Clarence,' said Charles. 'Barbara. I should discuss this matter with the men.'

Clarence couldn't mask the victory flooding his features.

'As you wish,' said Barbara curtseying. 'Though it means doing without my entertainment for you.'

As she spoke a group of scantily clad women appeared on the muddy slope.

They made their way down slipping, shrieking with delight and grabbing one another for support.

Charles's pensive expression lifted.

'I've instructed some players to act the fire in the city,' said Barbara. 'Much more fun than having the dull men drone it out to you.'

'How delightful,' murmured Charles.

'Perhaps,' added Barbara, 'I might say a few lines.' She nodded to the barge. 'There are costumes aboard.'

Charles smiled broadly.

'You lighten any occasion,' he said, offering her his arm. 'Even this bad business of fire.'

They began to board the boat, Clarence's face like thunder.

'Don't take it amiss,' said Amesbury with a companionable pat on his shoulder. 'She's cleverer than both of us.'

'She's a snake,' spat Clarence. 'She hasn't the cleverness of a man's sort. It's a low serpent's cunning she has.'

'Yes,' agreed Amesbury. 'And from what I hear she can swallow men whole.'

Chapter 48

The guard spat, and rubbed at his scarred face, causing a ripple of unintentional expressions. Then without a word, he disappeared back behind the wooden shop frontages.

The bundle of cockatoo feathers turned slowly above them.

After a moment the guard stepped back out and pulled roughly at Charlie's coat.

'No weapons,' he grunted.

Trying not to show his reluctance Charlie surrendered the knife from inside his coat.

'How is he today?' asked Charlie.

The guard glowered. 'Agitated,' he said. 'Full moon.'

Charlie let out a breath. It hadn't been the news he was hoping for.

'It's very important,' he said to Lily, 'that we keep things . . . calm in there.' He pressed air down with his hands.

She turned to him in surprise. 'Calm?'

'No raised voices. Excitement. Things could get nasty.'

The guard turned to Lily.

'You needn't think I'll let you maul me,' she said looking at his calloused hands. 'What do you imagine I carry inside my clothes?' She flattened her dress around her waist.

The guard considered this and then nodded for her to go forward. Charlie hid a smile.

They stepped into a corridor banded on all sides by planks like a mineshaft. A close meaty smell suggested beef pottage was boiling up ahead. The scarred guard was following at a close distance behind.

'What's that?' Lily whispered to Charlie, pointing to a collection of wires that ran alongside them.

'No whispering,' barked the guard. 'He doesn't like it.'

'Alarms,' said Charlie. 'Signals. The Oracle never comes out. Too many people who want his head. The wires lead to bells all over the Shadow Market. He works them from within. Don't touch them,' added Charlie as Lily put out a curious hand. 'Not unless you want a pack of smugglers to tear us limb from limb.'

The corridor ended in a packed-earth room lit by a cauldron fire. The wall was etched all over in crazed symbols and numbers. In the glow of the flame it was like stepping inside a maniac's brain.

Squatted low over the dark contents of the cauldron was a potbellied man with a clumsily shaven face, wearing a mismatch of smuggled lace and silk. His mouldering leather skullcap was crested with cockatoo feathers. He was scribbling frantically on the wall with chalk.

Beside him Charlie felt Lily tense.

'High tide and high profit,' the man was saying. 'But does lace fall, Wilkes? With fire taking all?'

The heat from the fire made the close quarters stifling. Charlie felt sweat break out on his face.

'Lily,' said Charlie, 'meet The Oracle.'

The man twitched and turned with surprising speed. Lily recoiled. Charlie held out a cautioning hand.

The Oracle's skin was so pallid that blue-green veins could be seen. Set against his mangy black skullcup and parched wine-stained lips he looked like a night-time creature recently emerged from his burrow.

But it was the eyes that made him such a frightening man to look on.

'Can he see?' whispered Lily. The Oracle's eyes were cloudy like a poached fish. Only the lightest pale blue swirled in their depths.

'All too well,' replied Charlie in measured tones.

The Oracle turned to consider them both with a hungry expression. Charlie held a cautioning hand to Lily. Now at standing height The Oracle was small. But the effect he had on the guard was profound. The burly man was bowing low as though in the presence of an emperor.

The Oracle's blackened lips smiled, revealing grey teeth.

'Charlie Tuesday!' announced The Oracle. 'The man with the memory.' His voice had a husky creak to it. Like a dry corpse in a long-lost vault.

'Mr Jenks is all manners today,' he added, waving towards the bowing guard. 'He upset Wilkes and we still don't know if the full reckoning has been had. Might be more than a finger in payment.' His eyes shifted to a large bandage on the guard's hand and he smiled. 'We shall have to see if Wilkes is feeling . . . merciful.'

Lily balled her small fists and swallowed. 'Who is Wilkes?' she asked quietly.

The Oracle gave her a vampire smile.

'My other half,' he said, tapping his head. 'My *better* half at times.' His voice rose suddenly. 'When he doesn't INTERFERE!' The shout echoed around the small room. He smiled another serpent grin.

The Oracle's clouded eyes were roaming over Lily now. His face had shifted to something more calculating. He looked at Charlie. 'And who might this be?'

'Her name is Lily Boswell,' said Charlie, unconsciously stepping a little in front of her. The Oracle noticed the gesture and his dark eyebrows raised. He gave a curious little shiver.

'You mustn't say such things, Wilkes,' he whispered. 'It is wicked. She's only a girl.'

Lily moved slightly behind Charlie. The Oracle moved forward, took her unresisting hand and rested his lips on it for slightly too long.

'You see, my dear?' he hissed. 'There's nothing to fear from me. Only Mr Wilkes and he stays out of the way. You're a gypsy?' he asked.

Lily glanced at Charlie then nodded.

'I can always tell by the eyes,' said The Oracle. 'A dark wildness to them. I can only imagine what secrets they hold.' He was considering her face, still holding her hand.

Then The Oracle's gaze turned sharply back to Charlie. 'Come to finish me off?' he demanded. His hand was at a deep scar by his eyebrow.

'I saved you from a gibbet at Tyburn,' said Charlie, keeping his tone even. 'I struck to disarm.'

The Oracle glanced down distractedly.

'Hard to know, hard to know,' he mumbled. His pale hand spidered to his face. Then the fish-eyes swivelled to Charlie.

'What do you want?' he asked.

'Information,' answered Charlie, 'on a ship.'

The sunken blue seemed to swirl in The Oracle's filmy gaze. 'Information costs money. More money than a thief taker has.'

'You owe me,' said Charlie. 'You had more than your half.'

The Oracle shook his head as though trying to dislodge some troublesome thought.

'Information the thief taker wants,' he whispered to himself. The Oracle tilted his head and appeared to listen intently. He straightened up.

'Wilkes has decided,' he said, 'to pay the thief taker fair return.'

'You may have your information, Charlie Tuesday,' said The Oracle. 'But then you'll be gone. Or Wilkes will set Mr Jenks to break your skull.' He gestured to the burly guard who had now retreated outside. 'Mr Wilkes can be kind as well as cruel,' added the Oracle. 'Do not forget it.'

Charlie nodded but Lily looked confused.

'This place charts the ships?' she asked, gazing at the array of dates, numbers and symbols. 'For smuggling?' She sounded confused.

'The Oracle knows of any cargo ship in and out of London,' said Charlie. 'Nothing gets past without his charting it.'

The Oracle smiled at the compliment.

'I break no law in charting these things,' he said to Lily. 'Perhaps a large import might stop up customs. That could leave a few smaller ships longer unguarded on the Thames approach. Or a sunk cargo could mean a better price on the black market.'

His attention returned to Charlie.

'I give no names.' There was a hardness to his voice now, and Charlie sensed a rising tension in him.

'I don't want any,' he said quickly, working to allay any possible switch in mood. 'We want information about a ship. One which sailed long ago.'

The dark eyebrows twitched in thought.

'I suppose I had better not ask your reasons?'

'Perhaps not.'

The Oracle thought for a moment.

'How long ago? This ship?'

'Seventeen years ago.'

The Oracle licked his grey teeth. 'I've no information from so long ago.'

Charlie felt the disappointment like a physical blow.

'The Shadow Trade has kept log for twenty-five years,' added The Oracle. 'But my predecessor was not literate.' His brow furrowed. 'There was a log of sorts – mostly pictures and shapes. Untidy,' he added grimacing. '*Dis*orderly.'

'Could we see the log?' asked Charlie.

'It's not nice to see,' said The Oracle. 'Not nice at all. I don't know if it could tell you much.' He'd begun clenching and unclenching his fist.

'It was a large ship,' said Charlie. He could see the signs of Wilkes emerging. But they had to take the risk. 'The Mermaid.'

The Oracle blinked rapidly and his mouth began moving.

'The tall ship which sailed the year the King was beheaded?' The Oracle's voice was undulating strangely. 'It's famed,' he added in a breathy whisper. 'That ship took all the noble supplicants. Those who threw themselves on the Prince-heir Charles and hoped to be remembered to his favour.'

Charlie and Lily exchanged glances.

'There are stories too,' continued The Oracle, licking his lips. 'Treasure. Gold.' His eyes flickered.

'We're not looking for treasure,' said Charlie quickly. 'Only a man who sailed on it.'

'There could be something,' said The Oracle carefully. 'A ship of that fame. Perhaps. Certainly it had wealth worth charting.'

'Might we see the log?' pressed Charlie.

The Oracle's eyes glittered in the gloom. 'Wilkes wants to know. Is your memory still as good as it was?'

'That depends,' said Charlie evenly.

'Perhaps you might tell me something,' said The Oracle. 'I've a smuggler who owes. I'd like to find him.' He pulled out a handful of money. 'This is the coin he paid with.'

Charlie regarded it. 'You owe me a debt,' he reminded him.

The Oracle's eyes shifted to Lily and then to the wall behind them. His pupils weaved over the symbols and numbers.

'But Wilkes thinks there's treasure,' he said. 'And Wilkes says there's an extra cost for treasure.'

Charlie ran a hand through his hair and made a decision.

'Ald Gate,' he said. 'By the sign of the painted sun. There's an official coin house there. That's where your man's coin was minted.'

The Oracle nodded in satisfaction and slid away the coins. Then he beckoned them to a low corner of the earthen cave.

'Here,' said The Oracle. 'This is the time of the treasure ship you seek.'

Charlie stared at the pictures. He could hardly believe it.

Chapter 49

'You took this from Barbara Castlemaine's apartments?' Lucy Walter was turning the dun-coloured ball in her hand. 'You're sure?'

Monmouth nodded. He was taking in his mother's appearance in shame. Lucy was tricked out in garish jewels, badly matched horsehair curls fixed to her head. Her wobbling bust was erupting from a tight-fitting magenta dress.

'Lady Castlemaine keeps fireballs,' added Monmouth. 'For what purpose I know not.'

Lucy laughed delightedly. 'Don't you know what this is?' She was pointing to a symbol stamped on the ball. It was a crown looped with knots.

Monmouth shook his head. 'Amesbury showed me that symbol,' he said, toying with his lacy cuffs. 'He asked me to look for it. To report if I saw it. He told me it was the mark of a rebel faction.'

Monmouth curled his lip.

'Can't you find a proper hairdresser?' he demanded. 'Your false curls look ridiculous. I will be a laughing stock if you appear in court.'

Lucy's eyes flashed hurt.

'And your dress,' he continued, gesturing at the low-cut neckline, 'your jewels. They are not fitting. You are mother to a great man,' he added, straightening his lace cuffs self-importantly. 'You dress like a harlot.'

Lucy's hand winged out and slapped his face. Monmouth reeled back in shock, touching his cheek. His eyes flashed fury and he raised his hand to retaliate. Then he noticed servants in the distance and pretended to be smoothing his hair.

'How dare you!' he hissed, his eyes sliding to the servants. 'I am the son of a King.'

'I am your mother,' said Lucy, the fire in her countenance ebbing a little. 'You must be careful how important you make yourself,' she added. 'Barbara has spies everywhere. She wants her children to be royal. Any excuse and she'll have you tried as a traitor.'

'You don't know anything about Lady Castlemaine,' said Monmouth. 'We have a better understanding nowadays. She thinks me a force to be reckoned with,' he added, smirking at the memory. Lady Castlemaine was in no doubt of Monmouth's virility.

'That's what she wants you to think,' sighed Lucy. She held the ball up.

'What do you think the symbol means?' asked Monmouth, looking at the crown and knots.

'That is the sign of the Sealed Knot,' said Lucy, furrowing her little brow. 'They were brutish men who fought for the King.' She gave a little shudder at the memory of heavyset, stinking soldiers arriving in Holland.

'They hated me,' Lucy added, in her usual habit of bringing the subject back to herself. 'The Sealed Knot wanted to plan war with your father. In Holland. But he preferred me to their battle-talk.' She smiled. 'Charles courted me like a true lady.'

'You were pregnant with me in Holland,' said Monmouth, who often grew exasperated by his mother's flagrant lies. 'And you had other men.'

'Oh well,' Lucy gave a vague wave of her hand. 'You know how things are. And Charles acknowledges you as his son. That's the important thing.'

Her dark eyes were considering the symbol again.

'You've not told Amesbury of this?'

'Not yet, but . . .'

'I'll take this to him myself,' said Lucy. 'And you mustn't talk of it. Amesbury has no business setting my son to spy.'

Chapter 50

Charlie and Lily stared. The corner of The Oracle's cave was completely covered in tiny pictures of ships. There were hundreds and hundreds, sketched small and detailing the contents of the hulls.

They were far more comprehensible than the elaborate symbols which spidered over the rest of the cave. At least ten years of London's shipping was detailed in miniature.

Charlie whistled. 'I'll wager even the Naval Office doesn't keep such comprehensive records,' he said.

'From long ago,' said The Oracle. 'I would have scrubbed them out,' he added, 'but Wilkes says "no" and I must heed him.'

Charlie knelt by the pictures. The rough-drawn shapes made more sense to him than The Oracle's crazed hatchings. There were signs he took to be emblematic of goods.

'Barrels for brandy?' suggested Lily, squatting down beside him.

'Or port,' said Charlie, looking at the shape. 'They're wide. Those are brandy,' he added, pointing to some smaller-drawn kegs. 'And those black powder.'

Charlie scanned down the column of symbols.

'Pipes for tobacco,' he decided, 'feathers might be birds.'

'There's no sign to say which boat,' said Lily. 'No numbers. No letters.'

'Nothing of which passengers might have sailed either,' noted Charlie. 'I suppose that's a lesser concern to a smuggler.'

The Oracle gave an angry hiss.

'Wilkes doesn't like that word,' he muttered.

'How might we know which was the Mermaid?' Lily asked, scanning the drawings.

'I've no idea how a mind like that works,' said The Oracle. He'd moved to the wall of the cave and began patting his symbols in a distracted rhythm. 'There's no order at all to the thinking. No order.' He worried at the cut on his face, picked up a piece of chalk and made a flurry of new neat symbols on the wall.

Lily looked nervously at Charlie. They needed to work quickly.

'Likely the ships are drawn in order of when they set sail,' decided Charlie. He examined the sketches, letting his finger trace the outlines.

'I think these ships sailed during the Civil War,' he said. 'Less goods, you see?'

Lily nodded.

The Oracle was crouched low now, the chalk poised in his hand. He stood, drew some more shapes, tapped the chalk and stood back. 'Low tide,' he muttered, his eyes twitching over the chalk markings. 'Fingers. Cut.'

'We should make haste,' whispered Charlie to Lily, recognising the signs. 'He's becoming agitated. Things could get dangerous.'

'These ships came afterwards,' replied Lily, tracking down. 'When trading was restored with Holland.' Her slim fingers rested on a column of ten boats.

'Here,' said Charlie, moving forward. 'That one.'

His hand rested on one of the larger ships.

'This could be a mermaid.'

'Strange kind of mermaid,' said Lily peering at the picture. 'Looks more like a sea monster.'

'But see there and there?' Charlie pointed to the other ships. 'An eagle, a lady. They're mastheads. None are well drawn.'

'Your sea-monster ship carried few goods,' admitted Lily, scrutinising the deck plan. 'That would fit if it was a passenger ship. But it tells us nothing of who sailed in it.'

Charlie let out a little sigh of frustration. He had been hoping for some better clue.

The Oracle gave a sudden shout of frustration.

Lily looked up, startled, but he returned to muttering to himself.

Charlie shot him a quick glance. He didn't know how long they had until Wilkes made an appearance.

'Wool was shipped,' he muttered, reassessing the image, 'this looks to be a little gold.'

He stopped. There was a picture of a chest. It was drawn much larger than the other symbols and in more detail. Charlie recognised it instantly. An intricate banded locking mechanism had been sketched across the sides and top.

'A chest . . .' began Lily. Charlie caught her wrist to stop her speaking. But the Oracle's sharp little blue eyes were already staring.

'Some cargo trunk,' said Charlie trying to sound nonchalant. 'Could be anything.'

'That is a trousseau,' said the Oracle, beside them again now. 'A locked wedding trunk.'

Chapter 51

The Oracle was looking at Charlie's key. He licked his black lips. Charlie eyed him. The signs of Wilkes were more evident now. There was a cruel twist to the mouth.

'Many valuable things in a wedding trunk,' The Oracle was saying, twitching a strand of dark hair between pale fingers. 'If there is one aboard a ship we try to record anything which would make it stand out. Even my foolish predecessor knew that.'

'What are those?' asked Lily. 'She was pointing to a number of arrows which had been drawn under the deck of the ship.

Charlie switched his gaze across.

'That is the sign of the broad arrow,' he said, tapping the shapes thoughtfully.

Something odd struck him about it.

'The broad arrow?' asked Lily.

'The broad arrow marks purchases for the country in the King's money,' supplied The Oracle. 'Military goods, things of that nature. Likely there were weapons on the ship.' His pale fingers had begun clenching and unclenching again.

'But why would the broad arrow be drawn among the barrels and bales?' Charlie puzzled out loud. 'This was the year the King was beheaded,' continued Charlie slowly. 'There was no military property to be shipped.'

They were all silent contemplating this.

'What property did the King still have, when his head rolled from the scaffold?' said Charlie eventually.

'Everything he had belonged to Parliament,' said Lily. 'Everything worth owning.'

Everything worth owning.

Charlie turned the problem over in his mind. What wasn't worth owning at the end of the Civil War?

Suddenly he knew the answer.

'Convicts.' Charlie slapped the wall with his palm, sure now of the answer. 'There were convicts on this ship.'

He turned to Lily.

'Convicts are military property. Even after the war was won. Some were kept in ships because the prisons were overflowing.'

'But this was a passenger ship,' said Lily. 'They would not have housed them there.'

'Passenger ships took prisoners who weren't dangerous,' interjected The Oracle. 'They kept them for a few voyages. Then returned and docked them in a London prison.'

Charlie looked at The Oracle's clouded eyes uneasily. He was showing too much interest.

Lily looked at Charlie. 'What does that tell us?'

He counted the arrows.

'It tells us there were fifteen men who travelled on The Mermaid, who might still languish in a London dungeon,' said Charlie.

'It was seventeen years ago. They'll be long dead.'

'Likely most of them,' admitted Charlie. 'But a few might live still. Poor men imprisoned do not get out alive. They are taxed for the cost of their cells and food, and then held for their debt to the prison.'

'We don't know which prison holds them,' said Lily.

Charlie chewed a finger. There were seven prisons in London, each with their own distinct character of felons.

'There's something different about these prisoners,' he decided. 'Some reason they were held at sea. They can't have been very dangerous. A ship is not particularly secure. Why would you choose some men over others, for a watery gaol?'

'Someone wanted them out of the way?' said Lily. For the smallest of moments Charlie thought he saw something flash in her face. Did she know something she wasn't telling?

'Perhaps,' said Charlie, hesitating. He blew out his cheeks in thought. 'New Gate prison wasn't built then,' he began slowly. 'The Clink is local. For those who commit crimes south of the river. Bridewell and Lud Gate are for debtors.'

He rubbed his forehead.

'That leaves the Fleet and Marshalsea on Borough.'

'And the Tower,' suggested Lily.

'That's for prisoners of great importance,' said Charlie. 'Not those who have been stowed on a ship for want of a place.'

His finger traced the shape of the arrows. Fifteen men, at the end of the war. Which small groups were captured at such a time?

'They are almost certainly all dead,' Lily was muttering.

'Perhaps. Perhaps not. In any case it is all we have,' said Charlie. He straightened thoughtfully. 'The Fleet's nearer the Thames,' he said. 'That's the most likely. And you have friends there,' he added meaningfully.

'It's already burned,' said Lily. 'You heard what the guards said.'

'Maybe not,' said Charlie. 'There's a chance.'

'Even if it still stands, it would be right in the heart of the blaze,' protested Lily.

'You can't get to the Fleet,' said the Oracle.

'I can get us through fire,' said Charlie. 'So long as the wind stays to the north.'

'Oh, I speak nothing of the fire,' said the Oracle.

His dry voice had deepened. The cloudy eyes had a hard brightness in their depths now, like flinty diamonds.

Charlie's stomach twisted. They'd left it too late.

'Wilkes is here now,' said The Oracle. 'You can't tell an old smuggler of treasure and expect to leave with your throat uncut.'

Chapter 52

The King was drunk. He called for more wine.

At the head of the barge three women in petticoats wrestled. The shortest, a dark-haired actress, faked a magnificent fall, rolling full across the little stage with her naked legs flying.

Charles sat up a little at the tantalising flashes between plump white thighs.

Barbara Castlemaine raised an eyebrow. 'I think she's cut her hair,' she observed gaily.

The King leaned back in his chair and raised a ringed finger. Instantly a servant appeared with a jewelled decanter of wine. He filled the King's goblet then turned to pour for Barbara, who shook her head.

'Sweetmeats?' suggested the servant. 'There are fresh candied nuts, marchpane fruits . . .'

Barbara gave him a dazzling smile. The servant caught her meaning immediately and retreated.

Smoke could be seen high above London in the distance. They were gliding past the large granaries at Scotland Yard.

'Why don't they use carts?' asked Barbara as stoic-faced men shovelled grain and shouldered sacks away.

'No carts left in the city,' said Amesbury. 'Not unless you've gold to transport.'

The dark-haired actress had come to sitting at an impressively dexterous angle, her legs splayed in front, body folded forward to conceal her upper thighs.

'I think her name is Nell Gwynn,' said Barbara, resting a hand on Charles's thigh. 'I could send for her to join us in the back of the barge.'

She gestured to where a little private tent had been constructed.

'Is she new to the company?' asked Charles.

Barbara considered. 'I'm not certain. Perhaps I remember her from some comedy or other.'

Noticing the attention she was attracting, Nell stood and bowed.

'We heard Your Majesty had his long hair shaved,' she announced. 'And so in His honour, I did the same.' She made a swooping gesture across her groin. 'God's truth I like it better,' she continued in a theatrical voice. 'For with this Great Fire I enjoy the extra breeze.'

Charles's smile fell away a little. The smoke on the horizon seemed to glower at him. He finished his wine in one draft.

The granary workers had seen the Royal Barge and they stopped to watch. A sound came, but whether a cheer or a jeer Charles couldn't be certain. He stood and waved.

A cheer, he was sure of it. Instantly Barbara was at his side.

'See how they love their King?' she said. 'It does them good to see England's Majesty.'

They passed the curve in the river and a horrified hush fell over the barge.

'The riverfront . . .' Charles couldn't believe it. 'It's completely destroyed.'

'No colours but black,' agreed Amesbury grimly. He eyed the single shade, stretching on and on up the river.

'Here were the fine wharfs full of trading stock,' said the King, his voice cracking. 'And here was once a church. Many churches. I never . . .' He stopped to rest his forehead in his hands. 'I had it from the Mayor that the fire would be under control. That buildings would be pulled down,' he managed. There were tears in his eyes.

'They do now pull them down, Your Majesty, but they cannot do it fast enough,' supplied Amesbury. 'And now the great masses flee for their lives and think no longer to save their city.'

Chapter 53

'There's no treasure . . .' began Charlie. But The Oracle moved to stand by his system of wires. He looped a finger through. Before they could stop him a loud bell could be heard echoing in the distance.

Charlie and Lily could only watch helplessly as the burly guard lumbered down the corridor towards them.

'This is no treasure for you,' repeated Charlie, keeping his voice even. 'Worthless papers only. I swear it.'

'Even so,' replied the Oracle. 'Wilkes should rather see for himself.'

The guard was in the cave now and The Oracle gestured towards Charlie.

'Take the thief taker's key,' he said.

Charlie stepped quickly towards Lily. He placed a careful hand on her waist.

'Let the girl go,' he reasoned, working a hand under Lily's bodice. 'She has nothing of value to you.' Charlie's fingers touched the blade hidden in her skirts.

The Oracle shook his head sadly.

'Women talk, Charlie, as well you know. Mr Jenks. Take the girl. Kill her quietly. You know how noise unsettles Wilkes.'

In a flash Charlie was behind The Oracle holding a knife to his throat.

The guard's eyes widened in surprise.

'Let the girl go,' Charlie nodded to the guard. 'Or he dies.'

The guard looked uncertainly at The Oracle.

'I searched him, I swear it,' he managed.

The Oracle's black lips were a straight line of rage.

'But you didn't search the girl,' he said, twitching against the blade at his throat.

The Oracle let out a cold chuckle. His guard moved uncertainly in front of Lily, unsure of how to protect his master.

'I knew you were fast, Charlie Tuesday,' said The Oracle. 'But I'd forgotten you were a sneak thief. And how foolish of me to forget a gypsy rat will always carry a knife.'

Charlie held the blade a little tighter and he stiffened.

'Let her go,' The Oracle muttered to the guard. 'But you pay for her escape, Charlie Tuesday,' he added. 'Wilkes will be sure of it.'

The guard had not moved from his position in front of Lily. The Oracle gave a little twitching nod.

'You may stand aside,' he said, annoyed. 'Let the girl leave.'

Instead the guard fell slowly forwards, an expression of frozen shock on his scarred face. As he hit the dirt floor Charlie saw a familiar knife in his back.

Lily knelt by the body, wrenched her blade free and looked up at the Oracle.

'Gypsy rats carry more than one knife,' she said. Her eyes switched to Charlie.

'We both go,' said Lily. Then she stood and ran.

Charlie hesitated for a shocked second. Then he pushed The Oracle aside and ran out after her.

Chapter 54

Blackstone held the flask up to candlelight. The alchemy chamber was small and dark. A chemical taint stained the air.

'Very beautiful,' he said. 'How do you make the crystals grow that way?'

'Quicksilver,' said the alchemist. 'And aqua fortis.' He was a handsome-featured man who seemed out of place in a secret underground chamber.

Blackstone moved closer. The alchemist was tall and muscular. But his height and size dwindled beside the other man's huge bulk.

'You're one of the cleverest men in England,' said Blackstone. 'Yet no one knows you work down here, beneath the Palace. In secret.' He sounded the last two words pointedly.

The alchemist pulled his long black coat a little tighter, as though Blackstone gave off cool air.

'I'm in the King's employ,' replied the alchemist carefully. 'He would rather I work in secret.'

Blackstone raised his eyebrows and returned the flask to the bench. The alchemist watched him uncomfortably. The array of metals and potions, crucibles and invented tools seemed to close around them.

'You don't like me down here,' observed Blackstone. 'But you must accept my authority.' He waved a royal sealed paper smugly. 'She gives me permission.'

The alchemist stared at the name. He hadn't believed it until now.

'She gained me entry to the secret tunnel which leads to this room,' continued Blackstone. 'And asks you supply as much lead as I ask for.'

The alchemist ran a hand through his thick wavy hair. He looked as though he was fighting back a retort. Blackstone was looking around the alchemy chamber now, taking in the expensive equipment.

'The King gives you ample funds then,' said Blackstone. He couldn't keep the bitterness from his voice. 'If you make baubles from mercury.'

'It's important work,' said the alchemist. 'We show that metals have life. Can grow.'

'You're sitting very pretty down here,' continued Blackstone. 'No one sees you come in or out. I should imagine you have access to anything you wish.'

'The King likes me near so I might report my findings.'

Blackstone's ice-blue eyes fixed on him and he stopped talking. The alchemic chamber suddenly felt claustrophobic.

'I remember this room,' said Blackstone moving to the damp walls. His hand traced the remains of two heavy bolts. 'I am all amazement His Majesty should wish alchemy here. Perhaps he was too young to know.'

The alchemist fingered a vial of silver beads nervously.

'You're a clever man,' said Blackstone moving back towards him. 'You'll have deduced things about this room. Underground. Hidden.' His eyes landed on the alchemist again. 'The old King certainly knew.'

'I had some . . . tools cleared away,' said the alchemist, his face twisting at the memory. 'Ugly, terrible things.'

'You didn't think to modify them for your purposes?' asked Blackstone. 'Good strong metal they were made from.'

'No,' said the alchemist sounding appalled. 'I didn't want anything of that nature here.'

Blackstone was regarding the stone wall again. His hands shifted across to a pattern etched on it. He stopped and stared.

'The Tree of Life?'

'It's the Kaballah,' said the alchemist. 'A mystic understanding of . . .'

'I know what it is,' snapped Blackstone.

He strode back to the workbench and fingered a crucible.

'You're broad-minded,' he said. 'Men like you can afford to be. Men like me, however . . .' Blackstone let the comment hang, his gaze sweeping around the room. 'We no longer have that luxury.'

Chapter 55

Charlie and Lily barrelled back past the fruit and fish stalls and into the main belly of the Shadow Market.

Behind them The Oracle emerged with a roar. Then he seized a bell pull and gave three great rings.

Lily turned towards the river exit but Charlie grabbed her by the skirts.

'Not to the river!' he hissed. 'You can't escape a smuggler on water.'

'Where then?' asked Lily, swinging desperately to survey the market floor.

Their eyes both fell on the tea-chest rope winch and the donkey.

'It goes somewhere above,' said Charlie.

'To a pack of smugglers!' protested Lily. 'They'll slice our throats before we get out of the tea chest.'

Charlie was calculating their distance from the river. Under Borough Street, he thought, south of St Oleffs.

'Maybe not,' he said. 'It's possible we're under Bermondsey Market. Perhaps the Shadow trade supplies the legitimate one. That winch could lead to the trade floor.'

'You're sure of that?'

Behind them a bell was ringing. A pack of guards appeared from the meat and fish corridor. The Shadow Market fell to an immediate hush.

'Not sure at all. But it's our best chance,' promised Charlie, grabbing Lily's hand. 'We must go now.'

They got to the winch and Charlie shoved Lily inside the crate. Her skirts stuck out and Charlie threw them in behind her.

A few eyes had turned to them now, struggling with the winch.

'We're too late,' said Lily. 'He comes.'

Charlie turned to see The Oracle had appeared in the main Shadow Market. He was holding up a hand to shield his eyes. All eyes were on him. The market floor was completely silent. In a moment The Oracle had sought out Lily and Charlie. His finger shot out to point.

'Stop them!' His husky voice broke the still air. 'Five guineas dead or alive!'

His words had an immediate effect. Guards by the doorway righted themselves and made for Charlie and Lily. The wider market was in disarray trying to understand what was happening.

'Keep your hands free of the rope,' shouted Charlie grabbing for the pulley. He seized and freed the counterweight as Lily wrenched in the last of her skirts. The crate went rolling upwards.

The guards were dodging through stalls now, toppling barrels and piles of fabric in their wake. Behind them The Oracle was running full pelt, his face like thunder.

'Stop those thieves!' he shouted.

Smugglers nearer to the winch were trying to understand who The Oracle meant to apprehend, looking in confusion to the unfamiliar dark-blond man pulling at the winch.

Charlie felt the crate seize and his arms burn under a sudden huge load. The counterweight had failed. He gritted his teeth, dug in and pulled with all his might. He could feel the crate jolting.

Either Lily was trying to climb the final distance, or she was putting up a fight against a pack of smugglers above.

Charlie looked back desperately. The guards were yards away. Then he remembered the donkey.

In a lightning move Charlie threw the rope around the donkey's neck and gave the rump a hard slap. The animal bucked and then charged in the direction of the approaching guards.

Darting free of the flying hooves Charlie pulled at the rope. It went suddenly slack. Lily was no longer in the crate. The counterweight had reset itself.

Charlie glanced at the guards who had regrouped themselves after the unexpected donkey charge. Then he wrapped the rope around his wrist and cut it free. The counterweight dropped, sweeping Charlie up the shaft just as the first guard made a grab for him.

He reached the top with a jolt which nearly shook him free from the rope and swung himself feet first through the narrow exit. Hitting the floor at a clumsy thump Charlie rolled, swore, then righted himself.

Lily was staring down at him. She extended a hand and he took it.

'Thank you,' he said, pulling himself up. 'You saved me back there. From The Oracle.'

She smiled. 'You promised me half the treasure. Where are we?'

Charlie was looking around. Relief flooded through him.

'We're at Bermondsey Market,' he said, taking in the smartly dressed traders. 'Let's go before The Oracle's men get here.'

They emerged on Maid Lane where nearby cattle were gazing warily at the burning city.

'The Fleet's not flamed yet,' said Charlie, looking at the direction of the fire. 'If we cross the river in the next hour . . .' There was a clutter of ferries and ships on the water. None were taking passengers south of the river.

'The Bridge,' decided Charlie. 'We can get to London Bridge. Cross the river that way.'

Lily bit her lip nervously.

'It's close wooden houses all round the head. If the wind sweeps east we'll be trapped on a burning bridge.'

Charlie pointed to the squat shape of the Tower of London to the east. 'All the King's men will be protecting the Tower. There'll be firebreaks from London Bridge to Tower Hill.'

His mind was working, charting their route.

'The Bridge takes us past the laundry houses,' he added. 'Where they use lye. Perhaps we may discover something of Blackstone's alchemy on the way.'

Chapter 56

The King looked up the river. The sumptuous barge was touring them eastwards. London Bridge was on the horizon. The huge waterwheels were chugging slowly.

'The waterwheels,' said the King. 'They should supply water to the whole city. There are pipes from Cornhill water tower from Bishops Gate to Westminster.'

'The pressure is gone,' admitted Clarence. 'Fools dig down into the pipes all over London.'

'But we have muster points,' protested the King. 'The engines alone should be able to use those pipes.'

'The pipes under London are rotted trunks of elm,' said Amesbury. 'They are easy to breach with a spade or a hoe. And there are only five engines in any case. The guilds have been negligent.'

The King was suddenly very sober. He turned to Clarence.

'You told me the flames wouldn't go south of Maiden Lane,' he said. 'Thames Street has warehouses of pitch and timber.'

'They hold it back on Thames Street,' said Clarence. 'We've press-ganged men.' He pointed. 'See where the steam rises? They fight the fire there.'

Charles laid down his wine goblet. He gestured for the actors to disperse.

'What else?' he said, pinching his forehead.

'Your Majesty?' Clarence smiled uncertainly.

'What else?' demanded the King. 'What else is being done?'

'Firebreaks . . .' began Clarence. He couldn't stop himself staring at the devastation.

'How does it approach the Tower?' asked the King, thinking of the enormous stores of gunpowder. 'If a flame was to reach it, it would blow the heart out of England.'

'The wind doesn't bluster that way,' reassured Amesbury.

Charles looked out at the endless abyss of fire.

'I've let them make a puppet king of me,' he said. 'Now my city burns.'

A blackened church caught his eye. Weeping people were pulling things from the ruins.

'Their livestock burned,' he murmured, looking at the charred remains being removed. 'Why do they retrieve the bones?' And then he realised.

'I had it in writing,' said the King, his voice thick, 'that no lives were endangered.'

'We record only nobles or guildsmen,' said Clarence. 'Commoners are not . . .' He caught the King's expression and looked away. 'They weren't deigned to be of note,' he mumbled.

The King stood.

'Land at Somerset steps,' he said, a steely glint in his eye. 'We'll convene Lord Somerset's house as a war room.'

'Your Majesty,' said Clarence, 'only Parliament can grant authority for such measures.'

'Parliament told me houses were being pulled down,' said Charles. 'There comes a time when a King must act.'

The barge drifted slowly to Somerset steps. Servants began readying the elaborate platforms needed to transport His Majesty's silver-buckled shoes over the mud.

'Put out the word that we need men to defend the Palace. Call it from the London Stone,' said the King.

The boat drifted closer to shore.

'Take Barbara back to the Palace,' said Charles. 'This is no business for women.'

Barbara's cheeks turned pink.

'Where shall I say to the courtiers that you have gone?' she demanded.

The King leapt to shore. 'I am going,' he said, 'to save my city.'

Chapter 57

'You think we should investigate some laundries?' Lily sounded wholly unconvinced.

'Not just any laundries,' said Charlie. 'London Bridge has the best. Speciality laundries. Starch for big collars. Blue albumen for the whitest shirts,' he waved his hands. 'Fine embroidery, water-silk, expensive dyed wool. And the best and strongest lye for whitening,' he concluded. 'If Blackstone is using lye, a laundry might tell us something of it.'

Charlie assessed the smoke in the distance.

'They're beating back the fire near the Fleet. You can see by the steam. We have a few hours. So long as the King made firebreaks we can get there.'

'The laundresses will have long fled,' Lily pointed out.

'True,' said Charlie. 'But we might learn something from their premises.'

'I suppose it's a better idea than a burned prison,' said Lily. She was looking to the horizon. 'See the smoke?'

Charlie nodded. The Fleet had burned hours ago. 'To London Bridge then?' he said.

Lily looked uneasily to the wide firebreaks on the north side.

'Very well,' she decided. 'But we should be quick about it.'

The south side of London Bridge was framed by traitors' heads swaying on fifteen-foot pikestaffs. The freshest still had gummy unseeing eyes and mouths twisted in a rictus of pain. Older remains had been picked clean. The vinegary smell of the rotting heads was sharp on the breeze.

Crows scrabbled clumsily on the lurching skulls as Charlie and Lily passed underneath. Ahead, London Bridge's twenty stone arches ran over the wide Thames.

Two huge waterwheels churned beneath them, passing water into London's rickety underground pipe network.

'The south side is better than the north,' observed Lily as tall half-timbered tenements and shops reared up before them. Large buildings leaned out from either side, supported by wooden struts butted against the outside of the bridge.

'Everything is deserted,' observed Charlie as the smoke-filled sky narrowed to a red-tinged slice above the dark shops and houses. 'It didn't take them long,' he added, thinking it was now late afternoon and he'd only been on the Bridge that morning.

'No one takes the chance, despite the firebreaks,' Charlie concluded. 'I don't like it.'

'Why not?' said Lily. 'It's much nicer without all the people.'

'I'm a thief taker,' said Charlie. 'People are useful to me.'

His eyes ranged over the empty shops and settled on an abandoned cheese shop.

'Are you hungry?' he asked Lily, realising he'd not eaten since morning.

She looked at him with interest.

'There's still cheese inside,' he said, sliding his eating knife out of his pocket and inserting it into the window casement.

'How do you know?' she asked, as he jimmied it open.

'There's no guild of cheese-makers,' he said, 'telling them how much cheese to make, or what price to sell it for. And harvest festivals approach. They'll have stockpiled.'

He gave an exploratory few tugs, then an expert wrench.

'My guess,' he continued, 'is they couldn't take all their cheese.'

'You didn't break the glass,' said Lily, impressed. Charlie was leaning into the window. A row of bulging cheesecloths were hanging on a pole, draining whey. He cut one free and retreated back.

'Here,' he said, opening the cloth and cutting her a slice.

'Shame we have no bread for it,' said Lily, taking it. 'Can you steal us some of that too?'

'I'm not a thief,' said Charlie. 'Thieves get caught.'

'What are you then?'

'An opportunist. Besides,' he added, 'I made no damage, and that cheese will likely be spoiled in any case.'

'I'll wager your wife didn't like your opportunism.'

'We weren't married,' said Charlie. 'But no. She didn't like it.'

He gestured they should walk. Were it not for the lack of people, he thought, they could be an ordinary man and wife, strolling the bridge, eating cheese.

'Is that why your woman left you?' asked Lily after a moment. 'She wanted you to give up what you knew? Settle down?'

'It was the uncertainty.' Charlie tried to think of a good way to explain. 'When I need money it comes. One way or another. It's always been that way with me. It's just,' he waved a hand, 'how it works. Maria did not like that. She grew up in a village, where you plant the seeds and reap the rewards. She didn't understand the cut and thrust of the city. I told her I would never see her starve.'

'A fine life to offer a woman,' said Lily with an arched eyebrow.

'Women don't understand,' replied Charlie. 'Just because something isn't regular, doesn't mean it's not dependable.'

Lily smiled. 'I'm a gypsy,' she said. 'I understand a little. But London is a hard place. You must see that.'

'Not if you've grown up an orphan,' said Charlie. 'You die or you find a way to make the city work for you.'

He gestured to the burning city of the horizon.

'There is so much wealth in London,' he said. 'Plenty spare when you know where to look. Perhaps there are sedan chairs by the doctors' houses on Compton Street. So a rich household is sick and the bake-houses over-bake today. Free bread.'

Charlie pointed east towards the Tower of London.

'Or a sherry ship docks early to fair weather,' he continued. 'There's surplus ale which would have gone to sailor's rations. We can buy a barrel for a song, sell it to a tavern and have free beer and money besides. I know where and when each market drives cattle, which fruit sellers have spoils on a hot day. And I have a hundred friends in the city besides. There is no place, no part where a man will not hide me.'

'You remind me of my father,' said Lily. 'He lived by his wits too. Not that it did him much good in the end.'

He noticed her hand had moved to the part of her bodice where the handkerchief was concealed.

'You truly mean to avenge him?' asked Charlie.

'Yes.' Lily was staring straight ahead. 'I came here to set my father at peace. I've survived enough dangers and dishonesty in London. I won't abandon my purpose now.'

'Blackstone is dangerous,' said Charlie.

'So am I.'

'You could forget your revenge and be happy,' suggested Charlie, thinking of Maria and her wisdom on such things. 'You're a beautiful woman,' he added, 'in London, you'd do well.'

'Ah, but there's also treasure,' said Lily, her mouth turning up a little. 'You promised me half. And you must know gypsies are mad for gold.' But he could tell that wasn't the reason Lily was still here.

They walked on in silence, with the thunder of the great blaze echoing. The buildings pressed around them, stacked on top of one another at overlapping angles as though by a childish giant hand. Their cluttered construction now almost blocked out the sky, shadowing the path an ominous red.

'This whole place is like a giant bonfire waiting to be lit,' muttered Lily, eyeing the jumbled wood buildings which crowded upwards and outwards so as to be almost touching.

Lily came to a sudden halt behind Charlie. He was standing by a barn-like building. It was large in London Bridge terms, with half-timbered wood walls and a mouldering thatch roof.

'This is it.' Charlie pointed up. 'The sign of the water butt.'

'How do we know where the laundry is?' asked Lily. 'There's no one to ask. The building's big.'

She looked up at the tall wood frontage scattered with grubby diamond-pane windows. A cluster of signs swung in the high wind, depicting various trades. A dentist and a fortune teller's among them.

'The laundry will be on the ground,' said Charlie. 'So they can use the river water. The door's locked though,' he added.

In reply Lily flung her little body against the oaken door. It repelled her backwards.

'Let me try,' said Charlie, moving her aside. He studied the keyhole for a practised second, then drew out his lock-picking earring.

'Small locks are easiest,' he said, inserting the end and twisting it expertly. He clicked aside three tumblers one by one.

'An old street-rat trick?' asked Lily as the door fell open.

'A thief taker's necessity,' he answered as they advanced inside.

Chapter 58

'So you try at alchemy?' The contempt in the Royal Alchemist's voice was clear.

Blackstone smiled. He looked back at the Tree of Life on the wall of the alchemist's chamber. It was strange to think they were deep below the King's palace.

'Not alchemy as you would know it. The *Royal* Alchemist,' he stressed the word contemptuously. 'I'm not of the coffee house chatterers. Men of your great learning would never let me in.'

He smiled a little.

'But I learned secrets all the same. It's brought me royal favour of a kind. As you know.' Blackstone's eyes roved around the alchemist's scattered papers. He picked one up. 'The green lion which ate the sun?' he said. 'The Royal Water, which dissolves all?'

'None may know my workings unless I wish it,' said the alchemist. 'The King pays me . . .'

'To find him gold,' supplied Blackstone. 'And we shouldn't want any common villain discovering that secret.' He gave a short barking laugh and tapped the papers disdainfully. 'Stories and pictures,' he scoffed. 'You make alchemy like a children's game.'

'You came for lead,' said the alchemist flatly. He glanced at Blackstone's heavy leather jerkin where the royal permission letter was concealed. 'I cannot refuse your lady's request,' he continued. 'Here is what I have.'

He slid a flat cloth-wrapped parcel across the table.

'This is all you have?'

'Cornish smugglers took a large part,' said the alchemist. His lip curled slightly. 'How much lead could a man like you need?'

There was a dangerous silence.

'You think me beneath you,' said Blackstone. 'Be a little careful. Men like me may rise up after all.' His large hand picked up a page of the alchemist's crabbed script.

Blackstone looked around the room. His eyes settled on a heavy sea chest.

'There's nothing valuable inside,' snapped the alchemist.

'I had no thoughts of that kind,' said Blackstone. 'My wife was gifted a similar trunk for our marriage. Yours stirred a memory, nothing more.'

A strange electricity was weaving in Blackstone's mind. Through his shattered memory, thoughts shifted, broken and uncertain.

Teresa was looking at the sea chest. 'The Sealed Knot make me a wedding gift?'

'They are grateful for your sacrifice,' said Blackstone.

'The sign of the Sealed Knot at the head,' said Teresa, holding the key. 'Lest I forget.' She pushed it into the lock and turned it. A complicated locking mechanism clicked and rolled. Teresa raised the lid.

Inside was a collection of little wood statues. They were crudely done, with paint to make the details. Suns and moons, astrology motifs and animals. Thirteen in all.

'Thirteen Blessings?' Teresa's mouth twisted strangely. 'Of course,' she smiled. 'The Sealed Knot could not give money. They took mine. Now they insult me with the Old Ways.'

'*Torr carved the blessings himself,*' said Blackstone. '*To wish us happiness in our marriage. He has an interest in mysticism and things of that nature. There is no harm in it,*' he added uncertainly, as Teresa began to unpack the trunk.

'*A sun?*' she held it up. '*To show masculinity.*' That strange smile again. '*Marriage brings me that at least. My great brute husband.*'

She pulled out more shapes. A cat, a moon, a star.

'*Hearth and home,*' she said. '*Dreams of a happy future.*' Teresa delved deeper and her voice shifted.

'*And look,*' she said. '*A heart.*' Her pale eyes settled on his. '*For love.*'

Thomas sat and took her cold hand. She didn't flinch away and he admired her for it. His new bride was sacred. Not like the hot sweating whores he'd dirtied himself with before. His body yearned for her purity.

Teresa caught the look on his face and looked away.

'*I will be an obedient wife to you,*' she mumbled.

Blackstone realised the alchemist was staring. Then he saw something else from the corner of his eye. A bulky shape covered with a black cloth. The alchemist must have concealed it hastily as Blackstone arrived.

'That is not for your eyes!' shouted the alchemist. But Blackstone was already pulling back the cloth.

'Well, well,' he murmured. 'This is a fine treason.'

Chapter 59

Charlie breathed in the damp air. Towards the back of the laundry the floor extended out over the river. A hazardous-looking lean-to of rotting planks allowed laundresses to hoist up water.

Enormous water butts were ranged in a state of disarray. To the back were a few smaller barrels, but most of the stock had been taken.

Lily followed Charlie inside.

'Why do they launder clothes here?' asked Lily, looking about her. 'There's hardly any room to dry.'

'Like I said, it's a starch laundry,' said Charlie. 'For rich folk. Collars and cuffs, not big wool skirts.' He pointed to the few remaining barrels. 'I'm guessing they fled with their coloured starch. And all the valuable lace and silk clothes. Those big butts were too cumbersome to carry.'

He approached the few barrels remaining.

'This might be lye,' he said, opening one up for a look.

The smell of ammonia hit him and he recoiled.

'That's piss,' he said, stepping back.

'There,' said Lily, pointing. 'That's their lye hopper.'

He swung to see a sturdy wooden trough filled with straw and ashes.

'This is for lye?' He approached it with interest. 'I thought laundresses kept a trough for pigs.'

'Water goes in the top,' said Lily, gesturing to a spout at the bottom of the trough. 'Lye comes out there. The barrel beneath has been taken.'

'How did you know that?'

'I like to keep my clothes clean.'

Charlie approached the lye trough. The straw was damp and pungent-smelling. There was a visible mark on the floor where the lye barrel had sat.

'Pass me your tinderbox,' said Charlie.

Lily handed it over, her face quizzical.

Charlie struck it and held the flame at the trough-spout, where a few drops of lye lingered.

'Nothing,' he said, as the flame scorched the wood. 'No blue fire.'

Charlie shut the tinderbox and inhaled. A strong smell of vinegar hung on the air. He swung around looking for the source.

'They keep a barrel of vinegar,' he said, noticing a squat open container within reach of the lye trough. 'That's not for clothes.'

'Laundresses dip their hands in it,' said Lily. 'Maybe to keep their skin white.'

'They've got the lye for that,' said Charlie. He considered the lye trough and then the vinegar. 'But lye burns the skin, doesn't it? Perhaps it stops the lye burning them.'

Lily looked at the hopper.

'Maybe,' she conceded.

'Only one way to know,' said Charlie.

He put an experimental finger into the spout at the bottom of the trough.

'What are you doing?' cried Lily. 'Lye burns . . .'

Charlie removed his finger. It was already beginning to heat. A red mark was blooming on his fingertip.

'Strong lye,' he observed.

Then he walked to the vinegar barrel and plunged his finger into the dark liquid.

Lily watched with fascinated horror.

Charlie waited for a moment.

'Vinegar stops the burn,' he said, removing his finger. There was a residue of yellow salt on his skin. He licked it cautiously and made a face.

'Sour,' he said. 'Interesting. So laundresses know a little alchemy.'

'I thought alchemy was making gold and elixirs.'

'Alchemy is about changing the nature of things,' said Charlie. 'Change something small and you can change something big. That's the theory. If vinegar can stop lye being lye, then that's a kind of alchemy.'

'Lead to gold,' said Lily understanding.

Charlie nodded. He sucked at the scar on his lip, taking in the rest of the laundry.

'We should take a little lye with us,' Charlie decided. 'Maybe we can find out more about it later. I only have a leather tankard,' he added, casting about the laundry for a suitable vessel. 'Do you have something which closes?'

'Try this,' Lily drew out an elaborately decorated gun-powder flask.

'Where did you get that?' he frowned, taking it from her. 'This is real carved horn. The silver filigree alone . . .'

'Men are not so careful,' she replied as he turned it appreciatively.

Charlie shook his head. 'Tip up the other end of the trough,' he said. 'I'll collect a little lye from the spout.'

'Why must I do the lifting?'

'Do you want to burn your pretty white hands?'

She moved to the end of the trough and with a heave, lifted one end. After a moment a modest trickle of lye streamed out of the spout. Charlie collected it, tutting as a few drops burned his palm.

'That's enough,' he said, waving his hand agitatedly and stoppering the flask. He dunked his hand in the vinegar and dried it on his patched breeches. 'Here.' He handed it back. She re-checked the stopper and slipped it inside her dress.

'Wait,' said Charlie. 'Do you smell that?'

'All I smell is vinegar and piss.'

Frowning, Charlie flung open the window. His nostrils were instantly assailed by the bitter smell of burning human hair.

'The traitors' heads,' he said. 'They're burning.'

Chapter 60

'It is no treason!' raged the alchemist as Blackstone pulled the cloth away.

Blackstone was examining the object underneath in wonder. He knelt so as to be eye level.

'Perfectly to size,' Blackstone muttered. 'All the buildings in the right order.' He ran a hand along one of the miniature streets. 'It is illegal to make a likeness of the city,' said Blackstone, 'without the King's permission.'

'I have permission from the Earl of Amesbury,' said the alchemist hotly. He stopped suddenly, realising Blackstone had manipulated him into divulging information. 'It's a private business,' finished the alchemist.

'I see Amesbury's hand all over this,' said Blackstone. 'He and I are old friends. Of a kind.' Blackstone pursed his heavy lips. 'We fought for the King during the war. But we had different notions of battle. Amesbury is regarded as a fine military leader,' he added thoughtfully. 'Because he won every battle. He has some notion of inspiring his troops. Fighting alongside them. Then he turned coat and joined Cromwell.'

Blackstone gave a scoffing little laugh.

'Do you know what Amesbury called me?'

The alchemist shook his head.

'The Wolf General,' said Blackstone. 'It was meant to be derisive. To show I ruled through fear.' His huge frame moved closer to the alchemist. The alchemist stepped backwards unthinkingly.

Blackstone smiled. 'When you terrify a man, you know where he will run,' he said. 'Fear is war's best weapon. It places men where you want them. I learned that here.' Blackstone waved his hand around the dank chamber. 'In this very room.'

He was looking back at the model of London now, at a tiny wooden St Paul's with its tall spire. 'You carved the model yourself?'

The alchemist nodded. He was battling with an unaccountable feeling of terror. This enormous man with his torture-scarred hands and dead eyes. The alchemist couldn't help but believe him capable of anything.

'Quite a talent,' said Blackstone. 'These red-painted buildings near Pudding Lane show the path of flames,' he added. 'Ingenious. Parliament took away the King's recent maps, didn't they? So Amesbury keeps a secret street plan down here. And now he asks you to discern something of this Great Fire,' continued Blackstone thoughtfully. He looked up at the alchemist. 'Pyromancy?' he suggested. 'You divine something from the flames?'

'It is no dark thing we do down here,' retorted the alchemist, 'no sorcery.'

The satisfied expression on Blackstone's face told the alchemist he'd wandered into another trap.

'You study the path of the fire,' decided Blackstone. 'So Amesbury believes something to be amiss with the way the fire moves. Or he plots to further the spread.'

He eyed the alchemist's face and smiled again. Then Blackstone pointed a thick finger and toppled the shops of Cheapside. The alchemist instinctively moved to right them and then caught the expression on Blackstone's face. His hand drew back.

'Let me help my old friend Amesbury,' continued Blackstone, sweeping a palm down towards Thames Street. 'All this,' he said, eyes glittering, 'all this has now burned.' His hand travelled up, levelling everything west of the Fleet.

'And all this will.'

Chapter 61

One glance towards Southwark was enough for Lily to see Charlie was right. Smoke was issuing from the long pikestaffs that crowded the south entrance to the Bridge.

The traitors' heads were burning. Fire had broken out on the south side.

Charlie made a logistical analysis. Their route back to Southwark was blocked by fire, and hot sparks flew on the breeze, whipping the wooden houses of the bridge into fast flame.

Charlie tried to see along the causeway where the fire had started. Then deep in the heart of the south-side flames, a blue light twinkled.

Charlie and Lily looked at one another.

'Blue fire,' said Charlie. He looked back up the frontages and then again to the fire. The south of the bridge could now be heard thundering into blaze.

Charlie looked north.

'We can still get off the north side,' he said. 'If we make haste.'

The traitors' heads were burning merrily now. One was facing Charlie, its eyeballs melting in two viscous streams down the grizzled face. It looked as though the traitor was crying for his city.

Charlie and Lily raced out of the laundry on to the narrow street. The wind was already sending thick smoke billowing down the straight. They fell back, choking and covering their faces from burning cinders.

'This way.' Charlie beckoned inside, covering his mouth. 'The rooms are all connected along the Bridge. There'll be another way out further down. Less smoke.'

He pulled Lily up a narrow wooden stair leading to the other business premises. They broke on to the second level and ran along a maze of interconnecting corridors. Charlie veered left, past a collection of quack physician premises and gore-covered barber-surgeon rooms. When he judged they must have outpaced the worst of the smoke he slowed. Up ahead was an open hayloft, built to drop hay from a height on to wagons beneath.

Charlie ran to the open edge, looked down and gave a shout of frustration.

Ladders were worth money and someone had removed it.

He looked back to see smoke was already filling the corridors they'd just run through. Lily appeared coughing and rubbing her eyes.

'The wind is so strong,' she gasped. 'It's like a bellows pushing the fire along the bridge.'

Charlie swung to the hay bales, picked the nearest up and began throwing them bodily out of the side of the hayloft.

'It's not so high,' he said, sweat breaking out on his lip as he worked. 'We can jump.'

Smoke had begun whirling and thickening beneath. Charged by the high wind it glowed with airborne debris.

Taking out his knife Charlie began sawing through the bales causing clouds of soft hay to tumble down on to the sturdier bales below. Cinders caught strands as it fell, sending burning hay back into their faces.

'Jump!' cried Charlie. He grabbed Lily's hand and flung them both from the hayloft.

They fell, legs cycling and bounced on to the soft hay. Lily cried in pain.

'What is it?' Charlie was at her side helping her up.

'It's nothing,' said Lily wincing. 'Only I fell on the gunpowder flask.'

'Serves you right for stealing it,' said Charlie, looking along the narrow streets of London Bridge. Fire was blazing through the south-side buildings. But they'd landed in a narrow alley which protected them from the worst of the wind-driven smoke. Surrounded by a bewildering maze of interconnected courtyards, Charlie tried to get his bearings.

'My dress!' Lily gave a sudden cry of terror. 'It burns!'

Charlie looked to her skirts in alarm. A kind of smoke seemed to come from the gold threads. A shrieking hiss was issuing up.

Charlie recognised the sound instantly. The bottle in Torr's cellar had made the same noise right before it exploded. Lily's gunpowder flask must have split, he realised. The lye had soaked into the fabric of her skirt.

What was making it hiss?

'Your dress!' he shouted. 'Take it off!'

Lily hesitated and Charlie ripped at the red silk, exposing a thick leather bodice underneath. A collection of necklaces around her neck swung free. A bronze chicken foot and an evil eye talisman.

Charlie tugged at Lily's skirts. A spark from the air landed. And suddenly Lily's dress was alight. Blue fire rolled across the gold threads.

She batted ineffectually at the flame, her face pure terror. She was pulling at her skirts when something swung free from her leather bodice.

Charlie watched open-mouthed.

It was a rosary. She was a Catholic.

Chapter 62

'A firestorm?' King Charles looked confused. He'd convened the sumptuous environs of Somerset House as a war room. Letters and reports had begun arriving from all over the city. And the latest intelligence from his Royal Alchemist was particularly troubling.

'That's what conditions predict,' said Amesbury. He was brandishing the letter. 'The fire grows so great, it could make its own weather.'

Clarence was shaking his head. His white wig jiggled.

'This sorcery is all very well in the dirty provinces,' he announced loudly. 'But here in London, we will brook no witchcraft.'

Amesbury held out his hands. 'Your alchemist makes a prediction, Your Majesty. He conjures no magic, as you know.'

'Pyromancy,' announced Clarence, waving chubby ringed fingers, 'is illegal. Like necromancy and all dark arts. You are not permitted to divine from smoke or flame . . .'

Amesbury was trying to keep the frustration from his voice.

'Your Majesty,' he said, turning to the King. 'This is no sorcery or witchcraft. The alchemist's study of cloud patterns, of air movement . . .'

'Another dark art!' interjected Clarence.

'The Royal Alchemist,' said Amesbury, 'has predicted storms with success for many years.'

'That's true, Clarence,' said Charles. 'Our alchemist has told us many clever things of weather.' He frowned. 'But if there were a storm, what matter? It would bring rain.'

Amesbury was shaking his head. 'I asked the same thing myself,' he said. 'In a firestorm rainfall is burned away high in the clouds. Long before it touches the ground.'

The King looked dubious. 'No fire is great enough to stop rain,' he said.

'The alchemist speaks of eyewitness accounts,' said Amesbury. 'In Africa.'

'This is England,' said Clarence, who disapproved hugely of the alchemist's habit of citing foreign scientific tracts. 'You can't suggest . . .'

'The conditions are right!' Amesbury was fighting to keep his temper. 'You only need go out in the city,' he said, glaring at Clarence, 'to know something happens to the weather. We've never known a fire burn this hot or high.'

He fixed the King with a firm stare.

'The alchemist says it will bring wind,' he said. 'Great winds, from all directions of the compass. Hurricane strength to fan the flames. Lightning strikes down bringing more fire. Dark clouds will eclipse the sun.'

Amesbury shook the alchemist's letter.

'The heat is strong enough to combust houses many streets away,' he continued. 'London becomes a living furnace.'

Clarence was openly sneering now. 'It's a nonsense,' he barked rudely. 'A complete nonsense. What he's describing. It's fire and brimstone. An Armageddon.'

'That,' said Amesbury, 'is what I'm trying to tell you.'

Chapter 63

Charlie was reeling. So Lily was a secret Catholic. She'd concealed it so well, he thought. The implications flashed before him. Catholics weren't loyal to the King. Could she be secretly working for Blackstone?

Lily was batting at her skirts, the rosary swinging low. Her dress was in blue flames.

'Keep still,' Charlie said coldly. 'It won't harm you. It's not like ordinary fire.'

He was watching the path of the blue flames. Only the gold threads burned.

Lye and gold.

Lily stopped beating her skirts and looked down.

The blue fire swirled in a last colourful eddy and then went out.

Lily looked at Charlie. She noticed the exposed rosary and gripped it guiltily in her fist.

'So you're a Catholic,' he said flatly.

Lily didn't answer. Her expression said it all.

'A secret Catholic,' said Charlie, surprised by just how deeply he felt the betrayal. 'You've played a clever game.'

The enormity of it was hitting him in waves. Lily's handker-chief. The story of her dead father. Was any of it true?

'I didn't know you were one of those who hated Catholics,' she replied.

His eyes widened.

'I'm not,' he said. 'In this city who you know keeps you alive. I never miss the opportunity to make a friend. But my friends don't lie to me.'

She didn't answer that.

'Did Blackstone really execute your father?' demanded Charlie. He was wondering whose side she was really on.

Lily's eyes shone sadly but she didn't deny the charge. Instead she looked to the fire.

'The flames come, Charlie.'

Smoke was thickening, pouring along from the burning buildings.

'The magistrate can decide how it goes with you,' Charlie decided. And gripping her wrists he made to drag her towards the north end of the bridge.

In a quick movement Lily's knee connected hard into Charlie's groin. Then she twitched out of his grip leaving him bent double and retching.

As he staggered back on the main thoroughfare of the Bridge, Lily was nowhere to be seen.

In the far distance Charlie caught something flicker out of the corner of his eye. A blue light, twitching at the north end of the bridge. Charlie froze. It seemed to be coming from the Skinners' Hall.

Then came the sound of an explosion.

Charlie's mouth dropped open in horror. The Guildhall was alight. The north end of the Bridge was now ablaze. Someone had fired both ends of London Bridge. Leaving him trapped in the middle.

Charlie made for the river. Wooden jetties crowded the water beneath London Bridge. It was dangerous to jump between them. But there were steps leading down. All he needed do was find a set, climb down and swim to safety on the north bank.

Lily was somewhere on the bridge and his conscience pricked him. He wasn't sure if she could swim. Suddenly the wail of a child pierced the air. Charlie froze. He'd thought the bridge was deserted. Surely the street children would have long gone?

The cry came again. Desperate and frightened. He guessed a child-thief must have stayed to loot, become confused by the smoke and was now trapped.

Charlie swung away from the river following the sound. It was leading him straight to the heart of the blaze. The roadway was filled with choking smoke. In the stifling heat and darkness Charlie fought to remember which direction he was facing. He caught sight of an abandoned water butt at the edge of his vision. Ripping a length of his shirt he dunked it in the dirty remnants before tying it around his nose and mouth. The mask helped him breathe but his eyes watered as biting fumes filled the air.

He could see the flames now as well as feel them. They had exploded through the windows of the buildings, spitting molten glass on to the streets below, and flaring upwards like great amber curtains. Fire spread outwards along rafters and with an agonising crack, the joists gave way and burning roof tiles began to hail down on the bridge below.

Charlie lurched in what he hoped was the direction of the sound, passing into a tangle of close wooden alleys. A badly made overhang offered scant protection from the raining debris. And underneath was Lily.

Chapter 64

Louise Keroulle broke into the room sobbing. Her plump legs propelled her across the thick rug.

The King and his men looked up in alarm.

'Your Majesty!' Louise gasped dramatically as she flung herself into his arms.

'What is the matter?' Charles looked from the sobbing form of Louise to his men.

Louise took a deep, shuddering breath.

'My . . . My people!' She squeezed her eyes tight shut, allowing tears to run down her pretty face. Her hand worried the expensive pearl embroidery on her dress.

In her distress she reverted to rapid French.

'They burn them and hang them!' she cried. 'Frenchmen and women. Catholics too. English people say the foreigners spread fire. Anywhere they see my people on the streets, they're beaten and worse. A man was hung from a shop-sign! A nobleman! I knew him.'

She put her head in her hands and sobbed.

Charles wrapped his arms around her and looked up at his men.

'Foreigners are being lynched,' he translated to the dumbfounded Amesbury and Clarence. 'She is crying for her people.'

Clarence let out a bark of disgust.

'The weak hearts of women!' he said, shaking his head. 'If foreigners and Catholics mean no harm they should stay indoors. We cannot be responsible if they venture out.'

Amesbury considered this.

'Clarence is right,' he decided. 'We must fight fires. We have no resources to protect foreigners silly enough to roam the streets.'

'It would be bad for relations with France,' said the King, still holding the weeping Louise to his chest, 'if ambassadors were lynched by an English mob.'

He released Louise and drummed his fingers on the table top.

'Without France's ships, Holland will invade,' he said. 'And what better time than when London is burning?'

Charles turned to Louise. He spoke carefully in French.

'You must go to the Royal Alchemist,' he said. 'He has a store of gold put aside.'

Amesbury's eyes glinted. He didn't speak French, but had recognised the word for 'gold'.

Charles reverted to English, beckoning to a servant.

'Paper,' he instructed. 'Sealing wax.'

He spoke French again.

'Take my authority to the alchemist,' said Charles to Louise. 'Take a plain carriage to Whitehall. Use the secret tunnels. Do not under any circumstances go out on the streets.'

Louise shook her head so hard her little curls bounced.

Paper and wax was placed in front of Charles. He took a pen, scribbled a fast note, rolled it then sealed it with his ring.

'Here,' he gave it to Louise. 'The alchemist will give you gold. Use it to arrange protection for the embassies. They can pay a guard to escort men to safety.'

Louise nodded again.

'If there are funds, Your Majesty,' said Amesbury carefully, 'they are better spent fighting fire.'

'Funds will be made for the fire,' said Charles. He turned to a servant. 'Can someone bring wine and cheese?' he demanded. 'It's already afternoon. I've not had a sip these long few hours.'

Chapter 65

Lily had with her not one child, but five. They clustered around buried in her skirts. Tiny fists clutched at Lily's clothes or hands.

She looked up at him in terror and despite himself Charlie felt his anger melt away. The frightened expressions of the children and hers seemed almost interchangeable.

'I'm not a traitor,' she said simply. 'I'm Catholic. But I'm for the King. I work for Amesbury and I told you the truth about Blackstone killing my father. But I didn't tell you my religion because . . . I didn't think it should matter,' she concluded, looking hurt.

Charlie watched her face. It was impossible to know if she was lying. Against his better judgement he found himself wanting to give her the benefit of the doubt.

'Why didn't you get off the Bridge?' asked Charlie, surprised by her apparent heroism.

'I can't bear the sound of children crying,' Lily muttered. The little boy in her lap was toying with her chicken-foot necklace.

'This won't protect them,' said Charlie, pointing at the over-hang. 'We need to get these children out.'

'How? Both sides of the bridge are burning.'

'There are steps down to the river,' said Charlie. 'They go under the bridge. Down to wooden jetties where the boats dock.'

Lily shook her head. 'They won't go down the steps,' she said, waving at the cluster of children. 'They fear the boatmen and lightermen.'

Charlie eyed the pale faces of the children. London Bridge loaded costly cargo. Waifs and strays grew up under the quick hands of boatmen.

The host of little faces looked up at him anxiously. To Charlie's relief he spotted a familiar child – it was the little girl who had guided him to the gambling den for a shilling. She was without the parchment-skinned baby she had previously carried.

'Where's the baby?' asked Charlie, kneeling down to address her.

The girl looked terrified, and Charlie realised he was still wearing his shirt-mask, giving him the appearance of a grubby highwayman. He took it off hastily.

With his face revealed the girl drew a shy arc with her toe on the dusty planked floor then looked up wide-eyed. 'Mama give him to the angels,' she replied. "Long with the other brothers. An' a sister,' she added.

'You remember me?' asked Charlie. 'That I gave you a shilling to be my guide and then a further shilling afterwards?'

He was rewarded with a firm nod. Charlie withdrew a shilling and pressed it into her warm hand. The smoke was beginning to close in around them and lines of sweat were coursing down his forehead.

'Can you lead your friends to the nearest steps?' said Charlie. 'The boatmen are all gone,' he added, as her countenance veered from pleasure at the coin to fear of the task. 'If you take them down then I shall give you all a shilling at the bottom and you a half crown besides. Do you understand?'

But the girl looked dubious. Charlie glanced back as a huge billow of smoke passed over them.

'Wha's half a crown?' she asked suspiciously. 'Why can I not have a shilling like the rest?'

'All right then,' he placated. 'You shall have your shilling like the rest, and I shall give you another for leading them, so that will be three shillings.'

The little girl acquiesced to this with all the gravitas of an ambassador sealing a trading agreement. And to his intense relief she began rounding up the other four children. After a moment they stood as one, awaiting further direction.

'Where are the nearest steps?' asked Charlie.

'That way,' said the girl uncertainly. She was pointing towards a growing pillar of fire which crested from the upper windows of two wooden buildings. The flames reached towards one another, forming a fiery arc over the straight. Broken glass twinkled rosily on the bridge below.

Charlie caught sight of the opening to the steps. A narrow hatch down past a gauntlet of burning houses.

Lily looked upwards at where the fire was roaring from the windows overhead. A tile smashed by her foot, showering them with hot shards, and then another fell, and another.

Charlie threw out his coat to protect the children. 'Go!' he said. 'Now!'

They raced towards the steps as the tiles had begun to rain thick and fast.

'This way,' said Charlie as a huge tile smashed within inches of them. 'Into the doorway.'

They sheltered for a moment under a narrow wooden porch. The hatch to the steps was tantalisingly close. But the tiles hailed down like mortar fire. Charlie looked above them. The porch was made of thick wooden planks, propped loosely rather than nailed securely.

He stood and heaved one free.

'What are you doing?' protested Lily as tile fragments ricocheted against her bare arms.

'Making a shield,' said Charlie, heaving the plank outwards. 'It will serve for them,' he added, grunting with the effort and nodding towards the children. 'We'll have to take our chances.'

He rested the plank against the house and caught the attention of the small girl.

'When I lever this plank over,' he said, 'you must run. Get to the next porch. Can you do that? Then from there you must all run to the steps.'

The girl looked up at the plank then along to the next porch. Her jaw set determinedly. She nodded.

'When I say go,' said Charlie, readying himself. 'Go!'

Chapter 66

Barbara Castlemaine opened the door carefully and ushered Blackstone quickly inside.

'Were you seen?' she asked.

Blackstone bowed low.

'No, Lady Castlemaine. I used the tunnels you suggested, with a torch to light my way.'

Barbara smiled. She'd taken advantage of her absence from the King to make hasty arrangements to see Blackstone.

'Charles uses those tunnels to bring pretty girls from the city,' she said. 'It pleases me that I may have my own intrigues by them.'

Blackstone smiled, but the expression did not reach his eyes. Barbara suppressed a shiver. He had always unnerved her. She hated dealing with Blackstone. All the Sealed Knot men had their horrors. A Civil War siege had starved Blackstone and his men to sticks. He'd come to Holland with his obscene bulk and dead eyes. She'd heard a rumour that rotting food had been discovered hoarded in his quarters.

But Barbara needed to fully vanquish Louise. If it took blacker arts to win, then so be it.

'The rumours are at their height,' said Barbara. 'Catholics throw fireballs.'

Her eyes were roving his face, testing for a reaction.

'That is what the people say,' returned Blackstone evenly.

His cold blue eyes were at her chest, and for a moment Barbara thought he meant to take advantage of their secret meeting. Then she realised. He was staring at her crucifix. Barbara's hand went to it self-consciously.

'You have converted?' Blackstone asked. There was something hungry in his tone.

'I . . . I have,' replied Barbara, inwardly cursing how he unnerved her. 'To the true Catholic faith,' she added, deliberately emboldening her words.

'His Majesty knows?' asked Blackstone.

'Oh yes,' said Barbara. 'Charles and I have no secrets.'

'Apart from our secret,' observed Blackstone.

Barbara gave a little laugh which sounded flat, even to her own ears.

Blackstone's hand went to a leather pouch under his arm. He surveyed Barbara's sumptuous apartment and his gaze rested on a hand-carved writing desk. Without a word he stalked towards it and laid down the pouch.

Barbara followed him to the table, her eyes fixed on Blackstone.

Blackstone unfurled the pouch. Inside were three squat balls, the colour of tallow.

They both looked at them.

'You understand,' said Barbara carefully. 'That I don't want to resort to this.'

Blackstone nodded.

Her eyes fell again to the pouch. 'How did you discover this alchemy?'

Blackstone smiled.

'A long time ago,' he said. 'I learned the art. Necessity, after the war. I returned penniless and joined a guild. The brothers taught me their secrets.'

'You rose to the Mayor's side,' said Barbara. 'I heard rumours he meant to honour you with an Alderman title.'

'Papers were lost.' Blackstone's eyes were dark with fury.

'Parliament would not recognise your claim, as a Catholic,' guessed Barbara, feeling uncomfortable.

'No.'

'Yet you have risen again,' said Barbara. 'Your talent makes you powerful. And you have royal favour.'

'I have used guild connections to my advantage,' agreed Blackstone, thinking of the army of boys he'd assembled over the past year. 'You must remember when we were in Holland, we both had nothing. You had your methods of gaining power, I had mine.'

'And how does your wife feel about your methods?' asked Barbara, her eyes flinty. 'Some say you returned from Holland with a great secret. That you and your wife made a very dangerous marriage.'

Blackstone's smile flickered. Images were playing back to him. Teresa's sad face as they signed the marriage papers.

This will tear England apart.

Barbara was watching his face, searching for clues.

'I also heard a legend,' she said, 'that some great power had been unleashed. Your brotherhood could turn lead into gold.'

'Stories, all. We made no marriage,' lied Blackstone shortly. 'And Teresa is dead.'

'I am sorry,' said Barbara. 'Teresa was a very beautiful woman. But it is fortunate that you committed no treason with her.' Her eyes locked on his, and Blackstone saw the determination behind their beauty. 'You may become valuable to me,' she said, eyeing the pouch. 'And unions made before His Majesty's triumphant return can be a deadly business.'

Chapter 67

London Bridge was crackling in flame. Charlie readied the plank for the children to run beneath. A burning pebble bounced up and struck a little boy's arm. His tiny mouth set in a square of anguish and he howled as though his heart would break.

'Hurry!' said Lily, 'before they get too scared to go.'

From high above them came a sound like a clap of thunder. The eaves of the house they sheltered by had given way to the flames and the towering buildings above swayed. They teetered, shuddered then threw off the top two floors. The upper storeys plummeted down, crashing towards them in a mass of fiery rubble.

Charlie grabbed the nearest children back. Lily gave a cry of horror, burying the little boy into the protection of her skirts and pulling another girl into her lap.

As the flaming dust settled they raised their heads. A great pile of building had landed between them and the steps. The fire, fanned by the falling rubble, flared with new vigour.

Charlie waved away dust and smoke. He thought he could make out a tiny passage of light underneath the fallen wood.

'I can see the river,' said Lily. 'There's a little space.'

Charlie and Lily looked at one another.

'It's big enough for the children,' said Charlie, pointing to a tiny opening. 'They may crawl through that crack.'

'But the flames,' said Lily.

'That space will hold for a moment,' said Charlie, assessing. 'Hardly any air. The wind isn't on that side. Fire needs to breathe and it needs to eat,' he added. 'No air for it there.'

The girl was looking up questioningly at Charlie. He knelt and grasped her shoulders. 'You can crawl through the opening?' he asked. She studied it for a moment then nodded. A huge flaming joist swung down suddenly in a cascade of cinders. Lily cried out in pain and rubbed at a scattering of angry burns which had appeared on her arm.

Charlie looked nervously to the burning pile between them and the steps. The crawl space wouldn't hold much longer.

'You must go down the ladder now very quickly,' continued Charlie. 'When you reach the bottom, stay under the stone arch, do you understand? And keep all the others with you.'

The girl bobbed her head.

'The stone arch,' repeated Charlie. 'Don't go on the wooden jetties. Say it back to me.'

'The stone arch,' repeated the girl, her eyes flicking nervously to Lily. 'Not the wood jetties.'

'Good. Very good,' praised Charlie. 'Then go now. Fast.'

The girl crawled for the opening followed by the other four children. They went one at a time on all fours, across the glass strewn floor. But one by one, with bloody knees and hands, they got to the steps. Then they waited fearfully as the girl began to shepherd them down.

'What if they don't go?' murmured Lily. The wind was blowing oven-hot heat and the children were crimson-faced and terrified.

They both watched as the girl stepped over the burning debris and helped the first child on to the steps.

'Quickly,' muttered Charlie, his eyes fixed on the collapsed building. 'Quickly.'

He turned to see Lily's hand clutched tight around her rosary. The remains gave a loud groan and a puff of smoke belched out from the crawl space.

'Get them down the ladder,' pleaded Charlie. 'Don't stop.'

One by one the other children vanished down. Then the girl's little head dropped out of view as she descended. Charlie let out the breath he hadn't realised he'd been holding.

'They're safe,' he said, relief flooding through him.

'They are,' said Lily, pointing to the blazing inferno that now came from all sides. 'But what about us?'

Chapter 68

The Duke of York was hemmed in by tedious nobles. With Charles absent from Whitehall, the dull business of protecting valuables fell to his brother.

Several attractive women were subtly pushing themselves through the crowd, angling to get closer. The Stuart brothers' weakness for women was well known. Families were sending their prettiest daughters to beg for carts and horses. A blonde girl in a white dress caught his eye. James raised a dark eyebrow. She was edging towards him. Then he saw her. James's heart quickened. Arabella Churchill. She'd managed to get into court.

Their eyes locked and she arched her eyebrows. Her gaze flitted to the blonde and she smiled broadly. James stepped towards her and the crowd parted.

'Your Grace.' Arabella smiled. 'I hear you help people guard their riches.'

'The roads are all blocked,' said James. 'I'd rather be at sea.'

'Ordering grubby sailors around?'

James smiled. 'I'd give my life for those grubby sailors.'

'You nearly did.'

'Which is why Charles keeps me on dry land,' said James ruefully. 'Helping with courtly matters.'

'Good,' said Arabella. 'Seeing your commanders torn apart by Dutch cannon fire should curb your seafaring. It's a miracle you escaped with a few cuts and a drenching of their blood.'

'All the same,' said James, 'I'd rather be with my men.'

'Than here?' Arabella stepped forward a little. He could smell her intoxicating perfume. 'With me?' She mouthed the words.

He moved to whisper in her ear. A ripple of scandal murmured through the assembled court.

'If I could take you with me,' said James, 'stow you beneath deck, that would be perfect.'

Arabella curtseyed and dropped back into the crowd. As she retreated, James caught the smallest tilt with her eyes.

Excitement flushed through him.

'Let me take a moment,' he announced loudly. 'I mean to eat in private, but I'll return soon.'

He began extricating himself from the crowds of nobles, trying to seem casual. Arabella was doing the same, shifting away from the richly dressed people.

The Duke of York broke free and hastened quickly to the long corridor joining the banquet hall to the private Parliament rooms.

Behind him he heard her little step but didn't dare look round. It was only as he unlocked the door to Clarence's office and slipped inside that he ventured to turn. She pushed herself into his arms and he pulled her in, shutting the door behind them.

'No one saw, James,' she whispered. 'I have a few minutes before I am missed.'

He moved her to the large table and sat her on it, pushing maps and paperwork aside. His hands travelled up under her skirts.

Arabella ran her hands under his shirt. Her fingertips brushed the scars of his recent naval attack.

'Quickly,' she whispered, her face flushed. James's hands fumbled at his clothing.

'You're good at this,' he observed as she opened her thighs, 'secret meetings.'

There was a knock at the door and they both froze.

'Arabella!' came a heavy male voice. 'Daughter, are you within?'

The Duke of York's mouth was at Arabella's neck. 'The door is locked,' he whispered, hands moving over her.

'I'm using the pot,' called Arabella as the Duke of York positioned himself between her legs. 'The buttered crab was bad,' she improvised.

There was a silence on the other side of the door.

'Be sure to open the window before you leave then,' called the voice. 'This is Clarence's office. You mustn't leave him a stink.'

Footsteps plodded away leaving Arabella and James clung together in paroxysms of laughter.

'We'll have to arrange things better,' said Arabella, thoughts of the barge and Barbara forgotten.

'We shall.' James arranged her among the piles of documents. Then he froze.

'What is it?' she hissed. He was picking up a paper.

'It's a demand,' he said. 'From a group calling themselves the Sealed Knot.'

'The soldiers from Holland?' she asked, glancing to the door.

'They were dangerous men,' said James. 'If they threaten it should be taken seriously.'

He shook his head, rearranging his thoughts.

'I have to tell Charles,' he said. 'There is a plot in the city. He must send troops. The Crown could be in danger.'

'James,' said Arabella, her expression suggesting she thought him dramatic. 'We have only a few moments. Do you want Clarence to find us on his desk? He has a key, you know.'

James put down the paper and took her chin in his hand.

'You're right,' he said, kissing her. 'It's probably nothing. The fire will never reach Whitehall.'

Chapter 69

'We must get to the side of the bridge,' said Charlie, shouting above the fire's roar. 'See there? On the other side of those flaming eaves? There's a brothel that isn't aflame. They'll have a trapdoor to the river, for taking in wine shipments.'

Charlie's eyes dropped to Lily's rosary.

'Best say a prayer,' he added, grabbing her wrist.

They ran out, weaving through the plummeting shrapnel, coughing as the smoke grew ever thicker around them. Fug and the flame closed on them, and Lily stumbled.

'Almost there!' gasped Charlie, pulling her upright. 'I can see the brothel!'

His hands hit the flat wood of the building and he groped for the door. The wooden bridge beneath them was deep in flames now and was starting to give way. A torrent of steam shrieked upwards as a section pitched into the Thames.

'Here!' Charlie's hand found a doorway, then the latch. They fell into the empty brothel gasping for air. The sweaty smell of well-used beds closed in on them, and Charlie realised he'd misjudged. No trapdoor to the river. This wasn't the kind of brothel that sold wine. In the glow of the fire Charlie could make out an obscene mural of King Charles and three naked women. The paint was flaking off in the heat.

'You said it wasn't burning!' Lily was looking in dismay at the peeling picture.

Charlie looked for windows. There was one, high up and tiny with thick wooden bars. His eyes settled on a staircase.

'This way.'

They raced up the staircase but the first two floors were the same. Tiny barred windows. No escape.

'The roof,' said Charlie pointing to a ladder.

They heaved themselves up on to the wooden shingled roof. All of the blazing bridge and London was laid out for them to see. For a moment they stood staring.

'There it is,' said Lily. 'Blue fire again.'

It winked out across the city. And another explosion wracked London. From their height above the city, Charlie had a clear view. The Draper's Hall had been flamed. And suddenly from the bird's-eye vantage point Charlie saw the pattern.

On the riverfront, fire had abated until the Fishmongers' Guild flamed. Then in the west, the Candlemakers' Hall hadn't simply fired. It had been blown to pieces. And now Charlie could see the tell-tale circle of gunpowder wreckage in the ruins of the Saddlers and the Drapers.

Guildhalls. Blackstone was firing the guilds.

He shot a look at Lily, wondering whether she'd seen it.

The more Charlie looked down on the blazing city the more he was sure of it.

Blackstone was using guilds to lead the fire west. Towards Whitehall. The King's Palace. The mystery of the round robin circled in Charlie's head again. Names in a circle. Was Blackstone using those common boys to spread flame? There was something obvious he was missing. Something about the round robin which could reveal Blackstone's tactics.

The roof shuddered beneath them. Then a spat of glowing embers landed on the wooden shingles. Wind roused them to a quiet flame.

'We'll have to jump into the river,' said Charlie, looking down at the water. It seemed very far away. Between each arch of the bridge was a wide jetty. And only a slim stretch of water in-between.

'Not much room to fall,' said Charlie. 'Can you swim to shore in your dress?'

Lily was staring at him in horror.

'You didn't say we'd have to jump in the water!'

'How else did you expect us to get off the bridge?'

'I don't know. I thought you had some trick.'

'I'm a thief taker, not a magician.'

Charlie looked to where the embers had landed. The roof was burning merrily now. Another scattering of embers landed.

'We have to jump,' he said.

Chapter 70

The creature in Blackstone's cellar peered up at the crack of light. It shuffled hopefully.

Maybe later a boy would come down. The creature licked its lips.

It was surrounded by bloodied objects and talismans. None were what it needed. But the creature knew patience. Patience and the old ways.

The creature remembered magic.

Thirteen wedding blessings.

And the marriage.

The marriage that had let forth all the dark things. Wealth untold, bound to fragile paper. The creature recalled it all. Mythic power. A mortal pen.

And the creature had heard things. Brother Blackstone had a wife.

Teresa.

She was here, in the cellar. Her remains were cursed. Evil.

The thought of her spirit brought a chill to the creature's soul. But the creature was stronger, much stronger than Teresa.

Blackstone's wife had confessed. The creature heard it all.

Teresa had told how Blackstone defiled her.

Dirties me. He dirties me.

Teresa had been dangerous. She knew the power of the papers. But the creature knew itself to be more dangerous still.

Carefully the creature began drawing out shapes in the mud of the floor.

It started with a broad circle. Then added a symbol and another circle. Slowly the shapes formed a kind of tree.

The creature breathed a little faster. This was the ancient source. Words came. Human sounds the creature hadn't made for some time.

I am more powerful now. I grow more powerful with every moment. This cellar will not hold me.

Blackstone knew it. He saw how the creature's strength grew. Teresa's witchcraft was no match for ancient powers.

The creature looked down at the shapes on the ground. It felt the confines of the cellar already weakening.

This was magic as old as time.

Chapter 71

'The waterwheels burn?' King Charles's mouth was set in a hard line. 'What does it mean?'

'Perhaps stronger currents on the river,' hedged Clarence. 'Loss of pressure in the pipes.'

'The river will break through the jetties at London Bridge,' said Amesbury bluntly. 'Deadly riptides. Boats overturned. And no water can be pumped.'

'The city's fire engines?' asked the King.

'We only know the location of three,' said Amesbury. 'Two have gone missing in the narrow backstreets.'

'What else?' the King demanded.

Clarence was looking at the floor.

'Fire has breached the Fleet,' he admitted. 'We weren't able to hold it back.'

Blood drained from Charles's face.

'Then fire goes to Whitehall,' he said. 'My children. *My children* are in the Palace.'

'Barbara won't let harm come to them,' said Amesbury gently.

'Go personally,' said Charles. 'Go to Barbara. Be sure the children are taken to safety. See it with your own eyes, do you understand?'

Amesbury nodded, but looked as though he wanted to disagree.

'Little Anne has a knitted poppet she can't sleep without,' added Charles, thinking of his eldest daughter. 'She likes me to tuck her into bed.'

Amesbury put a gentle hand on the King's shoulder.

'Look to save Whitehall,' he said. 'I will look after your family.'

Charles hesitated then closed his eyes.

'I . . . You're right,' he said. 'Thank you.' Charles pressed a hand to his forehead.

'Where is James?' he demanded. 'The Duke of York was tasked with intelligence. The Catholic plot to fire the city.'

Clarence rolled his eyes.

'If the Palace burns it's the end,' said the King. 'A plague and a palace burning. Englanders will take it as a sign.'

No one disagreed with him.

Chapter 72

'I can't.' Lily was staring fixedly at the water shaking her head. 'I can't jump.'

'You can't swim?' said Charlie, looking back down into the swirling Thames.

She didn't reply, only set her mouth in a narrow line. Charlie remembered suddenly. Lily's mother. Country mobs drowned gypsy women.

The fire was hot on their backs now and Charlie saw something was wrong with the water. It was flowing too fast.

He glanced back over his shoulder. Charlie's heart sank.

The waterwheels were burning.

'Step to the edge with me,' he coaxed, stepping over it so he stood on the wooden guttering. Lily stood rigid. Behind them the flames roared.

'The water,' said Lily. 'There are riptides, like the lighterman said.'

She was eyeing the fast-moving river. It had turned dark with debris. Chunks of the London Bridge jetties were beginning to break off.

'The jetties are weakening,' she said. 'They'll break and sweep us away.'

'The jetties are strong, well built,' said Charlie with more conviction than he felt. 'They're a dam slowing the water.'

Lily's knuckles were white, gripping the wooden barrier.

'It freezes solid in winter,' continued Charlie, desperately trying for a calm tone. 'We have Frost Fairs. Skating and hog roasts. It's slow water, Lily.'

'I'll drown' said Lily, 'I can't swim, and this dress will drag me to the depths.'

She was right, Charlie realised, taking in the heavy dress and tightly laced bodice.

He could feel the fire blistering his skin now, even through his thick coat.

'We need only float to under the arches' he said. 'The current is not strong. Hold my hand and I'll swim with you to shore. I won't let you go.'

Lily didn't reply, but he felt her hand snaking into his. He grasped it firmly.

Behind them another crash signalled the nearest building was collapsing. The jetty beneath them heaved off a supportive strut and the water swirled greedily, picking up speed.

Charlie made his move, pulling Lily forward.

'Wait!' Lily's face was alive with terror. 'I cannot,' she whispered. 'I cannot.' Perspiration was running down her neck. Her body was rigid. She flung a hand back, catching hold of a roof shingle.

'You go,' she said. 'I'll make my way out another way.'

Charlie looked out into the wide river. Then back at Lily. She tightened her grip on the roof tile.

'Go,' she said.

Charlie moved in a little closer. Lily tensed and he knew there was no chance of pulling her off the bridge by force.

'You might get back down the stair,' he said, defeated. 'If you climb through the debris you might get to the steps. The same way as the children.'

She nodded, though they both knew it was a lie.

'I'll meet you back in the city,' he said. There was a moment as they looked at one another. Both knowing there was no way out for Lily. Then Charlie took her face in his hands and kissed her.

For the smallest of moments she was caught unawares. Her hand loosened its grip on the roof tile. In that instant, Charlie fastened his hand like a vice on her wrist. Her eyes flicked up, angry, betrayed. But it was too late. With a wrench Charlie pulled her to the very edge of the roof. Then he jumped, pulling her with him.

As they fell through the warm air, Charlie realised he'd made a serious error of judgement. He'd not accounted for the strong wind. It caught Lily's large skirts, blowing them both back towards the bridge. The stone arch loomed towards them and Charlie's right shoulder connected with an agonising crack. They hit the water with a heavy splash.

Charlie flailed with his legs, but the current was too strong. And now the wooden loading bays finally gave way. The water tore through, restoring the current to its full force of nature. And as Charlie and Lily floundered in the eddying torrent it drove them from the protection of the arches out into the centre of the Thames.

Charlie wove his left arm around Lily's waist to keep her from being ripped away in the flow. She gasped, choked and her head went underwater. Charlie twisted helplessly as her face plunged down. The river rolled them around as he tried desperately to pull her head clear. Then she lolled limply like a rag doll.

Charlie bit back the pain of his shoulder. Lily was unconscious and her skirts were dragging them both down. Gasping with pain he managed to heave her head on to his chest, swimming on his back with his one good arm. Lily was a dead weight, but he thought she might still be breathing.

Charlie looked to both shorelines and steered to the flame-free bank of Southwark.

But the south bank was against the current, and no matter how hard Charlie swam, they were pushed back into the centre. Exhausted, his head began to duck below the waters. Desperate, Charlie kicked towards the opposite shore where the fire was eating angrily into the houses. This time the current was with them, and they half floated and half sank towards the bank.

Finally his feet touched the riverbed as the water became shallower. Charlie dragged his feet through the squelching mud, pulling Lily and her waterlogged skirts with difficulty. He gasped for air on the smoke-filled shore. Lily was still out cold.

Charlie turned to see that they'd drifted ashore outside the city wharfs. The huge warehouses contained hundreds of barrels of pitch and tar, thousands of yards of dry hemp rope, enormous bales of cotton, paper and flax all housed in buildings of thin parched wood. And dotted among all this merchandise were generous measures of gunpowder.

A thin stream of grey puffed gently from the nearest building and Charlie wondered hazily if a docker were enjoying a pipe somewhere among the wares.

Then the world exploded in a ball of flame. Something hot and heavy drove into his chest, driving him up and back down into the shallow water.

Charlie raised his head groggily. Lily was next to him, face down.

Using every last painful ounce of energy in his injured arm he turned her to face upright. Then he sank into unconsciousness.

Chapter 73

Blackstone woke in a cold sweat. It was night. But fire lit the city, casting an eerie red glow through the window.

Thin boys were ranged around him on the kitchen floor. For a moment he thought they were all dead. He was back there. Waking in the dark. Burning in the pit of his belly.

Slowly Blackstone heaved his great weight to standing. The boys slept heavily. They'd been bred to bed down on the floor. Not one stirred as he made his way down the cellar steps.

Blackstone drew a key from his pocket and unlocked the cellar door. A shuffling sound greeted him. He held up his candle. There she was. Teresa.

His wife was sat upright, surrounded by her magical things. As Blackstone drew nearer a rat darted across her face and disappeared into the black depths of the cellar.

Blackstone watched it go. He thought the cellar felt cooler today.

He seated himself opposite his wife. Mounded up by Teresa's dead things and bloodied talismans was Blackstone's food. He liked to keep it safe. Close by. Food didn't keep so well in the damp cellar, but war had removed Blackstone's discrimination.

The dream was still troubling him. He reached for a large half-eaten leg of mutton. It had already fed the boys below for weeks. Blackstone himself had fasted.

He took a knife and began carving meat. The slice through soft flesh. The pink layers mounding up. It soothed him. Blackstone took a slice of meat in bloated fingers and pushed it past his lips. He chewed mechanically.

Once, a long time ago, Blackstone had promised his men they'd eat like this. He thought his exact words had been: 'when it's over we'll eat like kings.'

He mentally probed. The cold terror that had woken him wasn't gone. But it had . . . rearranged itself. The food had numbed him. He cut more meat. Rolled it. Fed it into his mouth.

Then he took a breath.

'I dreamt of you,' he said.

Teresa didn't reply.

'I think,' he continued slowly, 'the devil puts you in my mind.'

Still no response.

'We have a priest,' continued Blackstone. 'I think he'll put these dreams aside.'

He paused, shaved more meat then stood to examine the hoard of food. The bread had been eaten. But there was flour. He peered closer into the sack. Black dents pocked the snowy surface. Weavils. He licked a finger, dipped and tested. The flour was gluey on his tongue but not unpleasant.

He turned back to Teresa. She looked cold, he thought. Blackstone selected a cloak for her, from the piles of clothes. A moth fluttered free. He draped the cloak carefully over her shoulders.

Teresa was angry with him, Blackstone could tell. Some days he brushed her hair and sang to her. But this was not one of those days. Revenge was not coming fast enough.

'God fans our flames,' he assured her. 'London will burn.' He paused. 'Perhaps the marriage papers too.'

Something tugged at the edge of Blackstone's memory. A flicker, no more. He suddenly had a feeling that his missing marriage papers were close.

Was it possible?

After all this time, could he retrieve the papers after all? The power of owning them again. It brought possibilities so rich he could taste them.

'Did you do this?' Blackstone asked Teresa. 'Do you send me a sign?'

He stared for a long time in the dark. Nothing. Perhaps it had been his imagination after all. But something was nagging him now. That the papers were here. Under his own roof.

Blackstone's mind travelled down to the kitchen, where the fireballs were stacked in neat, high piles. Did he have time to search the house? The wind had fuelled the flames better than he'd dared hope. But Blackstone was no fool. He no longer relied on God. Every detail had been taken care of. Every contingency thought through.

Blackstone looked down at the table. The jar of flour was empty. In his hand he held the stripped bone of the mutton joint. Even the cartilage had been gnawed to a nub. He regarded it for a minute, took out his sword and cracked the bone with the heavy handle. Then he began to suck out the marrow.

His wife stared back at him. Blank. Unseeing.

And deep in the dark another pair of eyes blinked out.

Chapter 74

Charlie awoke to the dark waters lapping at his feet. His head was sunk two inches into soft wet mud, and his face felt like scorched leather.

There was a moment of uncertainty and then Charlie knew. He was in hell.

Staring down at him from the jet-black sky was a single blood-red eye. Satan was watching through an air filthy with smuts and cinders.

Charlie raised a hand to his head and then sat up clumsily. He groaned in pain. His shoulder. His shoulder hurt. Then he saw the flaming warehouses.

He was on Thames Street. Now he remembered. Just before the warehouses exploded.

The relief was tempered by his injured shoulder. Charlie muttered a little prayer. It was fifteen shillings to cauterise and amputate. He sat up clumsily and was relieved to find his shoulder supported his weight. His reflection in the water showed new injuries. Burns peppered his face, neck and legs. The trusty leather coat bore a few extra scars but had protected him from chest to mid thigh.

Charlie winced, feeling a thick bruise under his hair and a painful stiffness in his neck. Falling unconscious in the river must have saved most of him from burning. The flames had rolled over the top of him.

How long had he been unconscious? He couldn't tell. It felt like a long time.

The city was burning much higher now. The fire had a fiendish quality. From the placement of the sun in the sky, it was midmorning. He'd lost a night and half a day.

Charlie sat more upright, wrenching his legs from the mud. Then he remembered. Lily. He couldn't see her on the shoreline. Swallowing, Charlie moved his eyes out to the river. No floating red dress there either.

He sat for a moment turning the possibilities over in his mind. Perhaps she had floated back out and been drowned by the river. Or maybe she'd regained consciousness and crept away.

Whilst thinking it over Charlie made a reflexive check of his possessions. He had after all, fallen unconscious in London. His purse and eating knife were still where they should be. A few coins, the tankard. All in order. His fingers reached up to his neck. They paused in disbelief then scrabbled frantically.

His key was gone. At once he knew.

Lily.

'No!' shouted Charlie, striking up a column of water with his clenched fist. 'No!'

He sat for a moment in blank angry despair.

'I knew it,' he muttered. 'I knew I couldn't trust that woman.'

It felt as though she'd taken a part of him.

Charlie punched the wet mud of the low tide again, but less forcefully. The paralysing feeling of desolation was easing now and something of his more usual sanguinity was inching back. He was a thief taker. There wasn't a corner of this city where she could expect to hide.

'And send her to the hangman as a thief besides,' Charlie thought grimly, picking himself up out of the mud.

He noticed for the first time that his shoulder had been tightly bound in red silk. Charlie moved it experimentally. It felt solid. Lily must have torn off part of her dress to bind it. She'd probably saved his arm before robbing him of his most treasured item.

Carefully Charlie pieced over what he knew.

Blackstone was leading the fire to Whitehall. The blue fire worked like a signal, Charlie was sure of it. A signal to fire a guild. Blackstone was using guildhalls and livery houses to tactically advance the flame. He must have guild contacts then. Only guildsmen were allowed in Livery Halls.

But he didn't think Lily knew that. All Lily knew was some convicts who'd sailed on the Mermaid might be in the Fleet. And the Fleet was burned. Where might she go next? Perhaps back to Amesbury, he decided. Try for access to official naval papers. Discover something more of the Mermaid.

Charlie raised a hand to his head, feeling out a bruise with a groan. If Blackstone was advancing the fire to Whitehall, he should try to get a warning to the King. Charlie rejected the idea as soon as it arose. His Majesty was plagued by commoners claiming plots and intrigues. Charlie would be dismissed as a scaremonger and possibly be given a beating into the bargain.

Shouts interrupted his thoughts. Heaving himself up, Charlie staggered to a slippery standing position and surveyed the fiery distance. A gang of men were emerging from the burning wharves. They were armed with cheap swords and cudgels. Charlie sensed their mood from yards away and instinct told him to run. But they were too close and he was trapped between the precipitous muddy shore and the burning city beyond.

'Hold!' shouted a gruff voice.

They were upon him in moments, splashing through the mud. A man with close-cropped hair and bad breath grabbed Charlie by the throat.

'Hold him!' shouted his companion, pulling up the rear. 'Looks like we might have another traitor to hang from the lamppost.'

Chapter 75

Barbara looked up in surprise. She had been in the midst of organising her children to leave the Palace when Lucy Walter had entered unannounced.

The King's first lover had aged, Barbara noticed. The stress of clutching her tenuous claim to courtly favour must be getting to Lucy.

'How did you get in?' Barbara asked, not bothering to disguise her contempt. Relations between the King's first lover and his longest-serving mistress had always been strained.

'My son, Monmouth.' Lucy Walter allowed herself a smile. 'Charles's *first* son,' she stressed the word smugly, 'he still has some loyalty to his mother.' She picked at the glue on a dark horsehair curl.

Barbara raised her eyebrows. 'Even though you deserted him in Holland?'

Lucy ignored the slight and knelt by Barbara's oldest child, who was shepherding the younger three to dress.

'You must be little Anne,' said Lucy, her dimpled face smiling. 'Are you four now?'

'Five,' said Anne. She was staring at Lucy's deeply lined cleavage. Barbara moved forward and took her hand.

Lucy rose, surveying the other children. She adjusted her deep-pink dress. The chaos of flowers and ribbons rippled.

'What little darlings,' she said. 'They take after you.'

'How kind of you to say it,' said Barbara evenly, running an unconscious hand over her own tasteful chemise-dress. 'Charles thinks they look like him.'

The smile dropped from Lucy's face. 'Charles provides well for you,' she said. 'These handsome apartments.'

'What do you want?'

'Leave my son alone. He's barely a man.'

Barbara managed a smile.

'Is that all? It was a fleeting thing. Only a little game I played with Clarence. I've no interest in Monmouth.'

'I know what you do,' replied Lucy. 'You hope to blacken Monmouth. That your boy will be King.' Her eyes dropped to Barbara's four-year-old son, Charles.

Barbara folded him in her skirts. 'Such is talk,' she said, sounding tired. 'Is this all you come for?'

Lucy bit her lip.

'I need carts,' she admitted. 'My fine dresses, jewels . . . Everything I own will burn.'

Barbara suddenly noticed Lucy was wearing an entire jewellery collection, heavy at her throat, wrists and fingers.

'And you come to me?' said Barbara.

'Charles won't hear me,' admitted Lucy, not meeting her eye. 'And I thought . . . you might feel you owed me a kindness. Because of these.'

She opened a pouch at her hip. Inside was a squat, fat ball stamped with a crown and knots.

Barbara was very still.

'What is that?' she asked. 'A fireball?'

'You should know very well,' said Lucy, 'since it was in your apartments. Monmouth,' she added, as Barbara opened her mouth to deny it, 'is not so foolish as you think.'

'How dare he,' muttered Barbara. 'What could a boy like Monmouth know of anything?'

'I'll write to the King,' threatened Lucy. 'Tell him of your deception.'

Barbara shook her head. 'No one would believe you,' she said. 'Your lies are the talk of Westminster.' She began to list them on her fingers. 'You are related to Henry Tudor on your mother's side and have a claim to Hampton Court Palace.' Barbara drew a second finger, 'You and Charles secretly married and Monmouth is the heir to all England.' Barbara shook her head as Lucy reddened.

'And we mustn't forget,' added Barbara, 'that the King of France himself wanted you for his Queen, but you rejected his advances.'

Barbara shook her head. 'You have no talent for lying,' she said gently. 'You've made yourself ridiculous.'

Lucy's face fell.

The youngest child, Charlotte, was tugging at Barbara's skirts now. Unthinkingly she heaved the little girl up on to her hip. Charlotte's tiny hand began reaching for her necklace.

'When fire comes, we discover what we truly hold dear,' said Barbara. She seemed to be arranging her thoughts, angling her neck away from the grasping fingers. 'You come to me for a cart? To keep your dresses from fire?' She kissed her daughter and set her down. 'I am more concerned with my children.'

Lucy reddened under the implication. 'I knew Monmouth would be safe,' she said. 'He's been under Charles's care since he was seven. I must look to my goods, or have nothing.'

'Charles will be sure Monmouth is protected,' said Barbara. 'He loves his children. Even yours.' She sighed. 'Talk to the footman,' she said. 'Once the children are safely taken there should be room in the last cart. You may store some dresses and trunks there.'

Lucy sagged in relief. She nodded, then began fiddling with a bracelet.

'I loved Charles,' she blurted. 'No matter what he told you. About the other men. I truly did love him, in my way. And Monmouth is his, I'm sure of it.' Her eyes were on Barbara's. 'Then you came to Holland and it was too late to make amends.' Lucy gave a little laugh. 'But I always thought I might. I didn't think you would stay so long, Lady Castlemaine.'

Lucy's dark eyes narrowed. 'Do you know what the people call you?'

Barbara shrugged. 'Whore?' she suggested, 'Harlot? Strumpet? I think Clarence calls me "England's ruin".'

But Lucy was shaking her head.

'No,' she said. 'They call you the uncrowned Queen.'

Chapter 76

'Are you a Catholic?' the man demanded of Charlie, pawing for a rosary. He held a crossbow in his free hand. His cropped hair suggested him to be Puritan.

'Do I look like a Catholic?' asked Charlie, batting the questing fingers away. He eyed the men. 'By whose authority do you come mauling citizens?'

The cropped-haired man stood a little more upright. The others clustered closer. Charlie noticed a wooden arm on one and a third man who looked like a weasel.

'The City Watch,' announced the leader proudly. 'Appointed by Parliament.'

Charlie rubbed his shoulder. He nodded to the crossbow.

'Expensive weapon,' noted Charlie, 'for a watchman.'

The man's eyes slid away and Charlie knew he'd guessed right. They'd been bribed by some noble or merchant to protect a private property.

'You're appointed by Parliament to find Catholics?' asked Charlie.

The leader's face faltered. He was chewing wormwood, Charlie realised. Which explained the bitter stink.

'To halt the fire,' replied the watchman. 'And to press any citizen to fight the flames.' He pointed to his crossbow meaningfully.

'Where do you fight fire?' asked Charlie, knowing they were about to press him into service.

The watchman signalled with his shoulder. 'South, near Maiden Lane.'

'The fire goes west,' said Charlie. 'The riverfront is already burned out.'

'We make an important stand,' said the watchman evenly, his eyes daring Charlie to disagree.

'The Strand,' said Charlie, 'is where you should make firebreaks. Between here and Westminster.'

The men eyed each other. The leader sucked his teeth.

'And risk our lives?' he suggested with a barking laugh. 'Those buildings fall.'

'Has Parliament given you no orders?' suggested Charlie. 'No muster stations?'

'Aye.' The leader spat wormwood. 'We've been ordered to fight fire. And press men to do likewise.'

'And if we see any Catholic dogs,' supplied the man with the wooden arm, 'we takes 'em and puts 'em in Bridewell.'

Charlie hesitated. The prisoners on the Mermaid flashed suddenly to mind.

Bridewell Prison. He'd forgotten that it was not only debtors. Political and religious prisoners were also held. And religion or politics might explain why a mysteriously small group were gaoled at sea.

'Unless they resist or throw insults,' weasel-face was sniggering. 'Then it's a worser fate.'

But Charlie was only half listening. The small group of convicts on the Mermaid. Fifteen men. A small sect. Seekers or Quakers. Such men weren't physically dangerous. But their words could undermine the fragile new republic. Better put them out to sea. Out of the way.

'Does Bridewell burn?' Charlie asked.

Weasel-face grinned evilly.

'Fire started up again near there this last hour. Those Catholics in Bridewell will be tight dust before the day is out.'

Charlie looked up at the smoke. He could be at Bridewell long before flames reached it. But he doubted these men would make it easy. Something else struck him.

'Lily's a Catholic,' he muttered to himself. 'Of course she knows Bridewell has religious prisoners.'

Charlie was suddenly sure she'd made the Bridewell connection immediately and kept it to herself. He was marvelling at the depths of her betrayal.

'Catholics started the fire,' said weasel-face, mishearing him. 'Everyone knows it. Catholics and foreigners. They love only Rome and would have us all in thrall to the foreign pope.'

The leader was nodding vigorously.

'They throw fireballs all over the city. What other business could a Catholic have in England,' he demanded, 'if not to plot?'

Charlie was thinking through the best route to Bridewell.

'I'm no good to fight fire,' he said, indicating his shoulder. 'Best find some other men.'

The leader hefted his crossbow.

'They all say that,' he grinned. '"Til we convince 'em otherwise.'

Weasel-face waved his cheap sword.

'Better you obey,' he said. 'If you don't want to fight the fire, then you hate England. Like the Catholics,' he concluded.

'And we've just lynched a nest of Catholics and foreigners from a shop sign,' supplied the man with the wooden arm. 'So you must do what we say.'

Chapter 77

Whitehall was in chaos. Servants had removed the first wave of valuables. But now the supply of carts and carriages was running out.

Queen Catherine of Braganza was vacating her apartments when the first familiar wave of miscarriage hit. She drove back a grimace with effort.

Her eyes sought her maidservant, Dolly. 'Oh, Your Majesty,' said Dolly, her face wracked with sympathy. 'Again?'

'It could be nothing.' Catherine let out a long breath and sat. 'There,' she said. 'I am better.' But she was twisting her rosary over and over in pale fingers.

Dolly raced to the door. The corridors were crowded with servants packing away Catherine's overtly Catholic furniture and possessions. The Portuguese Queen had never tried to disguise her religion.

Dolly was a resourceful girl, born to a middling family of dubious nobility. Dolly had risen to the Queen's side, because her captain father had bestowed her with two gifts – fluent Portuguese and a middle name of Bombay, honouring Catherine's dowry to Charles.

Dolly raised her voice to the servants.

'The Queen wishes to pray for London,' she improvised, shutting the doors. 'Her Majesty will say her prayers alone.'

Catherine eyed Dolly gratefully but was shaking her head.

'My ladies-in-waiting,' she said, reverting to Portuguese. They both knew protocol didn't allow lengthy privacy. The rosary was still skating over the Queen's fingers.

'News of the fire surprised you,' soothed Dolly. 'All will be well. They beat it back on the Strand. Fire won't reach the Palace.'

Catherine fixed her eyes on her favourite religious tapestry. A depiction of St Anna of Avila with a white dove. She slowed her breathing.

There was a knock at the door.

Catherine closed her eyes.

'It's her,' she said. 'Charles is occupied with fire. So she comes to torment me.'

'I can't send her away,' apologised Dolly. 'Not a Lady of the Bedchamber.'

The Queen gritted her teeth and breathed out.

'The King bestowed her with a great honour,' she managed. 'We must bear it with good grace.'

Dolly pulled back the door and there as predicted was Barbara Castlemaine. She looked less composed than usual. The decorative auburn curls had drooped a little and the self-satisfied look in her violet eyes was muted.

'Her Majesty, Queen Catherine of Braganza, receives you,' said Dolly, curtseying with as much disdain as she could manage.

Barbara shot her a look.

'I had forgotten you attended Her Majesty,' she murmured. 'Such a low-born girl.'

'Noble is as noble does,' said Dolly, anxiety for the Queen making her daring.

Barbara smiled icily. 'Perhaps in the City Guilds. Here in the Palace we value birth.'

Dolly glowered and retreated a little.

Catherine stood with difficulty.

'You're quite well?' asked Barbara, missing nothing.

Catherine managed a smile. She looked to Dolly. 'Can you tell her something?' she said, speaking Portuguese.

Barbara's pretty features puckered at the unfamiliar language.

'The Queen heard news of the fire and is distressed,' said Dolly smoothly, lying too fast for Barbara to doubt. 'Unlike some ladies she is sensitive,' added Dolly meaningfully.

'I don't doubt it,' said Barbara, deliberately speaking fast to confuse the Queen. 'Her Majesty fainted when Charles appointed me to her bedchamber.'

'Tell us why you are here,' said Catherine in thickly accented tones. Her face suggested she'd missed the jibe. 'Fire comes. Why do you not look to your own apartment?'

Barbara's face darkened. 'I saw your accounts. Some of your possessions became mixed up with mine, in the jostle to load the carts.'

Queen Catherine flushed crimson at the obvious lie.

'How dare you,' she began. 'You take advantage of the fire, to pry into my things.'

Her Majesty's English improved greatly when her temper was raised, Dolly noted.

'You give money,' continued Barbara, 'to Master Blackstone.' She arched an eyebrow. 'So it seems you would do battle with me.'

Chapter 78

Charlie looked to the men grappling with a firehook. They were skinny and sweating, faces resigned. Several had black eyes. The watchmen were keeping close guard, pointing out which houses should fall.

The long firehook was working on a half-destroyed house. Its rake-like head was pulling the last storey to a pile of broken fragments.

Charlie recognised the building they protected. It was the Cutlers' Hall. Hardly a key firebreak. Charlie turned to them accusingly.

'How much are the cutlers paying you,' he demanded, 'to press these poor men?'

The watchmen spat wormwood. 'We take no bribe,' he said, fingering the expensive crossbow. 'This hall is in the path of the fire. Houses must be pulled either side.'

'To save a burned-out riverfront?' said Charlie. 'Whitehall is in danger. You should be protecting the Palace.'

'The King already defends it,' said the watchman. 'Been issuing orders and promising ale these last few hours.'

Charlie considered. So the King already knew Whitehall was threatened. From what he'd seen from the riverfront, whatever fire-fighting His Majesty had orchestrated was too little too late.

'The Cutlers' Guild have only just finished paying for their new guildhall,' the watchman continued. 'They've no money for another if this burns. Many fine swords and pommels the cutlers make for this city,' he added.

Charlie shook his head in disgust.

'Have a heart,' he said. 'These men you press. They own little more than a wooden plate and a chair. You let their homes burn so they might save a nobleman's sword?'

'Money rules London,' said the watchman unapologetically. He waved his crossbow threateningly. 'And you don't have enough to desert your fire duties.'

Charlie looked to the beleaguered men.

Their unwieldy firehook was as tall as a house with three prongs at the top. At the base they coordinated clumsily to grapple private houses and shops either side of the Cutlers' Guild. Charlie saw instantly that they were pulling from the wrong side. The demolished building would fall north, straight into the path of the whirling cinders and high breeze.

'Hold!' he shouted, jogging to where the hook was fixing.

The nearest man turned to Charlie. He was shaven headed, with wheals on his scalp from wearing a cheap hog-hair wig. But he had a quiet authority despite meagre clothes and soot-streaked hands.

'I'm the parish man hereabouts' he said. 'John Waverly.'

'You pull the wrong way,' said Charlie, catching his breath. 'That building will send tinder straight to the flames.'

Waverly assessed the direction of the firehook and nodded. 'We had a kind of order. Then Parliament sent those jackals,' he said, pointing to the watchmen. 'And now all is chaos. They rove around pressing commoners who can't fight back. Throwing mixed orders.

So we have old and injured men. No cavalry, no one with experience of crisis. And confusion.'

'The watchmen have been paid by the Cutlers' Guild,' said Charlie. 'They care only for the guildhall.'

Waverly shook his head.

'They should be shamed. We're pressed here whilst our homes burn. We should be allowed to take our things to safety.'

The high winds were whipping heavy flaming ash into the air as he spoke. It was dropping on the dry rooftops of neighbouring houses.

'Raise and fix!' shouted the nearest watchman waving his cudgel. 'Pull that building!' He was pointing to a modest half-timbered house.

A female shout issued out. They looked up to see a woman. She had thrown open the little leaded window and was leaning halfway out.

'You have no authority!' she shouted. 'Only the King can grant permission to pull houses.'

The lead watchman's face twisted in annoyance.

'Who let that silly bitch back in her house?' he demanded.

Charlie looked at the Cutlers' sign. A gold elephant and castle, blackening in the smoke. He sensed an opportunity and turned to Waverly.

'Those watchmen know nothing of what they guard,' said Charlie. 'If they see riches inside the Cutlers' Guild, they might abandon their posts to loot. You and the others could escape to your homes.'

Waverly shook his head. 'The cutlers have cleared away their fine things,' he said. 'Trunks of swords. All kinds of expensive weapons. Huge tusks. All were carried away.'

'Guilds have sacred objects which can't be removed,' said Charlie. 'Relics to make promises with and share guild secrets.'

'I know it,' Waverly shrugged. 'I hear the fishmongers have a wooden carp. Such things are not worth looting.'

'Cutlers are wealthy,' said Charlie. 'They are no fishmongers or cooks. Their rites likely use fine swords or daggers.'

It was a guess but Waverly seemed to see the sense in it.

'None but guildsmen may look inside a guildhall,' he said uncertainly. 'They are closed to common men.'

'Yet no guildsmen are here to defend it,' said Charlie. 'They look to their own goods, whilst you are pressed here.'

Shouts were coming from the female house owner and the lead watchman.

'This is the time,' said Charlie. 'The leader is distracted.'

The watchman was by the occupied home now, waving a tinderbox. He punched a hole through the leaded window and lit the curtains.

'What think you now, mistress?' he demanded, looking up. 'I say fire comes. None will blame us for pulling a burning house.'

He turned back to the pressed men and spat wormwood.

'Raise and fix!' shouted the watchmen. 'She'll come out soon enough when she smells the smoke.'

Chapter 79

Queen Catherine's dark eyes looked to the ground. She looked back up at Barbara Castlemaine.

'Blackstone is kind to Catholics,' said the Queen. 'I give money for paupers of my religion. Nothing more.'

But Barbara knew a lie when she heard one. She moved a little closer.

'I think you know too well,' said Barbara, 'what kind of man Blackstone is. You dare use his alchemy against me?'

The Queen let out a long sigh.

'I have no wish to fight you, Lady Castlemaine,' she said. 'You have won. The King appointed you my personal lady, though I swore you would not be. You have four children by him. Two sons. I have none.' The words stuck a little. 'My great sadness,' Catherine continued, 'is not that I have lost.' She shook her head. 'It is that you, *Lady Castlemaine*,' she rolled the title grandly, 'are not grateful. Had I half your blessings I would smile the long day through. Yet you always want more.'

There was a shocked silence.

The Queen looked at Dolly.

'I feel unwell,' she said shortly in Portuguese. 'I will make my toilet alone.'

Catherine shuffled away leaving Dolly uncertain how to explain. It was unthinkable for Her Majesty to visit the bathroom without a servant.

Then something occurred to her.

'How would you know?' challenged Dolly as the Queen exited. 'How would you know his name?'

Barbara turned to her distractedly. She'd been watching the Queen absent herself in disbelief.

'Blackstone,' said Dolly. 'How would *you* know what kind of man he is?'

Barbara turned full force on Dolly.

'You dare to presume,' she said, her voice raising, 'to question me? You may not even *speak* to me. You are a gutter-born girl far above your station.'

'You are a cuckoo,' said Dolly, 'in the Queen's court.'

'I?' Barbara laughed. 'Look around you child. See you any of England in this chamber? Your Queen hates this country and always has. She doesn't speak our language. There is not a single English furnishing in her apartments. And she spends her days praying to Catholic idols for her homeland.'

Dolly set her mouth and was silent.

Sensing her opponent was on the ropes Barbara turned venomous.

'You know what they say?' she hissed. 'That Charles's advisors beg him to divorce. She cannot give him a child. They beg him to do it. He is too soft-hearted.'

Barbara raised herself a little taller and adjusted her silken dress.

'That is what you hope,' said Dolly. 'But you will never be Queen.'

Barbara's violet eyes widened in surprise.

'Is that what you think,' she said, 'that I want to be Queen? You silly girl. It is a prison sentence. The best freedom for a woman is mistress.'

'Until her looks fade,' said Dolly. 'Then a mistress's freedom seems hard bought.'

The Queen appeared in the doorway. She was deathly pale. The spite in Barbara's face ebbed away. She chewed her lip.

'Look to your lady,' whispered Barbara, keeping her eyes away from the Queen's skirts.

Dolly moved to the bed but Barbara shook her head.

'They examine the sheets for blood,' she said, waving an arm to the courtiers beyond the chamber. 'Use your own under-clothes.' Barbara's eyes flicked to the door. 'I'll keep her ladies away,' she muttered, hastening to it. 'Those harpies look for the first sign of weakness.'

Dolly nodded and something passed between them. Barbara rustled away. Queen Catherine sat.

'She isn't so bad,' said Dolly with a little smile.

'That's because she's won,' said Catherine with a pained expression. 'When she's losing she's capable of anything.'

She raised her dark eyes to Dolly.

'The King makes me ridiculous with his whores. I must be friend to Barbara, who plots to make her children royal. I must forebear Louise's whorish clothes and manners.' She shook her head. 'And the other one. The one who lies.'

'Lucy Walter,' supplied Dolly.

'Saying her son is true heir. Then denying it to my face. She should be hanged for treason.'

The Queen shook her head. The elaborately styled hair rattled.

'They think Barbara is the only ruthless woman in court,' she said, a sudden fire in her eyes. 'They think me meek, because I pray. But I know God's power. Do you know what I did, when they told me I must leave my beloved Catholic homeland and wed a Protestant King on a cold island?'

'You went to your shrine,' said Dolly uncertainly, because there was a feverish look in the Queen's pale face. 'In Lisbon.'

The Queen nodded.

'I went to my shrine in Lisbon. And I prayed to God above, that I might never bear this heathen country a child.'

Chapter 80

The watchman waved his crossbow at the pressed men. The house he'd just flamed was roaring to life.

'Pull the house!' he demanded. 'It fires!'

The house owner appeared shouting and gesticulating.

'Pull the Cutlers' Guild now whilst their attention is disturbed,' Charlie urged John. 'Use the firehooks. I'll get inside and throw out what relics I can find. The watchman will fall on them and you can escape.'

'How do I know you won't make off with the relics?' asked John.

'They're sacred things,' said Charlie. 'Every cutler in London would want my head. I couldn't fence them without being lynched.'

A gust of wind caused the nearby fire to roar suddenly.

'Now,' urged Charlie, pointing. 'Set the firehook there.'

'How can you be sure fire will go that way?'

Charlie hesitated. 'I was a cinder thief,' he admitted. 'A good one.'

He saw the warmth go out of Waverly's eyes. The parish man turned to the battered men.

'On my word!' he called. 'Heave!'

The firehook was raised, like a giant rake striking at the dark sky. The men wielding the thick pole stumbled under its weight and for a moment Charlie thought Waverly meant to ignore his advice. Then the parish man pointed to the Cutlers' Hall. The metal firehook was aligned to the roof, then its three huge prongs were sent smashing into the wooden shingles. The hook sunk deep into the top rafter.

Shouts went up from the watchmen. The leader made towards the firehook at a run, his crossbow raised. Charlie raced to the front of the Cutlers' Hall.

'You!' the watchman was raising his crossbow inexpertly. 'Get away from the Hall!'

Charlie eyed the solid guild. Unless the firehook worked there was no way in.

And the well-built hall was resisting its destroyers. Waverly and his men heaved, faces red from effort. But the timbers held firm.

A bolt shuddered deep into the wall next to Charlie. He looked to see the watchman loading for a second shot.

'Get back to your fire duties!' he called, taking a second aim.

'Heave,' shouted John, and the counterweight of the pole began to do its part. With a shriek of twisting timbers the joists began to give and the central beam was wrenched forward.

The half-timbered frontage of the Cutlers' Guild cracked then began to split.

'Go,' panted Waverly to Charlie as the men staggered back with the pole. Timber and plaster crashed down.

'Back!' shouted Waverly, as the momentum of the falling house picked up in pace and fell towards them in a tirade of splintered wood. 'Back!'

The front of the Cutlers' Guild was completely ripped away now, exposing the rooms inside. They were more elaborate than Charlie had ever imagined. No wonder the guilds kept their insides secret. They'd be robbed daily.

Rich decorations and strange murals adorned the walls. A huge carving bore the words 'Freemen of the City. Breed not birth right.'

Sparks from the nearby burning building were already wheeling through the air like glowing assassins. They began settling on the open walls of the guild, fanned by the high wind.

Charlie took a quick assessment. The downstairs was a large hall. This was where the cutlers held their dinners. To set trade prices for the swords and weapons they made.

Rings of candlewax and sword marks suggested ritualistic practices were carried out here. It reminded Charlie of an otherworldly church.

There were no trapdoors down. No tapestries to hide chambers or doors leading off.

Upstairs were a number of closed wooden doors. Charlie made for the stair and raced up. He vaulted over a step which was being fanned into flame and made it to the top.

He arrived on a landing which had been cleared of goods. There was a large map marked with jagged red crosses.

The map told of places in London where unlicensed cutlers were trading, Charlie guessed. The Cutlers' Guild would send men to destroy their goods and equipment.

The wall had been torn away, and Charlie could see the street and the watchmen below. A thud sounded above his head. He looked up. A crossbow dart. Charlie glanced down to see the watchman was reloading. He was a bad shot, Charlie had already deduced, looking at the arrow lodged high above him. But it wouldn't do to hang around. Quickly he assessed the closed doors. One bore a symbol he'd seen before.

A pyramid with an eye in it. The symbol for enlightenment used by alchemists all over the city.

Another bolt sailed through the air. It landed closer this time, lodging in the floor near his foot. Charlie opened the door with the symbol on it and dived inside.

The room was small, lined floor to ceiling with red fabric. A table held a collection of bones, laid out like some kind of holy relic. Embroidery depicted unfamiliar people and places. They were in the style of bible scenes. But there was nothing here Charlie had seen in any church. One showed a man in a red robe and gold ceremonial hat with a pointed staff. Another depicted a moon with a woman's face, over a rolling sea.

Tarot, Charlie thought, as the images settled into place. *These are tarot cards.*

Charlie made out frankincense on the air and some other burned smell. Then he saw the cutlers' livery and weapons. They were hung ceremonially on the far wall.

He'd been right about the expensive swords. There were seven, each exquisitely crafted in fine metals and jewels. They must be the works of the master cutler, thought Charlie. Kept secret and safe to show initiates what they might one day aspire to.

Quickly Charlie seized on them.

Charlie was halfway to the door when he saw the tapestry. It depicted a tree. A tree with symbols. 'The Tree of Life,' said Charlie, pausing to stare with the swords locked in his arms. What was it doing in the Cutlers' Guild? It occurred to him that Lily might know.

He didn't have time to dwell. Shouts from the street suggested the watchmen were moving in on the others. Quickly Charlie broke on to the landing and threw the priceless swords on to the soft mud of the street.

Waverly looked up at Charlie. Then across to the swords. Temptation glimmered in his eyes.

'If you take a sword,' shouted Charlie. 'The cutlers will hunt you for the rest of your days. Let the watchmen bear that burden and go to your wife.'

Waverly stood as the watchman moved towards the glistening treasure. Then Waverly pulled back, gesturing his men to follow him.

Charlie raced back down the stair. On the street watchmen closed on the swords. Charlie switched back into the city streets, leaving them to their treasure. Guild artefacts were a poisoned chalice. They couldn't be sold or fenced.

Charlie headed for Bridewell wondering if he'd be paid to find the cutlers' swords again when the fire was burned out.

Chapter 81

The priest stood, blinking against the candlelight, tattered clothes hanging from his muscular chest. He reminded Blackstone of a mangy bear, chained and alert as the dogs readied to strike.

Blackstone had made a makeshift church in the back room of his house. The boys had been amazed to find a raggedy priest there, ready to give them Holy Communion.

One by one the boys approached him. The priest lifted his heavy manacles, tipped wine, offered bread. Incense poured up from a smoking tankard by his feet.

'Body of Christ,' he intoned. 'Blood of Christ.'

The priest turned to Blackstone and there was the look again. Horror. Disgust. They'd known each other during the war. And though the priest was not a man easily shaken, Blackstone's transformation openly shocked him.

'You don't take the Eucharist?' he said to Blackstone as the boys retreated, chewing.

Blackstone shook his head. 'Will you hear my confession?' he asked.

The priest tipped up the jug of blessed wine and drank it to the dregs. 'You wish to confess to a heretic priest?'

'I have no other.'

'Very well.' The priest licked his lips. 'In here?'

Blackstone nodded. He waved the boys away.

'You're still bound by the laws of the Catholic church?' Blackstone asked the priest. 'Despite that?'

He was pointing to a tattoo just visible beneath the priest's ragged shirt. Its lines had bled and faded greenish over the years. But the shape was still clear. The Tree of Life. Its circles scattered the priest's chest, marred with deep scars.

The priest smiled.

'Thomas,' he said, 'I'm bound by priesthood. The same as I always was.' He tapped his chest. 'This is a different understanding,' he said. 'A meditation on life on earth. I'm still a Catholic.'

'Mystics and sorcery,' said Blackstone. 'That's what ruined us, Torr. That's what drove us apart.'

'No,' said Torr. 'You drove us apart.' His eyes flashed. 'You may keep me here, Thomas. You may force me to minister to your boys and take your confession. But you know these chains won't hold me.'

'They will,' said Blackstone. 'Consider them the price of your heresy.'

'My heresy created your cursed treasure,' said Torr. 'The treasure you stole. The papers you lost.'

His eyes met Blackstone's.

'What happened to you, Thomas?'

Blackstone looked back steadily. 'That man you knew is gone. Don't try to look for him.' His eyes were dead ice.

Torr shook his head.

'Conjuror's tricks,' said Blackstone dismissively. 'That's all you learned in Holland. Your interests brought you nothing.'

'They've brought me peace,' said Torr. 'Shouldn't you like that?'

'Then hear my confession,' demanded Blackstone gruffly, 'Let me be at peace for a while at least.'

'As you wish.' Torr made the sign of the cross.

'I have seen Teresa.' Blackstone's eyes were closed.

'You said Teresa was dead,' said Torr carefully.

'She came to me in a dream.'

Torr let out a breath. He had feared Blackstone had finally lost his mind.

'She told me . . .' Blackstone was speaking with difficulty. He stared at Torr. 'Teresa told me she was in hell.'

Torr opened his mouth to reply, but Blackstone continued.

'Her face was burned,' he said. 'And her long hair scorched away. She said . . . she said that demons bound her to a wheel. That they did things to her. Dreadful things.'

His face was expressionless.

'Teresa told me . . .' he continued stonily, 'that they make her confess. To signing the marriage certificate. They make her confess it over and over.'

'Tell me,' he whispered, 'that they can't hurt her in death as they did in life.'

'You're certain she took her own life?' asked Torr.

Blackstone shook his head.

'My memories are scattered. Plague took things. I can't be sure. Of anything. Most of that year is . . . nothing.'

But there was something. Even as Blackstone said the words he knew. Memories just at the edge of his grasping. A missing key.

'Thoughts come to me,' added Blackstone. 'Things I don't know . . . I don't know if they're real.' He was shaking his head, eyes closed tight in pain. 'My father and my sister. I think she wanted to marry. He was angry. Thought her disobedient. I remember . . . There's a picture in my head. Of him hurting her. Worse than anything he did to me.'

Blackstone's scarred fists were balled tightly.

'He can't have done what I think he did. My father was devout. Family was sacred to him.'

'From what I heard of your father,' said Torr, 'he was very strict with his household. Your mother and sister weren't allowed off the family estate.'

'Women must be strictly governed,' said Blackstone. 'Or they fall to base ways. You need only look to my poor wife,' he added.

'Teresa was responsible for her own life before God,' said Torr. 'She was obliged to preserve it for her own salvation. If, in her arrogance, she committed violence against God's gift, then she could not be allowed into heaven.'

'And if she wasn't a suicide? If I'm mistaken? Can she not be buried decently?'

Torr shook his head.

Blackstone took in a great gasp of air.

'She made spells,' said Torr. 'Witchcraft, Thomas.'

There was a pause.

'Then tell me what can be done.' Blackstone's voice came louder than he meant. He looked around and dropped it to a whisper. 'Tell me what can be done, Torr. For the Brotherhood. For the love we once bore each other. Tell me what can be done.'

Torr looked at his manacles, his dirty shirt.

'Teresa was a witch,' he said. His eyes lifted to meet Blackstone's. 'So you must make a holy sacrifice for her soul. Then you must burn her.'

Chapter 82

Prisoners were pelting out of the gates as Charlie neared Bridewell. Some stumbled on ulcerated legs. Others carried skin and bone children. Fire was already cresting the east side of the prison. Charlie could hear the screams of the Bedlam maniacs in the north quarter.

His breathing quickened. Bridewell was an enormous ranging sort of prison. Some cells were half a mile apart. He might not be too late.

The thick wooden door leading inside was ajar as Charlie approached. The prison was an ex-palace of Henry VIII with the thick walls and fortressing of a bygone military monarchy. So there was no heavy gatehouse. No portcullis.

Streams of prisoners were thinning now. The older and more infirm were hobbling. But Charlie still could hear howls of many more in the endless rooms beyond.

There were no gaolers and at first he assumed they'd fled. Bridewell was an open prison like the Fleet. It housed disorderly paupers, children and religious fundamentalists. But there were no officials by the benches where prisoners sat to be memorised.

Charlie moved into the deeper prison, his breathing quickening. Likely gaolers were roaming inside trying to restore order. In the chaos they might mistake him for a prisoner. But if he could find people still confined, he could release them in return for information. Better yet, he might find Lily.

Charlie passed into the first large room where prisoners could meet visitors. It was large, airy, built for a King. The floor was covered with lice-infested straw and a corner was stained in a high arc of urine and mounded with excrement.

He heard shouts from the courtyard beyond. Then another clutch of prisoners burst forth, stampeding through the visitor room towards the gate. Charlie flattened himself against the piss-soaked wall and watched them run. Then he moved into the large courtyard. It was slung with the deserted works of hard labour. Hempen ropes abandoned. Rope-beating hammers were ominously absent.

Charlie sucked at his scarred lip. He didn't like this. Somewhere in the prison someone wielded those hammers. And a desperate pauper was more dangerous than a gaoler.

Bridewell comprised two enormous courtyards bordered by a thick brick fortress building. It was five storeys high in places, elaborate and seemingly never-ending. To the side of the courtyard were Bridewell's long corridors and rooms. Charlie stepped inside. It was darker in here. Thick walls to protect a King and many rooms leading off. There were no candles or braziers, only slim patches of dim light from small high windows.

The row of doors were all open. He walked along, glancing quickly inside each large room. They were ranged with straw-filled cot beds, piled with filth and empty of people. The prisoners had all broken out. No guards to be seen. Something wasn't right. There was a scrabbling sound and Charlie froze. Then a chicken strutted from one of the cells, cocked an eye at the long corridor and began pecking at a stray pile of straw.

There was another movement out of the corner of his eye and Charlie dodged just in time. A burly man came hurtling from behind an open door. He held a thick-handled whip and a cudgel in his meaty hands. A gaoler, Charlie realised. And he was headed towards him with murder in his eyes.

Chapter 83

The map lay unrolled over Somerset House's largest table top. The King paced then turned in an angry movement.

'Why is there no recent map?' he demanded.

Clarence bowed uneasily and began toying with the hem of his doublet. 'The new maps are kept by Parliament, Your Majesty. For military reasons.'

'Military reasons?'

'Parliament decreed that Your Majesty's troops don't have maps of London,' he said carefully. 'A large body of armed militia . . .' his voice quavered. 'Soldiers might seize power. During Your Majesty's absence such a thing happened in Scotland . . .'

The King cut him off with an agitated wave.

'I know what happened in Scotland. Do not speak to me as though I were a child. Scotland is not why Parliament take maps from my Naval Office. It is *my* power they fear, not that of my army.'

He sat down, resting his hand on his forehead.

'Amesbury thinks this is a war,' he said, looking up. 'He recognises the hand of a general in the spread of the fire.'

Clarence looked shocked.

'It's a pincer movement,' said Amesbury, pointing to the map. 'Fire comes in strangely from the north and south. The Candlemakers' Guild burned, but it was nowhere near the main flame. Same with the Saddlers' Hall.'

Amesbury marked them out with his finger. 'It forces us to guard the flanks,' he concluded, 'whilst the fire turns west. To the Palace.'

'Amesbury fears for the Palace,' said Charles. 'But there's a lot of brick and stone between the Strand and Westminster.' He shook his head.

'Every day we're hounded by commoners claiming a plot on my crown,' he decided. 'I won't act by fear of plot. It's a simple fire, Amesbury. I won't doubt my people any longer.'

He stared at the map.

'Do you still think I should keep my troops from the city?' he demanded of Clarence.

'It's a fire,' said Clarence carefully. 'Not a military matter. Parliament law is quite clear that His Majesty's troops may only be deployed . . .'

'By God, Clarence!' Amesbury's fist slammed into the heavy table. 'Citizens are freely looting. Foreigners and Catholics are being lynched in the streets. Every gatehouse is a chaos of fists and escaping carts. If this isn't a military matter I don't know what is. Civil order is gone. Entirely gone!'

'London is burning,' agreed the King. 'It's time to act.' He put a hand to his forehead. 'Where is my brother?' he demanded. 'James was summoned hours ago. I need his knowledge of the city and the naval troops.'

'A letter was sent,' said Amesbury. 'He isn't in his apartments. I imagine he's with a girl.'

Charles shook his head. 'You misjudge my brother,' he said. 'James may seem feckless at court. But he's a seafaring man. No sailor doubts his leadership.'

'There's not a man in your navy who wouldn't give his life for the Duke of York,' agreed Amesbury. 'But we have a city on fire, not a ship under cannon fire.'

'James performs best in a crisis,' said Charles. 'He'll surprise you.' He thought for a moment. 'Call Monmouth,' he said. 'My son should learn of these things. He can take a battle post.'

Amesbury nodded but his mouth was set in a grim line. Charles was relying on a fifteen-year-old boy and the biggest lecher in court for his defences. This couldn't end well.

Chapter 84

Charlie dodged left as the gaoler struck. He took in his opponent. Beady eyes sunk deep in a well-fed face. Thick forearms. Sturdy legs.

The whip flailed towards Charlie's exposed shins. He jumped aside.

'Back!' commanded the gaoler. 'In the cells, dog!'

Charlie was too experienced to fight armed men willingly. Surgery was costly and uncertain. He could dodge until the outsized gaoler tired, land a few good blows. But he could sense uncertainty in the other man. So he tried for a trick.

'You strike at a King's man!' Charlie shouted, loading his voice with affront and entitlement.

The gaoler looked at Charlie's bare feet, then at his passably fashionable leather coat. Confusion rippled his heavy features.

Seizing the moment, Charlie pulled out the empty marriage papers he'd taken from Torr's cellar.

'I come from court,' he said, taking his chances the gaoler couldn't read. The frozen expression of panic told him he'd guessed correctly. 'King's orders,' he continued, waving the official-looking papers. 'I come to inform his gaolers of the fire.'

The gaoler lowered his whip uncertainly. He was still eyeing Charlie's feet.

'And I'll relay to His Majesty of the squalid conditions you keep,' continued Charlie. 'To avoid treading in shit from your prisoners I was forced to remove my shoes.'

The gaoler hesitated. 'They keep animals,' he said apologetically. 'It's mostly pig and chicken shit, you see. The prisoners make their leavings in the Fleet.'

The gaoler made a clumsy bow.

'Does His Majesty say we shall be paid for the prisoners?' he asked. His little eyes were shifting about. 'There is already fire on the north side,' he added. 'But we know not whether to release them. Does His Majesty say we'll still earn our shilling?'

Charlie nodded. 'Release them and you'll still be paid,' he said. 'You have the word of the King.'

The prospect of information on Lily occurred to him.

'A girl came here,' said Charlie. 'One of the King's favourites,' he improvised. 'Gypsy in looks. Dark-haired. Red dress . . .'

'The Catholic?' the gaoler cut him off. 'Catholic girl?'

Charlie hesitated. 'How would you know she was Catholic?'

'We searched her,' said the gaoler in a tone which suggested he had every right. 'Pretty girl,' he added. 'We always search 'em well. The nice ones. Searched her and found a rosary.'

'Did she have a key?' asked Charlie. 'A foreign-looking one? Double sided?'

The gaoler nodded. Charlie felt relief flood through him. She still had the key.

'Did she ask about some prisoners here?' asked Charlie. 'From long ago. On a ship?'

The gaoler nodded and rearranged his testicles.

'That's right,' he said. 'Asking about prisoners. You say she's a favourite with the King?'

'Yes,' said Charlie. 'Did you tell her what she wanted to know?'

The gaoler coughed out a sort of laugh and shook his head.

'No religious prisoners in Bridewell from so long ago. Cromwell made us set them free fifteen years back. Old Ironsides believed in freedom of worship,' he added, as though he disagreed strongly with this.

'How long ago was the girl here?' asked Charlie, ignoring his disappointment at the dead end. More important was finding his key.

'She's still here,' said the gaoler, as though this should be obvious.

Charlie's heart pounded.

'She's still here? Where?'

'She was a Catholic,' repeated the gaoler slowly, as though Charlie were slow of understanding. 'They're all over London start-ing fires.'

'So you told her nothing,' confirmed Charlie impatiently. 'Then where did she go?'

'We told her nothing,' agreed the gaoler. 'And we locked her up. In the High Cells. Where the bad people are.'

Chapter 85

Enoch was heaving the lead cauldron on to the rooftop. His bad eye was throbbing in the heat and sweat poured down his face.

Jacob was rolling a barrel up on to the roof. His initiation wound was paining him again. He stopped to stare at the blazing London skyline. Fire was everywhere. Master Blackstone's plan was working.

'Careful!' called Enoch, pointing to the barrel. 'It's Bringer of Death inside. Burns if you spill it.'

Jacob raised the crown and three knots on his forearm. It was burned deeper than any other initiate. 'You think I'll not be careful?'

They smiled at one another. There was camaraderie between the boys now.

'Steady the barrel,' Enoch instructed. 'You have the flame?'

Jacob nodded. 'We await the signal,' he said, wiping sweat from his face.

They stood for a moment, smoke flowing over them in great clouds, as the city around them burned.

'I think you were right,' said Jacob after a moment.

Enoch's bloodshot blind eye twitched.

'About the higher initiation,' continued Jacob. 'I don't think he ever means it for us low boys.'

'Don't matter now, does it?' said Enoch philosophically. 'All burns.'

'I think he tricked us,' continued Jacob. 'Told us we'd be part of an avenging army. But what he really wanted was our guild passwords.'

Enoch turned to him in interest.

'He asked you, didn't he,' said Jacob, knowing the answer, 'the motto to enter your guild?'

Enoch nodded.

'Me too,' said Jacob. 'Now he fires the guildhalls. That's how the signal works.'

Jacob pointed to the lead cauldron high on the roof.

'When we light it, they fire the Apothecaries' Hall. Your old hall,' he added, looking at Enoch's damaged eye.

'How did you know that's my guild?' asked Enoch.

'Seen a boiled eyeball before, in apothecary apprentices,' said Jacob. 'They make you stand too near the flasks when they bubble.' He heaved up a scrawny leg. 'Got my own,' he added. 'Carpenter's boy.' Enoch looked at a flattened knee-cap. 'From chiselling wood,' said Jacob proudly. 'Hours on your knees.'

They were silent for a moment, looking up at the huge flames.

'I'm leaving,' said Enoch suddenly. 'After this signal. I mean to run away.' He hesitated. 'Come with me.' His good eye settled on his friend imploringly.

Jacob looked away. 'Did you hear what Master Blackstone did this morning?' he said, not looking at his friend.

Enoch shook his head slowly.

'One of the boys brought a girl back,' said Jacob, fixing his gaze dead ahead to the city. 'Blackstone found them together.'

''S against the rules,' said Enoch, his voice tight, 'girls.'

Jacob nodded. 'Blackstone made him . . . He said the girl was wicked. They cleansed her.'

Both boys were silent for a moment. They had ideas of what this meant.

'Blackstone talks of unpure women in his sleep,' confessed Enoch, feeling sick. 'I've heard him. Says they fester and spread sin.'

Jacob looked away.

'He screams about his father too,' said Enoch. 'Like he's being tortured.'

Suddenly a blue flame flared in the distance. Enoch was on his feet, bad eye swivelling.

'There!' Enoch pointed. 'Ready the barrel.' Jacob heaved it up to the lead cauldron. But his foot slipped on the tiled roof and the barrel twisted from his grasp.

'No!' Enoch dived for the falling barrel.

The barrel hit the rooftop and split. Enoch closed his arms around it, soaking his chest in liquid. He screamed in agony. The Bringer of Death was burning into his skin.

Jacob raced to his aid, but Enoch waved him back.

'Send the signal,' he gasped, through gritted teeth. 'Or Blackstone will have your guts.'

Jacob hesitated. 'There's not enough left in the barrel.'

'There's half,' spat Enoch. 'It might be enough. He'll kill us both if we don't.'

Jacob heaved up the half-empty barrel and managed to fit it into the cauldron. Bringer of Death streamed into the lead. A fountain of steam poured up.

'Flame it!' managed Enoch as the agony bit deep into his chest.

Jacob wielded the flame and a font of blue fire rose majestically upwards. With only half the Bringer of Death, the light was smaller than usual.

The boys exchanged panicked glances. It wasn't high enough.

Then the fire was answered with another blue flame and then another. The final flame flared by the Apothecaries' Guild. The sonorous rumble of an explosion echoed out.

Enoch was gasping in pain. Jacob helped him off the rooftop and on to the street.

'Is it bad?' asked Enoch, taking in the crowded streets near Moor Gate. The gatehouse was packed in both directions.

'No,' lied Jacob, 'we'll find water.' He looked desperately to the citizens moving possessions out of London. Country folk, who'd heard how much their carts could be rented for, were trying to steer traps and horses into the blazing city.

'It won't work,' stammered Enoch, struggling to make words through the pain. 'The Elixir.'

'He burns!' shouted Jacob in panic. 'Help! Somebody!'

Heads turned in the crowded street. They saw the burned boy and recoiled. It was only then Enoch truly realised how bad the burn must be. Faces were contorted in horror. Enoch risked a glance down and felt vomit rise up. There was no skin left on his chest.

Jacob grabbed a pitcher of milk from a reluctant woman and threw it. Nothing. No relief. The burn continued to blaze.

'He won't live,' muttered the woman, snatching back her tankard and eyeing Enoch's burned body. 'Best get him to a priest.'

Enoch gritted his teeth. His good eye had rolled back in his head.

'No!' cried Jacob. He shook Enoch's fainting form. 'No.' Jacob's voice was firm. 'What you said before. You're right. We'll escape together.' He was shouting in Enoch's face, desperately looking for signs of life. The boy lolled, breathing fast.

'We'll go to the country, Enoch,' pressed Jacob, 'he'll never find us. We've both got trades . . .'

Enoch was trying to speak and Jacob brought his ear close to hear over the noise of the crowd and the fire.

'Anthony,' croaked Enoch.

'What?'

'That's my name.' Enoch managed a smile. 'Anthony Cary.'

Jacob took his hand. 'Peter Carpenter,' he said, shaking it.

Enoch bit his lip. 'Good to meet you,' he said. His bad eye was twitching violently back and forth. 'I'm done for,' he said. 'Get back to Blackstone and save yourself.'

'No,' Jacob hoisted his friend up. 'We're going to get you the Elixir. From Master Blackstone's cellar.'

Chapter 86

Charlie dived deeper into the stinking warren of old courtly rooms which housed London's poorest prisoners.

Fire was coming. Bridewell had turned perilous. The remaining prisoners were attacking their cell doors and killing guards.

The most secure cells in Bridewell were second storey, in the gallery. But besides this rudimentary knowledge, Charlie had scant idea where Lily might be. Or even how to get to the higher storeys. The prison was enormous and maze-like.

With relief Charlie reached an enormous grand staircase. The carved bannisters had been torn off and tiny pigs cavorted on the wide stair. They scattered as Charlie approached, little hooves resounding on the bare wood.

There were shouts behind him and Charlie saw a clutch of people. Vigilantes. They were manhandling a bloodied captive along the prison corridors.

'Are you a gaoler?' a broken-toothed man heading the gang rounded on Charlie. 'We can't find no gaolers,' he added, with an accusing shake of the captive.

'You can't imprison this man here,' said Charlie. 'The prison will burn.'

'He's a Frenchie!' shrieked a woman from deep in the mob. 'He's confessed to starting the fire!'

Charlie's eyes switched to the woman. She was thin-faced and venomous. Then he looked at the accused. The man's head lolled slightly and his face was battered. By his clothes he was clearly Dutch rather than French. And Charlie was willing to bet his confession hadn't come willingly. He eyed the little mob.

'He threw a fireball!' accused the broken-toothed leader. 'Liza here saw him.'

Charlie assessed the situation. The Dutchman was well dressed. Expensive clothing that would be quickly ripped from him the moment he entered a cell.

Charlie stepped forward and took the man roughly by the shoulders.

'You've done well to bring him here,' he said. 'I'll make sure he's locked away.'

'You're a gaoler then?' said the leader, suddenly looking uncertain. He eyed Charlie's thin legs. 'What if he struggles? We should help you bring him to the cell.'

'You've done your part,' said Charlie. 'The fire comes. The Apothecaries' Guild is only the other side of this wall,' he added. 'You shouldn't want to be here if that fires. Strange explosives and potions they keep inside.'

The little gang shuffled quickly away and Charlie put a proprietary arm on the bloodied Dutchman.

'Come,' he said, speaking in Dutch. 'Come with me. I'll take you to safety.'

At the sound of his native tongue the Dutchman sprang to life suddenly.

'It was a piece of bread!' he cried. 'That was all. A piece of bread I threw. For a pauper.'

'Shhh,' said Charlie. 'I'm no gaoler. Only wait until the mob has gone and you can be on your way.'

'You're Dutch?' asked the Dutchman.

Charlie shook his head. 'I'm a Londoner.'

'How came you to speak it?'

'I don't know,' said Charlie truthfully. 'From as far back as I can remember I've always spoken it.'

It was one of the unsolved mysteries of his orphan past that he didn't like to dwell on.

The Dutchman considered this. He seemed disinclined to trust another Englishman.

'You say fire comes here?' he asked.

Charlie nodded. 'On the north side. Over there,' he added, pointing at the far wide walls of Bridewell. 'So we have time yet. I'm looking for a prisoner in the gallery,' he added. 'Stay with me until we find you some different clothes.'

'Clothes?' the Dutchman looked confused.

'You can't go back on to the streets dressed that way,' said Charlie, gesturing to the man's foreign fashion. 'You'll be lynched.'

'But where can I get clothes in a prison?' The Dutchman was looking at Charlie's battered leather coat with some disdain.

'Prisoners have broken out,' said Charlie. 'Some will have died in the trying. Dead men don't need breeches.'

The Dutchman looked appalled but didn't protest.

Charlie led them both up the staircase and was confronted with an array of long corridors. Voices were echoing from deep within. But it was impossible to tell which direction. The high ceilings played tricks with the noise. Taking a guess Charlie picked a narrow corridor stretching south.

'Shouldn't you take the other way?' asked the Dutchman. 'You said you go to the gallery.'

Charlie hesitated. 'How would you know that?' he asked.

'I'm an architect,' said the Dutchman, adjusting his bloodied neckerchief. 'For the Dutch Royal household. I've made great study of Tudor palaces. Galleries are always south facing for the sunlight. So it would be built there.' He pointed to a thick wide corridor.

'What were you doing out on the streets?' asked Charlie, turning to follow the Dutchman's directions. 'An architect for royalty shouldn't be so foolish.'

The Dutchman passed a thoughtful hand over his blackened eye.

'A lady in the city,' he said smiling. 'I promised I would meet with her.'

They moved past high windows sending large shafts of sunlight down. But the rooms leading off were eerily deserted. Voices could be heard more clearly now though. Charlie's skin prickled. Prisoners were still locked in here. Deep in the depths.

'Was your lady worth the danger?' asked Charlie distractedly.

'Yes,' said the Dutchman. 'She was.'

They rounded on a wide arcing gallery and the Dutchman gasped. Ranged on the ground were the bloodied remains of a battle. Three prisoners lay dead, their scabbed legs splayed, bodies broken. Two had brutal head injuries, the third a scorch at his chest which spoke of cheap pistol fire.

Charlie knelt by the first body.

'Here,' he said. 'This man will fit you.' He looked up. 'Take off your clothes.'

The Dutchman hesitated.

'We'll change them over,' said Charlie pulling off the shirt. 'You can carry your nice ones under your arm,' he added at the expression of trepidation on the Dutchman's face. 'I don't try to rob you of them.'

The Dutchman took a breath and then began pulling off the ribbons at his white silk stockings. He rolled them down, then dropped away his breeches.

Charlie worked stoically, wrenching the remaining clothes off the dead man.

'You've done this before?' ventured the Dutchman, his face twisted in distaste.

Charlie spoke without looking up. 'I grew up in an orphan home,' he said. 'The beds often held a dead boy by morning. If you wanted to live you stole their clothes.' He handed the tattered garments to the Dutchman.

'Put them on,' he said, 'and go out the way we came. Do you know that way?'

'Down the gallery, past the grand stair and through the two quads,' said the Dutchman, displaying his knowledge of Tudor buildings.

Charlie nodded. 'Put them on,' he repeated, noticing the Dutchman had hesitated to dress.

'They're stinking,' complained the Dutchman as he raised the shirt to go over his head.

'You'll stink worse as a rotting corpse.'

Charlie looked back along to where a few gaol rooms were still closed.

'You're fortunate that mob brought you here,' he added. 'In St Giles they would have lynched you.'

The Dutchman pulled up the ragged breeches. He looked down at himself sadly.

'I have nothing to give you,' he said as he turned to go. 'Yet I owe you my life. Might I take your name at least?'

'Charlie Tuesday,' said Charlie.

'You're looking for a girl in here?' asked the Dutchman hesitating.

'Yes,' said Charlie.

'She is worth the danger?' suggested the Dutchman with an indulgent smile.

'No,' said Charlie firmly. 'She is not.'

Chapter 87

Barbara's face was haunted. 'Charles would never have agreed to it,' she whispered.

Amesbury looked away. He'd come to be sure Barbara's children were safe. But she'd interrogated him on how fire would affect the city prisons.

'We have no choice,' said Amesbury. 'We can't have prisoners escaping.'

Barbara shook her head as though she couldn't believe it.

'Monstrous,' she said. 'It's a monstrous thing you do.'

'And what would you do?' demanded Amesbury. 'Set them free? Women know nothing of . . .'

'*This* woman knows something of war,' said Barbara, the strength in her voice matching his. 'This woman travelled to Holland and bedded an exiled King. This woman listened to the campaigns, the strategies. The hopelessness.'

She ran an angry hand through her long hair.

'Charles would have married me,' said Barbara. 'In Holland. That's how little he believed he'd ever return to England. I said no. Because I had faith in him. I loved him too well to spoil the dowries and allegiances he could make.'

'And you have more power as a mistress,' said Amesbury.

Barbara looked annoyed. 'You weren't there,' she said. 'You chose the winning side. But I know what it is to lose at war. And I know this, Amesbury. Win or lose. *I would not burn men alive.*' Her violet eyes were aglow with fury.

'These are murderers,' said Amesbury. 'Child killers. Rapists. Men who would choke a whore rather than pay her shilling.'

'Do you think this shocks me?' demanded Barbara. 'Nothing men are capable of shocks me, Amesbury. Remember that.'

Amesbury sighed. 'Most are due to hang tomorrow,' he said.

'In the Clink!' said Barbara, 'not in Bridewell. Paupers and gentle lunatics.'

Amesbury shook his head. 'Bedlam has religious dissenters,' he said.

Barbara hesitated. 'Charles set them free,' she said.

'As did Cromwell,' said Amesbury. 'Being high up. It gives you the luxury of idealism. Practical matters fall to men like me.'

'The King commanded those men be released from prison,' said Barbara. 'Your duty is to carry out orders.'

'Bedlam is not a prison,' said Amesbury.

'You had the dissenters locked away for lunacy?' Barbara seemed torn between horror and admiration.

'England was torn apart by holiness,' said Amesbury. 'The streets are thick with religious plotters as it is. Imagine if more of them were loose, spreading their poison.'

'Bedlam is a dreadful place,' said Barbara.

'So you hear,' said Amesbury. 'You are fortunate. Stay here in your fine dresses. Leave the horrors of running a country to men like me.'

Chapter 88

Lily sat on the straw of her cell, hugging her knees defiantly. She listened to the streams of hysterical French and Dutch from wrongly imprisoned foreigners.

'Are you for business?' A man was tugging at her dress. She twitched her skirt away irritably. He eyed her evilly and laid a dirty hand on her arm.

'Gypsies are always for sale,' he observed. He was looking at the cheap necklaces and rings on her fingers.

Lily smiled. 'You're mistaken.' The man looked down at the blade in her hand.

'Provoke me further,' she warned, 'and you'll have nothing to proposition women with.'

The man spat, jiggled his groin suggestively and backed away muttering. He joined a group of prisoners and pointed towards her. Lily sensed something bad about to happen.

She moved to the prison door. It was an old Tudor creation. Thick and sturdy. The prison had modified it to have a small barred grating so prisoners could wave for the gaoler. To the back was a tiny window leading to the street, so prisoners might beg for food from passers-by. But today there was no hope of scraps.

Lily slipped her arms through and let them hang through the bars, feeling the free air beyond the dank cell. Something seized her wrist.

Lily started and instinctively balled her fists. Her rings. Even brass rings and coloured glass were worth something in Bridewell. Some escaped prisoner must have chanced on her vulnerable arms. She'd heard of London thieves who'd cut off a finger to get at a tight ring.

Then she saw a pair of familiar brown eyes at the prison door.

'Hello, Lily,' said a gruff voice. 'Where's my key?'

Lily beamed in relief.

Charlie had tried for menacing, but catching sight of her his voice didn't come out as planned. He caught hold of the prone forearm to shake it.

'How could you do it?' he accused. 'I saved your life!'

Lily smiled at him. 'I knew you would come,' she said. 'Hurry. Break me out. There's a hammer. At the end of the corridor. I saw one of the prisoners drop it as they fled. You can open the lock.'

'You think I come to free you?' Charlie was incensed. 'You robbed me! Of my most precious possession. And left me for dead on the banks of the Thames besides, when I near drowned myself dragging you to shore.'

'I didn't *want* to leave you, Charlie,' Lily said, looking over her shoulder at the other prisoners, who were watching silently. She dropped her voice to a whisper. 'Blackstone means to fire the Palace. I had to get a message to Amesbury. To warn the King.'

'Why did you steal my key?'

Lily threw out her hands exasperatedly. 'Think. The city is burning. What if I'd found the chest and let the papers burn for want of a key? You'd have never forgiven me.' She sounded hurt.

Charlie made a strangled sound. She looked so helpless, staring up at him through the bars. Already his firm knowledge that she'd left him for dead was slipping away. Something about her proximity was playing havoc with his normal rationality.

'You were out cold,' said Lily. 'On the riverbank. I tried to rouse you but you wouldn't wake. I knew you'd find me,' she added. 'You're clever enough to deduce that Bridewell is the place to look for religious prisoners.'

Charlie's head span. He didn't doubt she'd tell mistruth after mistruth for her own selfish gain. But before he could properly contemplate the issue there was an explosion.

They both started, but Charlie kept a firm hold on her wrist. Then he leaned back to get a better look at what had happened.

When his face reappeared it was grim.

'I think Blackstone has fired the Apothecaries' Guild,' he said. 'Fire comes to Bridewell quickly now.'

Lily's face was stricken.

'Let me out.'

'My key,' said Charlie. 'Do you still have it?'

She nodded.

'Give it to me.'

Lily set her mouth in reply. 'I'm not a fool, Charlie.'

'I . . .' he dropped her hand, offended. 'I wouldn't leave you here,' he said. 'You're a thief and a liar. But I'm not heartless.'

Lily was not convinced. 'Help me escape the gaol,' she said. 'Then I'll give you the key.'

'Tell me what you know of the Tree of Life,' said Charlie, thinking of what he'd seen in the Cutlers' Guild. 'You didn't tell me all you knew in Torr's cellar.'

Lily looked surprised.

'It's nothing,' she said. 'Just a story really, on how to lead a good life.'

'Like a religion?' demanded Charlie.

Lily shook her head. 'No. Tarot, Kaballah's Tree of Life. They're creation stories. They teach us the journey.' She glanced behind her. 'Let me out,' she said.

'That's it?' asked Charlie. 'A journey?'

Lily eyed the bars impatiently.

'In the beginning you have open-hearted willingness. Then come the tests,' she waved her hand, 'set-backs, things to be overcome. Finally you shed your old self and receive enlightenment. Charlie,' her voice grew insistent. 'You have to let me out. Now.'

She looked behind her. Prisoners were eyeing her with interest. 'Things are about to take a bad turn,' she added.

Charlie glanced back into the cell. The handful of men were talking and looking more intently at Lily now.

Charlie released her wrists.

'Over there,' said Lily gesturing. 'The hammer rolled under that bench.'

Several burly prisoners were heading her way.

Charlie picked it up, approached the thick door and swung. The heavy padlock rebounded. Another blow split it and on the third spun it away on to the wooden floor.

Charlie stepped away from the grating and pulled it open. Lily stood inside, her knife held outwards, a circle of prisoners eyeing her. He grabbed her arm. The prisoners inside surged at the door.

'Come,' he said, pulling her free as the other prisoners stampeded past. He eyed the colourful smoke breaking into the upper windows.

Lily was reaching in her dress.

'Here,' she said. 'Your key.'

She handed it to him, looking apologetic. Charlie took it and looped it over his head.

'We need to leave,' he said, relieved to have the key back. 'This whole prison will be aflame.'

'But what of the prisoners on the Mermaid?' asked Lily. 'If we find them we might find Blackstone. The King defends Whitehall,' she added, 'but Blackstone sabotages his plans at every turn. We must stop his blue fire.'

Charlie shook his head. 'Cromwell released the religious prisoners. A gaoler told me.'

'No.' Lily was holding his arm urgently.

'What?'

'I'll explain on the way,' she said. 'We need to get to Bedlam.'

Chapter 89

Barbara eyed her empty apartments. Amesbury looked uncomfortable.

'You talk as though I were weak,' said Barbara. 'Don't forget who has more sway with His Majesty.'

'His Majesty doesn't rule England,' said Amesbury. 'Parliament has the money. Parliament and the guilds.'

His face softened.

'Think of how it will look on the King,' said Amesbury. 'People already think him weak. If he releases felons. If murderers roam the streets . . .'

'Have you ever heard a man burn?' demanded Barbara.

Amesbury looked away.

'I never believed it of you,' said Barbara. 'Now I see what you are capable of.'

'I am capable of far worse,' said Amesbury shortly. 'My duty is to protect the King. I do my duty no matter what people say of me.'

'Then kill the dissenters in their cells,' said Barbara quietly. 'At least do that.'

Amesbury shook his head. 'There are not the funds. We'd need fifty hard men.'

'Not if you had guns and shot,' said Barbara, calculating.

'Guns and shot?' Amesbury was smiling at her naivety.

'Charles has a secret supply,' said Barbara, and Amesbury's smile fell away. 'Twenty guns. Powder. Shot. They're for his personal guard. In case of an assassination attempt.'

'How would you possibly . . .?'

'I can get them,' she said.

'Even if you could . . .' began Amesbury.

'I can.'

'Even if you could. And I don't doubt your influence on the King. We'd need men to fire them.'

'How much?'

'With the arsenal you describe, twenty men.'

'I didn't ask how many men,' said Barbara. 'I asked how much it would cost.'

'A guinea a man,' he said. 'For that I could find some willing.' He raised his old eyes to hers. 'But the King doesn't have so much. Nor would he give it for such a thing.'

Barbara was unfastening her emerald necklace. She pushed it into Amesbury's gnarled hand. Slowly his fingers closed around it. Then he stuffed it into his leather purse. Barbara's eyes shone as the bright jewels vanished. She turned away.

'Bedlam first,' she muttered.

Chapter 90

'I sent a message to Amesbury,' Lily explained as they raced through the smoking hallways of Bridewell. 'The King won't believe there's a plot. We must find Blackstone ourselves. They never released the religious prisoners,' she added. 'We might still find one who was held on the Mermaid.'

'But gaolers couldn't have kept them in Bridewell,' said Charlie, confused. 'Not if Cromwell commanded their release.'

'They didn't keep them in Bridewell,' said Lily. 'They declared religious dissenters insane.'

Charlie's stomach turned. 'They put them in Bedlam. The lunatic place?'

Lily nodded.

Charlie closed his eyes. He could hear the screams of maniacs drifting on the breeze. The Apothecaries' Guild was to the south side. If the wind stayed high it would gut the prison and fire the lunatic asylum in the blink of an eye.

'Why did you ask about the Tree of Life?' asked Lily as they followed the wails of Bedlam's madmen.

'I saw it in the Cutlers' Guild,' said Charlie. 'I thought there could be a connection with Torr's cellar.'

'The Tree of Life would be a good tool for a guild,' said Lily. 'Mastering a craft. It's a journey with trials and tests. Enlightenment at the end. Probably no more connection than that.'

Charlie considered this. Guilds regulated professional trade in London. They forced certain professions to join and set prices, or work elsewhere. But they exacted a standard of training and merchandise as well. From what he knew, guilds valued honesty and integrity. It made sense, he thought. 'But why hide it?' he pressed.

'The church doesn't like it,' said Lily. 'Tarot and other mystic things take power from ministers. Give men god-like powers over their own destiny.' Her dark eyes met with his. 'But since Cromwell,' she said, 'men begin to question, don't they? Religion is not fixed like it was.'

They broke out into a courtyard and suddenly the maniac screams took on a fever pitch.

'They get louder.' Lily's face was pale. 'The screams of the lunatics.'

Charlie nodded grimly.

'We're here.' He pointed to a mouldering doorway leading to an enclosed corridor.

Bedlam was a crumbling corner of Bridewell. A part deemed too rank and malodorous for common criminals.

'They've locked them in,' whispered Lily, pointing to the barred door. 'And left them to burn.'

'We'll break the lock,' said Charlie, hefting the hammer he'd used to break out Lily. 'Stay behind me in case any inside have broken free.'

Fire was already licking at the asylum windows on the far side, driving the occupants to a frenzy. As Charlie and Lily moved to the door, terrible howls rent the air.

Charlie raised the hammer and made short work of the aged padlock. The shrieks inside rose higher.

'Be ready to run,' murmured Charlie as he pulled the door open.

A surge of chittering rats poured free and they twisted back. The torrent of teeth and claws raced over their feet and Lily shrieked, kicking one free of her skirts.

Charlie stood still as the rush abated and the wails of the madhouse rose again.

'This way,' he said, gesturing Lily follow him through the door.

They both stopped in horror.

'Holy Jesus,' said Lily, drawing back. 'Are they human?'

Chapter 91

Something was happening with the weather. Blackstone could sense it. The boy, Jacob, had told him of the approaching fire. Plans to clear the house had been brought forward. In the meantime he was securing a cart.

Fire was coming sooner than he'd thought. He felt a sudden flash of . . . Was it fear? It was unthinkable Teresa be burned in the ignominy of a house fire. Blackstone needed a cart.

Blackstone had chosen where he would surrender his wife forever. High and glorious, the fire would be Teresa's holy revenge.

Fire will purge all.

His wife's soul would be cleansed as London fell. It was perfect.

The crush of carts at Ald Gate was perilous. Blackstone drew his sword and a document bearing the Royal Seal. He approached the owner of a large cart entering the city. It was already beset by well-dressed servants trying to secure it for their various households.

'Palace authority,' said Blackstone grandly, holding up the paper. 'Whatever your highest offer, I will double it.'

The driver looked down at him. He was a country farmer still wearing his battered straw hat and working breeches.

'Thirty pounds,' he said slowly, 'is the highest.'

'Sixty then,' said Blackstone quickly, brandishing the Royal Seal again. The cart owner spurred his horse and the servants fell back, looking murderously to Blackstone.

'What goods do you take?' asked the driver.

'My household,' said Blackstone. 'Private things. Some are already safe in Guildhall. But some must be kept away from prying eyes.'

The country cart driver gave a humourless laugh.

'That's London ways,' he said. 'Many thieves.'

Blackstone was mentally mapping his house. Important furnishings had been cleared in preparation. But he had a sudden powerful instinct that Teresa's wedding trunk should be kept safe. He thought it had been left empty in an upstairs bedroom. Ready to be taken with his other household goods to Guildhall.

The feeling spiralled away, replaced by a memory. A different trunk. Another time.

Hidden papers.

Blackstone never meant to steal the papers. He'd only meant to look at them. To imagine owning the secret. Perhaps fantasise of buying back his family's estate. Living in plenty again.

He'd been surprised at how badly they'd been hidden. Not even under lock and key. Concealed in a trunk of silly women's things. Poppets and ribbons. Luck charms and love talismans.

Then he'd seen a flash of pewter. Tobias and Sally Oakley, etched inexpertly in a heart. A wedding tankard.

Black rage had tunnelled through him. Teresa's dowry funded the war. But it seemed Tobias had married secretly, forgetting his obligations to fund the cause with an heiress. A love match with Lucy Walter's humble maid. No one had suspected. What man looked at Sally, when Lucy was near?

Realisation of the betrayal had destroyed Blackstone's last loyalty to the Brotherhood. Tobias hadn't fulfilled his duties. Blackstone had been starved, tortured and impoverished, whilst Tobias married for love. He imagined Tobias and Sally laughing at him. Mocking his life of poverty and miscarriage with a madwoman, whilst they bore healthy sons.

Even Torr had broken their vow of loyalty, keeping secrets with mystics and deriding the true faith. The Brotherhood of the Sealed Knot had all been a lie.

Blackstone had snatched up the papers, determined never again to believe in friendship.

None of them knew what Blackstone was truly capable of. What he'd been before the war. He and Teresa had made the marriage. The papers should belong to him. It was his time now. He'd finally find out what true power really meant. And take revenge on all those who'd been disloyal.

The cart was veering left now, keeping to the wider streets.

'This way,' said Blackstone, leading him through the smaller winding alleys of Ald Gate. They turned deeper into the backstreets, until the horse began to refuse.

'I won't get through,' protested the cart owner, as his vehicle began dragging at the sides of timber buildings. 'My horse is old. She'll bolt.'

But before he could utter another protest, Blackstone had driven a sword into his chest. The country man choked, staring down in utter shock before pitching forward. Blackstone dragged his body inside a deserted house and took possession of the cart.

It was such a shame, he thought, looking at the Royal Seal, that it had come to this. He'd been brought up loyal to the Crown.

As part of the Sealed Knot, he'd helped Charles escape England to the Continent whilst his father the King was beheaded. Hiding in cellars and priest-holes the young Charles had been exceptionally brave. But when the Brotherhood met him again in Holland. What a difference. The boy-Prince had become an adolescent debauchee, concerned only with girls and wine. They'd tried to talk war, whilst Charles's eye roved to pretty girls.

Then quite unexpectedly, Charles had approached Blackstone privately. He'd asked him to do the unthinkable. And Blackstone, blinded by the possibility of a future King's gratitude, had betrayed his Brotherhood. But now Blackstone knew. He knew what the word of Charles Stuart was worth.

Chapter 92

Bedlam was like stepping into a portal of hell.

'They've got out,' breathed Lily. 'They're out of their cells.'

The wide corridor of the asylum bore seven large doors. One was wide open. Scrawny ulcerated men loped on the straw-strewn floor, some on all fours, others dragging stumps of legs. They were shaven-headed, their scalps covered in welts and sores. Their clothing bore decades of soiling.

Other doors were still bolted. Behind the nearest, champing at the bars, was a wild-eyed woman. She was banging her shaven head and paused every few seconds before issuing a banshee shriek. Behind her was a man with a grossly swollen neck, his eyes almost bursting from the sockets. He was counting frantically, slapping a beat to the floor.

Charlie surveyed the asylum, urging his breathing to calm. The lunatics, though wild, didn't seem aggressive. They'd cowered and cringed away when the door opened.

He made an assessment of the seven doors. They were looking for a lunatic who'd been here a long time. Charlie's eyes roved the escaped maniacs, then the nearest cell. None in the first two cells seemed particularly old, but it was difficult to see from the corridor.

Perhaps further back into the madhouse. His gaze switched to the other rooms. Closed doors. Inhuman cries and guttural grunts. Smoke was filling the back of the prison.

'We should find a Bedlam physician,' said Charlie, thinking they needed to move fast.

'They've long gone,' said Lily. 'Maybe one of these cells is for religious types,' she added. She was looking warily at the madmen. But after an initial surge of interest in the newcomers, Bedlam's escaped occupants seemed to be amusing themselves.

'Dissenters,' she added, 'Baptists, Quakers, Ranters, Levellers. Perhaps they were put in a secret cell?' Lily was pointing to the back, where some smaller dark doors were ranged.

'Those rooms are treatment cells,' said Charlie. 'All the maniacs are housed here.' He considered. 'We'll take a good look in each cell,' he decided. 'Move through systematically. Perhaps there's even someone sane enough to talk to us.'

They approached the first door. The sewage stink of the Fleet mingled with the oncoming smoke.

'You said the fire goes to Whitehall?' asked Charlie as they stepped towards the first cell grating.

Lily nodded.

'I think so too,' said Charlie. 'Blackstone moves the flames by firing guilds. Fire shouldn't be moving west so quickly,' he added. 'Even with the high wind.'

He moved forward to peer through the grating of the cell door. A ghostly face with livid bloody lips appeared suddenly at the bars. Charlie moved back, pushing Lily behind him. The face at the cell gave a ghoulish smile and fell away. Charlie approached the grating again, his heart pounding.

The red-lipped ghost had retreated to a corner. He knelt and began smearing himself with matter from a dark pile. Another man crawled to join him.

'Too recent,' Charlie decided, surveying the occupants. A man who moaned and scratched himself looked directly at them. 'These are too young,' said Charlie.

'They don't look young,' whispered Lily, her face haunted.

'Many start life in the Foundling Home,' said Charlie grimly. 'That place makes boys old or dead quickly. Mostly dead,' he added.

'You were a Foundling,' said Lily, staring at the raving men. 'You lived.'

'I had someone to survive for,' said Charlie. 'My brother Rowan. I had to keep him fed.'

'You said he was your older brother,' said Lily, confused.

'Age doesn't matter. It's who gives up first,' said Charlie. He had a sudden memory of Rowan, pale and starving, asking if the game was over yet.

Lily was staring at an assortment of gruesome-looking tools.

'What do they do to them?' she asked, appalled.

'Each cell is owned by a different physician,' said Charlie. 'They try different things. Most believe that whips and chains help. Some think worse is needed.'

Charlie was eyeing a bubbling barrel of pitch next to the wicked-looking tools.

He moved back from the door, raised his hammer and shattered the bolt.

'What are you doing!' cried Lily as the sounds inside rose in terrible chorus.

'They'll not harm us,' said Charlie, throwing back the door. 'At least I hope not,' he added. Several of the lunatics had thrown themselves to the ground, gibbering. He left the door wide and moved to the second of the seven cells.

They could hear the roar of the flames now. Bedlam was catching alight.

Women populated the second cell. Old whores by the look of them. Some toothless and prattling, others shouting. One had her skirts raised and was chasing a mangy chicken.

Charlie raised the hammer and smashed it down. When he turned back to Lily she had frozen to the spot. Then he saw she was pointing at a pool of blood.

It was enormous, fanning out wide along the passage. He drew back his bare feet.

'Looks like we've found our man,' Charlie murmured, looking at the bleeding figure before them.

Chapter 93

Jacob and Enoch made it to within a quarter of a mile of Blackstone's house. It was obvious to both that Enoch was dying.

Then they saw the flames.

'It's come faster than Blackstone planned,' said Jacob, shifting the weight of his half-conscious friend.

Enoch's eyes fluttered. 'Leave me,' he said.

'No.'

'Master Blackstone goes to the Palace,' gasped Enoch. 'Go to him. Tell him his house is in the path of the fire.'

Jacob hesitated.

'If you don't,' managed Enoch, 'Blackstone will find you and gut you.'

Jacob was biting his lip.

'Don't sacrifice yourself for me,' urged Enoch. 'Isn't that our creed? In St Giles? I can get to the cellar without you.' Enoch breathed hard and righted himself. Jacob could see how much it pained him to do it.

'I'll get the Elixir,' said Enoch. 'Go to Blackstone.' He managed a crooked smile. 'Save both our skins.'

Jacob let out a breath. 'Breed not birth right,' he said, sounding the guildhall motto they'd learned as apprentice boys. 'I'll be back for you.'

'Work with honour,' said Enoch, through gritted teeth, 'and keep our word.'

Jacob nodded and sprinted off, leaving Enoch to make the distance alone. The pain was bad enough to make him crawl. But he dragged himself over the threshold of Blackstone's large half-timbered house.

The entrance to the cellar was ahead. A trapdoor. He crawled to the opening knowing he didn't have the strength to break a lock. But he found it opened easily.

A terrible smell wafted up. Enoch felt his mind swim with the pain. He manoeuvred his body on to the ladder. Partway on, he realised he couldn't do it. His injuries were too great. Then something lunged into the ladder. His grip jerked free and he pitched down into the dark.

———

Enoch lay sweating on the floor of Blackstone's cellar. The pain had been too much. He'd fainted. There was a noise he couldn't understand. Loud and terrible. Something brushed past his face and he recoiled.

His chest had settled to a heavy heat now. It blazed. But the worst had abated. Deep down Enoch thought he knew why. There was nothing left to burn.

Something flapped against him and he started. A harsh screech sounded.

Then Enoch realised.

A bird. He keeps a bird down here.

He wanted to laugh at his own foolishness. So Blackstone kept a rook or a raven. Squawking and large, but not ghostly or ghoulish. Enoch heard the bird hop away. He groped a hand weakly in the dark. His fingers touched a cold dirt floor.

Suddenly he was wracked with an agonising surge of heat. He gasped, contorting in pain. The Bringer of Death. It was still working on his body.

In the light of the open trapdoor his eyes were adjusting. Enoch was seeing things. Feverish horrors. An old woman in a green dress. A crown of leaves on her head. She was propped in a seated position, her head slumped. There was a dark space where her heart should have been.

He was cold now. A fierce prickling kind of cold. Enoch lay shivering. Parts of his body were numb, floating away.

Then he heard it. The unmistakable sound of a person breathing in the dark.

Enoch managed to twist his head and saw her. Blackstone's wife. Her long hair was white. And her eyes . . . She had eyes that rotted the soul.

The breathing was faster now, as though she were excited.

Enoch's chest contracted for the last time. And a chill moan of horror was the last sound he ever made.

Chapter 94

Charlie's eyes settled on a Bedlam physician dying beneath a bench.

'Is he one of the lunatics?' asked Lily, peering into the dark corner from where the blood rolled.

'No,' said Charlie. 'He's a physician, Catholic by his clothes. See his key?'

The man was old, with shoulder-length greasy white hair. A large key lay a few feet away from him and he lolled like a rag doll, arms spread wide. Charlie followed the trail of blood to the man's left arm. The hand was mostly missing, and blackened as though with gunpowder. What must have once been a torrent of blood had slowed to a trickle.

The physician looked up at him glassily with a half smile on his face.

'You're not an inmate.' He sounded confused.

Charlie knelt. 'No,' he said, assessing the man's injury. He could see instantly death was at hand. At least four pints of blood had streamed over the stone floor. 'Did you own the first cell?' he added.

The physician's blue lips parted.

'Until they set on me,' he said. 'Such is gratitude.'

Charlie remembered the starved and frightened inmates loping around the entrance of the asylum.

The gaoler nodded at the big key lying a few feet away.

'I had that key made by an ironmonger,' he said, nodding to the abandoned object. 'It works as a gun of sorts. A little black powder inside. A rudimentary firing mechanism. It was my protection, when I opened the door. If a group of felons chose to run at me.'

The smile widened.

'Never trust an ironmonger to do a gunsmith's work,' he concluded, eyes settling on the scorched remains of his hand.

Charlie moved forward. He pressed a gentle finger on the stump of the wrist. It was ice-cold.

'Nothing can be done,' said the physician, seeing Charlie's expression.

'Too much blood is lost,' said Charlie bluntly, thinking of the gruesome tools, and the frightened maniacs. He judged the physician in his fifties though. Perhaps he remembered something.

'Where you here when Cromwell ruled?' asked Charlie.

The old man nodded and coughed feebly. 'I was a young man then,' he said. 'Thought to stay a year and join a guild. But London is hard for Catholics. And here I am. An old man dying on a piss-soaked floor.'

He coughed again and a spurt of blood issued from his open wrist.

'There were some faith prisoners brought here,' said Charlie moving closer. 'Fifteen men. From a ship.'

The physician's dying eyes narrowed. His blue lips set.

'I spent my life under Protestants,' he replied. 'Now my faith takes me to heaven. You may go to hell.'

Lily knelt and put her slim fingers on his uninjured hand. She drew out her rosary and kissed it.

'I'm a Catholic,' she said. 'As your fellow, I ask it of you.'

The man's face softened.

'You're young,' he said. 'I hope times are less hard for you than for me.'

'Heaven will soothe all injustices,' said Lily.

The physician looked at Charlie, then back to Lily.

'Many faith prisoners in those times,' he said, speaking only to Lily now. 'Many got loose.' He tapped his head with difficulty. 'They were cunning, the dissenters,' he said. 'Cleverer than the other lunatics. We had to take measures. Be sure they didn't escape.'

'These had been held on a ship called the Mermaid,' said Charlie, eyeing the slowing trickle of blood at the gaoler's hand. 'They would likely have been unloaded at the head of the Fleet River.'

The gaoler looked thoughtful.

'They would have stunk of the ballast,' suggested Charlie, thinking of where ship prisoners were usually kept – low in the hull where stagnant seawater and sewage of the ship mingled with the sand used to stabilise the keel.

The gaoler's nose wrinkled as if in memory.

'There was a group of dissenters,' he said slowly. 'Stinking of rotten seawater. Baptists, I believe.'

'Are any still here?' pressed Charlie, hope bursting in his chest. 'Did any live?'

'No,' the gaoler shook his head. 'Their ship was cursed. It brought a gaol fever.'

His gaze dropped to his arm again.

'One did live,' he corrected himself. 'Only one.'

'Is he here?' pressed Lily.

'Perhaps,' said the physician. 'He escaped three times. Might have taken advantage of the fire and confusion. No one to guard him. We put him in the cold cell.'

'The cold cell?' asked Lily.

The physician shivered in reply.

'A terrible thing,' he murmured, 'to be cold. A terrible thing.'

Something flashed in his face. As though he was sorry for something. Then his eyes grew filmy.

Lily gripped his hand, but Charlie pulled her back.

'He's gone,' he said. 'We need to find the cold cell.'

The physician had a set of keys at his hip, and Charlie knelt to unhook them. There were large ones for the doors and smaller keys for manacles and other restraints.

Smoke was streaming steadily through the window now. Lunatics had begun venturing free from their cells, eyeing the open door suspiciously. One began shouting about the apocalypse.

Charlie was taking in the building. Past the seven living cells was a cluster of dark treatment rooms. They skulked at the back, with no grating to peer through.

'What's a cold cell?' asked Lily.

'Bedlam's best treatment,' said Charlie. 'It's a kind of icehouse. Expensive, but Lady Castlemaine gives money for it.'

'Ice?'

'They pull it from the river in winter,' said Charlie. 'As long as you keep it layered in straw, store it somewhere deep and cool, it stays frozen most of the year. It cools the blood,' he added, 'a kinder way to help lunacy.'

He scanned the floor, the walls. Then he spotted a thin stream of water running over the stone floor.

'Unless,' he added, following it, 'your building sets on fire.'

The flow of water led to a grimy door at the back of the asylum. There was no hatch, no grating. Charlie bent down and touched the ground.

'Ice cold,' he said straightening. He examined the lock and held up the bunch of keys he'd taken from the physician. After a moment he selected the right-sized key. Lily hung back as the tumblers clicked open. Ice-cold air rolled out at them. And two blue eyes blinked out from filthy straw.

Chapter 95

Amesbury was packing a large cart when Barbara arrived.

'I thought I'd find you here,' she said. 'Mean you to turn coat again?'

'Charles will lose this battle,' said Amesbury. 'Whitehall will burn. I go to Oxford. Parliament will find me some position.'

'You underestimate Charles,' said Barbara.

Amesbury shook his head. 'Charles is probably chin-deep in chubby white thighs as we speak.'

Barbara laughed. 'Yet we need such a heart in our King,' she said. 'For what is England if not the most fickle of mistresses?'

Amesbury raised his eyebrows.

'England betrayed Charles,' said Barbara. 'Exiled him, killed his family. None but the biggest of hearts could forgive it.'

'Certainly,' she added, 'loving *me* seems easy in comparison.' She treated Amesbury to a disarming smile. 'And I think Charles loves England. Very much.'

Amesbury was shaking his head. 'We cannot save Whitehall with these resources.'

Barbara put her hand on his.

'Don't go,' she said. 'You've won enough battles. Won't you stay and lose one? Make all those other poor generals feel better?'

Amesbury paused.

'You love him too,' said Barbara, 'I know you do. We all do. Underneath it all he is a good King. Isn't that what you always wanted to fight for?'

'And what of you, Lady Castlemaine?' Amesbury's dark eyes were on hers.

'What of me?' Barbara looked uncertain.

'I know you've been meeting with Blackstone,' said Amesbury.

'Blackstone?' Barbara's denial was brittle. 'I've nothing to do with that man. Why should I? We've not met since he was in Holland.'

'What do you know of him?' asked Amesbury.

'He was with the Sealed Knot.' Barbara looked incredulous. 'They were very religious. Communed with mystics. Alchemists. I hardly saw them.'

'Fireballs,' said Amesbury, 'have been turning up all over the Palace. In your apartments. In Queen Catherine's chambers . . .'

Barbara was shaking her head.

'It is a nonsense,' she said. 'Queen Catherine of Braganza, throwing fireballs?' she began laughing.

'They were stamped with the sign of the Sealed Knot,' said Amesbury.

The laugh died on Barbara's lips.

'Wait.' She closed her eyes. 'I have something to confess.'

Chapter 96

The prisoner blinked up at them from the filthy straw. The remains of his clothing was in the old Royalist style. But the colours had long since leached away and his lace collar and cuffs were in grubby tatters. His long white beard and hair were grimed with dirt, making his blue eyes seem particularly vivid as he stared up at them.

He gave a humourless grin as they entered, revealing speckled brown teeth. A wicked-looking iron manacle sat heavy at his ankle, the skin around it worn to sores.

'He's not a lunatic,' whispered Lily, leaning in to Charlie. 'Look at his eyes.'

Charlie nodded. The man looked sane enough to him. The prisoner twisted on his straw, wrapping his arms tighter around his scrawny body. Ice blocks were piled to the edges of the damp room and the man's skin was almost blue.

Charlie moved closer, taking off his coat and throwing it over the prisoner's freezing shoulders. The man looked up in confusion. He was staring at Charlie's face.

'Are you a gaoler?' he said, peering closer. 'I've seen you before.'

Charlie shook his head. 'We haven't met.'

The prisoner scratched the sores at his manacle in a habitual way.

'I must be mistaken,' he muttered. 'You're a minister then? Come to save my soul?' he growled. 'I have already told the other Protestants, I live as a Baptist and will meet my Maker the same way.'

Wordlessly Lily drew out her rosary.

The prisoner grunted and scratched his armpit.

'Then to what do I owe the pleasure?' he asked.

'You sailed on the Mermaid,' said Charlie.

The prisoner looked surprised.

'That was a long time ago,' he said eventually. He gave an involuntary shiver that he hardly seemed to notice. Then he seemed to suddenly notice Charlie's coat and pulled it tighter around his scrawny body.

'I did,' he said after a moment. 'Forty days and nights. In the stinking depths of the hull. It still haunts my sleep at times. Makes me glad to wake up in this palace that you see.'

He waved a hand to indicate the dank cell.

'We are hunting one of the passengers,' said Charlie. 'A Catholic named Blackstone.'

'You want information? What can you give me in return?' The prisoner eyed them craftily.

Charlie's pulse quickened. He couldn't tell if the man knew something or was working them.

Charlie pointed to the manacles. 'Your freedom.'

Again, the blue eyes shifted in surprise.

'And who are you to offer such a thing?' he whispered.

In answer Charlie held out the bunch of keys. The prisoner's gaze riveted to them. He moved a scrawny leg out from under him with effort.

'Then unlock me,' he breathed. 'And I will tell you what I know.'

Charlie shook his head. 'We do not know yet if you know anything.'

The prisoner ran a tongue over his dry lips, his eyes assessing them.

'Perhaps,' he said slowly, 'freedom does not mean so much to me as you think.' He shot a glance up at the narrow window. 'From what I hear, things are not so good out there for Baptists. The new King has betrayed us, is that not right? Like his father before him.' He addressed this last remark to Lily. 'No freedom of worship?'

Lily gave the slightest nod of her head.

'God's appointee on earth,' spat the prisoner. 'I fought for him. The old King. Until I found God's truth in the Baptists.'

He shook his head angrily.

'His Royal Majesty betrayed all his soldiers. Not that it did him any good in the end.' He scratched at his leg thoughtfully.

'The Mermaid,' he said, seeming to have reached a conclusion. 'She was filled with those seeking the young exiled heir in Holland. Not that us prisoners saw a great deal of them, down in the hull.'

'Blackstone would have been around twenty-five years old,' said Charlie. 'Dressed for the Royalist cause. Noble clothes. Can you tell us anything of him?'

The prisoner's blue eyes met with Charlie's. 'I did not see a man named Blackstone,' he said.

Charlie sighed out in disappointment. 'You are quite sure?'

The prisoner nodded, his eyes drifting again to the window.

'It seems tender-heartedness was in short supply after the war,' he said. 'So you may leave me here to rot, for I have nothing to tell you.'

The prisoner watched them, waiting for them to leave.

Charlie moved towards him and he twitched.

'Do what you will,' he said. 'You'll do nothing the good-hearted physicians have not already done and worse.'

Charlie had the prisoner's filthy leg in his hands.

'Keep still,' he muttered. 'Keep still while I unlock the manacle.'

The prisoner's eyes widened. Mutely he stilled his thin leg. His hands were shaking.

'He could be dangerous,' hissed Lily, eyeing the dirty prisoner.

'More dangerous than you?' replied Charlie, as he knelt on the wet straw and selected the right key.

The manacle fell away revealing a band of stinking red flesh. The prisoner's hands rubbed at the wound. He looked up wonderingly.

'Come,' said Charlie, taking his ice-cold arm and helping him to his uncertain feet. 'I will guide you out. Once you are in the city you never saw us.'

The prisoner nodded, his hands already combing at his beard.

'Fire is to the west,' added Charlie. 'Soon it will be inside the walls.' They staggered out, with Charlie supporting the prisoner on his shoulder. Bloody screams were curdling the asylum air. Charlie picked up the hemp hammer where he'd left it. There were four more cells to unlock and he worked quickly, hefting the hammer and shattering the locks. The whole corridor was a thick wall of smoke now. It was hard to see around the corner to the main entrance.

The prisoner was looking on in mute wonderment. 'They won't run,' he said. 'They're too scared of the physicians. Best look to yourself.'

'People sometimes surprise you,' said Charlie, 'when fire comes.'

Suddenly a gunshot sounded in the far gloom, back towards the main entrance.

Charlie froze. Musket fire. A soldier's weapon. Then came screams and hooting. Fists on flesh.

Smoke had thickened in the air now. Charlie risked a glance around the corner. He darted back, breathing hard. A little pack of armed men were being set on by the lunatics.

'Soldiers,' he said grimly. 'Seems as though they didn't expect the lunatics to be out of their cells.'

'Why are they here?' asked Lily.

Charlie glanced round again then flattened himself back out of view.

'My supposing?' he said. 'They've come to do for the lunatics. Kinder than letting them burn.'

The prisoner gave a black-toothed smile. 'Better than letting them loose,' he corrected. 'Half the men in here are religious dissenters.'

'What about us?' cried Lily in horror.

'I don't suppose,' said Charlie, 'they'll believe us sane citizens who've broken in.'

Chapter 97

Enoch was laid out on the wood floor of Blackstone's house. He'd been prepared for burial with an improvised winding sheet. His eyes were closed with coins.

'He was burned,' said Jacob, looking sadly at his friend. 'The barrel slipped.'

'He was dead when I found him,' explained Abraham. As an initiate of the highest level, he'd been permitted to retrieve the body from Blackstone's cellar. Abraham wore second-hand military breeches and a hair shirt that rubbed open sores on his chest. He'd been charged with clearing Blackstone's house after Jacob reported fire.

They were both looking at the corpse. Behind them was the heaving and dragging of furniture being lifted and packed. Blackstone's boys were packing up at speed. Fire was coming.

'Where did you find the coins?' asked Jacob.

Abraham looked at him in surprise. 'This is how I found him.'

A chill rippled through Jacob. He was seeing something else now. There were deep scratches on the face.

'There's a raven loose down there,' said Abraham, following his gaze. 'It probably had a peck at him, after he died.' The long marks were curved, as though made by a beak.

'The winding sheet,' said Jacob. 'It's a woman's dress.' His eyes lifted to Abraham's. Then he tugged away the fabric.

They both recoiled. Marked on Enoch's burned chest were circles and mysterious symbols. They formed a rudimentary tree shape.

'He looks more like a sacrifice than a burial,' said Jacob, staring. He drew back from the body and looked at Abraham accusingly.

'Who did this to him?'

'I don't know.' Abraham spoke with the firmness of a boy who didn't ask questions.

'There's something down there, isn't there?' said Jacob. 'Enoch heard it at night.'

Abraham hesitated. 'I'm not permitted to take a candle into the cellar,' he admitted in a tight whisper. 'Your friend was directly under the trapdoor. All else was darkness. But one time . . . I thought I heard breathing,' he admitted.

'His rosary's gone,' said Jacob sharply. 'Where is his rosary?'

'I don't know,' said Abraham. He took the other boy by the shoulders. 'Fire comes,' he said. 'Sooner than expected. We must prepare Master Blackstone's things for the cart.' He pointed to the other boys sweating and loading.

'Now,' he instructed. 'Or there'll be consequences.'

Numbly Jacob allowed himself to be led.

He joined the sweating boys, arranging trunks, heaving rugs and candlesticks.

'Fire will be here within the hour,' said Abraham. 'Master Blackstone needs his things packed up and packed well.'

'Where does he take them?' asked Jacob.

'Guildhall,' said Abraham. 'If we can get a cart.' He paused to scratch under his hair shirt. A louse was dislodged and fell wriggling to the ground. 'Did you clear upstairs?' he asked the boys.

'All but a big sea chest,' said one. 'It was too heavy to move.'

Abraham cast his gaze around. It rested on Jacob. 'You and me then,' he decided. 'We'll get it down.'

The boys moved into the landing. There were five doors leading off, all open and empty but one.

'His sister's room,' explained Abraham as they approached.

'I didn't know he had a sister,' said Jacob.

'She died during the war.'

Abraham opened the door. A gentle female face smiled out from behind a shroud of incense. Both boys drew back in amazement.

Chapter 98

The screams of the lunatics were blood-curdling and musket fire crashed around Bedlam.

'Stay back,' said Charlie. 'There has to be another way out.' He turned to the prisoner. 'You escaped before,' he said. 'Can we get out from here?'

'I got out into the Fleet River,' said the prisoner. 'Dropped out through the privy holes. But they've bricked them up smaller since.'

He was pointing inside a cell, where a fist-sized hole winked daylight from the outside.

'There might still be a way,' decided Charlie. He was looking at the brazier with the cauldron of pitch. 'Those men have guns,' he said. 'So they'll have black powder. We put a powder flask in that hole. Blow a big enough opening to escape.'

'Even if you could get black powder we'd need a fuse,' protested Lily. 'Unless you want to lose a hand lighting it.'

'The pitch could work,' said Charlie, eyeing the smoking tar used for treating lunatics. More shots fired and he made his decision. 'It's all we have,' he said. 'Take the pitch. Make the best fuse you can and wait for me there.'

Lily hesitated and then nodded. She eyed the aged prisoner and then put out an arm for him to lean on. Charlie stepped into the fray.

The soldiers had been caught off guard. But now they were winning the battle. Two lunatics had been shot dead. A third lay dying. A few lunged and hung off the soldiers. Others cowered in their cells.

The door to Bedlam was wide open and a few inmates were moving tentatively towards daylight. But most were docile as the soldiers rounded them up for execution.

Charlie ducked low and made for a soldier grappling with a scrawny inmate. The two swung wildly, fists flying. A powder flask hung low on the soldier's hip and Charlie's fingers closed around it. Sensing the theft the soldier tore away. But not before Charlie had ripped free the flask.

'The lunatic has black powder!' shouted the soldier as Charlie raced towards the cell where Lily and the prisoner waited.

And as Charlie made for the open door a stampede of soldiers followed behind.

Chapter 99

Blackstone's sister's room held a simple altar, with a picture of a woman. Fresh candles and incense burned.

Abraham spoke first.

'It's a shrine,' he said, shrugging his shoulders to rearrange the hair shirt. 'To his sister.'

He was eyeing a large portrait of a gentle-faced girl with pale eyes and soft flowing hair.

'She was lovely,' said Jacob, staring. 'Must have been young when she died.' He took in the rest of the shrine. It was carved wood, depicting St Benedict holding a poisoned chalice.

'I've seen this before,' said Jacob. 'When I was part of the Carpenters' Guild.' He turned uneasily to Abraham. 'They do it when a person has been cursed. To ward off evil.'

Abraham stepped back as though the floor were red hot.

He took in the rest of the plain chamber. The only other object in the room was the large sea chest.

'Leave the shrine,' he said, crossing himself. 'Come help me with the chest.'

'I think we should leave the chest too,' said Jacob, looking at the shrine. 'I don't think Master Blackstone should know we've been in this room.'

Abraham thought. 'If the chest is worth something,' he said, 'Master Blackstone will be very angry we let it burn.'

They eyed it appraisingly.

'Looks like it's worth a bit,' Jacob conceded, with a sideways glance at Abraham. Jacob ran bitten-down fingernails across an intricate locking mechanism.

'It's a wedding chest,' said Abraham. 'Dutch or Frenchie.'

'How do you know?'

'I unload at the wharves,' said Abraham. 'Seen things like this before.' He winked. 'Smugglers pay a song to know when things like this arrive in port,' he boasted.

'It's locked.' Jacob was pulling at the lid. He gave the lock an experimental prod with a calloused finger. 'What do you think's inside?'

Abraham slapped his hand away. Jacob was making him uneasy. By his reckoning the newest recruit was not nearly frightened enough of the Grand Master. Because Abraham had seen things. Seen what Blackstone could do. And worse. How readily he did them. Hardly any excuse was necessary. The new boy needed learning before it was too late. Abraham was true to the cause. He believed in the power of the initiation. But he wanted no more hanging boys in the cellar.

'What's inside will be your guts if you go sneaking,' replied Abraham. He drew back, considering. 'See the initials? I think this is the wife's wedding trunk,' he said.

'Blackstone's wife?'

Abraham nodded. 'The suicide,' he said meaningfully. He scratched a sore on his shoulder. 'Talk is,' Abraham said, his eyes sliding back to the shrine, 'the wife killed the sister. With black magic.'

'How do you know that?'

'Talks in his sleep doesn't he? You must have heard it.'

Both boys looked uneasily at the gentle face glimmering behind the candles.

'Why would he leave his wife's wedding trunk here?' asked Jacob. 'Her things are down in the cellar.'

There was another uneasy silence. They'd all walked through Teresa Blackstone's strange possessions during their initiation rite.

'The chest is too heavy, even for Blackstone,' said Abraham, assessing the solid shape. 'You'd need two men. Maybe he didn't want anyone else in here.'

'We should leave,' said Jacob.

'No.' Abraham reached a decision. 'My orders were to clear the house. A good son does not question.'

He bent, fitted his hands and puffed out his cheeks with effort. 'Help me,' he grunted.

Reluctantly Jacob grasped one end of the chest.

'Where'd he learn the alchemy then?' panted Jacob as they heaved out the chest.

'Holland,' said Abraham, with a gasp as they made it to the stair. 'I heard he sailed there . . .' he puffed air, 'learned it from the source. The mystics.'

They dropped the chest with a heavy thud.

Abraham wiped his brow and looked down the street. Flames were coming. He turned to Jacob in alarm.

'There should be a cart here,' he said. 'A cart to take Master Blackstone's things.'

The colour had drained from his cheeks.

Jacob watched the flames in the distance.

'Fire'll be here soon,' Jacob guessed. 'What will Master Blackstone do if his things burn?' He was looking at the piles of possessions. Clothes, plate and furniture.

'Help the other boys. Start moving everything to the street,' said Abraham. 'I'll keep a watch for the cart.'

Jacob nodded and headed deeper into the house. But as he reached the trapdoor to the cellar he hesitated. Enoch's death taunted him. Something was down there, he knew it. Something dangerous.

Curiosity burned at him. He was gripped with a strange compulsion to open the trapdoor. It was so strong. As though forces beyond his control drew him closer.

And before Jacob could help himself, he was prising open the trapdoor.

As it opened his arm flew to cover his mouth. The smell. It was incredible.

Then he saw it. Enoch's rosary. It had been hung on a rung of the rope ladder down. The rosary glimmered in the semi-darkness. Like bait.

Jacob thought of his friend. He couldn't let Enoch be buried without his rosary.

Throwing a leg over the trapdoor entrance, Jacob began descending the rope ladder. Deep in the dark a candle flame twinkled. He made towards it like a sleepwalker and a rush of terrible stench rolled up to meet him.

At first Jacob attributed it to the piles of mouldering food. He'd never seen anything like it. There was enough to feed an army here. But rotting away. Stinking. A nest of rats writhed over what might have been a side of beef, now liquefied and reeking. Sugar loaves were spotted with mould and spoiled. Sacks of grain and flour ran with weevils. Pitchers of fetid green water might have once held milk.

Then Jacob saw her. Blackstone's wife. He wanted to look away but his eyes were riveted. Was that . . . skin? Or something else?

The sound of the cellar door jolted him from his torpor. And there, enormous in the entrance, was Blackstone.

His icy eyes rested silently on Jacob. An ocean of silence seemed to pass.

'I . . . I came to get Enoch's rosary,' stuttered Jacob.

'This is my wife's room,' said Blackstone. 'No one may look on her.' His voice turned steely. Jacob knew his fate was sealed.

'I didn't . . . I don't.' Jacob was casting his eyes everywhere but Her. 'The fire comes,' he said desperately. 'Your things will burn. There's . . . a chest,' he stuttered, 'your wife's. A wedding trunk I think.'

Blackstone hesitated.

'I'd forgotten her chest,' he said thoughtfully. 'It was too heavy to be moved and empty in any case.' Blackstone wondered if Teresa had hidden the key somewhere. He was remembering the wedding blessings, torched and blackened.

Blackstone put a hand to his scarred head. He had an image of the missing key. Then nothing.

'The wedding trunk should be with my wife,' he decided.

Something else occurred to him.

'You were in my sister's room,' said Blackstone.

'We were told to clear the house,' managed Jacob.

Blackstone inhaled deeply. His eyes settled on his wife. 'The ribbons and poppets,' he said, 'I thought it a harmless fancy. A foolish woman's trickery.' He was shaking his head.

'She will burn,' said Blackstone slowly. 'And it will be on a pyre to make the city weep. I'll make her a bonfire so great that God himself will open up the heavens to receive her.'

His eyes switched back to Jacob.

'Gunpowder must be used,' he said, 'to make the hottest flame. She must also have a sacrifice. An offering to be sure her soul is freed.'

Jacob felt fear tighten his stomach.

'You will help me,' Blackstone decided.

Chapter 100

Bedlam was in smoking turmoil. Charlie got inside the thick cell door and pulled it shut just as a pack of soldiers herded towards the grating.

'Lock it up!' shouted Lily as Charlie fumbled for the right key. He found it, plunged it into the keyhole and turned the lock as the first man flung himself against the door. The door rebounded and held.

There were shouts and pounding of rifle butts as the soldiers assaulted the heavy wood. Then the barrel of a musket came through the grating in the door.

'Get down!' shouted Charlie as a spray of fire ricocheted around the room. Lily ducked, one hand over her head, the other pulling the prisoner down. Charlie's eyes fixed on the small privy hole. Lily had laid a thin line of pitch. Too narrow to light, he thought.

'There wasn't enough pitch,' explained Lily, following his line of sight as Charlie ducked down beside her.

'It might still fire,' he muttered. 'Give me your tinderbox.'

She handed it over with shaking fingers. On the other side of the door they could hear the soldier fumbling to reload his musket.

'Be careful,' she whispered, pointing to the open grating in the cell door. 'They're reloading.'

'I didn't know you cared.'

'I care about escaping.'

Charlie made across the cell on his hands and knees. He'd tucked the black powder into the privy hole and raced back out of sight before the soldier could raise his gun again. Then he struck the tinderbox against the pitch.

It flared and for a few seconds a cheerful orange flame weaved up the line. Then it reached the bottom of the wall and died.

Charlie cursed. Behind them something heavy slammed into the door. He heard the wood split. He looked up to where the soldier with the musket was angling for a clear shot.

'Charlie,' said Lily, realising what he intended to do. 'Don't.'

But he was already halfway across the cell. A shot from the powerful musket would light the powder flask. Guns had a full few seconds' delay. Charlie was confident he could duck and roll before the shot hit.

The soldier had put his muzzle full through the grating this time, to be sure of a clear shot. Charlie stood up in clear line of sight, the flask of black powder behind him. The soldier's finger tightened on the trigger.

'Don't shoot,' came the voice of another soldier from outside the cell. 'He's no lunatic. He's got black powder in that privy hole. Take the shot and you'll blow the wall out.'

The soldier hesitated. Charlie's heart sank. Then Lily jumped to her feet, grabbed the musket barrel and pulled it hard through the grating. The soldier's face slammed into the bars. In his surprise his finger pulled the trigger. Charlie dived, rolled and the shot went off, driving a blast of fire into the small cell.

The gunpowder exploded loudly, driving brick fragments in all directions.

For a moment the air was too tight in gun-smoke to breathe. And then the fumes cleared through the sunlit hole in the prison wall.

They all made for it.

'You got out this way?' protested Charlie, looking down at the sheer drop. 'It's a clear thirty feet to the Fleet.'

'I'm a Baptist,' said the prisoner. 'It's my faith. God receives me safely in water.'

Lily rolled her eyes. Charlie was eyeing the stinking streaked wall. It looked slippery. But the brick was uneven and the mortar crumbling away.

'We can climb,' said Charlie, swinging a leg over the side of the blast hole. 'Come on.' He climbed on to the outer wall, feeling for holds with his bare feet. 'It's not too hard,' he promised Lily, holding out a hand. 'Plenty of raised bricks to catch a hold.'

She hesitated and then pulled her skirts close to her body and climbed out on to the prison wall, hanging on to the remaining brickwork. Warm air blew over them. Below, the Fleet rippled.

Lily began climbing down. Charlie glanced back to the prisoner. The soldiers had renewed their pounding on the door now, perhaps deciding to save musket fire. It had split down the middle and was giving way.

'Can you climb?' Charlie asked the prisoner. 'If you stay here you'll be captured or executed.'

'I'm not of a mind to climb,' said the prisoner, with a nod at his manacle-savaged ankle. 'But I won't meet my death today. Not at the hands of them.'

He had a strange expression on his face and he looked down to the low Fleet River.

'Your coat,' said the prisoner suddenly. Charlie realised his coat was still resting over the man's skinny shoulders.

'Take it back.' The prisoner heaved it off and passed it over.

Charlie took it with one hand and rested the leather in the crook of his arm.

373

'You won't survive the river this time,' said Charlie, nodding to the Fleet. 'The water is low after the hot summer.'

The prisoner nodded. 'You may be right,' he said. He hesitated. 'You're a good man,' he said, nodding to the coat. 'And though you're no Baptist, I owe you a courtesy. I didn't tell you the truth,' he continued, 'back in the cell.'

Charlie froze halfway out of the prison wall. There was a crashing sound. A musket butt appeared through a gap in the thick door.

'I do remember something about the Mermaid which might help you,' continued the prisoner.

'What?' Charlie was eyeing the door desperately.

The prisoner shot him a crafty glance.

'I did see a man,' he said after a moment. 'As we were brought out on to deck. I don't know if he was your Blackstone. But he was perhaps the right age, and dressed as a cavalier. In Royalist clothes.'

Lily and Charlie exchanged glances.

The prisoner nodded. 'He was selling a gun,' he said. 'I heard him talking of it.'

Charlie was turning this over. Guns could be traced. Even seventeen years ago.

'What makes you think him the man we seek?' asked Charlie.

'There were two men with him,' said the prisoner, staring at Charlie. 'One was dressed ragged like a hermit. With a tattoo. Circles. Some mystic thing. The other man . . .'

The prisoner stared Charlie full in the face. 'The other man looked just like you,' he said. 'That's why I thought I recognised you. When I first saw you.'

Charlie felt the blood in his veins turn to ice. The prisoner licked his lips.

'Just like you,' he repeated. Then he turned to the water, opened his arms wide and jumped into the Fleet River.

Chapter 101

'Whitehall will burn,' said Amesbury. 'Within the hour.'

King Charles put down his wine glass with shaking hands. Safe within the luxurious walls of Somerset House, he'd been able to talk strategy from a distance. Now what he held dear would burn.

He glanced at the Duke of York. His brother James had arrived from Whitehall just in time to witness the kingdom slip away.

'The children?' The King's voice trembled.

'Headed to safety,' assured Amesbury. 'I saw with my own eyes. They'll be halfway to Oxford by this evening.'

'The Palace has been cleared? The Queen?'

Amesbury nodded. 'She's also to Oxford. They packed much of your apartments. The tapestries and furnishings in the Great Hall will burn. It can't be helped. There weren't enough carts.'

Charles took a breath. He felt strangely calm.

'Then this is the end,' he said with a weak smile.

'It's not over,' said the Duke of York angrily. 'You are King.'

'A plague and a burned Palace,' said Charles. 'A Catholic Queen who cannot birth a child. I can never recover from this.'

'You can stay at Oxford for the winter,' said James. 'Rebuild . . .'

But Charles shook his head. 'Amesbury knows it, James. Look at his face. A Palace isn't a house. It's a symbol.'

Charles stood. He walked to the map. A courtier caught him mid-stumble and he steadied himself. Charles picked up his wine and took a deep draft.

'It's our family tradition,' he said, smiling, 'losing the throne.'

The Duke of York stood.

'Our tradition is not losing the throne,' he said. 'It's fighting without enough men.' He gestured to the wider city. 'We have not enough men now,' he said. 'Will you stand and fight?'

Charles looked at him with tired eyes. 'I'm getting old,' he said. 'I've no fight left.'

The Duke of York eased the wine from Charles's hand.

'Remember Holland?' he said.

'Holland.' The King gave a smile. 'They were good days.'

'We did what we pleased,' said James. 'No expectations we'd marry a sour foreign princess. No duties of state.'

'I truly thought,' said Charles, 'I'd buy a French farm and live with a pretty girl and a clutch of bonny children. Perhaps I'd have been happier.'

'But then Barbara arrived,' said James. 'And brought you to your senses. And here we all are. Back in England, just as she said, with you as King.'

'London is in ruins,' said Charles. 'A King needs something to rule over.'

'I say we can still save Whitehall,' said the Duke of York. 'This isn't a fire, Charles. It's a war.' His eyes flashed. 'You and I have much experience at war.' He cast a quick look at Amesbury. 'Despite how we may appear nowadays.'

Charles looked to Amesbury. His face said it all. It was a fool's mission.

'Something is happening to the weather,' said Amesbury. 'The firestorm which the alchemist warned us of. It is very dangerous even to be on the streets.'

'You think it's hopeless to defend the Palace?' asked Charles.

'Hopeless and foolish,' said Amesbury.

'Lead from the front,' insisted James. 'As in battle. We can win this.'

Charles considered. He and his brother had never won a battle yet.

'You always pick the winning side,' he said to Amesbury. 'If it's truly hopeless why are you still here?'

'Perhaps I'm getting old too,' said Amesbury. 'Disloyalty is a young man's luxury.'

Charles smiled. He stood. 'One last stand then,' he said. 'Stuarts may lose battles, but we are pig-headed enough to go out and dirty ourselves in the fight.'

'You are the general,' said the Duke of York. 'Where are your orders?'

'How many men do we have?' asked Charles.

'Not enough,' said Amesbury.

'Less than a hundred,' said James. 'But perhaps we can band some sailors together.'

Charles eyed the map.

'St Paul's is a powerful landmark,' he said.

'St Paul's won't burn,' said James.

'The spire is scaffolded,' Amesbury pointed out.

'I had forgotten the scaffold,' said Charles. 'The architects came to blows, didn't they, over who should be chosen to redesign the cathedral.'

James frowned at the memory. 'Young Christopher Wren. Suggested some soaring cupola. We chose Roger Pratt's practical straight spire. Less costly.'

Charles thought for a moment.

'If it's a war,' he said slowly, 'we'll need battle stations.' The idea seemed to galvanise his thoughts. He stared at the map.

'We defend the west,' he said, stabbing a finger. 'Here, at Temple Bar. This is where Westminster begins.'

'Where the lawyers are,' agreed Amesbury. 'If fire breaches Temple, it's a straight gallop to Whitehall.'

Charles nodded.

'Fire can reach Temple, from both the south and the north.' He pointed. 'James, you'll defend the north, by the Fleet River. You'll make our strongest defence. Clarence and Monmouth will defend the south. The Post Office.'

'Monmouth and Clarence?' Amesbury looked appalled. 'Clarence might be cunning, I suppose. But he's never fought in a war. And Monmouth is a boy. The Post Office is a vital part of England's commerce.'

'Monmouth is feckless and vain,' agreed Charles. 'But so was I at his age. War made me a man. It will him too. And you underestimate Clarence,' he added. 'He'll do the right thing, when it comes to it.'

Charles turned back to the map. 'Amesbury,' he said, 'you and I defend Temple.'

There was an authority in his voice Amesbury hadn't heard before. As though the King had been sleeping all these years and was now waking up.

'Three stations then,' agreed James. 'Temple Bar, Fetter Lane and Holborn. Thirty troops on each with orders to press a hundred more men.'

Charles nodded. 'A good thought, to press men,' he agreed. 'Your naval experience serves us well.'

He looked at Amesbury.

'My purse can give five pounds per station,' he said. 'Three shillings a man. Will it serve?'

'Better food,' said Amesbury. 'If you press common men, offer food. Ale, bread.'

Charles nodded. 'Very well then. Rally the troops with the loudest voices. I want word shouted from every station. Any commoner that stands to fight the fire shall have a pound of cheese, a good loaf and ten pints of ale to sustain him through the night. And two extra shillings per man besides.'

The King thought for a moment. 'Monmouth can hold a post with Clarence,' he said to James. 'Amesbury, go to the alchemist. Find out what you can about the firestorm.' He paused. 'If you truly think there's a plot,' he added, 'we must try to strategise around that as well.'

Amesbury nodded.

The King turned to his brother. 'You and I then,' he said. 'From the front.'

James put a hand on his shoulder.

'From the front.'

Chapter 102

Charlie and Lily raced away from Bedlam and on to the burned-out Strand. Back towards Bedlam the faint sounds of gunshots had died.

'The soldiers have run out of shot,' said Charlie. 'I think a good few lunatics got out whilst they tried to kill us.'

'I hope so,' said Lily with feeling. She turned to Charlie.

'So a man who looked like you was on the Mermaid? With Blackstone and Torr. Your father?'

Charlie nodded.

'It seems that way,' he agreed. 'I know nothing about my father. Only that he died when I was small.'

'How did he die?' asked Lily.

Charlie considered. 'I don't know,' he said. 'I don't know if I ever knew. It was more a feeling I carried with me. I suppose my mother must have told us. I think my brother may have known more about my father. He didn't speak of it. Now Rowan is gone too.'

'Perhaps he was a supplicant for the King,' said Lily. 'Maybe he was one of the Sealed Knot. What does it matter? We still know nothing about Blackstone.'

'We know everything about Blackstone,' said Charlie. 'You forget. I'm a thief taker. Tracking property is my skill. The Baptist told us Blackstone sold a set of guns.'

'You think we can find Blackstone's guns? After seventeen years?'

'Better,' said Charlie. 'We can find Blackstone's address.'

'How?'

'There is a network of sold goods and contraband in the city,' said Charlie. 'Pawn shops. Taverns where you buy smuggled wares, or goods stolen to order. I know all of them.' Charlie rubbed his bent nose. 'There are only two pawn shops who take guns,' he continued. 'Only one who would deal with a Royalist after the civil war.'

'And the pawn shop could tell us something?'

Charlie nodded. 'Guns are very expensive. And you cannot easily fence arms in London since the war. Thieves always come unstuck,' he added. 'Pawn shops take details from the gun-maker.'

'So where is this pawn shop?'

'Near All Hallows church,' said Charlie.

Lily's face fell.

'But there is all burned,' she protested. 'All have fled with their goods.'

'Pawnbrokers aren't guildsmen or nobility,' said Charlie. 'By the time All Hallows burned all the carts and boats had gone to rich people. They'd have no option but to bury their goods.'

'Which means?'

'Unless our pawnbroker wants to be looted, he'll be back already, digging them up.'

⌣

They made south, over the burned and broken path that the fire had already ravaged and followed the riverfront for safety from the flames. There were no coaches and carts anymore. Just a mournful multitude tramping on foot, their arms and shoulders weighed down with belongings.

The expensive jewellery shops of Bishops Gate were husks. The Royal Exchange a sooty ruin. Scraps of burned things danced on the breeze. And in the distance, the great mighty roar and flames of the fire still burned westwards.

'The sun sets,' said Charlie, looking to the blood-red sun. 'You'd hardly know it. Fire lights the city bright as day.'

'And heats the air,' said Lily, sweating. It was desert dry, and warmth poured from the ashes and burned rubble.

Charlie saw a run of exposed cellars where the road had collapsed. Burned wine barrels, rolls of silk and linen turned to ash, butter and cheeses split and scorched.

'There's not enough money in England,' murmured Lily, 'to pay back these goods.'

London Wall lay bare and desolate when they arrived. Its tangle of tall buildings cowed and humbled to ash. In the centre of it all, the London Stone stood alone glowing faintly.

'It's like a lone survivor,' said Lily, eyeing the luminescent stone. 'Looking at everything it's lost.'

'At least the stone survived,' said Charlie. 'A bad omen should it have cracked.'

'I thought you didn't believe in omens.'

'The London Stone is different.'

'It hasn't done much good so far,' said Lily.

Charlie was taking in the ugly devastation. As an orphan he'd grown up floating between the close family structures and social ranks that tie Londoners to the clay earth. So he'd made his own ancestry in the dense buildings and dirt alleys of London. He'd woven his soul into labyrinthine streets and crowded taverns. Now all was burned and he felt suddenly adrift.

'Looters are already here,' noted Charlie, looking at a man and a boy picking through the debris. They were working the edges of the burned buildings, coughing as smoke plumed from the spongy ash.

'Have a care for the smoulder,' called Charlie to the boy. 'Where there is smoke is fire.'

The young looter wore a tatter of flour sacking for a shirt, torn to show ribs under paper-thin skin. He nodded uncertainly, but his pencil-thin limbs continued stalking the hot remains.

The older man wiped a line of sweat from his brow. 'Still does dreadful warm here,' he commented, looking to Charlie. 'Think you it smoulders?'

Charlie nodded. There was something on the warm air. A whispered promise of unfinished business.

'Don't go inside the buildings,' advised Charlie. 'Smoke can choke a man quickly.'

The man took off the dog-eared wedge of material that served for his hat and waved it in front of his face. 'Perhaps,' he said suspiciously. 'But I think if it flares again the flames will be small and we'll have a goodly time to escape.'

They moved towards the shell of a burned-out cottage, the man using a stick to poke around the fire's leavings and the boy plunging his hands into the charred embers, cursing occasionally as they met with a burning fragment.

Charlie frowned at them and turned back to Lily.

'On their own heads,' he muttered.

Lily was looking at the gutted remains.

'Can you tell from the rubble?' she asked, prodding a chunk of smoking wood, 'where the pawn shop was?'

Charlie was taking in the shapes of the burned-out carnage.

'We're standing in Fen Church,' he said. 'So over there.'

Lily was shaking her head.

'This was some noble's house, Charlie. Look at the burned things. That's a piece of plate. And some parts of linens were there.' She knelt and eased free the remains of a burned box. Inside was a blackened ribbon, scorched where it had held hair. The rest was fine ash that fell through her fingers.

'It's not a noble house,' said Charlie. 'It was a church. Commoners tried to protect what they had here. That's why you see domestic things.' He pointed.

'People use the churches to protect their things from fire,' continued Charlie. 'Thick stone,' he added, slapping a standing fragment of wall and causing scorched bricks to fall. 'Those who can't afford carts or boats rely on God's protection.'

'They lost it all,' said Lily sadly. 'And they didn't have much to begin with.' She was looking at a scorched sack of grain. 'What of those with expensive goods?' she added. 'Jewellers, fur trades?'

'Those are guild trades,' said Charlie distractedly, leading her over the debris. 'They have the Guildhall to store their fine things. It has a vault buried twenty feet underground with walls two feet thick.'

He paused to take in the angle of the sun and the shape of the ruins.

'The pawn shop is over there.' He pointed at a crowd of men digging at some shrubs. 'Likely he'll be with those other shopkeepers unearthing their goods.'

Lily hesitated as they passed a charred corpse. Some unlucky Londoner had tried to rescue their possessions from the flames.

'They'll say that no one died,' she added sadly. 'That's how nobles will tell it. No one will record the commoners who burned.'

'This way,' said Charlie.

As they crunched over the burned ground a gentle breeze whispered through the piles of decimated buildings and possessions. It stirred a malevolent glow in the embers, watching them through a hundred red eyes.

Chapter 103

Charlie and Lily found a clutch of sweating men digging purposefully by a patch of skeleton-black bushes. For a moment Charlie thought the pawnbroker wasn't among them. And then he saw him, leaning on his shovel looking mournfully to the smoke above. A pile of muddy goods lay by his feet.

'Brookes!' Charlie approached him warmly. The pawnbroker's far-away look was replaced by surprise then pleasure. He was a silver-haired man who'd moulded into the fabric of his shop over the years. Outside his small shop he looked lost and strange.

Brookes clapped Charlie on the shoulder. Then his eyes rested on Lily.

'This is Lily,' said Charlie. 'A friend.'

Brookes raised his white eyebrows.

'You need not fear, I do not come to sell,' said Lily.

'You know each other?' asked Charlie.

'She's come to pawn things before,' mumbled Brookes, in a tone which suggested the transaction hadn't been a pleasant one.

Lily smiled innocently.

'You saved your goods?' asked Charlie, pointing to the beginnings of an open pit. Inside was a dense packed trove of possessions.

The first layer revealed blackened cooking pots, bone-handled knives, fusty wigs and linen bed sheets.

'My goods, yes,' said Brookes, stooping to heave out a skillet. He dusted away soil and dropped it to one side. 'But I have nowhere to house them. The shop is all burned. The fire still rages. My shop boy goes to Watford where we have a cousin with a donkey.'

Charlie knelt to help him, pulling free some cheap bolts of cloth.

'People say the fire will reach the Palace,' continued Brooks. 'Perhaps there'll be nothing to come back for. If Whitehall burns people will doubt the Crown.'

They both stared up at the red-black clouds covering the sky. The bloody maw of the flames crashed a great crescendo in the distance. The air was parched.

'All here was vanquished,' continued Brookes. 'It was like civil war all over again. The fire had laid up its wide army all around then attacked us mercilessly.'

He shook his head sadly.

'Many poor people thought the church would save them. No flames could breach the walls. But the roof. The roof of St Swithins was wooden shingle. Flaming ashes dropped down.' Brookes mimed the action with a palm of ash scooped from the ground. 'I saw myself when flames had exploded through the tall windows,' he added. 'It tore the weeping face from the Virgin Mary and showered the street in stained glass. Like jewels. Until the looters came.'

'Didn't they fight the fire on Cannon Street?' asked Charlie.

Brookes shook his head and heaved out a small, sturdy chest. Charlie helped him brush away soil and set it right.

'It came like a stealth attack,' said Brookes. 'The people were distracted trying to save the church. The heat had skulked along St Swithin's Lane, warming the dry timbers of the homes, readying them for the next wave of force. Then came a blast of gale wind. It drove smoke into our faces and suddenly all the houses were alight.'

Brookes paused.

'But you don't come for news of the fire,' he decided.

Charlie shook his head. 'I'm looking for a Royalist who pawned a set of guns. Seventeen years ago.'

They'd unearthed a new layer of pawned possessions now. Piles of dresses, underclothes, breeches and stockings lay exposed. Hose, belts, coats, and boxes brimming with buttons and buckles.

'A set of guns?' Brookes pulled free a bundle of shoes. 'They'll be in my records. But they're all in St Paul's Cathedral.'

'St Paul's?'

'Safest place in the city for paper,' said Brookes. 'The stationers and booksellers of Paternoster Row began it,' he added. 'St Paul's will never burn.'

'Could we get your records out?' asked Charlie with a rising sense of hopelessness.

Brookes shook his head.

'The vaults at St Paul's are sealed up so tight not the tiniest spark can get inside. Fire rages that way. Those with papers in the vault are determined it will not burn. Ah!' he added, 'my sledge.'

They turned to see a beleaguered-looking donkey led by a frightened boy. Both animal and herder were looking this way and that at the burned city.

'You can see the flame from Watford,' said the boy. 'The people all say it's a curse. On the King and his godless ways.'

'Never mind the King,' said Brookes, pointing to the pit. 'Load the sledge.'

A clutch of tools had been revealed under the clothing. Handsaws and hammers. The boy worked to pull free a scythe and began heaping the sledge at impressive speed. Charlie helped Brookes heave up a set of hoes.

'Perhaps you remember the man,' tried Charlie, aware time was running out. 'Thomas Blackstone. Tall. Dark hair, blue eyes. Very large. Grossly so.'

Brookes shook his head and didn't stop loading.

'He came after the war,' pressed Charlie. 'Few Royalists pawned guns at such a time.'

'More than you might imagine,' said Brookes, straightening. But he looked as though he might be remembering something. He looked distractedly to Lily. She was dipping her hand into a rescued button box and letting the contents fall through her fingers.

'He has a smell of death about him, this Blackstone,' supplied Lily. 'Dangerous. A general during the war. Docked from a ship called the Mermaid.'

This seemed to prompt a memory.

'There was a general,' said Brookes slowly. 'Now you say of a ship it puts me in mind of him.'

Chapter 104

Monmouth was adjusting the seed pearls on his black doublet. He pulled at the reins on his horse, coughing at the smoke. His long lashes blinked against the smuts and cinders.

'You've found me a bad horse, Clarence,' he accused, twisting in an effort to regain control. 'She nearly had me off when we fled from that mob.'

'She has the best temperament in the Royal Stables,' said Clarence, giving his own steed a soothing pat. 'She behaved valiantly. But the smoke frightens her.'

They looked to the General Post Office. It was a fine brick building with long windows in new glass.

'We'll defend it with our lives,' said Monmouth grandly, still wrestling the horse. 'Where are the men?'

'These are what we have,' said Clarence, gesturing to the thirty palace guards. 'We must press commoners to make one hundred.'

Monmouth blanched a little. 'Very good,' he muttered. His horse jerked her head and Monmouth gave her a spiteful kick. Cries went up in the distance. Mobs were on full attack now, battering Catholics and lynching foreigners.

'Common people,' muttered Monmouth. 'If I were King I'd have them hanged for looking so disagreeable.' He glanced at Clarence irritably.

'Do you really think it's true?' asked Monmouth. 'That Parliament would have me as King?'

'The Queen births no children,' said Clarence carefully. 'The Duke of York has Catholic sympathies. I can imagine it said, that a good Protestant should rule.'

Monmouth seemed to swell.

'I would look very fine with a crown,' he said. 'Royal jewels ornamenting me. I have the bearing for it, that's what people say.'

Clarence's eyes flashing a warning. Monmouth's ambition was troubling him. The boy seemed increasingly deluded of late.

'Why are you twisting like that, Clarence?' asked Monmouth. 'Do lice trouble you?'

'A few possessions,' admitted Clarence, 'inside my doublet. And I wear extra clothes too. My house will burn within the hour,' he added, looking steadily to the enormous Post Office.

Monmouth raised his eyebrows. 'They couldn't get you a cart?'

'They did, but I sent it to the Naval Office,' said Clarence. 'Important paperwork there. There's rumours the Dutch could attack whilst England is weak. We need our defences in place.'

He moved a fat white hand inside his doublet and brought forth a little miniature. A portrait of a plain-looking girl.

'It's strange,' said Clarence, 'I always thought I'd protect my fine furnishings. In the end I only wanted a few items.'

Monmouth peered at the miniature.

'Your wife?' he suggested.

'My daughter,' said Clarence thoughtfully. 'She died in child-birth, recently, but I hadn't seen her for years. I didn't approve of her marriage and wouldn't pay her dowry. My daughter never forgave me,' said Clarence, tucking the miniature back in his doublet.

'The sins of Eve,' said Monmouth, 'are borne by women.'

'She died alone,' said Clarence, hardly listening. 'There was no money for a live-in nurse. By the time her husband came back with the midwife it was too late. And now all burns, I realise that I lost everything long ago.'

Clarence looked to the assembled soldiers.

'Fire comes, Your Grace,' he said. 'We should begin pressing men.'

'It looks a good deal in the distance,' said Monmouth uncertainly. He leaned down and refastened a ribbon that had untied on his breeches. 'Once the people see us fine men on horses, they'll rush to our aid. No need to endanger ourselves unduly.'

A guard was approaching.

'High tide comes,' said Clarence, looking hopefully to the Thames. 'Pipes in the west will fill with water again. Perhaps there is a chance . . .'

'The Fleet River is blocked with debris,' said the guard, shaking his head. 'The only way to clear it is gunpowder. We have no long fuses.'

'Have we no brave men?' asked Monmouth. He glanced at the King's guard. 'None who'll risk themselves for the city?'

The guard looked at Monmouth, high on his horse in his spotless clothing.

'None under this command,' he said.

There was a long silence. Then Clarence began sliding from his horse.

'I'll go,' he said.

Monmouth turned to him in shock.

'You could lose a hand!' he said. 'It's a commoner's job.'

Clarence was removing his snowy wig.

'Better an old man lose a hand than a young one,' he said. 'Have men roll the gunpowder by the blockage. I'll light the fuse.'

The guard was looking dubiously at Clarence. The fat old man might lose more than a hand. He didn't look fast on his feet. But a slim chance was better than none, he reasoned.

'Bring the gunpowder!' called the guard.

Chapter 105

Brookes was frowning in thought. 'A Royalist who'd come back from Holland,' he said. 'I have a memory he pawned something valuable. Might have been guns, though I couldn't say for certain.'

'Do you remember anything else about him?' asked Charlie.

Brookes shook his head. 'It was a long time ago,' he said.

'You would have taken his residence,' said Charlie. 'If he pawned guns.'

'I would have,' said Brookes. 'It would be written in my records.'

'The records we can't get to?' said Lily, turning out a weasel-skin coat and a pair of leather stays.

Brookes looked at her and then back to the boy loading.

'You're sure you remember nothing of his guns?' pressed Charlie.

Brookes shook his head slowly. 'Couldn't even say for sure that's what he pawned. Many guns, Charlie. Many guns in seventeen years.' He turned to the boy. 'We can't fit the larger tools,' he decided. 'Leave them. Take the buttons and buckles.'

'What of his reasons for pawning?' asked Charlie. 'If it was something valuable you must have asked the reason?'

The boy had almost fully loaded the sledge and Brookes was looking sadly at the possessions he'd have to leave to looters.

Brookes hesitated. 'You're right,' he said. 'I do have some recollection of that.' He frowned trying to urge the memory. 'This man had sailed back from Holland and I asked of our exiled King,' said Brookes. 'And he said . . . He said something of putting his faith in new giants. Those who warded for breed not birth.' Brookes looked at his goods. 'I remember it,' he said, 'because my wife was growing beans at the time and she made some joke. Jack and the beanstalk or some such.'

Lily and Charlie looked at one another. Lily mouthed the words to herself.

New giants.

'Do you know what he meant?' asked Charlie finally. Brookes shrugged. 'A family motto?' he suggested. 'I was more interested that he'd met the exiled King.'

'A strange kind of motto, breeding over birth' said Charlie, but Brookes was focused on wedging extra goods on to the sledge.

The slightest rustling had begun to sound from the nearby ruins, and a fine mist of smoke was shrugging slowly up into the sky. The donkey let out a baleful sound.

'You should go now,' said Charlie, surveying the devastated remains. 'There are still unburned embers here. The wind hasn't died out. And something happens to the west.'

He was looking to the red clouds that had begun to swirl like Armageddon.

Brookes nodded and slapped the unhappy donkey.

'Always take the word of Charlie Tuesday,' he winked, 'when fire is at hand.'

There was a sudden shout from near Fen Church. Charlie looked up, half expecting to see rekindled flame.

One of the looters had pulled free a droop of metal, melted to an indeterminate shape and studded with black cinders. He was holding it up triumphantly. Charlie watched as the father wandered over to where his son stood, stepping with difficulty where the rubble beneath him broke anew and plunged him ankle deep into soot.

They should leave, Charlie decided. The embers were burning too hot. And he could see a muddy haze begin to drift from the ash. But the problem of the guns was nagging at him.

'Pistols,' said Charlie, thinking aloud. 'Giants for breed not birth.' It sounded faintly *familiar* somehow. Like a colloquialism he'd heard before. He scanned his memory.

'Giants in the city?' said Lily.

'There are wooden giants at Guildhall,' said Charlie slowly. 'Gog and Magog. Statues from an old legend. Men say . . .' He turned it in his head. 'Men say Gog and Magog watch over trade and care not for Kings.'

He looked at Lily.

'Breed not birth,' she said.

Suddenly things fell into place.

Chapter 106

Torr sat straight-backed, eyes closed. His damp prison vanished away.

The gunshot wound throbbed. He was dying, he knew. But his mystic meditations lifted him beyond pain and anger. It was a kind of magic.

Torr had lived by the sword and expected to die a soldier's death. He'd never thought it would come at the hand of his brother at arms.

Torr placed a steady hand on his bloody sternum. Slowly he worked through the Tree of Life tattoo.

Foundation, Mercy, Wisdom, Victory.

His fingers settled at the very top, where a crown was tattooed. And without meaning to Torr found himself back there. Holland. The secret alchemy chamber. Holding the marriage papers.

The power.

Even now, all these years later, Torr could taste it. Crucible embers smouldering. The glow of knowledge.

A little roll of papers. Torr could feel them now, resting in his hand. He could see Teresa, dressed all in black. Tears streaming down her horrified face.

This is treason. The Brotherhood will kill us.

A little roll of papers that could destroy a Kingdom. It was temptation. Torr knew it now. His years with mystics had helped him commune with his higher self. Temptation and pride. They had driven him to it. He repented of it now, but it was too late.

We should never have made the marriage!

But it was no good. The thing had been done.

The ultimate marriage.

Torr could only hope that Sally Oakley had hidden the papers well. If Blackstone found them, he would be capable of anything.

He let his mind run deeper, back to poor Teresa Blackstone. Hers had been the most shocking confession he'd ever heard. Her husky voice, explaining the terrible things Blackstone made her do. It still haunted him.

The gunshot wound pulsed a spasm of pain. Torr's eyes jerked open. It was no good. The nightmare reality flooded back. He called to mind the last time he'd seen his captor.

'You never would reveal to me,' said Blackstone, 'the secrets of your mystic sect.'

'You weren't deemed worthy,' said Torr. 'And I swore never to reveal the secrets.'

Blackstone was looking at the tree of life tattoo, his mouth moving.

'I think this must be sulphur,' he said, looking up to Torr's face. 'Sulphur mixed with quicksilver perhaps.'

Torr shook his head.

'It isn't a code for you to unravel. It's a journey.'

Blackstone stabbed a finger at the trunk of the tree. Torr flinched.

'Foundation,' he said. 'The trunk is the foundation stone. The golden elixir. So these branches must be the formula. The ingredients.'

Torr sighed and looked away.

'You never did understand, Thomas. I pity you that. If it's wealth you seek, best look to the papers you stole.'

'When Teresa's soul is freed,' said Blackstone, 'she'll reveal the papers to me. I'm sure of it. They're close.'

'Why did you make Teresa do it?' asked Torr.

Guilt flashed across Blackstone's face.

'Two people,' he said. 'We needed two people.'

'You could have chosen someone else.'

'Teresa was pure,' said Blackstone. 'Pure, obedient and loyal.'

'She was an innocent soul,' said Torr, shaking his head. 'You made her hunted. She must have feared the Brotherhood would kill her slow.'

'But they didn't,' said Blackstone. 'I protected her.'

'In a damp cellar?' said Torr. 'It's no wonder she turned to witch-craft and dark things.'

Blackstone's eyes flashed.

'That was Sally Oakley's doing,' he said. 'Filling her mind with it.' He shook his head. 'You made the marriage, Torr. You're as guilty as I. Worse. Without your powers it never could have happened. You changed everything.'

'I thought I did right,' said Torr. 'But we made a monster, you and I. We mined gold from humble lead.'

'And what of Sally Oakley? Letting her practise pagan things.'

'Sally was from the country,' said Torr. 'Perhaps she even did a little good with her charms and herbs.' Torr eyed Blackstone.

'You broke your word,' he said. 'To Tobias. You said you'd protect Sally and keep her safe as a maid in your household until he returned from sea.'

Blackstone's eyes flashed.

'Broke my word to a traitor?' he demanded. 'Tobias Oakley loved a maid-servant more than our cause. And Sally meddled with things she shouldn't.'

Torr was shaking his head.

'*You should have better counsel with yourself,*' *he said.* '*Charles Stuart. He was the one who left us talking war and thrones, whilst he rutted with pretty girls. You twisted your rage to Tobias.*'

Blackstone gave a thin smile. '*Tobias married a penniless maid. What did she bring the cause? My wife's dowry funded our last battle.*'

'*Is that what you hoped to do with the papers?*' *asked Torr.* '*Get back Teresa's dowry?*'

Blackstone allowed himself a smile.

'*I thought about it often,*' *he said.* '*Such power. To have such power . . .*' *He closed his eyes.* '*Years ago I would have made gold,*' *he said.* '*Riches. Now,*' *he smiled,* '*I will topple England.*'

Torr looked away.

'*Fire comes,*' *said Blackstone.* '*I have chosen a fitting sacrifice for Teresa. As she burns, so London will fall. All will be cleansed.*'

Blackstone closed his eyes at the image. Then he opened them again.

'*I can't take you with me.*' *He gave Torr a little smile.* '*You know how sure I must be of my plans. You're unpredictable.*'

Torr looked down to see the pistol in Blackstone's hands.

He spread his arms wide. '*God grant me the grace,*' *said Torr,* '*to accept the things I cannot change.*'

Blackstone pointed the pistol. '*Grace,*' *he said thoughtfully.* '*I haven't heard that word in a long time.*' *And he fired the gun.*

Chapter 107

'I've had it all wrong,' said Charlie as realisation dawned. 'I thought of Blackstone as a clever alchemist. But he is nothing so skilled. Remember the way he fires the city? The guildhalls?'

Lily nodded.

'He is a guild man,' said Charlie. 'I'm sure of it. Think. Blackstone loses everything in the war. His secrets are stolen. All he has of value is a set of pistols.'

'Enough to buy a place in a guild,' breathed Lily.

The light gusts had became a stronger kind of exhalation, steadily kindling the loose embers. Charlie listened. It was coming from the west.

'Whatever schemes or alchemy the Sealed Knot made in Holland, they did not work,' said Charlie, thinking aloud. 'Blackstone joined a guild. And whichever guild it was,' he added, 'taught Blackstone some fraternity secrets to make blue fire.'

He looked north to the blaze. 'If Blackstone's a guildman he likely stored goods in Guildhall,' he continued. 'There could be some clue to his whereabouts. His chest could even be there too, waiting for us.'

'The papers,' said Lily. 'Whatever secrets they hold, I'll wager it's enough to stop Blackstone in his tracks.'

'Guildhall has fire engines,' said Charlie. 'So long as they put them to use, we likely have a few hours before the flames reach there.'

A sudden sharp wind was pouring forth along Cannon Street.

'Something is coming,' said Charlie. 'We need to leave.' Instinctively he turned to where the looters were picking through a building. Flames had struck up again.

Charlie felt it before he saw it. The fire was making its own weather.

'Get away from the ruins!' shouted Charlie as flames poked their heads from the rubble. The father and son looters were confused, looking at one another, not knowing which way to turn. The flames had danced out to dazzle. But it was the smoke, wreathing luxuriantly through the air, that was wrapping them in its deadly embrace.

Charlie raced towards the burned-out cottage knowing he was already too late. Smoke was stealing quiet fingers down the throats of the looters, and he was too far away. The old man began wheezing first, dropping to his knees as the fumes took hold. In panic his son knelt to grasp his father's shoulders. Fires were winking to life all over the sooty ruins now, like a pack of little devils. Father and son were trapped in the flames. And in the distance the London Stone seemed to glow hotter.

Wind blew sharp and fierce, streaming in from every compass point.

Charlie was halfway to the looters when he heard it. A great sigh like a heart breaking. Then the London Stone shuddered and cracked.

Beyond, in the rest of the city, Londoners would swear this to be the time they heard a giant rumble sweep over them. Like the harbinger of apocalyptic force. The ground trembled and the standing buildings shook in the heat as though rattled by a mighty hand.

In the heart of the city fire sunk deep as if to garner its strength, and then towered up, sucking in its own immense winds that streamed in from every side.

'What's happening?' Lily cried as scalding gales blew out her skirts, spitting hot dust and splinters.

Charlie froze, partway towards the trapped looters and turned back to Lily.

A hurricane was pouring in from every direction, hurling forth everything in its path. The fire in the west gave a great thunderous bellow and surged high into the sky.

'Get down!' Charlie shouted. The blast of air was spiralling larger debris from the ruins. Lily ducked. A splintered chair leg spun over her head and embedded itself deep in a blackened wall.

In the burned-out cottage the son had stumbled to his feet, looking for a path through the flames. A flying barrel caught him unawares, smashing his skull and knocking him to the floor. Neither father nor son were conscious as flames scorched away their hair and clothing in quick acrid billows.

Charlie took hold of Lily.

'We need to get out of the wind!' he shouted over the howl of the gale. Heavy debris was picking up now, driven towards the hungry flames by the oncoming hurricane.

'Behind a building,' he called as dust and dirt were driven into their eyes and mouths. Charlie's eyes locked on Fenchurch Street. 'This way,' he decided.

'What's happening?' cried Lily as they forged against the wind. 'It's like the world is ending.' A sack exploded against the cobbles at their feet, blasting them with a spray of flour.

'Something to do with the heat of the fire,' said Charlie as they battled towards Fenchurch Street. 'The heat pulls in so much air. It makes a kind of storm.'

A crack of lightning forked in the distance.

Charlie glanced back to the burned-out cottage. Having shaved and stripped the two looters the fire was devouring its quarry. Melted skin and crackling fat blazed anew in the reawakening furnace.

Above the city the heavy smoke began to swirl and sway, as if something was stirring the elements. And on the ground the people knew it. Armageddon was coming to claim London.

The firestorm had arrived.

Charlie watched helplessly as flames tore through the streets. It was moving faster. He thought at least double the speed. Which meant around one hundred houses an hour were burning.

'Guildhall,' panted Charlie, as they moved behind the shelter of a burned-out house. 'We can still get there.'

Lily looked uncertainly to the boiling sky.

'My father told me,' she said, 'of far off lands, where fire grew hot enough to make a tempest. I thought it was a campfire story.'

'The wind blows inland,' said Charlie. 'We can cut up Cornhill.'

'Do you think it will reach Guildhall?' asked Lily.

Charlie nodded.

'With the wind as it is,' he said, 'Guildhall will burn soon.'

Chapter 108

'We'll put her chest there,' Blackstone said, pointing.

'In the enclave?' said Jacob.

Blackstone nodded.

Jacob fitted his arms to begin heaving the large trunk. Blackstone moved to help him.

'It's heavy,' panted Jacob, 'for an empty chest.'

'This was her wedding trunk,' said Blackstone, as it was manoeuvred into position. 'It came with thirteen blessings inside.' There was a tone to his voice which Jacob hadn't heard before. Regret.

'Lots of folk still make the old ways,' said Jacob. 'Totems for hearth and home, luck and love.'

Blackstone's eyes fixed on him sharply.

'A great evil,' he said, 'those old ways. They are against the Catholic faith.'

Blackstone was staring at the chest, as though remembering something.

Jacob dropped his head, confused. Teresa's possessions were all spell-craft. Poppets bound in ribbon, switches of willow and oak.

'Yes,' he mumbled.

'Arrange those there.' Blackstone was pointing.

Jacob began moving through Teresa's things with shaking hands. They were things he didn't like to touch. Dark magic and bloodied talismans.

Blackstone watched as he worked.

'In Holland,' he said, 'much was made of alternative faith. Mysticism. Different ways to experience God.'

Jacob kept his mouth shut tight.

'Heathen practices,' said Blackstone. 'But I found them useful. I learned my own conjuring tricks from their rites and death practices.'

His eyes swung to Jacob.

'I returned to England and joined a guild,' he said. 'They taught me secrets too. How lye can be flamed blue. Ways to make a demon in a bottle that will set alight.'

Jacob was working stoically on moving Teresa's terrible things. His eyes were darting, trying to find a way to escape.

'Do you know what we build here?' asked Blackstone.

Jacob shook his head.

'This is a fortification,' said Blackstone. 'Like every great general I know every inch of it.'

Jacob was waiting for his moment. He'd been watching Blackstone. The Thing he called his wife. That was the key to escaping. Jacob would do some damage. Drop a candle. Upend a table. Blackstone would be distracted. Jacob would escape. He knew the backstreets well. And he was fast on his feet. All he needed to do, was wait for his moment.

Chapter 109

'It's like hell itself,' said Lily as the white stone walls of Guildhall came into view. 'Everyone looks to themselves.'

The wide courtyard was thick with armed men loading goods. Guild merchants were grappling to hold fast their carts and possessions. Droves of poorer Londoners were hanging on carts, pleading and tussling to load their meagre goods. Fights were breaking out and drivers brandished whips and cudgels.

'People think judgement comes,' said Charlie, watching two men and a screeching woman throw punches. 'It's pure fear they act by.'

Gog and Magog had loomed large over Guildhall for as long as anyone could remember. The wooden giants conferred protection for the city merchants. But today they had ropes slung around their necks. As Charlie and Lily approached the first statue was felled. Gog hit the ground with an ominous crack, his benevolent face split in two.

A terrified horse reared up, sending the contents of a wooden cart flying free. Tumbling barrels split apart on the cobbles. Salt spilled out in snowy drifts and people dived to fill their tankards.

Warm winds were whipping the people into a frenzy and the firefighting had broken down. A large fire engine stood unused.

There was a muddy puddle nearby where men had dug out the pipes. But the pressure was run out and the water pooled to nothing.

Two apprentice boys jostled past carrying a large painting. It was an enormous tree bearing the guild trades across its branches, root and trunk. Picked out in gold leaf were the names of the Lord Mayors.

Charlie watched it go past. The old song London boys learned to memorise the guilds sounded in his head.

The Mayor of London's Guilds. Butchers, saddlers, soapmakers, goldsmiths, carpenters, cooks, barber surgeons, vintners, drapers, coopers, cutlers, skinners, fishmongers.

Charlie froze.

'Lily,' he said, 'give me the round robin.'

'But why . . .?'

'Give it to me.'

She rustled in her dress and handed it over, looking annoyed. Charlie snatched it up.

'We've been carrying a clue to Blackstone all along.' Charlie pointed to the round robin. 'This paper of common men's names. They're not names. They're guilds.'

Lily peered at the paper, mouthing the words.

'Saddler, Goldsmith, Cooper . . .'

She looked up at Charlie in amazement.

'Cutler, Cook, Barber,' she read. Her eyes flicked up to Charlie. 'The Cutlers' Guild. The Worshipful Company of Cooks, the Barbers' Company.' She looked at him. 'You have it right. They are guilds, every one.'

'Nine names,' said Charlie. 'And there are ten guilds in the city. So whichever guild is not on here,' he stabbed the paper, 'that is Blackstone's guild.'

They looked back at the map in earnest. Lily's finger shot out.

'Here!' she said. 'Soapmaker. Blackstone is of the Soapmakers' Guild.'

They looked at one another.

'Lye,' said Lily. 'Lye is not just for laundresses. The best soap-makers use lye.'

'So Blackstone uses lye,' said Charlie. 'To make balls of soap. That's how he comes to know the alchemy. The guild of soapmakers taught him their secrets.'

'Which guilds store their goods here?' Charlie called to one of the apprentice boys struggling with the painting.

'All of them.' The boy seemed confused by the question. 'Every guildsman is entitled to keep possessions in the vaults,' he added, pointing to a heavily bolted and locked door. 'But the vaults are full. No one allowed in.'

Charlie and Lily looked at one another. The entrance seemed impregnable.

'Did a man come bearing this mark?' asked Charlie, holding up his key. 'A soapmaker?' But the boy only shook his head and hurried away.

'We need to get inside,' said Charlie, eyeing the ornate stone-carved front of Guildhall. A huge door decorated with gargoyle heads was open a crack.

'Perhaps if we can get into Guildhall,' he suggested, 'there'll be another way down to the vaults.'

'There's no way into Guildhall,' said Lily, looking at the burly men on the door. 'It's heavily guarded.'

'They'll guard it until fire is at the door,' agreed Charlie, look-ing at a well-dressed Alderman with two large guards. 'Knowing the guilds they'll be some sign or secret words to get inside.'

'Do you know it?'

Charlie shook his head.

'Being part of a guild is about integrity,' he said. 'Keeping your word. Working hard. Freemen believe that noble deeds outweigh noble birth.'

'Freemen?'

'It's the title of a man once he's joined a guild,' said Charlie. 'A freeman of the city.'

Charlie eyed the entrance thoughtfully. He turned his key.

'All guilds have a motto or some such. The right words would get us inside.'

He thought for a moment. 'They won't let us in the Guild without authority,' he said. 'But Guildhall is part of St Lawrence Jewry church. The Mayor's church. By rights every Londoner should be entitled to say their prayers inside. Come on,' he decided. 'Nothing ventured nothing gained.'

And he walked purposefully to the door with Lily shuffling uncertainly behind. The Alderman was looking at Charlie's feet as they approached.

'The crypts are full,' said the Alderman. 'And for guildsmen only.'

'I wish to enter the church,' said Charlie. 'To say a prayer for the city.'

The guards rearranged themselves.

'The church is for freemen of the guilds only,' said the Alderman. 'And fire will be here soon. You'd best get yourself and your wife to safety.'

'I'm London born,' said Charlie. 'The King decrees I have the right to pray in the Mayor's church.'

The Alderman shook his head. 'The King might say so. But he has no sway here. Here is Guildhall law. And we say our men only.'

Charlie held up his key. 'I'm of the guilds,' he improvised. 'I've already brought goods. For Master Blackstone. Of the soapmakers.'

The Alderman looked at him. 'I don't recognise the sign,' he said. 'Each guild has their own marks and practices I suppose.'

'Fire comes,' said Charlie, desperately turning over what could gain them entry. 'Master Blackstone wants a prayer said to be sure it won't burn.'

'The whole of Guildhall could burn and the crypt will hold,' said the Alderman. 'It's stood since old King Stephen.' His tone became sardonic. 'I hear Blackstone's soap is bought by the King's ladies,' he added. 'So he might use Barbara Castlemaine's personal quarters.' The Alderman winked at the guard.

'I hear she is generous with them,' sniggered the guard.

'Guilds only in the church.' The Alderman's eyes settled back on Charlie. He seemed to be waiting for something.

'Lord guide us,' said Charlie, trying for the Lord Mayor of London's motto. The Alderman's face shifted. It hadn't been the answer he was looking for.

'We must hope so,' he replied, looking up to the heavens. 'Tell Master Blackstone he must come in person if he wishes entry. Or send a boy of the guild.' He waved his hand and the guard adjusted his stance.

Charlie's heart sank. There was no other way into Guildhall. He felt something at his ear. Lily was leaning close.

'Freemen of the City. Breed not birth right,' she whispered.

Charlie looked at her. Then he repeated the words to the Alderman, who was looking at Lily.

There was a slight pause. Then the Alderman nodded and moved away from the door.

'That's Guildhall password,' he said. 'So I must let you enter. Work with honour and keep our word,' he added. 'You might go in the church if you wish but you are foolish. Our firefighters have fallen to disarray. If flames come we can't hold them.'

Chapter 110

Amesbury's face was wracked with confusion.

'So lead into gold. It isn't real?'

'Not in the way it's commonly understood,' replied the alchemist. 'There are men who spend their lives trying to make gold. But they're not true alchemists.'

'But the Philosopher's Stone . . .'

'Is a story,' said the alchemist. 'A story to separate the unworthy from true alchemists. Alchemists don't grub for treasure,' he added. 'We seek to change the leaden mortal mind to the gold of enlightenment.'

'This is your lead into gold? The Magnus Opus?' said Amesbury. 'Your great work?'

The alchemist nodded. 'Enlightenment is the work of a lifetime. The path is different for everyone. Kaballah shows us steps to meditate upon. Tarot maps the journey. I believe some guilds have their own practices. The masons meditate upon death.'

Amesbury was nodding slowly.

'Torr's lead into gold,' he said, 'was a means to acquire riches.'

'Torr is a master of allegory,' said the alchemist. 'Spinning stories to hide truths. I think his lead to gold tells a different story. A power more . . . earthly.'

'The universal marriage,' said Amesbury. 'That's part of the story. The most sacred and powerful marriage.'

'That suggests more practical alchemy,' said the alchemist. 'The masculine and feminine. A marriage of the elements.'

Amesbury's brow furrowed in thought. 'Blackstone married a madwoman,' he said. 'She couldn't bear him children. No one knows why. There was some fine horrors which happened because of civil war. Royalists married to secure money for war. There were precious few love matches.' Amesbury seemed to be turning this around in his mind.

'For alchemists gold is metaphorical,' said the alchemist.

Amesbury felt there was some very obvious answer, but it kept sliding around at the edge of his thoughts.

'The only person who can answer your questions is Torr,' said the alchemist. 'He made the story. He knows the truth at the heart of the allegory.'

'I fear Torr,' said Amesbury, 'is long gone.'

'What of the other plot you spoke of?' asked the alchemist. 'You found fireballs in the royal apartments. Stamped with the sign of the Sealed Knot.'

Amesbury waved his hand distractedly.

'I was mistaken,' he said. 'An old member of the Sealed Knot joined a guild and had a fancy to use the symbol on his soap.' He mimed with his hands. 'Soap-balls, fireballs,' he shrugged. 'They can look almost identical.'

Amesbury gave a little smile. 'The courtly women were sneaking Blackstone into the Palace, trying to keep their soap purchases secret,' he said, conspiratorially. 'They were ashamed the King would learn of their measures to look youthful.'

To Amesbury's surprise the alchemist laughed.

'Women will go to greater lengths for vanity than anything I have ever encountered,' he said.

'It caused a lot of confusion,' said Amesbury. 'Barbara Castlemaine I can understand,' he added. 'When her looks fade, she'll have nothing. But I didn't expect such behaviour from the Queen.'

The alchemist shrugged. 'Women,' he said simply, 'will be all our undoing.'

Chapter 111

'How did you know the Guildhall password?' asked Charlie as they moved inside the cool interior of St Lawrence Jewry.

'It was written on their painting,' said Lily. 'The one they were taking to safety. And I've seen it written before. Every guild has a tapestry or a wooden carving with those words.'

'Not such a good secret,' observed Charlie.

'No,' said Lily. 'Perhaps they're not so concerned with hiding away as people imagine.'

They were in the vast church now. It was stripped completely bare and deserted.

'This way,' said Charlie. 'That door leads straight into Guildhall.'

They followed it through.

'No one to guard,' observed Lily.

'Nothing to guard,' corrected Charlie as they moved into the vast white stone interior of Guildhall. 'It's been cleared. Not even a tapestry or a candlestick left. All is in the vault.'

He pointed to the solid stone floor beneath their feet.

'What should we do?' asked Lily. 'We wanted to be in the vaults. We're only in the church. The entrance is outside and guarded.'

Charlie was looking around for a possible way down. There was none apparent.

'Guildhall vaults are an old crypt,' said Charlie, thinking aloud. 'Those big giants. Gog and Magog. They are Roman leavings. This whole place is an old Roman church.'

He rubbed his forehead.

'In old churches, there is always another route into the crypt. Under the altar.'

'How do you know that?' asked Lily.

'I've chased a few tomb raiders in my time. They always break in through the altar.'

'So how do we find the altar?' Lily was looking into Guildhall's grand vaulted ceiling. 'This building hasn't been a church for hundreds of years.'

Charlie was taking an angle of the sun.

'Altars are east facing,' he said, pointing to the back of the building. 'We will try there.'

They moved to the back of the grand hall and Charlie studied the black mosaic floor carefully.

'Here,' he said finally. 'And here. See it is brighter in colour. It makes a cross shape. If it was an altar, it was big,' he added.

Lily nodded.

'So where is the crypt entrance?' she said, studying the floor. 'There is nothing to mark it.'

Charlie scanned to where the centre of the altar would have been. He strode over and dropped to his knees.

'See here?' he said triumphantly. 'This is newer and a little higher. This mosaic has been added. The tiles are not so worn at the edges.'

Glancing about he removed his knife and inserted it down the side of a tile. It lifted out easily. Underneath was wood and Charlie worked to remove three more tiles.

'We can get in here,' he said. 'It is only planks over the old stone entrance.'

Using both arms he heaved and pulled back the wooden covering. A cloud of dusty smoke cleared to reveal a narrow set of steps.

'There is a way down!' he exclaimed, looking excitedly at Lily. She grinned and moved behind him as he lowered himself on to the stair.

The steps were steep and bowed into the middle from centuries of use. They turned in a sharp spiral downwards.

At the bottom of the steps Charlie stopped in wonder. The crypt was enormous, stretching the length of the entire Guildhall above. It was crested with a thick ceiling of vaulted stone, supported by heavy branching pillars. And it was stuffed to bursting point with merchants' valuables.

Charlie breathed out. It was a thieves' paradise.

'Look at this,' he whispered as Lily bumped into him in her haste to get off the dark stair. She gave a gratifying gasp at the sight of the booty.

'Every rich merchant in London must hide his goods here,' said Charlie.

'So how might we find Blackstone's valuables?' asked Lily, scanning the gloom.

Charlie followed the direction of her gaze. The Guildhall crypt was like a stone forest of branching pillars. Some possessions seemed to obey a kind of order. But most seemed randomly flung.

'Household things there,' Charlie muttered. 'Furniture and the like. That pile has many barrels, perhaps for vintners . . . It's by guild,' he decided eventually. 'But we need to know what order they are arranged.'

'By letter?' suggested Lily, studying the piles. 'Brewers, carpenters?'

Charlie shook his head.

'Remember these are guilds. They all have their secret codes and systems. It would be nothing so simple.'

'The Tree of Life?' suggested Lily. 'You saw it in the Cutlers' Guild.'

'No,' said Charlie. 'The cutlers are wealthy. Educated. They might teach these mystical practices. But a fishmonger or a barber?' he shook his head. 'Their initiation ceremonies will be a keg of beer and an argument.'

Lily scanned the piles, then marched towards a sturdy looking barrel and split open the top with a closed fist.

'Do you discover something?' asked Charlie, frowning at the ordinary looking barrel.

'Wine,' she said, leaning down and scooping several handfuls to her mouth. 'Helps me to think.'

Lily sucked her teeth and wiped her mouth. Then she sat and looked out into the wide crypt.

'It's so still down here,' she said. 'Peaceful. Hard to imagine out there the world is ending.'

Charlie took out his tankard and scooped out some wine. He sat by her and offered her a sip. She took it and passed the tankard back.

'Maybe it is,' said Charlie, taking a long swig. The cool quiet of Guildhall was a sudden relief. 'But I think this fire has been in the making a long time.'

He took another swig and passed the wine back to Lily.

'Do you think to leave the city?' she said. 'Now so much is burned?'

Charlie shook his head. 'What of you?' he asked. 'Do you miss your gypsy caravan?' He couldn't imagine being nostalgic for the dirty dangerous countryside.

'I miss…' she paused. 'The fireside stories. The camaraderie of it. You don't find that in the city.'

'You do,' said Charlie, thinking of the Bucket of Blood. 'Sometimes country people don't know where to look.'

'Maybe,' said Lily. 'But it's people that make home. When Blackstone killed my father, he took away my place in the world.'

Her eyes flashed pain. And for the first time Charlie had an understanding of how much sadness she'd carried.

'You left everything you knew to avenge your father,' he said. 'Takes bravery, that. More than I can imagine.'

She didn't answer, only took out her knife and scraped at the stone floor.

'I don't want vengeance,' she said. 'I want my father's soul to be at peace.'

'What makes you think it isn't?'

Lily bit her lip. 'There was a bird at his grave,' she said. 'A little blackbird. With a yellow beak.'

She glanced up at Charlie then down to the floor again.

'I knew at once.' She was twisting the blade now. 'It was the soul of my father.' Her dark eyes were on Charlie's now. 'City people don't believe such things,' she said. 'But when a gypsy dies wrongly, they do not go to a better place. They stay in the mortal world, until they're avenged.'

Lily looked back at the knife.

'My father taught me everything,' she said. 'He made sure I would never be defenceless. I will not let his soul wander the earth.'

They sat in silence, contemplating Guildhall crypt.

'We are alike in something then,' said Charlie thoughtfully. 'Blackstone took away my place in the world too. I might have family.'

'You think you might have lands due? Titles?'

Charlie shook his head.

'I'm not concerned for that. I live well enough. But sometimes I feel like . . . I don't know who I am,' he said. It was the first time he'd said it out loud, and the words felt strange. 'I should like to know,' he concluded.

'You think knowing your family would tell you who you are?'

'Maybe not.'

Charlie surveyed the crypt again, trying to make order from the chaos.

'We should try and find Blackstone's chest,' Lily said. She took the tankard from him and drained it.

Charlie stood. He closed his eyes. There was an order. He was sure of it. His gaze settled on the nearest pile of goods in the crypt. Among the medley of general possessions was a disproportionate quantity of leather.

'Skinners,' he decided, looking to the next pile. 'Next to the vintners.'

Something was tugging at his thief taker's instinct. Here was London's true heart, laid out in this crypt. Wealth. Commodities. Each guild had a separate huge jumbling pile. What distinguished where each stored their things?

Then the pattern settled into place. It was so simple. Charlie found himself smiling. He didn't know how he hadn't seen it before.

Chapter 112

The Fleet waterfront was ablaze as Clarence slipped and slid through the stinking riverbed. The blockage was before him. An enormous cart had come off the bridge in the mayhem to leave the city. It lay splintered into three huge parts. Two shire horses were sprawled dead. Fire debris, ash and general detritus in the river had caught on the cart and horses, building a dam.

Clarence's eyes rested on the gunpowder. Images of civil war veterans, hobbling on mangled limbs, flashed through his mind.

Two barrels, joined by the shortest of fuses. A beam of wood crashed down from a burning building, sending down a shower of sparks. He ducked clumsily as they hissed harmlessly on the wet mud.

Clarence was breathing heavily now. He took out his tinderbox, hands shaking. But as he approached the gunpowder, he knew he couldn't do it.

The blocked Fleet was much more slippery and precipitous than he'd anticipated. He'd never make it out. It had been a fantasy to imagine that he, of all men, could escape exploding gunpowder on a slimy riverbed.

Clarence took a breath. He'd tell them the fuses were too damp, the tinder wouldn't flare. They'd know him a cowardly old man who'd never been on a battlefield. But he'd escape with his life.

Then he heard a noise. A low whinny. One of the horses was still alive. A mare.

She rolled an eye towards him, bloodshot and terrified. At least two of her legs were broken. Clarence stamped towards her, sliding in the mud. He laid his hands soothingly on the mare's neck. Her heartbeat fluttered fast under his fingers.

'You've been lying here all alone,' said Clarence, looking to her shattered body. 'In pain and frightened.'

He realised he didn't have a sword to put her out of her misery.

Clarence tightened his grip on the tinderbox. 'I can end your suffering,' he decided. The gunpowder would blow everything to dust.

He made to move away towards the powder kegs, but the horse snorted.

'Easy girl,' breathed Clarence. 'Easy.'

Clarence looked to the fuses, then to the frightened animal.

The snaking flame would terrify her further. He should stay, to comfort her. Keeping a soothing hand on the horse, Clarence eased out a foot, and brought the short fuse line nearer.

The mare's chest was moving rapidly, her eyes flicking in confusion.

Clarence sat against her huge body, feeling light-headed.

'There's nothing to fear,' he said, patting the horse's sweating neck. 'I won't leave you here alone to die.' Clarence looked to the open kegs.

'In a moment there will be a loud noise,' he said. 'Then all this pain and suffering will be over. It will be very quick, I promise you.'

Clarence rubbed the horse's nose. He thought she understood him.

'Very quick,' he said. 'And I'm here with you all the while.'

421

Then he sparked the flint. The horse started as the flame grew. He stroked her flank. Then the fuse hissed and snaked.

'Nothing to fear,' said Clarence, resting his head against the horse's. He felt her breathing relax a little. He stroked her dusty mane. There were a few sad-looking flowers entwined in it, drooped and closed.

'My daughter made me daisy chains,' said Clarence, turning them in his chubby fingers. 'Long ones. I wore them more proudly than any chain of office. I never told her that.'

There was a booming explosion. Clarence felt himself lifted up. He tightened his grip around the mare's neck. Somewhere another barrel detonated. There was a sound of water rushing. Then nothing.

Chapter 113

Charlie scanned the medley of Guildhall crypt, surprised he'd not deduced the arrangement straight away.

'The order is based on the sacred god of all guilds,' said Charlie, grinning at Lily.

'Which is?'

'Money.'

Lily smiled. 'The piles are in order of the richest guilds?'

Charlie nodded. 'The wealthiest get the safest place. Simple as that.' His eye roved the crypt. 'Goldsmiths right in the centre. Everything spans out from that.'

'Where would soapmakers be?' asked Lily.

'Somewhere in the middle,' said Charlie, picking over the piles. He reached a barrier of goods stacked to ceiling height and began climbing over it. 'Soapmakers sell to fine ladies,' he added. 'There's money in vanity.'

They moved further into the possessions. It was darker and lower towards the centre. More like a cellar. Charlie felt the familiar unease close around him with the damp air.

'Why don't you like cellars?' asked Lily. She was watching him and Charlie realised his discomfort must have shown on his face.

'As a boy,' he said, moving over piles of leather goods, 'I lived in Blackstone's house. There was something in his cellar. A witch. I was very afraid of her.'

Charlie peered through the gloom and made out the edges of another pile. Saddlers. And there. Cooks. He cycled through his knowledge of the London trades and their incomes. Saddlers beat cooks, but came under soapmakers. Charlie switched left.

'A witch?' Lily was following behind him.

'Blackstone's wife,' said Charlie. 'Rowan, my brother, was drawn to her. He'd take her things. Tributes. Dead mice and the like. She'd make spells for him. Blood magic.'

'Did she have powers?' asked Lily, her eyes widening.

'I don't know,' said Charlie. 'But she was dangerous. She showed me a bloodied poppet once. A corn dolly. Told me she'd killed Blackstone's sister.'

Charlie had a sudden image of Teresa Blackstone, holding a blood-filled chalice, chanting. He gave an involuntary shudder, moving over piles of saddles and reins.

'Here,' he called back. 'This side.'

Charlie was standing motionless as Lily made her way over the mound of goods. She looked in dismay at the pile he stood by. It seemed to be one of the larger ones.

'How will we ever find Blackstone's things in here?' she asked.

Charlie pointed. 'There.'

A rush of sadness was washing over him. He'd recognised an item in the pile. Something from long ago.

Lily followed the direction of his finger. She looked back at him.

'I only see a bundle of cloth,' she said confused.

'Do you not see?' said Charlie. 'It is the same stitching as your handkerchief.'

Charlie strode into the pile and pulled it gently free.

'You can recognise stitching at a distance?' said Lily, confused.

'I've seen it before,' said Charlie. 'It was my mother's.'

It was the strangest feeling to be handling her things. Part of him wanted to put them back. To tuck them in the pile and pretend he'd never found them. There was a deep feeling of unease at the pit of his stomach.

'So this must be Blackstone's pile.' Lily was pointing excitedly. 'And there! Blackstone's chest!'

Chapter 114

The King rode out having made a tactical change of outfit. A thick pig-skin tabard now hung heavily from his broad shoulders and he wore high boots of the buccaneer style with thick wool stockings.

'We're losing,' said Amesbury bluntly. 'A firestorm sweeps the city. It sucks in air and fires out heat from buildings. Witnesses say the ruins on Gresham Street exploded again in flame. An inferno sweeps over Guildhall.'

'The merchant goods?' asked the King.

'I don't think even the crypt can protect them. The heat. No man has seen anything like it. It explodes stone.' Amesbury's face was grim.

'The city will be bankrupted,' said Charles. 'Thousands and thousands of pounds in that crypt. The wharfs of timber and metals. There are no commodities left in London.'

He shook his head. 'You must have faced worse odds in battle,' he suggested hopefully.

'No.' Amesbury shook his head. 'I never faced a worse enemy than this. It comes from all sides. It has a furious power. We've lost an engine and there's no pressure in the pipes for the ones we have.'

'The waterwheels,' asked Charles. 'Burned beyond repair?'

'So I hear it,' said Amesbury.

'James defends the Fleet,' said Charles. 'Send a fire engine to him. They can fill it straight from the river.' He wiped sweat. 'If my brother can hold off fire there, we have a chance to save the Palace,' he said.

'The Fleet is blocked,' said Amesbury. 'A large cart fell yesterday.'

'No,' said Charles, bringing out a letter signed by Monmouth.

'My son cleared the blockage himself,' said Charles proudly. 'He lit gunpowder with a short fuse at great personal risk.' The King sat higher on his horse. 'Monmouth has become a good soldier.'

Amesbury said nothing.

Charles eyed the wall of fire. His troops were stoically shovelling, fitting firehooks. But the pressed men were barely trying.

'Why don't they work harder?' asked Charles. 'It's their city they save.'

'They've nothing worth saving,' said Amesbury. 'They're homeless and beaten. The only thing they're here for is ale and bread.'

He turned in surprise. King Charles was off his horse and heading towards the blaze.

Amesbury swore and hurried after him. It was dangerous near the fire. Not to mention the general ill-feeling in the city towards the King.

But Charles was displaying a hitherto unseen common touch. Amesbury watched as he took a shovel from a wide-eyed commoner and directed the man to help with an undermanned firehook.

'Come on, men!' called Charles above the blaze. 'We can win this yet.'

Amesbury was speechless. An old man sidled up and gave him a toothless grin.

'I've been watching from the sidelines,' he admitted. 'I've an art for dodging press gangs. But if the King is fighting, well, there's something in that isn't there?'

And to Amesbury's surprise the old man trotted towards the blaze and began scooping soil with his hands and tossing it.

The other commoners had also been galvanised into action. They shovelled harder and cheered as the firehook demolished the top storey of the nearest building. It collapsed in a shower of splinters and a young man pulled the King bodily away from the tumbling debris.

Amesbury was impressed. He knew the power of leading from the front. And though the King couldn't hope to save the Palace, he would certainly go out in a blaze of glory.

Chapter 115

Charlie followed the direction of Lily's gaze. She was tugging a household trunk from the pile.

'That's not it,' he said. 'The chest we seek is a sea chest.'

Lily's face fell. She ceased pulling.

Charlie was taking in the heap of goods. There was something wrong and it took him a moment to work it through.

'None of his wife's things are here,' said Charlie.

'What?'

'His wife, Teresa,' said Charlie. 'Nothing of hers is in this pile. It is only his things. Blackstone's. Her wedding chest must be somewhere else.'

Lily was searching the pile for evidence of Blackstone's whereabouts. She tugged at household furniture and tapestries.

'Maybe there's a clue in my mother's things.' Charlie settled on to his haunches and unrolled the embroidery. A pewter tankard and three corn dollies wrapped in ribbons dropped free.

Charlie stared at them.

A pewter tankard. Poppets.

'You're sure it's your mother's?' asked Lily, moving to stare down at the fabric.

'She took these things from Blackstone's house,' said Charlie, nodding as he ran his hands over the fabric, 'before he murdered her. I recognise them. But I'd . . . forgotten them.'

As a child Charlie never questioned the little corn poppets. Now questions were coming thick and fast.

'Why would Blackstone have kept them?' asked Lily.

'I don't know.' An uncomfortable idea was shifting in his mind. Perhaps Blackstone had given his mother's things to Teresa. So she might perform some finding spell or curse. He pushed it away.

Charlie stared at his mother's possessions. It felt like he was dreaming. They brought with them a feeling, rather than a memory. Something soft and warm. Tinged with a deep fear.

Charlie turned a corn dolly. It was dulled to a dun colour. Corn stubble pointed up at the head like a crown and it was bound with faded ribbons.

'How did they get here?' asked Lily.

'Blackstone must have kept or hidden them,' said Charlie. 'She was a maid. These were what she put aside as proof she would not turn thief.' He frowned as the unexpected memory shuffled into place. 'I remember her wrapping this bundle and handing it to the mistress of the house. She was . . . sad I think.'

His attention was back on the corn dollies. There were three. Two small and one larger.

'Poppet magic?' asked Lily, looking at the doll.

'I . . . I don't know.'

Lily frowned and eased the larger dolly gently from his fingers.

'It is a harmless thing,' she said. 'A dolly for protection is all.'

'Then why were they not burned and buried? Only witches keep poppets past the harvest.'

'No,' said Lily. 'Many country folk practise the old ways. Poppets and ribbons for luck and love. Herb medicines.' She looked at him. 'There's no harm in it.'

Charlie didn't reply.

'Truly.' Lily put her hand on his. 'See the white ribbon? It's for protection. Against evil spirits and bad things. Three dollies.' She looked at him. 'You, your mother and brother?'

'Perhaps,' said Charlie.

'Then your mother thought something bad came,' said Lily. 'And tried to protect you all.' She took the smallest dolly. 'You should keep this,' she said, pushing it towards him.

Charlie hesitated, then put it in his coat. He moved his attention to examine the cloth.

'It's a sampler,' he said. 'That's why it uses the same stitches as your handkerchief.'

'What's a sampler?'

'Seamstresses plan the stitches and colours they mean to use on a larger work,' Charlie explained. 'They refer back to the sampler as they stitch.'

'Like drawing a plan for a building?' suggested Lily. Charlie nodded.

'It hung on the wall,' he added. 'I remember it. My mother must have used it to sew many things.'

He turned his attention to the tankard and ring.

It was an ordinary tankard, slightly battered. On the side was engraved Sally Oakley and Tobias Oakley circled with two hearts. The names were inscribed in a rustic kind of way, the heart shapes imperfect.

Tobias Oakley.

'My father's name,' he said, tracing the letters. 'I never knew it before.'

'The ring is good,' Lily pointed out. 'Her wedding ring?'

Charlie lifted and turned it. It bore the mark of the Goldsmiths' Guild on the inside. 'It has a guild hallmark,' he said. 'Made by a

London goldsmith. I don't remember this ring,' he added, examining the gold band and ruby. 'But you're right, it is good.'

'Perhaps your father was a wealthy Royalist,' suggested Lily. 'Who lost his life and wealth to the Civil War.'

'Then why did my mother work as a maid for Blackstone?' asked Charlie. 'If Tobias Oakley was from a fine family my mother would have been a respectable widow. Someone would have taken care of her.'

The mystery of it was swirling in his mind. He picked up the sampler again.

Tobias Oakley. And a ruby ring.

Then came a memory, fresh and clear.

Charlie was staring at the cloth. 'I can see it clearly,' he said. 'This sampler, hanging on a wall. Even the view from the window.' He spoke slowly as though it were an effort to drag up the words.

Lily waited for him to continue.

'I remember,' said Charlie swallowing. 'I remember Blackstone's house.'

Lily gave a gasp of excitement. 'There must be something there to reveal his plans.'

'It was in the old part of the city.' Charlie was speaking like a sleepwalker. 'Blackstone's house was on a small street. There was a . . . a sign of the Merlin's Head.' He closed his eyes. 'A smell. Some industry.' He tried to pull it out of the air and then it materialised. 'Brewery,' he said. 'There was a brewery at the bottom of the garden.'

His eyes snapped open. 'Breweries are by Puddle Dock,' he said. 'Fire goes there now.'

Above them was a sudden thunderous crack. Charlie's gaze flew upwards. The thick stone ceiling above them shuddered. And then a large split ran fast from pillar to pillar and spread into a network of fissures. There was another boom above them and then the crack widened to a fist-size opening, raining rubble down on them.

Guildhall crypt was splitting apart.

Chapter 116

Teresa Blackstone's circle of power was almost complete.

The Thing lay at the centre, bony hands crossed over her chest. Blackstone and Jacob had surrounded her with a wide thicket of her strange possessions. Aged and broken furniture formed the outer ring. Towards the centre, her more personal effects. Dresses hung like ghoulish women. They were an old courtly style that Jacob had only seen in pictures. Wide skirted and moth eaten.

It reminded him of a fairy tale he'd once heard as a boy. Sleeping Beauty. Only things had been mixed up. The wicked witch was at the centre. A kiss would open her rotting eyes and she would swallow her hapless rescuer.

Blackstone was staring. 'Her dress,' he muttered.

Jacob swallowed. He couldn't tell from the remains what she'd been wearing when she died.

'The gown she was married in.' Blackstone decided. His gaze landed on an old green dress, elaborately skirted and embroidered with winding yellow ferns.

'Look away,' he barked to Jacob. 'You mustn't see her undress.'

Jacob turned, thinking now was the time to take flight. He risked a glance back over his shoulder to see Blackstone's ice-blue eyes trained on him.

'You think to run,' said Blackstone.

Jacob shook his head to deny it.

'I have a pistol trained on you,' said Blackstone. 'If you run you will regret it.'

Jacob sagged visibly. He hadn't counted on a pistol. His escape plans needed to be revised. A weapon. Get close. But the idea of striking Blackstone filled him with paralysing terror.

Blackstone was crooning an eerie tune, working The Thing into her new dress.

He fitted the green sleeves and cloak, talking all the while. Jacob noticed one of the corpse's arms was now broken at a bizarre angle.

'Sleep now,' Blackstone was saying. 'This pyre will send you to heaven. I will make the last signal and you will be at peace.' He glared up at Jacob suddenly.

'Why do you stare?' he demanded.

Jacob looked away. 'I . . . no reason,' he said, searching for a suitable answer. 'I thought your wife wore a black gown,' he said, 'on your wedding day.'

Jacob didn't know why he said it. Only that it was one of those stories the boys told. As soon as the words were out of his mouth he regretted them.

But Blackstone looked thoughtful. 'Who told you that?' he asked.

''S just . . . a story,' Jacob managed. 'The boys said it when I joined.'

Blackstone's gaze had switched to another dress. A black one, hanging by the body.

'That wedding,' he said, deep in memory, 'that wedding cursed us. But the marriage gave us great powers too.'

He gave a strange little smile.

'At least it should have,' he said. 'Were King Charles a man of his word.'

Blackstone's face twisted at the memory.

He and Teresa had stood solemnly at the altar. She'd worn a black dress, tears streaming down her face. Torr stood before them. The air was filled with smoking crucibles and the smell of chemicals.

The exiled Charles had arrived late, wearing a wine-stained shirt, with silly half-dressed Lucy Walter on his arm. Despite their smiles and promises only a few days before, both were clearly disturbed by Torr's dark laboratory. They'd been warned of the alchemy, but not been prepared for the reality.

Lucy eyed the strange tools in horror and flashed Blackstone a quick look of distaste. And when Charles caught sight of Teresa, silently sobbing, Blackstone had feared he would have the marriage aborted.

But the King-to-be had made the right smiles and empty promises. Promises he had no intention of keeping. The unholy marriage had taken less than a minute.

Lead into gold, Torr had said. His hands were shaking as he recorded the union which would change the world. *People will say we made the philosopher's stone.*

But the legend they'd forged was far more powerful.

Blackstone remembered his wife's face and wondered if it was that day which had truly broken her. The day they'd unleashed the potential for wealth untold.

Chapter 117

'The firestorm!' said Charlie as the ceiling split above them. 'It's come to Guildhall.'

'The vaults can withstand it,' said Lily. 'Those pillars are thick enough to . . .'

Her words were drowned out by a crash as a portion of stone ceiling broke free.

'Better we don't wait to find out,' said Charlie. His eyes were ranging the crypt, assessing for the best escape. The stonework had collapsed in the direction they had come in. Above them a split was running into a river of cracks.

'The fire comes so quickly,' said Lily. 'It must be a fierce flame.'

Charlie held up a finger, feeling the airflow.

'There's fire above, in St Lawrence Poultney,' he decided, 'over there, where we came into the vault.'

'How do you know?'

'I know how fire moves,' he said. 'Trust me.'

'Why would I do that?'

Charlie was looking in the other direction. Using the airflow he could picture the fire above. It was settling itself over the church, like a great hulking monster, sucking up the air.

'It's not yet in Guildhall,' he muttered. Air beneath that part was dead and still.

'This way,' said Charlie. Weaving between the piles of possessions he headed towards the Guildhall exit. 'Everyone will have fled the flames,' he said. 'We can break the door and come up in the main courtyard.

Behind him he heard Lily fall in step.

'You can get us out safely?' she asked nervously as the ceiling made an ominous groan.

'I can,' Charlie promised. His eyes slid to a pile of Carpenters' Guild merchandise. Wooden furnishings and half-finished carvings.

'Safer to climb over this pile than go in-between,' said Charlie, clambering up. He swung himself over the brink of swaying tables as Lily brought up the rear.

Charlie rolled and tipped himself down from the pile to the stone crypt floor. Above him Lily was balancing atop a pile of chairs. Judging the base of the pile Charlie grasped a table leg and pulled hard. The chairs vanished beneath Lily, sending her tumbling headlong down the side of the pile. Charlie stepped forward and neatly caught her in his arms.

'You did that on purpose,' she accused, straightening up and removing his hand from where it had slid down. 'There was no need to climb over that pile.'

'I didn't think you'd fall for it,' grinned Charlie, assessing their escape. 'Card sharp like you. Losing your touch?'

'Just get us out of here.'

They were by the main door out of Guildhall crypt now. It had been sealed tight. Guildsmen had used wax to stop up the edges of the door, so no spark could get inside.

'The door must be a foot thick,' said Lily. 'Can you pick the lock?'

Charlie shook his head. He glanced around. There was a stone statue by the door and he levelled a kick at it. Charlie stepped back as it toppled. The neck shattered and he stooped to pick up the stone head.

'Big locks sometimes have a weakness,' he explained, taking aim with the stone head. 'Hit them at the right point and they spring.'

'Have you ever sprung one before?'

'A few times. If they're badly made.'

Eyeing the lock he fixed on the top right corner.

'What makes you think this lock is badly made?' asked Lily.

'I'm an optimist.' Charlie smashed the stone head against it. Nothing happened.

Lily raised her eyebrows.

Charlie examined the dent he'd made in the lock.

'It's too well made,' he admitted. 'Push at the door,' he said, directing Lily. 'Putting pressure on the catch will help.'

She leaned her little body against it and Charlie smashed again.

'It's no good,' he said, 'the door's too big. We'd need three big men to lean on it.'

Charlie glanced towards the way they'd entered the vault. He turned the stone head, an idea forming. Smoke had begun filtering in.

'We can use the fire,' he said.

'What?' Lily sounded alarmed.

'Fire moves air,' said Charlie. 'We use it to pin the door.'

He glanced back to the other side of the vault, where smoke was creeping in.

'The pressure might be enough,' he decided. 'But we need to get some airflow here.' He drew out his eating knife and worked it into the keyhole.

Wax flaked free. Then a cloud of dust spat out towards them.

'It'll work,' said Charlie, starting work on the edges of the doors. 'There's a big fire up there. It's hungry for air.'

On the far side of the vault a few tongues of flame peeked inquisitively through, drawn by the new air flow.

'You're bringing in flame,' said Lily, taking out a knife of her own and helping to flake away the wax. 'I hope you know what you're doing.'

'Nearly enough air,' said Charlie as the door creaked in protest. 'Stand back,' he added. 'When I break the lock fire will rush towards us.'

'You never mentioned that part.'

'Just stand back.'

Wielding the head like a club, Charlie staggered back and took aim at the wooden door. Lily flattened herself against the wall.

'Make it count,' she said. 'I don't want to be down here when it burns.'

'It's burning hot,' muttered Charlie as air whistled past them. He raised the statue head. 'Where we stand is about to become a fireball.'

Taking aim he hit the top corner of the lock. A roaring could be heard as the fire surged. Then the lock sprang with a loud click.

'Thank God,' said Lily, moving to the door.

Charlie pulled her back and as he did the door flew open.

Fire roared through the long vault, crossing the entire length in a single stride.

'Keep to the wall!' cried Charlie, shielding Lily with his body.

A ball of fire rolled up the stair beyond, setting the wooden steps alight.

Charlie waited a moment for the airflow to subside. The fireball died back, but now several piles of possessions were alight.

Lily was looking in horror to the flaming stair.

'It's burning!' she said.

'Orange flame,' said Charlie. 'It gives more light than heat. We can get through it, if we're fast.'

He grabbed at Lily's clothing.

'Ready!' he shouted. 'Now!'

Without waiting for her reply he hurled them both through the flame and on to the burning stair.

'Move fast,' gasped Charlie, pulling her behind, 'Don't give the flames time to catch you.'

Gasping for air they staggered up, with the fire seething beneath them. There was another door at the top, bolted but not locked. Guildhall courtyard was on the other side.

Charlie threw the bolt across and flung open the door and landed on the warm flagstones of Guildhall. Lily arrived behind him.

'You were right,' she said, taking in the deserted space. 'Everyone fled the fire.'

Behind them flames were licking at the mighty hall. The wide courtyard seemed strangely calm.

'The firestorm has passed over,' said Charlie. 'It burrows deeper into the city's heart.' He was looking west where flames were driving high.

They stood for a long moment, breathing hard and watching the fire.

'You're bleeding,' said Lily. She moved to touch his face, where a line of blood ran from under his hair.

Reflexively his fingers went to touch the injury and met hers. Lily pulled her hand away quickly and reddened. But she didn't move her eyes from his.

'It is only a scratch,' he decided.

'You still have the head,' said Lily, after a moment, eyeing the statue head under Charlie's arm. 'Who is our rescuer?'

He turned it and examined the face.

'Emperor Brutus,' he said with a half smile. 'Looks like Brutus has given some protection after all. Even after his giants have been toppled.'

He dropped it on to the floor.

'We should get to Puddle Dock,' he said. 'We may still have time before Blackstone's house burns.'

Chapter 118

Details were assailing Charlie as they raced through burning rubble to Puddle Dock. A brick chimney and hearth. Wooden walls. They needed to move fast.

As they ran down St Andrew's Hill they could see ugly flames streaming up from the breweries. Londoners were openly looting the nearby wharfs. There was a great boom to the west and a cascade of flames erupted.

'The Coopers' Hall,' said Charlie. 'Blackstone draws the fire on towards the Palace.'

From the crest of the hill Charlie could see the rooftops of a little street. His heart skipped a beat. Thick brick chimneys enclosed by wood. He must have seen them twenty times or more on his way into the city walls. But now he was seeing them in a new light.

'We're not too late,' Charlie pointed. Fire had started up on the street, making a high crackle as the wood houses began to burn. 'I can still get in with those flames.'

'I'm an old cinder thief,' he added as Lily shot him an unbelieving look. 'I've got furniture out of worse fires without a blister.'

They pelted down towards the riverfront as the wind switched direction. A wall of black smoke rolled over them and they coughed and choked.

'It comes,' said Lily. 'The firestorm comes.'

From all directions air currents began to lift. Charlie felt the hairs on the back of his neck stand up. His skin prickled.

As the smoke passed, they saw flames towering high from the wooden rooftops. Houses were already being reduced to ash.

Lily slackened her pace.

'There's still time!' shouted Charlie over the smoke. But Lily was bent double and fighting to breathe.

'You go!' she managed.

Charlie ran through the graveyard of a burned-out church. Where the ground had been over-filled with plague victims the scourge of flames had burst apart the soft earth. He vaulted over broken tombs and haphazard corpses, their skin turned to charcoal and clothes burned away.

Stone crypts were shattered open. Dismembered limbs of statues were scattered all about with human ones. A man was prodding in the dust with a stick and pocketing chunks of the melted church bells.

Charlie passed the smoking remains of the church. He saw charred bodies inside where people had hidden.

As Charlie swung to the edge of Blackstone's street, several houses at the far end were already burned to ash. Others were wreathed in flame. Brick chimneys had pitched away and smashed on to the cobbles.

Charlie skidded to a halt, taking in the carnage. But he couldn't distinguish from the blazing fronts the house of his childhood.

Then he saw it. The sign of the Merlin's Head. He blinked in disbelief. It was still there, after all those years. All beyond the sign had burned to the ground and the house next to it was in high flame.

Charlie let out a breath. The picture in his mind was of the Merlin's head swinging next to Blackstone's house. The flaming building. This must be it.

The windows were simple cottage style, open holes barred with wood. Charlie grasped a bar and pulled himself up to see inside. The interior was thick with flames and smoke. It wasn't familiar at all.

Lily arrived by his side panting.

'Is this it?' she gasped. 'This is Blackstone's house?'

'I . . . I don't know,' he admitted, drawing back a little. Something didn't feel right.

'The Merlin's Head.' Lily was pointing. It was swinging violently back and forth in the high breeze. And then Charlie saw his mistake.

'It has two sides,' he said, drawing back from the blazing house. 'The Merlin's Head is a two-sided sign.'

He switched his attention to the house on the other side of it. The one which was burned to ashes.

'That was Blackstone's,' he said. 'We're too late.'

The house had been burned to the ground. Nothing remained but smoking ruins.

Fire had beaten them.

Chapter 119

Flames were roaring through the Post Office roof.

Monmouth's face was blank terror.

'We can't save it.' The guard was shaking his head. 'We should have pressed men, Your Grace. Now there aren't enough troops.'

'Send a message to my father the King,' said Monmouth. 'Tell him the Post Office is defended well and we're beating back the fire.'

The guard looked at him dumbstruck. 'The flames . . .' he began.

'It will hurt my father's morale,' said Monmouth, 'to be told the Post Office burns.'

'But he must know for tactical reasons,' said the guard. 'Your Grace, he must be told. The Duke of York defends the Fleet. If fire comes unawares from the south . . .'

But Monmouth's lip was curling petulantly. 'Do as I say,' he said. 'The King made me commander here. I'll not have him think his son a failure.'

Monmouth coughed. 'The smoke is too thick,' he said. 'My lace and cuffs are already dirtied.' He looked with disdain to the filthy men, sweating and daubed with soot. 'I mean to retreat a little,' said Monmouth. 'We can't have Palace guards see their nobility shabbier than they. Keep the men fighting the fire. I'm sure they'll best it soon.' He was already turning his horse.

'The men will work harder if they see their leader!' called the guard. But his words fell on deaf ears. Monmouth was already beckoning for an exhausted guard to pass him a tankard of ale.

Monmouth tilted his head slightly. Men were racing from the Post Office, clutching bundles of mail. Screams could be heard on the high breeze.

The guard arrived at his side, tugging the reins of his horse.

'We must make haste, Your Grace,' said the guard. 'A church burns two streets away. People are still inside.'

Monmouth glared at the guard and tugged his reins free.

'My father wants me to hold the Post Office,' said Monmouth. 'The west wing can still be saved,' he said, 'we must keep men here.'

'There's nothing in that part,' said the guard. 'We've taken as much post as can be carried. Fire has breached our defence. Monmouth, we can save those people.'

'They are commoners?' inquired Monmouth, 'in the church?'

The guard nodded.

'Then their deaths won't be recorded,' said Monmouth. 'We've no way to know which commoners died and which lived.' He looked to the blazing Post Office. 'But people will know,' he said, 'that Monmouth's efforts saved the west wing.'

The guard sagged a little on his horse. He was too old for this. 'The King makes you commander,' he said.

'We'll not be short of commoners once this fire is out,' said Monmouth. 'Look to the Post Office.'

Chapter 120

'All is burned,' said Charlie, studying the ashen remains. 'Everything.'

The burned-out building glowed with heat. Half the upper storey had fallen in and all the roof was burned away. The blackened walls of the ground floor were lit in the red glow of the Great Fire.

Charlie's eyes travelled down half a wall. Up ahead was the remains of a staircase, burned to cinders and fallen to one side.

Charlie looked up and then down again.

'There,' he said, pointing. 'That was the room.' Something cold and hard had settled in his stomach. 'The floor burned through,' he added. 'So whatever was inside fell here.'

They both looked to the layer of charred timbers and soot.

'The house had been cleared already,' said Charlie. 'The chest was banded in metal. Some of that would remain.'

Half-heartedly they searched the rubble. Then Charlie used the ruined stair to raise his head to the second storey. It was burned out and empty.

'The chest isn't here,' said Charlie.

'Look at this,' said Lily. She was looking at one of the scorched walls. 'Something here didn't burn completely. A painting or an etching.' Lily turned her head, trying to get a better look. Then she reached up and unhooked a blackened picture frame. It fell to pieces in her hands.

'What is it?' asked Charlie. He knelt. 'A family tree?'

The remnants bore miniature portraits with names underneath. Leaves and branches connected them into a large tree.

'That's what it looks like,' said Lily. 'It's hard to tell with the scorching. But it's very beautifully done,' she added, looking at the detailing in the leaves and branches twisting around the faces. 'They must have been an important family. Before the war.'

Charlie picked up the pieces carefully. There were five little pieces of paper in all. He tried to fit them together.

'Do you remember it?' asked Lily.

'No.' Charlie's lips were moving.

'Lady Harriet Blackstone,' said Lily helpfully. 'There's a Lord here.' She looked at the little faces. 'By the dates I'd guess they're Blackstone's parents,' she said. 'They look stern don't they?' She tapped the numbers. 'Both died at the beginning of the Civil War,' she added.

'I don't see Blackstone,' said Charlie, examining the faces.

'He's not here,' said Lily. 'I don't see his name. Or Teresa's.'

'There's no one from his wife's family,' said Charlie. 'Every name here is Blackstone.' He looked up at Lily. 'A coincidence don't you think? Only Blackstone's family members survived the fire?'

Lily was nodding. 'Blackstone removed his wife's family,' she said slowly. 'And left this half to burn.' She picked up another piece.

'This face has been scrubbed out,' she said, holding it up.

Charlie felt a flash of fear in his gut.

He took the scrap of portrait.

'I remember it,' he said, looking at Lily. 'This is . . . This was Blackstone's sister. I . . .' Charlie closed his eyes. He had a sudden powerful image.

Teresa Blackstone, her face twisted in hatred. She was casting a spell, working soot over the little portrait. Her finger twisted over and over until all the face had been rubbed away.

'Teresa scrubbed this face out,' he said.

Lily looked at the ruined picture.

'She must have hated Blackstone's sister,' she said. 'To do so much damage. Do you really think she killed her?'

'Teresa said she did,' said Charlie. 'But I don't know. Blackstone . . . He loved his sister, I think. He kept her dresses and a rosary for her. And he was angry with Teresa for destroying his sister's picture. My mother told us Blackstone's sister was killed in the war and we should never speak of her.'

They looked at one another.

'The wife hated the sister,' said Lily. 'Why?'

Charlie shook his head.

'The other half of this family tree would tell us,' he said. 'I'm sure of it.'

Charlie's finger traced back up through Blackstone's family, looking for more clues. There was something odd about this family. He wasn't sure what.

His fingertips touched the family crest, drawn starkly at the top of the tree.

'This crest.' His hand rested on it. 'I've seen it. There's a private chapel. In St Paul's Cathedral.'

'Must have been an important family,' said Lily. 'Once upon a time. To have a chapel in London's cathedral.'

'We need to find Blackstone,' decided Charlie, moving to stand. 'If the chest is unburned somewhere it will be with him.'

'The family tree tells us nothing of his plans,' said Lily.

'Perhaps not,' Charlie conceded. Although something whispered at the edge of his mind, that maybe there was a clue there.

'Blackstone is a strategist,' said Charlie. 'Everything he does is planned.'

He mapped the guilds in his head and a realisation struck.

'The last guild to fire was the Coopers' Hall,' he said. 'We saw it as we came over St Andrew's Hill. So there's only one guild left.'

Charlie was mapping through the city.

'He's fired all but the Carpenters near Tower Hill,' he said. 'Why leave that one unburned?'

'It's nowhere near Whitehall,' supplied Lily. 'It's of no use to him.'

'No.' Charlie was shaking his head. 'Blackstone is a general. He understands tactics. If he'd wanted to burn Whitehall, he'd have fired the Carpenters' Guild first. To draw troops east.'

'So he doesn't mean to fire Whitehall?'

Charlie shook his head. Things were fitting into place.

'He uses it as a pawn. Blackstone knows the King will rush to defend the Palace in the west. But he leaves the east undefended. The Tower.'

Lily's mouth dropped open. 'England's munitions base,' she said.

'The Carpenters' Guild is near the Tower,' said Charlie. He was picturing the chaos of flames, rubble and escaping Londoners and his heart sank. It would take them hours.

'We won't get there in time,' said Lily.

'Maybe we can,' said Charlie. 'Generals plan from afar. I don't think Blackstone would risk firing it himself. He'll signal with his blue fire.'

Charlie chewed a nail thoughtfully.

'If we intercept a signal we can break the chain. The Carpenters' Guild won't burn. It might be enough to save the Tower.'

'But we don't know where Blackstone will signal from,' Lily pointed out. 'It might be further from where we are than the Carpenters' Guild.'

Charlie sighed impatiently. 'Where . . .? Where would you be sure would not fire?'

'Whitehall?' suggested Lily. 'If his plan is to use the Palace as a feint then he knows it will be safe.'

'Whitehall is too far west,' said Charlie. 'He could not be sure his flame would be seen. Even if he gets up high.'

He frowned in thought.

'Somewhere high,' he muttered. 'Somewhere safe.' But the only safe places he could think of were low down. Underground. Cellars. And then it hit him.

Charlie closed his eyes. 'There's something else,' he said. 'Perhaps it was only a nightmare. But I think Blackstone had a cellar.'

Chapter 121

'Everything has been cleared,' said Charlie, standing and assessing the charred layout of Blackstone's home. 'Apart from half a painting. What if Blackstone couldn't get a cart? Maybe he stored his wife's things in the cellar.'

'It's what most people do during fire,' said Lily. 'But I don't see a cellar here.' She was looking to the solid floor. 'Planks on earth,' she said.

'The cellar was . . .' Charlie closed his eyes, remembering. A thick feeling of unease came over him. 'It wasn't like an ordinary cellar,' he said. 'More like a cave.'

'You're sure you're remembering right?' said Lily, sounding disbelieving.

'No,' he admitted. 'But the entrance was in the kitchen.' He moved to the back of the building. 'Here.'

Charlie was moving towards where he thought the kitchen would have been. Hot ash and soot covered the ground. He kicked aside a chunk of burned rafter and it disintegrated into live sparks. 'It was here,' he said. 'A great door leading down.'

'Be careful,' murmured Lily. 'The floor could collapse.'

But Charlie was shaking his head. 'It isn't here,' he said, torn between disappointment and relief. 'No doorway. I suppose it must have been a dream after all.' It was a strange thought. The images were so clear. He stood for a moment, uncertain of what to do next.

Lily considered the rubble. Then she moved to stand beside him. To his surprise she dropped to her hands and knees.

'Things are often smaller than you remember as a child,' she said, dusting aside the soot. 'Perhaps it's not as large an opening as you think.'

Her fingers slid into the gaps of the charred floorboards. Then she stood up and stamped her foot. A perfect square of ash vanished into the ground.

'There,' she said proudly. 'Cellar door.'

Charlie looked down. A bolt of dread hit his stomach.

'It is small,' said Charlie uncertainly. He dropped to his knees, feeling for the ring to open it with his hands. His fingers closed instead on a burned nub of rope.

'I remember,' he said, dread building. 'It had a rope handle.' He took out his eating knife and levered open the edge of the door. It stuck and then opened jerkily, hinges shrieking. A cloud of ash tumbled down, obscuring the bottom completely. They waited for it to clear. Charlie felt his stomach tighten. Images of Teresa Blackstone's dead things were rising up. Something about this cellar was the stuff of his nightmares. And he couldn't shake the feeling there was something down here. Something evil.

There was a swinging rope ladder and Charlie climbed on to it, trying to dismiss the foreboding curling around him.

The smoke made it hard to see. But he could make out damp stone walls which seemed to lead on forever.

'Lily,' he called up, 'pass me your tinderbox.' He felt the cool metal touch his hand and he took it. Fumbling, he tried to spark the tinderbox whilst keeping a hand on the ladder. The first drive of the flint across the fire-steel sent out a shower of sparks.

Charlie glimpsed a Royalist coat of arms and then all faded to black. He froze. There was something down here with him. In the darkness he felt every other sense heighten.

At the edges of his hearing Charlie could make out a ragged animal kind of breathing. With shaking hands he made another try on the tinderbox. The flint struck, flared but the tinder failed to light. Suddenly something jolted hard into the ladder.

Charlie grappled to right himself. The momentum of the attack sent him swinging wide with the hand holding the tinderbox waving desperately in the black. Another jerk broke his grip. He felt himself fall into the dark.

Chapter 122

Blackstone was looking up at the beautiful stained glass.

'It seems a pity,' he murmured, 'that this must burn. It was once a magnificent place for Catholic worship,' he added. 'Imagine how it must have looked, with the incense swinging and the Latin words. Even a Protestant must have found himself moved by such beauty.'

His eyes lighted on The Thing.

'But my wife must have her sacrifice,' he said.

Jacob was looking at the gunpowder.

'Drape the cloth there.' Blackstone was pointing. 'I'll bring her across.'

'In the enclave?'

Blackstone nodded. 'There is a protected space for me here. No one else might use this part.' He gave another thin smile. 'An advantage of my fine family name.'

With a sinking heart Jacob stepped away from the candelabra. That had been his weapon of choice. He draped the cloth, keeping one eye over his shoulder.

Blackstone's eyes were lighted tenderly on The Thing. Jacob's gaze roamed desperately around the small chamber. There was nothing to fling or break at hand. His only choice was to run. But Blackstone's huge form was blocking the route out.

Reverently, Blackstone stooped and picked up The Thing. And as he did, Jacob raced away. He knocked against Blackstone's solid body. Blackstone's hand shot out low. He held a needle blade which Jacob hadn't seen. The knife tore through Jacob's calf, slashing muscles away from bone.

Jacob let out a cry of pain and staggered. He took another few steps. Blood poured from his leg. Blackstone was moving away from him, carrying The Thing to her resting place.

Jacob's gaze locked on the far wall where the door was. It seemed a long way. Past piles of possessions. His leg felt cold now. He hobbled. The pain made him spin left. Gritting his teeth he righted himself, extending an arm for balance.

He risked a glance behind him. Blackstone was laying The Thing gently down. Jacob felt a surge of hope. He swallowed, grunted in pain and began hobbling.

The stacks of goods were forming something of a maze and Jacob found himself confronted with two routes. One was stacked either side with chairs and looked dark. The other was dappled in light. Sweating with pain, Jacob took the light way.

He'd dropped to all fours by the time he realised it was a dead end. The possessions had led him into a closed room. A large vestry.

His jaw twitched in fear. He couldn't escape the feeling that Blackstone had planned this. Planned for him to enter this closed away place. But how could he have known which route he'd take?

Jacob felt a chill all over now. The energy to move at all was flagging. In the beginning blood had poured hot over his foot. But now his toes were wet and cold.

Even before Blackstone arrived behind him, Jacob knew he was going to die. He turned to face his killer, his lips white.

Blackstone was holding the needle blade.

'A useful tool,' he said. 'But more useful still is your fear.' His icy eyes glittered. 'You think you can escape me, boy? I know your every move. Even before you do.'

Jacob shook his head.

'You should have taken the left path,' said Blackstone. 'That would have led you outside. You might have even lived.' Blackstone indicated to Jacob's injured leg. 'But I knew you wouldn't. Pain, you see. A little pain is all it takes to disturb the thoughts.'

He moved in close to Jacob and lowered his voice to a whisper.

'You ran right, to the vestry,' he said. 'Because your left leg hurt you.'

'How could you know . . .?'

'Experience,' said Blackstone. 'I learned the hard way, to keep my head. And I always know, where fear will drive a man.'

Chapter 123

Charlie fell hard on the damp floor of the cellar. The landing knocked all the breath out of him and he scrabbled up on to all fours, trying to sense where the attacker might be.

There was a familiar rank smell. Blackstone had been hoarding food down here. Charlie had forgotten this was one of his traits.

'Charlie!' He could hear Lily making her way down the ladder.

'Stay away!' he shouted. A heavy shape careered into him. Charlie ducked low and rolled. He hit damp brick wall and his injured shoulder jarred in pain.

Breathing heavily he grasped the tinderbox with both hands and struck at the fire-steel. A larger shower of sparks flew, illuminating a set of yellow teeth inches from his face. A black tongue snaked out and licked the lips. Then the flint died without lighting the tinder.

Charlie scrabbled as fast as he could backwards. His spine cracked into a cold stone wall and he realised he was no longer holding the flint. He must have dropped it somewhere towards the middle of the pit.

'Charlie?' Lily was down in the cellar now. Charlie's stomach tightened. He heard the creature head for Lily in the dark.

A single thought held. Get the flint back. He needed to see what they were fighting. Creeping on his hands and knees Charlie swept an exploratory hand out in front of him. The darkness was so absolute it had a texture all of its own. Nothing was visible, not even his own pale hands questing the floor.

In the black he heard Lily scream.

Charlie inched across the floor, trying to keep the deafening sound of his movements to a minimum.

The attack came from nowhere and he felt the blow of the creature strike. He twisted, trying to throw it off. And as he did so he felt the sharp shape of the flint press into his palm.

He struck at the tinderbox and this time the tinder caught. A high flame illuminated the entire confines of the dingy cellar, blinding him.

As he blinked away the dancing shapes before his eyes he heard a gasp – a more human sound than the previous brutish noises. Then his eyes dropped to the ground to see a man crouched on the floor. He was deathly pale and panting in agony. But the pain and fear in his expression receded as his eyes met Charlie's.

'By all that is Holy,' said the man, as the flare of the tinderbox faded and died. 'Tobias Oakley's son lived.'

Chapter 124

The Duke of York stood with his naval commander at his side. Both looked stern-faced into the impending flames. All around men were heaping earth and mud on dismembered buildings.

The sun was setting. They could see a blood-red sliver at the base of the black clouds. Night was coming.

'It is a war,' said James, looking to Lud Gate Hill. 'And here comes the first wave.'

He adjusted his grip on the shovel. Behind them troops were frantically pulling houses.

The naval commander was looking uncertainly towards the Post Office.

'You're sure Monmouth held back the flames?' he said. 'It seems fire is high that way.'

James nodded. 'Monmouth wrote personally,' he said. 'To tell me he holds it. So we defend the east.'

He caught the commander's expression.

'The Fleet now flows,' said James. 'So we know Monmouth tells us true. He cleared the blockage and holds the Post Office.'

There was a flash of gold in the distance, and their hearts lifted. The famous Clerkenwell fire engine being dragged steadily towards them.

'It comes in time' said James. 'Thank God. Then we still have a chance.' He ran to help the men.

With no horses to draw the engine it had been a task of inhuman strength to drag the deadweight of copper and brass along the uneven cobbles of Bishops Gate and through the cloying mud of Snow Lane.

'The tide is not yet high enough for pressure in the pipes,' explained James. 'We must take it nearer the Fleet.'

The exhausted men looked uncertainly at the muddy trickle of river. Then they began to manoeuvre the deadweight, inch by painful inch, towards the stinking Fleet.

'It will come down Lud Gate Hill,' said James, returning to his post and looking to where the flames had now grown larger. 'We've made a large firebreak. We now have an engine. I only hope there are troops enough to beat it back.'

James eyed his men. They were the best naval recruits he could find at such short notice. He trusted them all with his life. Together they'd fared high seas and cannon fire worse than this.

'The fury is upon us,' announced James, looking to the flames. 'Into battle then.'

He turned to ready the men, when a shout went up.

'The fire! It comes from behind!'

The Duke of York wheeled. The flames had launched a surprise attack from the Post Office. Instead of coming down Lud Gate Hill it had sailed high in the wind, falling on Salisbury House behind them. James's mouth dropped open in horror.

'Monmouth said he kept fire back,' he whispered. 'He lied.'

'It's breached our strongest defence!' shouted James.

Their careful battle plan fell to instant chaos.

'Turn the engine!' bellowed James. 'You men turn it to Salisbury House.' The group of men halted, some pulling one way, some another.

On the soft earth of the riverbank, the huge engine unbalanced then teetered. Several men leapt aside as a ton of shining metal careered towards them. Then slowly, the fire engine toppled sideways and fell with a heavy splash into the Fleet. A wave of reeking low-tide water soaked the men. Then a hideous sucking sound went up.

They watched in silent horror as the equipment sank in a slow stream of bubbles like some mythological creature returning to the deep.

Behind them the fire gave a great roar as if proclaiming its triumph over the ineffectiveness of its would-be vanquishers.

Salisbury House was full ablaze, trapping their escape. And now the fire launched its frontal assault, tunnelling down Lud Gate Hill.

They were trapped in the stifling blaze.

'We've no choice,' said the Duke of York, his face blistering in the heat. One of his heavily dressed men was swooning. 'Retreat!' he bellowed.

Stumbling and sweating the Duke of York's regiment ran for their lives.

Chapter 125

The cloud of ash had cleared now and a shaft of daylight shone down into the cellar. It took Charlie a moment. Then he made the connection.

'You are Torr?' guessed Charlie. 'Blackstone's been holding you here?'

Torr nodded. He had the air of a soldier about him, battle-worn and dangerous.

Charlie and Lily glanced at one another. He was muscular beyond his years, with a large tattoo of an elaborate Tree of Life showing at his neck.

'He's dying,' whispered Lily. 'Look.'

In the dim light Torr's hands appeared black. Then Charlie saw they were drenched with blood. A deep bloom of red was at his stomach.

'A scratch,' said Torr, but his teeth were gritted.

'Come up out of the cellar,' said Charlie.

Torr shook his head, looking at the ladder. 'I couldn't make the first rung,' he said. 'This is where it ends.'

He glanced at the light from the trapdoor.

'Blackstone's boys thought me a creature, roaming in the dark,' said Torr. 'I was down here so long in the dark I began to believe it myself. But I always thought my moment would come. I would find the right tool. Escape.'

Torr's eyes settled back on Charlie and Lily.

'Were it not for my meditations,' he said, 'I should have gone mad down here.' He glanced at the Tree of Life, scraped into the ground. 'The human mind is the greatest power. If only the church could understand.'

'You knew my father?' asked Charlie, taking Torr in.

'Tobias died at sea,' said Torr. He smiled faintly. 'He was a hard man, your father. Full of duty and family. A good fighter. Sally brought out something soft in him.'

'Where's Blackstone?' asked Lily, as Charlie turned this over.

But Torr only shook his head. He leaned back against the cellar wall, the last fight gone out of him now. They didn't have long, Charlie realised.

'You performed his marriage, didn't you?' asked Charlie. 'You were the minister.'

Torr's eyes widened a little and his lips moved as if working something out. He was looking at Charlie's key.

'Your mother?' he managed. 'Hid his papers?'

'She was Blackstone's maid,' said Charlie. 'He killed her for it.'

Torr frowned slightly. 'Not Blackstone's maid,' he mumbled. 'Sally Oakley was maid to . . . Lucy Walter.'

Charlie hesitated.

'I can't tell you about the marriage papers,' Torr added. 'Blackstone confessed to me. I'm his priest. To tell you his crime would have me burn in hell.'

He was looking at Charlie's key again.

'I made your key,' said Torr. 'Lead into gold, hidden within the Sealed Knot. Your mother hid the papers in Teresa's trunk.' He was nodding to himself.

'If you find the papers,' said Torr, 'you must destroy them.' His face was earnest. 'They must be destroyed.'

'The secrets of lead to gold,' said Lily, confused. 'They should be shared.'

'Lead to gold.' Torr chuckled quietly and then winced. 'That was my story.' He looked at Lily. 'I studied with mystics and alchemists in Holland,' he said carefully. 'A story with a grain of truth, will conceal a thing better than a lie. That's what I learned.' He reached out a pale hand and touched the key. Charlie felt the coldness of his fingers.

Torr nodded. 'A clever woman, Sally Oakley. 'She knew the old ways.' He smiled to himself.

'Can you tell us where Blackstone went?' pressed Charlie.

Torr shook his head. 'Blackstone makes a funeral pyre for Teresa. He means to send his last signal as she burns. He makes her the highest and most holy fire,' added Torr, making the words carefully.

'If we found the papers,' said Charlie, 'could we force Blackstone to halt his firing of the city?'

Torr smiled a little. 'Stories twist and turn over the telling,' he said. 'There is nothing good in those papers. They are a power which no man should hold.'

He laid back slightly against the damp wall.

'But I should think,' added Torr, 'that the man who has those papers would have power over England herself.'

They were silent for a moment. Torr gasped in pain.

'Your father,' Torr said, looking at Charlie. Torr seemed to be drifting further away from them now. His voice was growing quiet. 'Tobias was a good man,' he managed. 'He should never have trusted Blackstone.'

Torr's eyes were clouding. He lifted his gaze to the cellar ceiling.

'Thomas and Teresa made the most powerful marriage,' he said. 'The marriage at the heart of it all.' Torr's eyelids were drooping. 'It was my greatest regret,' he managed. 'God forgive me.'

Torr's hands lost their grip on his rosary. His fingers fumbled, pushing something into Charlie's unresisting hand.

'Perhaps you are like your mother,' he said. 'You see things others do not.'

He tapped Charlie's hand.

'A good alchemist,' he said, 'questions his known truths. He looks at the big picture.'

Then Torr's body slumped and his eyes closed for the last time.

Chapter 126

King Charles's large wig had been tossed aside. He worked with his shaven head sweating, tossing muddy water on to the blaze.

They saw the flames and Charles knew they were done for.

'James hasn't held it back,' said the King. 'Fire comes to Temple Bar.'

There was no stopping the blaze now. The King's soldiers were working a firehook. Commoners were shovelling soil on demolished houses. It wasn't enough.

'Back!' called Charles. 'Back! Regroup!'

The men retreated, the heat beating them back.

Everything had failed. The pipes still ran dry. Low tide kept supplies of water inaccessible. Shovels of dry earth weren't working. They'd realised too late that suffocating the flames was hopeless. The winds relit the fire as soon as it was doused. Firebreaks were the only effective thing.

Charles looked behind him. His heart sank. A warren of wooden buildings as far as the eye could see. Then he had a sudden memory.

'What road runs behind those buildings?' asked Charles.

'Bell Yard,' said Amesbury. 'It goes to Temple Bar. Where the lawyers are.'

'Is Lincoln's Inn Fields still there?' asked Charles.

Amesbury nodded, wiping sweat from his brow. Charles considered.

'That bank of buildings,' he said. 'If we can pull those down we'd make a large break.' His jaw set. 'If we work quickly and break through to Lincoln's Inn Fields it might be enough.'

A swirl of heat began to ripple in the air.

Amesbury looked at the clouds above. 'There aren't enough fire-hooks to do it,' he said. 'We have only three. The rest were abandoned when we fled the Fleet.'

Dust and debris were picking up on the breeze again.

'We need to retreat, Your Majesty,' said Amesbury. 'Leave this work to the firefighters. It's a firestorm. You risk being killed.'

Charles shook his head. 'No,' he said. 'I ran from plague and I always regretted it. England has survived horrors far worse than fire. I won't abandon her again.'

Charles turned to the assembled men. Three firehooks only.

'Send to Holborn and Fetter Lane,' he said. 'Get their fire-hooks. Get their men. Have all pitch on to this bank of buildings.'

Chapter 127

Charlie watched as Torr's eyes closed. He opened his hand.

Torr had given him a leather pouch. It was decorated in coloured glass.

Lily picked it up and unstoppered the top.

'It's just a bottle of vinegar,' she said, passing it to Charlie. He tasted it. She was right.

'Vinegar neutralises lye,' said Charlie, sitting back on his haunches. 'Maybe Torr hopes we can stop Blackstone's signal with it.'

'There's not nearly enough,' said Lily. 'Those blue flames would need a bucket of vinegar.'

Charlie examined the decorations on the pouch.

'Letters and numbers. I can't make out any words,' he added.

'It's in Latin,' said Lily, reading the writing. 'Johannes is John. It's a bible reference. John 2:1-11.'

'Do you know it?'

Lily thought. 'I think that one is the Marriage at Cana,' she said. 'When Jesus turned water to wine.'

They looked at one another. Nothing unusual or mystical about it.

'You could buy pouches like this at the leather market,' said Charlie. 'Along with tankards referencing when Jesus walked over water.'

Charlie housed it in his coat with a shrug. 'Could come in useful,' he decided.

He thought of Torr's last words.

'He means us to question what we know,' he said. 'To look at the big picture. The papers are not what we think.' He thought for a moment. 'A story with a grain of truth,' he said. 'An allegory. The papers don't turn lead into gold. They're not a formula or a recipe for an alchemist.' Charlie was picturing what he remembered of the papers. Blackstone and Teresa's looping signatures.

He frowned in concentration. A kind of theory was settling into place.

'A commoner to royalty,' he said. 'That's a kind of lead to gold is it not?'

'Blackstone's marriage made him royal?' said Lily.

'Perhaps.' Charlie was working through the theory. 'Blackstone marries into royalty,' he said, sounding it out, 'he betrays his Brotherhood, who are now against the King. Perhaps the marriage is disputed. Denied, but the papers prove it.'

But even as he said it Charlie knew this didn't quite fit.

'There were female relatives on the King's side, after the Civil War,' said Lily. 'Placeless. Open to a marriage they would have previously shunned. Perhaps Blackstone married some distant cousin of the King.' She wrinkled her nose. 'But I can hardly imagine a lady marrying Blackstone for love.'

'Better we find the papers,' decided Charlie. 'And solve the riddle that way. Nothing of Teresa's was in Guildhall,' he added. 'I think Blackstone means to burn Teresa's things along with her body. We must discover where he makes his pyre.'

'You're a thief taker,' said Lily. 'You must be able to figure it.'

'To be a thief taker you must walk in another man's shoes,' said Charlie. 'Imagine how he sees the world and from that deduce his next move.' He drummed fingers on his scarred lip. 'Blackstone is difficult,' he added. 'Most men are motivated by money or love. He seeks only revenge.'

Charlie considered.

'Blackstone loved his wife,' he said. 'Whoever she was. If he has a weakness, that will be it.'

He replayed the conversation with Torr back in his mind. Something struck him.

'Torr said "the highest and most holy",' he said. 'Blackstone makes his wife's pyre the highest and most holy.'

He thought for a moment.

'I think Torr was leaving us a clue,' said Charlie. 'Most holy. Where's the holiest place for a Catholic?'

Lily spread her hands. 'Rome.'

'In London?'

'There are churches with Catholic history,' said Lily doubtfully, 'St Dunstan in the West, St Mary Moorfields.'

Charlie was deep in thought, his mind working. 'Highest,' he muttered. 'Perhaps he didn't mean high flames. The highest point in London is Lud Gate Hill.'

'No Catholic churches there,' said Lily. 'Nothing but the Old Bailey.'

'No Catholic churches,' said Charlie. 'But a cathedral. St Paul's Cathedral is at the highest point in the city.' He looked at Lily. 'And it's the holiest place in London.'

'The highest and most holy,' Lily was turning the words around. 'It fits, I suppose.'

'I think that's what Torr was trying to tell us,' said Charlie, grow-ing more certain with every passing moment. 'Blackstone loved his wife. He wants to take revenge on the King. It's fitting, is it not?

Burn her remains in the holiest place in the city. Send a message to the King by burning London's best-loved landmark.'

Lily was nodding.

'If we can get there in time,' continued Charlie, 'we might find the papers before they burn. And stop Blackstone from sending his last signal.'

'St Paul's Cathedral,' murmured Lily. 'That is the very heart of the fire.'

Chapter 128

Blackstone was taking in the vaulted ceilings.

Cromwell had used this holy place as stables. He had no respect for godly grandeur.

Blackstone gave a cold smile. 'But then again,' he muttered to himself, 'neither does fire.'

He was looking at the mounds of possessions. Valuables and domestic goods lay in disordered piles. Ahead was a wide set of stone steps leading to the roof.

Blackstone began heaving the great barrel up.

Teresa was in her circle. Gunpowder had been laid around her. As her soul was cleansed, London's holiest building would be shaken to its foundations.

A fitting sacrifice.

Blackstone paused. He could see the door to the rooftop now. His boys were in place at the Carpenters' Guild. When Blackstone signalled with blue fire, the Tower could not be defended.

His skin prickled in the dry air. Fire came.

Blackstone thought of Teresa on her holy pyre. All her worldly goods around her. Her cursed wedding trunk. The black dress she'd worn for the ceremony.

His thoughts went to his long-dead sister. Then to the day he'd found Teresa dead, her own knife deep in her belly. The images seemed to flash over one another.

Teresa with the knife. His sister. Blood.

I killed your sister.

He'd never blamed Teresa. Blackstone had secured her dowry for the Sealed Knot. But it was her he'd wanted.

Blessed blood.

That's what Blackstone's father had said of his bride, before the soldiers came.

Teresa had blessed blood.

She wasn't royal, or highborn. She was far more special than that. They'd made the ultimate marriage. Blackstone still remembered their wedding night. The revulsion on Teresa's face as she'd regarded his large body.

If you must do it, husband, I will bear it.

Thoughts were coming thick and fast now. Teresa, burning on a wheel in hell. Blackstone began pushing the barrel again, mapping through his strategy.

First, send the signal. The Carpenters' Guild would burn and the Tower would be impossible to defend. Then he would descend to Teresa. Once he'd lit the gunpowder, London's greatest landmark would be obliterated. His wife would be cleansed as the traitor King lost his Kingdom.

All sin would be purged.

Blackstone was nearly on the roof now. The end of his great plan was in sight.

Chapter 129

Charlie and Lily were running across the hot soot of Foster Lane. Above them thunder swirled.

They made it on to Watling Street which stood eerily empty, lead-windowed fabric shops cleared of stock.

Charlie looked up at the sky. It was deep night-time. But fire lit the city bright as day.

The towering edifice of St Paul's was in view now and he stopped short. The cross-shaped building was enormous. It sprawled into its own quarter of the old city, big as a village. Smoke wreathed its endless grey rooftops like clouds.

'We have it wrong,' Charlie said, looking up at the huge structure. 'Blackstone doesn't make his signal here.' He looked at Lily. 'He couldn't make a flame large enough. It would be hidden in all the smoke.'

'Then Blackstone has misjudged it?' suggested Lily. 'He did not expect the fire to be so great?'

Charlie shook his head. Nothing he knew of Blackstone suggested a man who planned poorly.

'We have the place wrong,' he said, frowning. 'Blackstone plans to signal from somewhere else.' Charlie shook his head. 'Highest and most holy. I was so sure . . . Unless . . .'

Something occurred to him.

'Wait,' he said, 'we have it right. This is where he will make his signal.'

'But how?' said Lily. 'If you say he can't make a flame big enough.'

'The roof,' said Charlie. 'The roof is lead. All Blackstone need do is pour his lye down the tiles. The Cathedral will flame like a blue torch.'

Charlie was certain now. St Paul's fit so exactly with what he knew of Blackstone. A grand gesture to take revenge.

Red clouds eddied above them. There was a long rumble of thunder.

A warren of backstreets led to St Paul's, but each route held different perils.

Paternoster Row was the stationers' street; dry books and paper. The alleys could trap them in smoke and flame. And the merchant streets were lined with cellars that could collapse. Not to mention gunpowder and muskets to deter robbers.

'Back alleys are safest,' said Charlie, deciding fire was more predictable than gunpowder.

An explosion sounded behind them. Lightning had struck deep in the back alleys. Wind billowed through setting the close wood houses alight.

'Fine merchants then,' said Charlie.

He looked to the blaze of alleys behind them and to the gunpowder basements ahead. Something was wrong with the airflow. He turned to Lily.

'Run,' he said.

They raced at full pelt along Watling Street. Ahead of them a flame exploded from a merchant's window in a tinkering of glass. Then it vanished down into the belly of the furthest building.

Within seconds they heard the first basement fire. The ground beneath their feet shuddered and then the shop to the side of them exploded. Lily lurched as cobblestones vanished beneath her feet. Charlie pulled her away as a cloud of burned coffee fumes puffed up.

From the direction of Paternoster Row a wave of fire surged forth. The wattle-and-daub homes of Friday Street had ignited. Behind them a wall of heat shimmered and then charged out, sucking up the draft of ventilation greedily and flinging it out as a white-hot force.

A cellar ahead of them detonated in a spray of burning lavender oil.

'This way!' Charlie zigzagged away from the collapsing ground and Lily followed close behind. They pelted over cobblestones.

'It's the firestorm,' panted Charlie. He swung, trying to predict where the next blast would come from. Up ahead Carter Lane seemed to ripple. Then the corn dollies hanging from the eaves of shops burst into flame.

'Back,' said Charlie, flinging out an arm to protect Lily. The half-timbered shops shook off a scattering of plaster, then combusted before their eyes.

There was only one way to St Paul's now.

Charlie wheeled towards Lud Gate Hill. He smelled it before he saw it. The scorching aroma of lead smelting. Then he saw it. A river of melted lead was pouring down the narrow street.

Lily raised her eyes in horror.

'Holy Jesus!' she said. 'St Paul's!'

The building was on fire. The towering east wall was rolling in dripping lead. It cascaded down the side of the towering side of the building, splashing on to the cobbles below.

Charlie pointed.

'The lead roof,' he panted. 'It's melting in the heat.'

A waterfall of grey metal was cascading from St Paul's. People below were trying to escape as hot lead splashed and scalded. A man looting a shop turned too late. Lead burned his legs and he fell. Fiery molten metal rolled over him as he screamed and flailed.

Charlie's gaze swung wildly.

On the ground the lead was forming a fast-moving torrent. It spilled down Lud Gate Hill and poured through the narrow back-streets. People were screaming and running, caught in the unexpected surge. The streets glowed fiery red.

Charlie and Lily were trapped between flaming streets and scalding lead.

There was a flash of lightning and Charlie caught the shape of a bulky figure high on St Paul's.

Blackstone.

'He's on the cathedral roof,' gasped Lily.

'We must hurry,' said Charlie.

Chapter 130

The King raised and fixed, raised and fixed. The sky was dark but the city was bright heat. His muscles ached. Next to him the troops were visibly flagging. They knew the truth. The fight was impossible.

The last floor of the building was rent to timber. They paused for a moment, exhausted. Flames leered down at them from the city beyond.

'Your Majesty,' gasped one of the troops, 'the men are tired. We cannot beat it.' He was shouting over the deafening roar of the fire.

The King clasped his blistered hands to the firehook. 'Temple Bar is where Westminster Parish begins,' he said. 'We cannot let fire cross. Raise!' he shouted, 'fix!'

Reluctantly the men shuffled to take their posts. They all knew it was hopeless. Lawyers had begun streaming forth from Temple Bar. The legal heart of London had fallen foul of its own expertise. No lawyer would pull another's property without official documentation. Now their precious gold and papers burned.

The Duke of York arrived by Charles's side. Behind him came a small troop of men carrying a single extra firehook.

'Where are the other firehooks, James?' asked Charles, his gaze fixed up to the wavering pole in his own hands.

'Lost, broken.' James coughed against the thick smoke. 'What does it matter in any case?'

'We fight to the end,' said Charles. 'Bring this bank of buildings down. We can still do some good.'

'Raise and fix!' called James. His men began swinging the pole into place.

'How goes the fire to the north?' shouted Charles.

'Regrouped west in Cloak's Lane and cut us off,' admitted James. 'We had to run. Jonathan's Coffee House blew behind us,' he added.

'One good thing,' said Charles heaving back. 'I always hated those coffee shops.'

The building shrieked against the firehook and unexpectedly gave way. Charles and the other men were propelled back. Huge timbers and joists tumbled towards them. James grasped his brother and pulled him out of the way. A soldier shouted in pain. They looked to see a beam had passed clean through his arm.

'Get that man to a surgeon,' shouted Charles.

James shook his head. 'He won't make it an hour.'

'Your Majesty!' A shout came from the troops and Charles turned, expecting to see more injury. Instead one of his soldiers was pointing. Charles followed the direction of his finger.

Water was bubbling up from the ground. From where the underground elm-pipes had been breached.

'I don't believe it!' said Charles. He turned triumphantly to James. 'I knew this fire would be the making of Monmouth. That water comes from the Fleet! My son blew the blockage. High tide will help us. The west pipes flow again!'

James was wondering at the truth of Monmouth's bravery. He would have words with Monmouth later. If there was still a Kingdom to defend.

They watched as water erupted in several more little spurting spots. Fire spat and retreated from the wet ground.

'Set to!' bellowed Charles. 'Get this water on the blaze!'

The exhausted men surged forward. It was the first good omen they'd had since the fire started. They dug in, hurling water and angling the firehooks.

'We can pull here now!' said Charles, pointing to a building they'd left standing, for fear of it fuelling fire on the dry ground. 'It will fall in the water.'

Charles gripped with blistered fingers and pulled back on one of the higher storeys. It fell sizzling on to the wet ground.

The partially demolished building afforded an unexpected view. Charles's men drew back, wonder glowing on their tired faces.

There, like an earthly paradise, was the yellowed grass of Lincoln Fields.

'Get to the firehook!' shouted Charles. 'If we can topple this building we might stand a chance yet.'

Chapter 131

Charlie looked up to the nearest building. It was half-timbered with black beams. Hot lead was running fast towards them.

He looked up. Blackstone had vanished from sight.

'He hasn't flamed the roof yet,' Charlie called to Lily. 'There's still time.'

'We can't get there.' Lily was looking to the fiery lead covering the streets. 'The route is blocked.'

'Climb on to the half timber,' shouted Charlie. 'We can scale up and use the rooftops.'

'Are you mad?' shouted Lily above the roar of the blaze. 'Those buildings are aflame!'

Charlie heaved himself on to the first beam. 'Use your finger-tips,' he called. 'It's easier than it looks from the street.'

Lily pulled herself on to the sill just as the first flow of lead snaked past. She stared down at the smoking metal in disbelief. Then she began clambering upwards.

Charlie reached the second-storey window, which had a jutting window box.

'Bridge with your legs!' he shouted, bracing himself against the opposite building. 'And walk up.'

Beneath him Lily was positioned with her back braced. Her eyes were closed and she seemed to be praying. Charlie grasped thatch, hauled himself on to the roof, then reached down with both hands to hoist her up.

They stood on the uneven thatch and breathed hard.

Below them screams issued up. Guttering from St Paul's had burst and was directing a font of molten metal into the fleeing crowd. Lead was rolling down the hill in a heavy torrent. Londoners were racing in all directions as burning lead from the roof splashed down towards them.

Charlie glanced across the rooftops. Blackstone had vanished from sight.

His sixth sense for London's jumble of dark buildings was firing. He gauged the gaps between the roofs, plotting a route.

'This way.' Charlie ran and jumped the divide, his heels sinking into thatch.

Charlie looked out at the higher buildings of Carter Lane, mapping the levels through which the fire might pass. 'That room contains hay,' he muttered, plotting a route around it. 'That roof is painted with pitch.' He gauged the distance. 'We get on to a tile roof,' said Charlie, pointing. 'Stay on tile and go only where I do.'

The thatch under them had started to crackle with flames. Charlie ran to the edge of the roof and jumped to the next.

They were closing the gap now, nearing the cathedral.

Ahead of them the straw roof collapsed inwards like a great yawning mouth. Charlie dodged, hopped across two more roofs and then his feet hit tile. Lily landed next to him, her shoes leaving imprints in the softened tiles.

'We can make it,' said Charlie, 'St Paul's graveyard is the other side of that building.'

'It's too far away!'

'We can make it.'

Chapter 132

Blackstone looked out on to the blazing city. All but one guildhall had been burned to the ground. He counted twenty churches still burning. The Royal Exchange and Post Office were smoking ash.

London was ruined.

Blackstone rested the barrel on the apex of the roof. Then he assessed.

Strange things were happening to his mind.

Down on the street, he could have sworn he saw a familiar face. Tobias Oakley.

It couldn't be, of course. Oakley had died years ago. After betraying his brotherhood.

Sally Oakley. Everything was her fault.

Torr had liked Sally too. He'd gone deep into mysticism and wanted to learn of the Old Ways. Sally, a country maid from Wales, had taught him her silly spells. Rites with ribbons and poppets.

He had a sudden image of Sally weaving poppets to protect her sons. She'd known what Blackstone was capable of, when Tobias didn't.

Because Tobias remembered the old soldier. The Brotherhood man who would have given his life for the King. A man who fought until nightfall in the rain, then slept on the battlefield and rose at dawn to fight again.

After the King's great betrayal, Blackstone wasn't that man any longer. And only Sally Oakley saw it. But it hadn't saved her.

Blackstone felt his feet shift. The lead was soft beneath his boots. Pliable. On the east side it was melting. Torrents poured on to the people below.

Blackstone shifted the barrel. Better move it along where the roof was firmer. He wanted to be sure of a grand flame. A blue fire that would be seen all over London.

Chapter 133

Charlie dodged over softening roof tiles and jumped clear as a section of roof flared into flames.

Lily was at his side, sweating.

Charlie was alive with the forgotten skill now.

'Through there,' he said, pointing to a run of buildings.

The heavens rumbled and a dart of lightning shot down. It smashed a chimney stack, showering Lily and Charlie with burning brick.

'Jump!' shouted Charlie, pulling Lily to the side. They pitched away from the broken shingle and landed on an adjoining rooftop. The house they'd abandoned roared a protest, then lurched downwards.

'What now?' asked Lily, shaking as she surveyed the destroyed buildings to the left and right of them.

'Between those two buildings,' said Charlie. 'Fast,' he added, 'the bricks might explode. It's the only way,' he added, catching her horrified expression.

As they made for the gauntlet, bricks began detonating around them. Lily yelled in pain as sharp shrapnel hit her bare arms.

'Keep clear of the black ones,' said Charlie, ducking as mortar flew at them.

He pointed. 'Fix your eyes on the wall ahead. That's where we can climb up.'

He reached a wooden wall, but it was smoother than he anticipated. Charlie ran his fingers over the flat wood, testing for climbing holds.

A knife thudded to within an inch of his fingers. Charlie turned in shock to see Lily pelting towards him, another knife poised to throw. It thudded two feet higher than the first.

Without waiting to explain she lodged her foot on the first knife and sprung up on to the second.

'Climb up!' she shouted. 'Use the knives.'

Too surprised to protest Charlie levered himself up on the first knife and gripped the second. With effort he pulled over and on to the higher roof.

Lily was waiting for him at the top. 'Which way now?' she asked.

'Through this window,' said Charlie, breaking it open. 'St Paul's is on the other side of this building.'

'It's rented rooms,' panted Lily, catching her breath. 'Locked doors.'

'Only ground floors and Catholics lock their doors in London tenements,' said Charlie. 'The rooms will connect. We're only a stairwell away.'

Chapter 134

Charlie and Lily burst out into St Paul's graveyard. Her mighty roof surged with tongues of flame.

'No blue fire,' said Charlie. 'Maybe Blackstone waits for something. We need to get inside.'

His gaze dropped to the vault entrance. It was completely sealed. The stationers had filed it to bursting with books and papers.

'They've made that vault the biggest danger in the city,' muttered Charlie. He was taking in the candlewax that sealed the doors. 'Any breach of the cathedral floor,' he said, 'and fire will rip through those papers fast as gunpowder.'

His cinder thief experience was telling him to turn and run. A huge building atop a vault of dry tinder. It would blow like a cannon if fire got underneath.

'The vestry,' said Charlie, pointing at the church. 'There's no flame on the west side yet. We can get in that way.'

'People have already broken the window,' said Lily, eyeing the shattered stained glass as they climbed up at the vestry.

'Commoners turn desperate to store goods,' said Charlie, easing himself through. 'This is the last unburned church.'

As they slipped through and landed, Charlie covered his mouth.

There was a smell on the air that was all too familiar.

'Blackstone's here,' he breathed. 'Somewhere in the church. He hoards food. I can smell it.'

Lily looked around the vestry. It was crammed with pitifully cheap goods. Broken chairs and makeshift tables had been jumbled in. Alongside sacks of flour, barrels of ale and half-eaten sides of meat.

'This is Blackstone's?' Lily was looking around her.

'No,' Charlie shook his head. 'This is commoner's stuff. Cheap barrels of preserves, smuggled goods from the Shadow Market.'

He looked through the piles to the vestry beyond. It seemed as though every Londoner had stored goods here.

'Teresa's pyre is somewhere out there,' said Charlie. 'In the cathedral.' He was eyeing the huge space, which ranged on and out of view.

'The altar?' suggested Lily. 'That would be the holiest place.'

'No,' said Charlie. 'I don't think he'd put her out in the open. Something happened to Teresa Blackstone during the war. She never went outside.'

'There's a vault,' said Lily uncertainly.

'It's jammed floor to ceiling with books and papers from Paternoster Row,' said Charlie. 'And sealed up so tight not even a spark could get in.'

He looked down the long body of the cathedral. Charlie pointed to a section with a number of private chapels spiralling off the sides.

'Remember Blackstone's family tree?' he said. 'The crest. I've seen it in this church. I think they have a private chapel here. That would be the place.'

They began heading towards the private chapels, entering the cavernous space of the mighty cathedral.

Suddenly Charlie heard Lily gasp in pain. He felt something red hot drop on his arm. Charlie looked down to see a drop of grey liquid.

'The roof,' he called back to Lily. The enormous arc of lead above them was spilling drops.

There was another splash, this time towards the back of the nave. And then the drops started to become regular, like light rain. Hot lead sprayed up as it splattered and cooled on the stone floor.

Lily exclaimed as boiling drops splattered her bare arms. Charlie's gaze swung around the huge space. His eyes lighted under the belfry where no lead fell. The leaded spire was tall enough to resist the melting heat.

'This way.' Charlie threw his coat over both of their heads, and they raced to the belfry like young lovers escaping a rainstorm. The metal splashed on their skin in hot coin-sized spatters and drummed hard on to Charlie's thick coat, but they emerged singed and panting under the belfry.

'What now?' said Lily despairingly, looking out to the unceasing barrage. It echoed around the cathedral, building to a crescendo. 'We can't get to the chapels.'

Charlie looked across the cathedral. Eventually the roof would run out of lead. The burning deluge would stop. But they didn't have time for that.

'St Paul's is aflame,' said Charlie. 'Blackstone's pawns are all in place.'

He looked up to see the spire curling away above them.

'We can get to the roof,' said Charlie. 'The belfry has a stair up to the steeple.'

'But Blackstone will be armed,' said Lily, following behind uncertainly. 'We have nothing to defend ourselves. We need the papers . . .'

'We can't get to them in time,' said Charlie. He looked at her. 'We have to take our chances.'

'You've waited your whole life for those papers,' protested Lily. 'London is as good as burned in any case. If they hold riches as Torr says . . .'

'There is more to this than treasure,' said Charlie. 'I have waited my whole life for the papers. I can wait a while longer. Stay and search if you wish. I know how gold holds sway with gypsies.'

He put a foot on the ladder to the spire and hoisted himself up.

'Then toss me the key,' called Lily hopefully, ignoring the slight.

She cast around the overflowing cathedral and then pushed up behind him.

'You owe me half the treasure,' she grumbled. 'I cannot very well claim it if you are burned alive.' But Charlie noticed she didn't manage to keep her voice as casual as she'd intended.

They inched upwards, coughing against the rising smoke. Ancient rickety steps coiled around the narrow spire, barely a foot's width across. And as the angle of the building became more acute, it forced them to lean outwards as they climbed.

'Do you think we have a chance?' Lily called up.

'Blackstone will have got on to the roof by the main stair,' said Charlie. 'We'll come out a different way. He won't be expecting us. We'll have the element of surprise at least.'

They drew level to the enormous bells. They sat sedentary, each the size of a small house. A mass of thick coloured ropes tumbled down from their innards.

'There are hand-holds,' called Charlie, pressing himself against the inside of the winding spire. 'But they are well worn. Be careful.'

'There is a seventy-foot drop,' panted Lily, swinging to grasp the hold behind him. 'You need not tell me to be careful.'

As they reached the mid-point, Charlie's hands found the edges of a small door secreted in the edge of the spire. It led out on to the roof.

'Here,' he called. 'This is the way.'

Lily breathed out. She retrieved a knife from her skirt.

'I'm right behind you,' she said.

Chapter 135

'I don't believe it.' Amesbury's soot-streaked face was raised to the burned-out walls of Chancery.

The troops had dropped the firehook and turned to look. One pointed.

'We've met the fields!'

The gaggle of men turned to one another hardly able to believe it. A grassy firebreak stood between Westminster and Temple Bar. All around lay flattened buildings.

Charles let the shovel in his hand drop. James was dousing the last of the rubble. Deeper in the city flames still roared. But the west had been barricaded. 'Do you think it's enough?' asked Charles. 'Fire has got to St Paul's,' he added, looking with devastation to the cathedral in the distance.

James nodded. 'A quarter-mile stretch of demolished buildings lays between the Strand and Westminster,' he said. 'Most remaining in the west are stone. Lead or slate tiles. The wind dies. Fire is fading even now.'

Charles allowed himself a cautious breath out.

'We've done it then,' he said. 'The Palace is safe?'

James clapped his brother on the back in reply. Then both looked out to the roaring inferno in the city beyond. Deep in the city, lightning still forked across the sky. There was a storm in the east.

A rider was approaching, expertly steering his horse through the mire of smoking rubble.

Charles recognised him.

'Monmouth!' he hailed. 'We think Whitehall is protected by firebreaks. Your bravery has been rewarded. Now we should fortify in the north and south.'

But Monmouth's face was ashen.

'They say fire goes east now.' He looked as though he might cry. 'Will this fire never abate?' he wailed.

'He's like a fainting woman,' muttered Amesbury, eyeing Monmouth with disgust.

'To St Giles? The slums?' said Charles, less certainly now. The wind blew west. East had never concerned them.

'Not to the slums. To the Tower.'

Charles felt icy fear run through him. The Tower held the country's entire munitions. Gunpowder. Arms.

'My God,' breathed Charles. 'We've no men there.'

'There are three hundred houses between London Bridge and the Tower of London,' said Monmouth.

'Wooden houses,' said Charles. He turned to Amesbury. 'How can it have got so far east?' he whispered. 'The wind goes west.'

Amesbury spoke carefully. 'Were there a plot,' he said, 'this would be a good strategic move. Draw your resources west. Leave the Tower undefended.'

'Think you it then? This has the marks of a plot? To attack the Tower?' The King was white as Amesbury nodded.

'If it is a plot,' said Charles, 'then we've walked straight into it. The east is completely defenceless. All our resources and engines have been drawn west. We've handed them London on a plate.'

Amesbury's face was grim. 'I think this has the marks of a well-schemed attack.'

'You're sure?' asked the King.

Amesbury shrugged. 'It's what I would do,' he said.

Chapter 136

Charlie pushed the spire door open and climbed out. The huge roofs of St Paul's rolled out before him. There were smoking flames in some parts, but others were a wide expanse of lead tiles.

There was no sign of Blackstone beneath the scalding sky.

The spire where Charlie stood was wreathed in wooden scaffolding. He grabbed the nearest thick strut, clambering down on to the roof. Behind him, he heard Lily emerge.

'I can't see Blackstone,' called Charlie, above the inferno of burning London.

They both stared out on to the blazing city, holding tightly to the scaffold.

'My God,' said Lily. 'All is gone.'

A third of the city was a smoking shell. The blaze all around St Paul's spread out to embrace another third, with a half-mile of glowing embers in its wake.

'The Tower still stands,' said Charlie, squinting into the distance. 'There are no blue flames on the roof. And the Carpenters' Guild hasn't been fired. There is time.'

He cast his eye across the rooftops. The steepled roofs enclosed a multitude of areas where Blackstone could cast his lye. The east side of roof was melted almost all away now, revealing the open joists. But huge quarters of the enormous cross-shaped roof were intact.

Above them the dark sky boiled and churned. Lightning was striking down all over the city, sending up plumes of fire and destruction.

There was a sudden movement, a half rooftop away from where they stood.

'There!' hissed Charlie.

Blackstone loomed like a demon against the blood-red sky. He was heaving a huge barrel into position on the apex of a thickly leaded roof.

'I can get him.' Lily raised her knife.

'You're sure?' said Charlie, looking at the smoky distance. 'If you miss he'll know we're here.'

'When have you known me miss?' Lily adjusted her grip on the scaffold, securing her footing. Then she breathed out, and drew back to throw.

Blackstone ducked down, sending his cascade of lye pouring down the roof. Great clouds of hissing steam rose up.

Lily cursed and adjusted her aim.

'Now!' said Charlie. 'Before he flames it.'

Thunder crashed directly above their heads, and the scaffold shifted. Lily's hand jerked free and she slipped.

Charlie put out his arms to stop her fall and her momentum pulled him from the scaffold. They slid three sharp feet down the steep spire. Charlie's feet hit the base, shattering tile and he broke Lily's fall.

He righted himself, breathing heavily, and looked towards Blackstone.

'No,' said Charlie, refusing to believe it.

Blue fire zigzagged along the roof. It rolled down like a fiery fountain, then roared upwards triumphantly.

They could only look in horror as the west roof blazed blue. Then at the Carpenters' Guild, they saw an answering blue light. Lily put her hands over her mouth.

'The guild is fired,' said Charlie, trying to keep the hopelessness from his voice. 'The Tower will burn.' He looked up to the storm. 'The papers,' he decided. 'Perhaps we can still stop Blackstone.'

'He's already won,' said Lily. 'All of England's defences are in the Tower.'

Lightning cracked, illuminating the rooftops. Lily started.

'We're concealed by the scaffold,' Charlie reassured her. 'Blackstone hasn't seen us.'

'I was more concerned about being stood on a steeple during a thunderstorm,' said Lily.

'This steeple was hit by lightning twenty years ago,' Charlie said. 'Lightning never strikes . . .'

Light flashed and the steeple exploded. A shower of burning lead and timber rained on to the roof, tearing huge holes and tumbling into the vaulted chasm below.

Charlie ducked reflexively, throwing out his arm to protect Lily. On the west roof Blackstone whipped around to follow the source of the light. His eyes fell on Charlie.

Then on his key.

Charlie grasped it instinctively, shielding the symbol with his fist. But it was too late. Blackstone's mouth twisted slowly upwards. He had seen the key. And he knew what it meant. In the next moment Blackstone's hand was at his hip, reaching for a pistol.

'Lily,' said Charlie, 'get . . .'

Blackstone's gunshot blew her backwards. Charlie snatched at her dress but the silken fabric tore through his fingers. He could only watch as Lily fell back, crashing through the weakened spire and down into the cathedral below.

Chapter 137

'Lily!' Charlie dived for the gap her body had made. He climbed back inside the spire. The bell ropes were swinging. Deep below the monstrous chasm of the cathedral seemed to taunt him.

In the dark depths Charlie couldn't even make out her broken body.

His eyes blurred. 'Lily,' he whispered.

'I'm not dead yet,' called a breathless voice. 'Only cut me down.'

Charlie looked in the direction of the voice and saw her hanging. She was upside down, her leg tangled up in the mass of bell ropes.

'Help me,' she gasped, struggling, 'my foot is trapped.'

As she spoke the rope slipped and she dropped screaming for six feet, before halting with a jolt. The massive bell attached to her rope shuddered.

'Lily!' he cried. 'Were you shot?'

'No,' she shouted, 'I twisted away and slipped. Get me down.'

Charlie looked up. Lightning had flamed the spire. Fire lit the rafters. The joists which held the bell pulls were burning.

His eyes followed the rope twisted at Lily's ankle. The slightest struggle would unloop it and send her crashing seventy feet down. 'Don't move!' he shouted. 'I'm coming.'

Charlie closed his eyes. 'Things would be so much simpler,' he muttered, 'on my own.' And then he jumped.

Charlie landed with both arms and legs wrapped around the nearest bell rope. He slid then halted himself. Lily was two ropes away and twelve feet beneath him. Manoeuvring the next heavy rope with his legs, Charlie wrapped it around his foot, pulled it towards him and swung across.

'I'm nearly there!' he shouted, looking up to where she hung. 'Hold on!'

'I don't plan,' gasped Lily, 'to let go.'

Charlie looked up into the rafters and then down to the cathedral floor. The bell attached to Lily's rope was huge. Twenty feet high at least. And the organ stretched up to a third of the cathedral height. If the bell were rung, it might lower Lily enough distance to reach the top of the organ.

'Do you trust me?' he asked. 'Never mind,' he added, seeing her expression. 'The bell you hang from. It is too heavy for you to ring.'

'I do not try to peal the bell!'

'If I jump on to your rope we will be heavy enough together,' continued Charlie. 'The bell will turn,' he said, glancing at it again. 'So the rope will drop. I think it will bring us low enough to drop on to the top of the organ.'

'I am caught,' said Lily.

'I will probably have time to cut you free,' said Charlie, 'before the bell swings up again.'

'You *probably* have time?'

'The rafters are burning,' said Charlie. 'Your other choice is the cathedral floor.' He took a breath. 'Put out your hand,' he said.

Lily paused and then her little fingers snaked out in the gloom. He grasped them.

'Ready!' he shouted, placing his knife in his teeth. 'Now!'

Pulling her towards him, Charlie climbed on to her rope. They hung stationary, Lily upside down, Charlie level with her calves.

'It hasn't worked,' gasped Lily. 'We don't weigh enough to move the bell.'

'Wait,' said Charlie leaning back against the rope as far as he dared.

For a moment nothing happened. Then slowly the great bell began to move down, clanging a muted peal.

Charlie climbed up over Lily, bringing his head level with her suspended feet. Then, working one-handed, he took the blade from his mouth and began sawing frantically at where the rope had caught above her ankle.

At the rafters the bell reached its ascent with a sonorous clang. Charlie looked down. The top of the ornate organ was less than five feet away, but he was only halfway through Lily's rope.

Having reached its apex, the bell began to swing back the other way. Charlie watched helplessly as the organ grew small beneath them.

Lily was struggling beneath him.

'Stop moving!' he shouted, looking up at the rafters. 'The ropes are on fire.'

Lily looked upwards and froze. The fire had caught the thick bell ropes.

'The next drop,' said Charlie. 'It is the only chance we have.'

The rope next to them screamed a final protest and sped coiling down into the dark cathedral.

'When I shout,' said Charlie, 'let go.'

Lily's eyes were closed in prayer as the bell gathered speed on the descent, sending them tunnelling down towards the organ.

Charlie watched the fire. Their rope would not last the downwards peal. He took hold of Lily by the waist and pulled her lower half up, to be level with him. His knife was at her ankle.

'Ready?' he said as they sped down.

She nodded as two more blazing ropes hit the cathedral floor.

The rope jerked as it rang the bell. Then it untwisted sharply down as fire snapped two of the three threads.

'Now!' Charlie's knife sliced through the last portion, sending them both flying downwards. They sailed through the air for a moment, then landed in a heap on top of the organ. The fall knocked the breath out of them.

'Your ankle is not hurt?' asked Charlie, rising to his feet.

Lily shook her head. She took Charlie's outstretched hand.

'The papers,' said Charlie. 'Blackstone knows where they are.'

'Blackstone will come down the main stair,' said Lily. 'We can get to the chapel before him.'

There was a splintering shriek of glass and they both twisted in the direction of the sound. It had come from the nearest window, which had thrown off a portion of brightly coloured glass.

'The stained glass,' said Charlie. 'It's held together with lead.'

The rainbow of beautiful glass was shifting and twisting in the heat. Various bible scenes were depicted in lush colours.

Something occurred to Charlie. Torr's last words.

Alchemists look at the big picture.

What if Torr had meant it literally? The ultimate irony for an allegory spinner. What if Torr meant they should look at a picture of the Wedding of Cana?

Charlie's eyes tracked the stained-glass windows. It wasn't an uncommon scene to depict. And he was sure he'd seen it in St Paul's.

Charlie's eyes settled on the right window, just as the bride and groom shattered and fell across the stone floor. Then Jesus and Mary, gazing benignly on water pitchers, fractured into a thousand coloured pieces.

He shook his head. There was nothing there. Just an ordinary bible scene.

The last portion of window showed two disciples. They splintered apart raining down. For some reason, Charlie couldn't place these particular men.

Something about the way the marriage was set out didn't quite make sense. The bride, the groom. Jesus and Mary. Disciples. And then it hit him.

They're not disciples. They're witnesses. Witnesses to the marriage ceremony.

Suddenly Charlie knew what the marriage papers were.

Torr's last words.

To be an alchemist you must question known truths.

With a sinking heart Charlie realised he'd shown Blackstone where to find the greatest power in England.

'We must find the papers,' said Charlie, throwing a leg over the side of the organ. 'I know what they hold.'

And without waiting for her, he began making his way down.

'What?' shouted Lily, following after him.

'I thought you needed three people for a wedding,' said Charlie. 'A bride, a groom, a minister. The stained glass reminded me. A true wedding needs five people in total.'

'Five?' Lily looked confused.

'All this time,' said Charlie, clambering down the ornately carved organ, 'I thought Thomas and Teresa's names on the certificate meant they got married.'

'It didn't mean that?'

'No.' Charlie dropped to the ground. The molten rain had eased now and only a few scant drops fell between the belfry and the private chapels.

'Two witnesses.' Charlie scanned for the best route. 'To make things legal. Thomas and Teresa signed those marriage papers, because they were witnesses. At someone else's wedding.'

He pointed to the front of St Paul's, where a familiar crest hung.

'Lead into gold,' breathed Lily. 'A commoner into royalty. You had it right.'

'The right idea,' said Charlie. 'The wrong commoner.'

Chapter 138

The King wheeled on his horse. The fire had come too quickly. He knew it and the men knew it too.

The Carpenters' Hall had fired. Flames had burst through the guild without warning. Any hope they had of securing extra commoners had vanished. Flames now came from all directions. They'd fought all through the night, but still had no hope of winning.

'It's not as fierce as we've fought,' said Charles. 'But we've a tenth of the men.'

'Orders have been sent,' said James. 'I'll have twenty naval men here within the hour.'

'It won't do us any good.'

'Sailors race up rigging,' said James. 'They can climb the buildings and settle the firehooks. Each naval man is worth two troops. They'll pull buildings twice as fast.'

'Even so,' said Charles. 'Even with sailors, we haven't enough men.' He was looking at the Tower, thinking.

'How much gunpowder is in the Tower?' asked Charles.

'Two hundred barrels at least,' replied James, making a quick calculation of the arsenal. 'Once fire hits, the whole Tower will explode.'

'Send men,' said Charles. 'Start rolling out the barrels.'

'There's no time,' said James. 'We can't clear out that amount of gunpowder. You'd best set your troops to make firebreaks. Slow the blaze.'

'Send men,' ordered Charles. 'Remove the gunpowder.'

The Duke of York opened his mouth to protest and then decided against it. His brother would lose the crown tonight. There was no harm in obeying his last ill-judged order.

Chapter 139

Two candles winked out in the gloom of St Paul's crypt.

Teresa Blackstone's empty eye sockets glared out accusingly. They watched as two shadowy figures approached the edge of her magic circle. Then whispered voices echoed.

'This is it,' said Charlie, looking up at the crest. 'Blackstone's family chapel.'

It was a narrow room leading off the main cathedral. Carved wood screens partially barricaded the entrance. A high stained-glass window cast twisting colours on to the weaving nest of Teresa Blackstone's possessions.

'The smell.' Lily was covering her nose. 'It's unbearable.'

'The light comes from deeper inside,' said Charlie. He was moving like a sleepwalker. 'There.'

Charlie had stopped

'These are her things,' he said. 'Teresa's.'

They had reached the edge of a jumble of possessions which glowed from behind by an eerie light. At first they seemed to be household items. Books, a few chairs. But as their eyes adjusted to the candlelight everything was wrong.

The furniture was broken and old. Little animal corpses lay in piles in and around the broken furnishings. Birds, mice and squirrels had been wrapped into corn dollies, their dead eyes peering out. Some had been crowned in leaves and others tied with ribbon and anointed with candlewax.

'Poppets?' whispered Lily uncertainly. She was looking at the decorated animal corpses.

'It was for magic,' said Charlie trying to remember. 'She collected them. I think . . . Rowan brought her some of them.'

A memory was flickering through his mind. Two boys descending into a cellar. Ribbons. Blood.

'What are the branches?' whispered Lily. She was staring at the twisted dead foliage that tumbled over the edges of a broken chair. It was knotted at points, giving the appearance of a crazed nest.

'Oak for strength,' said Charlie, 'willow for power. Purple ribbon for enchantment.'

His hand sought out the faded purple ribbon that held his key.

Lily glanced at him and then back. She was staring at them both reflected in a broken mirror. The glass forked Charlie's face with an ugly crack.

'This is all household furniture,' said Charlie. 'I don't see her personal things.'

'It's a circle,' he added. 'The way her things are arranged. A witch's circle. So she will be at the centre.'

Charlie's mind was rolling with dark remembered things.

I am the magic, I am the power.

'You're sure you want to go on?' asked Lily.

Charlie nodded, eyeing the pile. 'There will be a way in,' he said. 'If Blackstone means to burn her then he must have left a path.'

He began moving around the edge of the broken furniture and knotted branches. After only a few steps he found where the possessions were parted by a foot.

'Here,' he called. 'By the east,' he added, mentally remapping the church above. 'This is all symbolism. Her better things are here,' he added, moving towards the candles.

A tapestry had been draped barring the way ahead and pewter plates and cutlery were arranged on the ground. Pinned to it was a torn part of a picture.

'The missing part of his family tree,' said Charlie. 'Teresa's half.'

'It's empty,' said Lily, turning to Charlie. 'The only face is hers.'

Charlie's mind was ticking. The portrait of Teresa's face was so familiar.

He could see it in his nightmares. Charlie tried to separate the dark shifting memories, to apply thief-taker logic. The face. There was something about Teresa's face. But then it slipped and danced away and shadows crowded in.

'Come, we must find the chest,' Charlie decided, moving the tapestry. His fingers seemed to tingle as they swept it aside.

Beyond the fabric lay a circle of flickering candles.

Charlie's eyes tracked around the low light, searching for the chest.

Then he saw the body.

The lips had rotted back in a ghoulish toothy smile, but part of the cheeks and upper face remained. A curtain of white hair cascaded over the plinth. The familiar features had been eaten away. A leering crone lay beneath.

The empty sockets seemed to wink out at Charlie. As though she could work dark magic from beyond the grave.

One drop of blood, Charlie Oakley.

He felt Lily bump against him as she stopped short.

'Gunpowder.' Lily pointed. Teresa's remains were circled with kindling and faggots of wood. In among them were kegs of black powder. The lids were off, and fuses were set, ready to blaze through the pyre.

'When he lights the fuses this whole chapel will blow,' said Charlie.

He moved a little closer to the body.

'It was not the dress she died in,' said Charlie. 'You can see how she was mauled into it.'

The green fabric was in the old court style. Wide at the bottom with thick lace at the neck and wrists. Teresa's arm had been twisted at an obscene angle through the narrow bodice.

'Her wedding gown?' suggested Lily, regarding the elaborate lace. She moved closer to the body and examined the plinth.

Charlie nodded, drawing back.

A tablecloth lay covering something low on the ground and Charlie pulled it away. It was only when he heard Lily gasp that he truly understood what he'd revealed.

Three jars had been arranged around the base of the plinth. Crowns of drooping flowers decorated their rims but did not hide the contents.

'Are they . . .?' Lily could not say the words.

'They must be hers,' Charlie said. 'She must have preserved them. After they . . . After they were born early.'

Each jar was filled with clear liquid. And floating inside an unformed child.

'They're deformed,' said Lily, eyes riveted to the grisly embalmings.

Charlie swallowed.

'I've seen this before,' said Lily, looking sick, 'in the country. When the blood is too close.'

Charlie looked at her, uncertain of her meaning.

'Sisters and brothers,' said Lily. 'The children come wrong. Early.'

Charlie covered his mouth in shock.

'Teresa Blackstone's missing family tree,' he said. 'She didn't have one, because hers was Blackstone's. They were brother and sister.'

Chapter 140

Lightning crackled above as Blackstone raced down the stairs.

Within this very cathedral was the key to the greatest power in England. Blackstone felt the thrill of it course through him.

The key. Teresa's wedding chest.

It slotted into place now. After all these years. Clever Sally Oakley. She knew no one would look in the wedding trunk. It was a cursed thing.

Blackstone's mind pulsed with the thunderstorm ahead. Jumbled images were colliding.

Charlie Oakley. He looks just like his father.

Somewhere in the reaches of his mind, Blackstone thought he'd seen Sally's grown-up son before. But the memory kept spinning away.

Then a bright solid picture settled. His gentle sister, washing his wounds. Her beautiful face taut with concern. His father's voice.

Next I will test your brother's faith on the rack. As the martyr St Devota endured.

Blackstone grew up to know his older sister as an angel. Set on high. Glacial perfection and beauty. He wasn't sure when he'd begun to feel differently towards her.

Blessed blood. His father's words. *Our family is of blessed blood.* Teresa was pure. Her blood must be kept unsullied. Husbands were suggested. His sister even had a notion of a suitor. But Blackstone couldn't let her marry outside the family. Not to a dirty half-breed. He refused to see their family's money leave their estate.

After soldiers had killed Blackstone's parents, there was no one alive who knew his sister's face. And Teresa had been raised to such total obedience, she hardly even thought to object.

Before coming to Blackstone's estate, the soldiers had passed through a nearby village. It had been easy to find a murdered girl. Blackstone had burned the face of the corpse, in case it was recognised.

After burying the body as his sister's, Blackstone collected her dowry as the natural heir. Then he'd passed it off as his new wife's money and bought himself great favour in the Sealed Knot.

Blackstone's every sense was alert. Straight away he heard it. He allowed himself a cold smile. Sally Oakley's son was in Blackstone's best fortification. All the power of England would soon be his.

Chapter 141

'Blackstone married his sister,' breathed Lily. 'And hid her away from the world.'

'Old noble families marry close to keep the bloodline,' said Charlie. 'Perhaps war twisted Blackstone. He used his sister's dowry to fight the war,' he added.

'But the Royalists lost,' said Lily.

'And his sister went mad with their crime,' said Charlie. The puzzle was unravelling. 'That's why Teresa scrubbed out the portrait. It was her own picture. Blackstone must have had a new picture drawn. Of Teresa as his wife.'

'So his sister didn't die,' said Lily. 'She became someone else.'

'And Teresa turned to witchcraft,' said Charlie. 'After everything she'd sacrificed, losing the war must have been the bitterest blow.'

'But it's not Teresa's and Thomas's marriage papers which were hidden,' said Lily. 'They both witnessed a marriage far more powerful.'

'We must find her chest,' said Charlie, tearing his eyes away from the ghoulish jars. 'He laid her out in a wedding dress. It must be near.'

The candles flickered as they scanned around. Dresses were hung at the circle edge like a parade of ghostly women with shoes tucked neatly beneath.

'There?' suggested Lily, pointing to a small leather box.

Charlie shook his head.

'It's large. We are missing something.'

His eyes scanned the broken and bloodied things, the little vermin poppets. Suddenly there was a sinister clicking, like a pistol being cocked.

He turned sharply, expecting to see Blackstone's looming form at the edge of the circle. There was nothing there and Charlie turned back in confusion. It must have been the sound of the fire, he realised. Stone shrieking and twisting in the wider cathedral. He looked overhead and saw the wooden surrounds of the little chapel were smoking. They needed to move quickly.

Charlie looked back to the corpse and froze.

Teresa moved.

He blinked, staring at the corpse. Lily was investigating a pile of woven branches strewn near the remains.

'Did you see that?' Charlie's voice was tight.

'What?'

'She moved,' said Charlie, pointing. 'Teresa's body. Her mouth is wider open. Like she's trying to tell us something.'

Lily crossed the narrow space and laid a hand on his arm.

'Charlie,' she said softly. 'She's dead. She can't hurt you now. The dead don't move.'

'I could have sworn . . .'

'It's your imagination,' said Lily. 'You were scared of her as a boy. Now you imagine her greater than she is.'

Charlie felt his heartbeat slow. His gaze settled on Teresa's remains. She looked less frightening now. The witch who haunted his childhood was a woman who had undergone horrors. Something in the dark seemed to whisper to him that his mother felt the same.

A thought occurred to Charlie. Teresa was an ordinary woman, so there would be no grand altar to place her on. His eyes dropped to the plinth on which she lay. It was covered in a plain wool cloth. But the fabric did not quite fall completely to the floor. A tell-tale glimmer of metal winked out.

'The chest,' said Charlie quietly. 'She lays on it. It's under Teresa.'

Chapter 142

For a few seconds Charlie and Lily stood looking at the covered chest.

'If you touch her,' boomed a voice, 'you will be sorry for it.'

They both started around. Blackstone's huge bulk barred the exit from the crazed nest of Teresa's possessions. His mass of plague scars glinted in the candlelight, bald and livid against the remaining thick black hair.

Blackstone held a pistol in his hand.

'Tobias's son,' he said quietly. 'After all these years.'

Lily glanced at Charlie.

'Sally Oakley hid my papers well,' continued Blackstone. 'And now you have led me right to them.'

He aimed the pistol at Charlie. 'The key.'

Charlie looked up to the burning ceiling. The chapel had its own wooden surround that had caught and was sending up tongues of flame.

Blackstone tilted his head, keeping the pistol trained on his quarry. Amusement flickered on his bloated features.

'Fear,' he said, 'is a useful thing. I can predict your thoughts.'

'It's not the only predictor,' said Charlie. 'When fire comes, people also save the things they love.'

Charlie ducked and threw a well-judged kick. It cracked into the wooden wall, sending a blazing shower of splinters down into the crypt.

Blackstone's arms flew up. Then he lunged to where his wife lay.

Charlie grabbed Lily, pulling them towards the entrance to Teresa's den. He scooped up a fragment of burning rafter.

'The papers,' he said to Lily. 'They must be destroyed.'

The sparks had died harmlessly away and Blackstone swung the pistol. He hesitated.

Charlie was holding the long splinter of wood, blowing the glowing end to a flame.

Blackstone glanced at the open gunpowder kegs, then back to Charlie.

'That box holds powers,' said Blackstone. 'Powers you cannot imagine. Powers I thought were lost until you led me to them.'

'I don't need to imagine,' said Charlie. 'I know.'

Blackstone smiled. 'If you knew what those papers held . . .' he began.

Charlie watched Blackstone's face.

'It was the exiled Charles Stuart who got married, all those years ago,' said Charlie. 'To his first mistress. Lucy Walter.'

Charlie paused.

'Those papers make Lucy England's Queen and Monmouth the legitimate heir,' he added. 'A commoner into royalty. Lead into gold.'

Something like fear skirted across Blackstone's face.

'You hoped to gain favour with the King,' said Charlie. 'You and Torr betrayed your brotherhood by helping the King marry. The dowries, the political allegiances that make a throne. All gone. Destroyed. They must have hated you. You'd given the Kingdom they fought to restore, for a whore.'

Blackstone smiled thinly.

'I learned twice,' he said, 'that the word of a Stuart King is worth nothing. First the father betrayed me. Then the son. Charles regretted his haste. Things with Lucy turned sour and he wanted to forget I ever helped him.'

Blackstone shook his head.

'Torr was preaching forgiveness and humility. But I knew. The only way to be certain is to take what you want.'

'But then my mother took it from you,' said Charlie, with a hard edge to his voice. 'And you killed her.'

'And now I have the papers again,' said Blackstone. 'I will give them to Monmouth,' he continued. 'The boy is as greedy and stupid as his mother. I will easily persuade him to fight for his birth-right.'

Blackstone smiled. 'Civil war,' he said. 'King Charles will not survive it.'

He looked at the barrels of gunpowder surrounding Teresa.

'Those papers must be destroyed,' said Charlie. 'They will tear England apart.'

Something seemed to clarify on Blackstone's face.

'You will have heard that your father is dead,' he said carefully. 'It is not so. There is a letter in that chest from Tobias.'

Blackstone smiled.

'You have your father's cleverness about you,' he said. 'He wouldn't have you surrender your birth-right to a traitor King.'

Charlie could feel the key burning. He tightened his grip on the flaming wood.

'You have lands due to you,' said Blackstone. 'Don't you want to go home?' His face was tired suddenly and Charlie thought he saw something of the old soldier.

'London is my home,' said Charlie. As he spoke a great rumble was heard in the distance. It reverberated around the old cathedral like an earthquake.

Blackstone smiled. 'Hear that?' he said. 'Fire has reached the Tower. Your traitor King has lost his Kingdom. London is gone,' concluded Blackstone. 'A smoking shell.'

'No,' said Charlie. 'She will rise again.' He blew again on the wooden shard in his hand. Flame flared high.

'You can claim your estate,' said Blackstone. 'The King will give anything for those papers. Lands, fine houses . . .'

'That's your dream,' said Charlie. 'Perhaps it was my father's. It isn't mine.'

And he threw the fiery ember into an open keg of gunpowder.

Charlie grabbed Lily's arm and pulled her towards the gap in Teresa's possessions. They dived through it, hitting the stone floor and rolling.

Inside the circle Blackstone staggered back, firing his pistol. Shot reverberated around the private chapel.

A wave of heat and noise exploded. It drove apart Teresa's possessions, exploding the chest beneath her and blowing her corpse to dust. Fire roared.

The blast drove Charlie and Lily backwards. They were propelled skidding over the chapel floor, out into the main cathedral.

There was an ominous rumbling sound. The ground beneath their feet shook.

'The crypt underneath us,' said Charlie. 'All is paper.' As he spoke a great section of roof shrieked above them and a house-sized piece of stone vaulting plummeted down. It hit the tiled floor with a mighty boom, splitting straight into the crypt below.

'The scaffold on the roof falls,' said Charlie. He scanned the cathedral. 'The main doors,' he decided. 'That way.'

Softened lead tiles splattered on the stone floor. Then burning beams began hurtling through the air like flaming spears.

There was a crash of cindery sparks and then all was strangely silent. Apart from an ominous rushing of air. The floor of the cathedral seemed to ripple.

Charlie knew what was about to happen. The vault full of paper was about to meet a flaming backdraft.

'Run,' said Charlie. 'Now.'

As he spoke the ground opened up only a few feet from where they stood. Flames rushed up as they sped away towards the back of the cathedral.

'The east floor will give way first,' shouted Charlie, mentally mapping the crypt. 'Keep to the west side.'

Blackstone emerged with a roar from the chapel. He was beating out fire from his clothes. With no time to reload his pistol, he dug in his clothes and brought out a bottle of lye.

Blackstone took careful aim and hurled it. The bottle smashed against the stone floor by Charlie's bare feet, forcing him to dodge left. Charlie felt the contents spray on his calf and then a dreadful burning pain. He staggered, gritting his teeth.

The leather pouch of vinegar. He delved into his coat as they fled. The pouch felt light in his hand. Charlie untwisted the stopper, and shook the contents towards his blazing leg. A few drops of vinegar splashed out. The pain ebbed slightly. It was enough to think straight, but not to stop the burn.

Another shot fired and the pouch went spinning from Charlie's grip. He watched helplessly as the last drops puddled away to nothing.

Charlie looked ahead. Two directions.

Left to the main doors, right to the vestry.

The lye on his left leg bit deep.

'The vestry!' Charlie gasped, trying to use his uninjured leg for extra speed. 'Go right.'

Chapter 143

Blackstone allowed himself a quiet smile as the ground gave way across the eastern part of the church. Tobias's boy was panicking. It was always the way. He was almost sorry for how easy it would be.

He smiled. 'Tobias Oakley,' he muttered. 'I hope you are watching. The grave will not protect you from my revenge.'

He made a cool assessment. Tobias's boy was injured and running to the vestry, just as Blackstone hoped. The bottle of lye had been deliberately thrown to force him away from the exit. Foot soldiers invariably ran for cover under fire. Like rats to their holes. Without thinking through the outcomes.

Blackstone calculated. A good general knew every part of the battlefield and he knew every part of St Paul's. The vestry was where the commoners put their scant possessions. Barrels of food. Beer. A few bales of herbs. No weapons. He had checked it only hours ago. There was nothing there the boy could use. Not even a keg of gunpowder.

His leg would have burned through to the bone by now. He would be maddened by pain. But the girl . . . Could she be a threat? Blackstone had learned never to underestimate women. The cathedral was burning now. Approach carefully and break her neck quickly, he decided. There would be enough time to take his revenge on Tobias's boy.

Blackstone reloaded his pistol and felt for the bottle of lye in his cloak. Scald the face and shoot the stomach, he decided. Let Tobias's son bleed it out whilst the flames finished the job.

***

Blackstone tried the vestry door carefully. It had been barricaded shut. Interesting. Blind panic or was there some plan afoot? There were always two doors to a vestry. Perhaps Tobias's son had formulated some rudimentary attack. He hoped so. It seemed a shame how easy it had become.

Approaching the second door Blackstone found it open. As he opened it a cloud of fragrant smoke hit him in the face. As he expected it was piled high with possessions. Common things.

***

A bale of herbs had been set alight by the door. He shook his head at their idiocy. Smoke. He had fought in cannon and gun smog. His eyes adjusted and he saw Tobias's boy slumped by a barrel. His hand was at the tap and beer trickled over his burning leg.

'It will not help you,' said Blackstone. 'Lye cannot be washed away.'

Then he saw the crypt door had been opened. So that was the plan. Draw fire underneath the vestry. Distract him with smoke. Then direct him to stand where the floor would collapse. It was not a bad plan at all. Particularly considering it had been formulated at such speed. But Blackstone had all the advantage. He had planned. He knew the terrain.

Then from nowhere a knife appeared from the smoke. The girl. Blackstone dodged, shocked by her speed. She brought the knife around in a perfect arc. He twisted away, but the knife slashed his cheek. Blackstone was impressed. Such skill. It seemed a shame to kill her. The blade had missed his neck by inches.

In a practised move he tossed up his sword, caught the blade and swung the huge handle hard into the girl's stomach. She folded in half and slumped to the floor, clutching her belly. Blackstone swung back his enormous leg and made two powerful kicks to her prone form. She made a moan he was familiar with from battle. It was the satisfying sound of fainting pain.

Blackstone was assailed by the most wonderful certain feeling. London was toppled and in a few moments he would emerge triumphant to claim his prize. The girl had been unexpectedly fast. But his battle skill had not failed him. Now God had served him up yet another just reward. Revenge on the boy. Finally, after all this time, the heavens were favouring him.

Blackstone turned, fingering the lye in his cloak. Perhaps he would have time to douse more than the face. He took out his gunpowder flask and began reloading his pistol.

Blackstone approached Tobias's son. Belongings had been placed strangely and he found himself taking a circuitous route. He frowned.

His mind wasn't working as sharply as he was used to. Blackstone's fingers weren't moving as he wanted either. Something was slowing his movements. It didn't matter. Elation was soaring through him.

'Do not take it to heart,' he said, tamping the gunpowder clumsily. 'Your father wasn't as good as I was either. I knew you would run to the vestry. I calculated it. Fear made you predictable.'

'So did I,' said Tobias's son. 'And what you did not calculate is that every common man owns a barrel of vinegar pickles.'

Realisation hit Blackstone. It wasn't beer flowing from the tap. Tobias's son was dousing his wound with vinegar. A stream of pickle juices staunched his lye burn.

Then Tobias's son stood.

Chapter 144

'I can tell you something else about common men,' said Charlie, as the burn in his leg ebbed away. 'They buy smuggled goods. The smoke you breathe is called opium.'

Blackstone swung in confusion. Somewhere towards the vanquished shape of the girl and the door to the vestry he could see the smoking bale. It had been placed so he breathed the smoke but they didn't. A current of air drew silkily over him. It meant something. He didn't know what.

For the first time since he could remember, Blackstone felt uncertain. He tried to summon his knowledge of the cathedral and found that he couldn't. Tobias's boy had laid the room out, he could see that now. Blackstone had been drawn to stand with the large stained-glass window behind him. There was something wrong about that. But he couldn't work out what. Thoughts rolled like warm treacle. He couldn't gather them together.

Charlie took aim and sent a candlestick winging towards the stained glass window. It dented the lead fixings and smashed away two small portions of glass. Just enough to force a current of air whistling into the still cathedral.

Blackstone turned slowly. His eyes lifted to the stained glass window behind him. It seemed to be shimmering. The Virgin Mary stared at him. She had a face he knew. Sally Oakley, leaden tears running across her cheeks.

'No,' he whispered. 'You died.'

The cathedral seemed to take a giant breath. The whistling sound rose to a shriek. A network of cracks split out from the holes in the stained glass. Then the entire window bowed inwards as air rushed to fuel the fire.

'This is not a war,' said Charlie. 'It is a fire. Fire doesn't fear its own skin, or seek riches. All fire wants is food. You have released a monster you can't control.'

'You think you can control fire?' asked Blackstone.

'No man commands fire,' said Charlie. 'But I can predict where it will go.'

The window smashed apart in an explosion of coloured glass. Blackstone held up his hands as the glass shards pelted him. He looked wonderingly at his arms. They were sliced to the bone, but the wounds didn't hurt him.

Then the ground beneath him shuddered as air rushed through the crypt beneath.

Blackstone staggered as the floor split apart.

A great split appeared in the floor, showing the burning books and papers below. They glowed like hellfire. He staggered again. The ground was uneven. It was hard to stay upright.

His last thought was the pistol. Blackstone thought it was loaded. He could fell a man across a battlefield after a day and night's hard fight. Tobias's son would waste time saving the girl. Tobias was the same. Sally Oakley had always been his weakness.

Blackstone aimed the pistol. His mind swirled like a thick fog.

He had been right. Tobias was pawing at Sally's unconscious form. The pistol sights wavered and then fixed. A chest shot was safest. He couldn't miss.

Charlie looked up from Lily's collapsed figure. Blackstone's gun barrel was pointed square at his chest.

Then a knife whistled through the air and lodged deep in Blackstone's throat. His eyes widened in amazement and his hand went to the knife. He tugged at it in puzzlement but it had been driven too deep.

The ground shuddered beneath him. Blackstone slipped, twisted, then fell headlong into the fiery bonfire of papers below. Beside Charlie, Lily dropped her knife arm.

Below them Blackstone gasped as the fire burned his hair and clothes. Then he stood with arms outstretched.

'Teresa,' he choked as blood filled his throat. 'Is it you?'

He staggered forward into the fire. And then the flames masked him out.

Chapter 145

Lily doubled over again, clutching her stomach.

'Here.' Charlie grabbed a burning stem of opium poppy. 'Breathe this. It will take the pain away.'

Lily inhaled gratefully and stood a little more upright.

'Better,' she agreed. 'We need to get out of here.'

The stone floor split and collapsed a few feet away as Charlie helped her out of the vestry. Out in the wide cathedral all was chaos. The huge roof had split open revealing the dark sky above. Possessions were aflame and the floor had collapsed into a fiery pit.

Charlie took it in with the practised eye of a cinder thief.

'This way,' he said, drawing them away from the main air flow.

———

They broke out into St Paul's graveyard gasping from the smoke. Behind them the mighty cathedral blazed. London's most iconic landmark was destroyed. The great spire had smashed through the burning roof. The paper-filled crypt had blown apart the thick walls and sent all tumbling down.

Above them the dark sky crackled. A sliver of yellow sun peaked low beneath the black clouds. It was morning. Charlie felt a cinder land on his face. Then another fell. And another. But they didn't seem to be burning him.

Charlie brought his hand to brush them away and was surprised to find it wet.

'Lily,' he grinned. 'Rain.'

She tipped her head back and smiled up at it.

'The wind has died as well,' she said. 'Perhaps it will do some good.'

They looked up at the flaming cathedral. There was no saving it. Somewhere deep inside were the papers, blazing in Teresa's wedding trunk.

'Did you mean it?' asked Lily. 'About your father? You really don't want to know?'

Charlie shrugged. 'It hardly matters now. Perhaps it is best some things stay buried.'

'Oh,' said Lily. 'Because if you want them, I have the papers.'

Charlie stared at her. 'You have the papers?'

'Yes.' Lily nodded.

'Why? How?' Charlie could barely get the words out.

'I had your key,' said Lily. 'I made a copy. On my way to Bridewell Prison. I spy for Amesbury,' she added, 'I know men who will forge a key in a few hours.'

'How did you take the papers from the chest?' asked Charlie.

'You were distracted by Teresa's magical things,' said Lily.

Charlie was thinking back. 'I thought the body moved,' he said. 'It was you. Opening the chest.'

Seeing Charlie's expression Lily pulled them out of her bodice. 'Don't be angry,' she said. 'I had my reasons.'

Mutely he took them.

'Torr said they were dangerous to England in the wrong hands,' said Lily. 'It was only when you fired the chest I knew you could be trusted with the papers. They could bring down England you know,' she added earnestly.

'Is not a man's word . . .' Charlie stopped speaking and shook his head. His gaze dropped to the papers.

'Women,' he muttered.

'Aren't you going to look at them?' asked Lily. 'You've waited long enough.

Charlie shot her an incredulous glance. Then shaking his head, he unrolled them.

Chapter 146

The King turned to his troops. Everyone was covered in a fine dust-ing of gunpowder.

'You thought well,' admitted James. 'To use gunpowder.'

'It was your naval men who placed the barrels right,' said Charles. 'They raced up those buildings like monkeys.'

'They're good men,' said James. 'I'd give my life for them and they for me. But your plan was what saved us. It was a good one. A barrel of gunpowder is worth twenty men.'

They looked at the smoking devastation where buildings had been. It had only taken a few well-placed barrels of gunpowder to make a wide enough firebreak. Gunpowder smoke scented the air. Sooty-faced men grinned at the victory. The Tower was safe.

The wind was dying down and, unexpectedly, rain began to fall. A muted cheer went up. The smoking shell of the city began to whisper and hiss.

Amesbury was looking admiringly to the King and his brother.

'Say what you will about the Stuart brothers,' he said, looking to the Tower, 'they come into their own in a crisis.'

'We must rebuild without delay,' said the King. He was looking at St Paul's still burning in the distance. 'Did we not have plans for the cathedral in any case?'

Amesbury nodded. 'Sir Roger Pratt drew up plans for a very high spire.'

'There was another architect, was there not?' The King was remembering.

'Christopher Wren,' said Amesbury. 'It was decided he hasn't the experience for such a project.'

'Bring me his plans again,' said Charles. 'He suggested a domed cupola I think, which I remember liking. Time for something new, perhaps.'

He thought for a moment. 'The London Stone is now broken in two you say?'

'Split in half,' agreed Amesbury.

'Then we will have Mr Wren set a piece of it at the altar in our glorious new St Paul's,' he decided. 'The other can be set in its original place on Cannon Street. That will afford our great capital dual protection I should think. From the Roman Gods and the Christian angels besides. I'll wager Londoners will be swearing on the stone in five hundred years' time.'

Amesbury nodded. The King certainly had style. But he had no understanding of finances. London was bankrupt.

'But first we must go to Hatton Gardens,' muttered the King, 'where the refugees gather. We should attend to the poor as well as the rich.'

Chapter 147

The first paper, Charlie had seen before. A Fleet wedding certificate signed by Thomas and Teresa Blackstone. He made out the word 'witnesses' above their names. Then further up the firm signature of Charles Stuart. And a looping 'Lucy Walter', written smaller beneath it.

Even though he had known what the papers held, Charlie found his hands shaking.

'This could bring down the Crown,' he said.

Lily nodded. 'It could start a foreign war,' she said. 'King Charles was given Bombay and Tangier for his Portuguese wife. Portugal should not like to know her marriage is not legal.'

'Or another civil war,' said Charlie. 'Monmouth is Protestant. People may prefer him to the Duke of York, with his Catholic wife and children.'

He unrolled the other paper. It was written in Dutch with a Dutch seal and he frowned as he made out the names. It was addressed to Sally and signed Tobias.

'I can't read it,' said Lily. Her eyes were on Charlie.

He tried to see what was written, but his eyes were swimming. Peering hard he made out a few words. 'Miss you' and 'home'.

Charlie rolled up the papers.

'Do you think he is there still?' asked Lily. 'In Holland?'

'No,' said Charlie. 'I think he died at sea.'

As soon as Charlie said the words he was certain of them. He folded the letter carefully and slid it inside his coat.

'It is enough,' he said, 'to know it.'

'What of your father's lands?' asked Lily.

'Maybe Blackstone told the truth, maybe he didn't,' said Charlie. 'But no land in England truly belongs to a man. Civil War taught us that. Besides,' he added with a grin, 'I grew up in London. I've no business in the country.'

Lily smiled. 'There's not much of London left,' she pointed out.

'You'd be surprised,' said Charlie, 'how little of London is out there,' he pointed, 'and how much is in here,' he said, tapping his chest. 'So long as people are here to remember how things were, they'll rebuild. More quickly than you might think. If there's money to be made, there's no stopping them.'

Charlie's eyes swept the smouldering remains of St Paul's graveyard. He took a few steps and dropped the certificate into a patch that still flamed.

Lily moved towards him. For a moment Charlie thought she meant to retrieve the papers. Instead she took out the mermaid handkerchief and dropped it into the flames.

They watched as paper and cloth smoked and then flared.

'Do you trust me now?' asked Lily, as black ash swallowed up the King's signature.

'No,' said Charlie. 'A little,' he qualified. 'Why did you give me the papers? You could have destroyed them.'

'Maybe I've grown fond of you.'

Charlie considered her expression.

'I was wrong about you,' he decided. 'You do have a tell.'

'I do?'

'It just says something different to what I thought.'

Lily tried for a casual tone as he moved closer. 'What do you think it says?'

'I cannot easily put it into words.'

'Oh.' She sounded disappointed.

'I can show you,' said Charlie. And he kissed her.

Three days after the Great Fire

Lucy Walter knocked tentatively on King Charles's bedchamber. She adjusted her low-cut pink dress and repositioned a horsehair curl.

'Come in!' called the King.

Lucy entered to find the King standing with his brother James, Amesbury and a short man with a tall wig she didn't recognise.

Lucy curtseyed low. 'Less security outside your rooms of late,' she observed.

'Charles is currently the most popular King in Europe,' said James.

'And there are no plotters left in any case,' added Amesbury. 'Discontented men tend to be poor. And they suffered worse from the fire. Most are still camping out in Hatton Gardens.'

'I've sent orders to the surrounding towns and cities to receive refugees,' said Charles distractedly. He was looking at a large map.

'This is Christopher Wren,' he said as an afterthought, gesturing the introduction. 'These are his plans for the new city.'

'The streets make the Kaballah Tree of Life,' said Wren, mistaking Lucy for someone of importance. 'St Paul's Cathedral is the heart of it. And see here how it spans out.'

Lucy glanced at it, then back at Charles.

'Barbara was very kind,' said Lucy haltingly. 'She gave me a carriage and cart. I owe her everything I own,' she added, sounding as though the confession pained her.

Charles looked up at her. 'Barbara can be very kind,' he said. 'Just not often to me.' And he gave Lucy the dazzling smile that had first made her fall in love with him. 'She's out arranging charitable donations,' added Charles. 'Making sure the homeless have food and shelter. Better you're gone before she gets back,' he added. 'Giving away money puts her in a foul temper.'

'You're very popular in the city,' said Lucy. 'People say you single-handedly held up the blazing wall of St Dunstan in the West. That's not my story,' she added, catching his expression. 'The people say it.'

'I'll pass your thanks to Barbara,' murmured Charles, making clear she was dismissed.

'There was something else,' blurted Lucy. 'Some small thing,' she added as they all turned to stare. 'There was talk, of the Sealed Knot having some papers,' she said, looking directly at Charles. 'Some alchemy things. Lead into gold, nonsense like that.' She gave an embarrassed cough.

'Oh?' Charles was looking at her with a warning expression.

'I didn't take as good care of them as I should have,' admitted Lucy, 'in Holland.'

Charles's eyes widened.

'But Amesbury tells me they burned,' she concluded. 'And if they hadn't, if they ever showed up, I would burn them myself. Worthless things that they were.'

Charles nodded slowly to show he understood, whilst James and Wren looked confused. Amesbury frowned for a moment and then smiled as though working something through.

They all looked back to the London plans as Lucy exited.

'I like them very much,' said Charles. 'The streets laid out like this. You say it's a kind of journey? With enlightenment at the end?'

Wren nodded. 'It's something the stonemasons advocate. Or free-masons I should say,' he corrected himself. 'They make a great study of symbolism and mystic ideas. I think it makes them better at their craft.'

'This fine domed roof,' said Charles. 'I always liked it. But it wasn't possible to get it through Parliament. I think I've bought myself enough grace to insist upon it now, don't you think?'

'It will be the pride of London,' said Wren happily. 'Hundreds of years from now, people will gaze up at St Paul's and think Charles II made a modern wonder for London.'

Amesbury tapped the London sketches.

'Perhaps we should be cautious about making these mystic free-mason things. Feelings about religion run high after the fire. People blame Catholics.'

'The Freemasons were accepted by Oliver Cromwell,' said the King. 'I will be no less tolerant. And besides, Amesbury, the Freemasons might have some strange ideas of how the world came into being, but they make some fine buildings with their notions of symbolism and such.'

Charles considered for a moment.

'There should be a monument,' he decided. 'Near to Pudding Lane. Something which offers thanks to the heavens. Wren, you must speak with the Royal Alchemist. He can advise you on astrology and so forth.'

'The Royal Alchemist?'

'Isaac Newton,' said the King. 'He makes some alchemy for me in secret,' he added, catching Wren's face. 'As well as helping us catch coin counterfeiters.'

'I'll arrange to meet with him,' said Wren. 'What should you like this monument to be called?'

Charles frowned. 'I'm sure I shall think of something,' he said. 'But for now, we'll just call it "The Monument".'

Seven days after the Great Fire

Charlie surveyed the hoards of sailors crammed in the Bucket of Blood.

The King had called back almost all his navy to help rebuild the city. And with their usual brothels and taverns burned, Covent Garden was stuffed to the rafters with sailors.

Among the jolly tars Charlie noticed a familiar face. Bitey was throwing back a leather tankard of beer, wiping his filthy beard. As Charlie moved closer, a muscular weight slammed against his knees. He lurched, then righted himself on a nearby table.

Bitey looked up, grinning. His pig, Juniper, began chomping on Charlie's breeches.

'You survived the fire then?' said Charlie, pushing her large head away with difficulty. 'And found your pig?'

'Survived and flourished,' said Bitey proudly. 'My room in Covent Garden is worth its weight in gold. I have three refugees paying me rent whilst they rebuild.'

Bitey nodded to a gaming table where coins and cards flew.

'I'm not the only one doing well,' he added. 'That widow has made a small fortune from those sailors. Poor lads never saw a Covent Garden hustle before.'

Charlie glanced over. The female card player was dressed in plain black, a modest white cap hiding part of her face. Charlie thought there was something familiar about the curve of her mouth. Then he grinned.

———

'Beware of the widow,' said Charlie, as he approached the table, 'she's more practised at cards than she looks.'

From the far end of the table Lily recognised Charlie and beamed. The sailors she'd been card sharping glared at her, realising the pay they'd just lost was no accident.

'What brings you to the Bucket of Blood?' asked Charlie.

'You.' She gave him a disarming smile. 'And boatloads of landed sailors,' she added.

Lily stood. Seeing she was hemmed in by people, she climbed up on the table. The sailors dived for their cards and money as her black skirts swept across. Charlie put up his hands and lifted her down.

'I thought you might have gone back to the country,' he said, keeping her close. 'City in ruins and all that.'

'No,' said Lily, stepping back a little. She was still holding her winning hand of cards and she tapped them on his chest. 'Once you've been in London a time, it gets under your skin. And this part didn't burn.' She gestured to the dark walls of the Bucket, lined with its usual malodorous clientele. 'Still enough of the city left to make a living.'

'Why did you leave?' asked Charlie, remembering the last time he'd seen her. They'd spent a few happy days together in Covent Garden. Then Lily had vanished without explanation. He'd assumed she was on some urgent spying mission for Amesbury.

'Important business,' she shrugged enigmatically, her dark eyes on his.

Charlie raised his eyebrows.

'Amesbury wanted to know about Blackstone,' she admitted. 'I told him what I knew.'

'Which was?'

'Blackstone was one of the old plotters,' she said. 'But now fire has burned away that festering part. The King wants to rebuild a clean new city,' she added. 'That's the talk in court.'

'He's too late,' smiled Charlie. 'Londoners are already putting their city back together, more or less the same way as they left it.' He smiled at the thought of the narrow alleys and haphazard roads being stoically reassembled. No notion of city planning would deter a Londoner from the serious business of making money.

'There was one more reason I came back,' said Lily.

'Oh?'

'The paper,' she said, 'from your dead father.'

'What about it?' Charlie could feel Tobias Oakley's letter lodged deep in his leather coat.

'Did you manage to read it yet?' She was turning the playing cards in her hand.

He grinned. After all this time she was suddenly so easy to read.

Lily caught his expression and put the hand of cards on the table behind her.

'I have a job for you,' she said, 'involving treasure. Buried treasure.'

'There's no such thing,' said Charlie evenly.

'I'm not hiring you for your opinion. But I might offer you one quarter of the findings.' Her dark eyes flashed excitedly.

'You don't find a good thief taker,' said Charlie, 'he finds you. What makes you think I'm interested in your assignation?'

She slipped off the ruby ring she'd pickpocketed from the aristocrat in Fetter Lane.

'Remember this?'

'Of course I do,' grinned Charlie. 'You stole it the first time I saw you. Then you burned a house down. That kind of thing stays in the memory.'

'You knew,' said Lily slowly. 'You knew from the first, what this ring was.'

'Maybe,' admitted Charlie. 'I had my suspicions. But I was pre-occupied with other things. You know,' he added, 'I'm employed to take the ring back.'

'So take it.' She handed it over, keeping her eyes on his.

Charlie took the ring slowly, not breaking the gaze. His heart was pounding as he glanced down at the ruby.

'Worthless,' he said, handing it back.

Lily was smiling.

'So you'll help me?' she said, turning it carefully in her palm. 'Another adventure?' She raised the ring. Sunlight sparkled in the red depths. 'I know you know what this ring is,' she added.

'Do I?' His hands were on her waist. 'Maybe I'll take some convincing.'

'I would warn you it could be dangerous work,' said Lily.

'I wouldn't expect anything less,' he replied.

'Then shall we go, Charlie Tuesday, and make our fortunes?'

Lily slipped the ring on her finger, then put her little hand in his. And together they walked out into the din of Covent Garden, back towards the smouldering remains of their city.

Truth is stranger than fiction. Which of these events really happened?

One of the following facts is false. Do you know which? Go to www.thethieftaker.com/firecatcher. Guess correctly to unlock a free secret history of *Fire Catcher*.

1. The Great Fire caused a weather phenomenon known as a firestorm. This threw out walls of heat, drew in high winds and struck down lightning, firing up more buildings.
2. Barbara Castlemaine turned her seductions to the fifteen-year-old Monmouth.
3. A Shadow Market of illegal goods operated under London's South Bank.
4. The roof of St Paul's Cathedral melted during the Great Fire, flowing rivers of molten lead down Lud Gate Hill.
5. King Charles II's quick-thinking use of gunpowder during the fire saved the Tower, and most likely England.

About the Author

Richard Bolls

C.S. Quinn is the bestselling author of *The Thief Taker*. Prior to writing fiction she was a travel and lifestyle journalist for *The Times*, the *Guardian* and the *Mirror*, alongside many magazines. In her early academic career, Quinn's background in historic research won prestigious post-graduate funding from the British Arts Council. Quinn pooled these resources, combining historical research with first-hand experiences in far-flung places to create Charlie Tuesday's London.